Gail Hamilton

Stumbling-Blocks

Gail Hamilton

Stumbling-Blocks

ISBN/EAN: 9783337369460

Printed in Europe, USA, Canada, Australia, Japan

Cover: Foto ©Andreas Hilbeck / pixelio.de

More available books at **www.hansebooks.com**

STUMBLING-BLOCKS

BY

GAIL HAMILTON

AUTHOR OF "COUNTRY LIVING AND COUNTRY THINKING,"
"GALA-DAYS," ETC.

BOSTON
TICKNOR AND FIELDS
1865

FOURTH EDITION.

•

UNIVERSITY PRESS:
WELCH, BIGELOW, AND COMPANY,
CAMBRIDGE.

Contents.

I.

THE OUTS AND THE INS.

THE World and the Church are two opposing forces. To make everything move easily, the Church ought to be entirely composed of good people and the World of bad. As matters stand, there are a great many sinners in the Church and a great many saints in the World. Moreover, the people who are good are not good all the way through, and the people who are bad have many excellent qualities, — which complicates the case still further. Also, the Church is and should be aggressive, for the avowed design of its Leader is to reign till he hath put all things under his feet. But its chief weapon should be love; and because it will not confine itself to this weapon, it is far less aggressive than it should be. Instead of loving the sinner while hating the sin, it often falls into a way of loving itself and hating the sinner. The World, being a very observant, as

1   ▲

well as a very wicked World, sees this, and falls
to making reprisals. It gathers together the sins
of Christians, and builds thereof a bulwark for itself against Christianity, behind which it pours its
small shot into the Church.   In all this the World
is entirely wrong, though the Church is very far
from right.   The World, in the first place, makes
the mistake of thinking that, when a man "joins
the church," he steps out of the sphere of ordinary humanity, is to be measured by different
standards, and is amenable to new laws, — standards and laws which have no relation to other men.
His faults and foibles immediately assume a new
importance.   His movements are watched with
careful scrutiny, and criticised with rigid severity.
Failings become vices ; faults, crimes ; and an imperfect man, a hypocrite.   Constitutional tendencies to particular sins, formerly unmarked or but
slightly noticed, are first exaggerated, and then
turned into an occasion for innuendoes and sneers,
if not against the Christian religion, at least against
its profession and its professors.

This is all wrong.   It is founded on a wrong
idea.   What is it to "join the church"?   "Does
he profess to be a *good* man?" I once heard a
person ask ; and many people seem to fancy that
when a man joins the church he professes to be
good, — better than other people ; and they accordingly set themselves to work to ascertain and
prove that he is not.   But is there a church in the

land that requires its members to make a profession of goodness? I never heard of such a one. Those who enter into church covenants profess to love Christ, and promise to obey his commands, and to watch over each other; but I never heard a single individual declare himself to be good, holy, righteous. "Joining the church" is rather a profession of belief in and love of God, and of an intention to do his will. This is done, first, because Christ is supposed to have ordained some such profession; secondly, because each man, endowing his own weakness with his brother's strength, is supposed thereby to be better able to resist temptation, and to grow in grace; and, thirdly, because the Christianization of the world is expected to be sooner effected by ranging the guns, than by letting each man fire his shot at random. I know no other profession and no other purpose. In what respect, then, does this place a man on a new plane? He simply promises to do what it is the imperative duty of every human being to do. No possible vow can increase its imperativeness. The acknowledgment of obligation does not create obligation. The recognition of relation does not establish relation. Every human being owes allegiance to God. All that he has and all that he is belongs now and forever to God. No contract can increase, and no absence of contract can diminish, the weight of such obligation.

It follows, then, that church-members and non-church-members are to be judged by the same rule. No duties are incumbent on the one that are not incumbent on the other. I do not mean to imply that the standard by which Christians are measured should be lowered. Lowered? Heaven forbid! No one is in danger of failing because he sets his mark too high. The grander the attempt, the grander the achievement. It is only by following on to know the Lord, that we learn to know him at all. Let not one jot or tittle be taken from the measure of the stature of the fulness of Christ. But what I do say is, that a non-church-member has no right to consider an act sinful in a church-member that would not be sinful in himself; nor a sinful act to be any more so in the one than in the other. If it is wrong for a church-member to steal, to commit forgery, to drink wine, to gamble, to play cards, to mend his tools on Sunday, to stay away from church, to be crabbed, fretful, impatient, violent-tempered, it is also wrong, and equally wrong, for a non-church-member. For a man to excuse wrong-doing in himself, on the plea that he does not belong to the church, or to exaggerate it in others on the plea that they do, is absurd. He ought to belong to the church. He ought to have that state of heart and will which would justify him in joining it. If it is the duty of one, it is the duty of all. If Christ has left,

and if the history of the world gives, intimations
that the glory of God and the good of man can be
best promoted by organization, then it is the duty,
not of A and B only, but of the whole alphabet,
to organize. If A and B, who have signed the
compact, do not live according to it, it is not for
C, who stands aloof, to complain of them, or to ex-
ult over them. His own guilt is farther back than
theirs. However wrong they may be, they have
taken one step towards the right, which he has not.

If two children in a family sign a paper, signi-
fying that they will love, respect, and obey their
parents, do they owe love, honor, and obedience
any more than the other children, who have not
signed it? If, notwithstanding their written agreement, they fall into disobedience, does it indicate
that they are more blameworthy than the other
children who also fall into disobedience? Not at
all. It only shows that the contract, in their case,
has failed of its intended effect.

Just so, it may be said, violation of church covenant shows the invalidity of such covenants. It
does in that one case; that is all. It indicates
that in that individual the principle of evil has
overleaped the restraints; that he was wrong in
supposing that he loved Christ, and willed to serve
him; or that, loving him, it was with a faint and
fluctuating emotion, and not with that perfect love
against which the waves of temptation surge and
dash and break in vain.

I do not propose to enter into a discussion of the effectiveness of church organization. I wish only to say that the dereliction of one, two, or a dozen, or a hundred individuals, does not show it to be worthless. So long as men have the power to deceive themselves and to deceive others, so long will there be many in the church who are not of the church. In order to demonstrate that church organization is useless, it will be necessary to divide our country, or any nominally Christian country, into two classes, — those who belong to a church, and those who do not; and then to show that morality and religion, purity of heart and life and practical benevolence, are equally distributed between these two classes. It may not be that this will solve the problem, but nothing short of this will. Even should we be able to find no good in such organizations, indications of Christ's will still remaining, there would be no choice as to our duty. I do not think, however, that the result of such an investigation would throw the question back upon the teachings of Christ.

Again, the fact that a man commits sin after joining the church does not necessarily prove him to be a hypocrite or a self-deceiver. Sin — a sin — is too widely spread, and too deeply rooted in the human heart, to be extirpated in a moment. The axe has, indeed, been laid at the root of the tree. Its gnarled trunk, unseemly branches, and poisonous leaves have disappeared, and the man

fondly believes that his sin will trouble him no
more; but anon green shoots sprout up round
about, showing him that the roots are there, drinking in sustenance from the springs of his life.
Then he digs about them, diving deep into the
soil, undermining, plucking up, trampling under
foot, and burning; but it may be the work of a
lifetime, and never, never in this world shall the
garden of his soul go back to the velvet verdure
of Eden, but remain a rugged, upheaved patch, —
fertile, it may be, but irregular; productive, but
uncouth; a vineyard of the Lord, but not the land
of Beulah.

For it is the baleful nature of all sin, that, though
never so bitterly repented of, it leaves a scar.

If a man has lived in selfishness, if he has rioted
in wine and wantonness, if he has found his pleasure in heaping up wealth, if he has never restrained his tongue or his temper, it is not improbable that, after his conversion, even though it be
real, he will sometimes lapse into his former wrong
habits. He will see Christ, but it will be through
a glass, darkly, and the glass will be colored by
the peculiarities of his own character. The ava-
ricious man will have many a hard fight against
avarice, and will perhaps sometimes succumb. The
untruthful man will keep out many a lie that
comes battering at his barred gate, though a sly
little falsehood may elude his vigilance, nay, even
take advantage of it, and worm itself in through

a crevice. The World will not see the many con-
tests, the frequent victories, but only the one defeat ;
and seeing this, will be ready to exclaim, "If *this*
is what comes of your Christianity, I am very well
content without it."

World, you are in the wrong. This is not what
comes of Christianity : it is what comes in spite
of it. The errors that you see result, not from
Christianity, but from a deficiency of it. The man
has it, but not enough. It is not sufficient to say
that he is a sinner after he professes to have become a Christian. You must show that, without
it, he would have sinned no more. Until you
know what religion has done for him, as well as
what it has left undone, you are not a competent
judge. And may it not be suspected that the
extreme alacrity with which you discover and exhibit his errors is not owing solely to your hatred
of shams and your love of sincerity and truth, but
in great measure to a strong, though perhaps unconscious, desire to justify the position which you
yourself have adopted, and which your conscience
continually warns you is an unsafe and untenable
one ?

II.

THE FITNESS OF THINGS.

UT however wrong the World may be in the positions which it assumes, the Church is verily guilty concerning her brother. By her folly and her wickedness she places stumbling-blocks in the way of the World. By setting great value on incidentals, and small value on essentials, she confounds moral distinctions, and offends Christ's little ones. She too often exalts forms and neglects principles. She adheres to the letter, and disregards the spirit.

For instance, going to church and to church-meetings, maintaining family worship, leading in social prayer, reading the Bible, committing it to memory, warning the impenitent, and endeavoring to lead them to the truth, are undoubtedly right things to do; but they are not proofs of Christianity in the soul, — only indications. They are the incidents, not the essentials of religion. We know that there are conceivable circumstances in

1 *

which a man can be an eminent Christian without going to church; but no circumstances can arise which shall render Christianity consistent with dishonesty. A cripple may be a saint, but a thief never.

The incidental is not objectionable. It is good for just what it is. Tithes of mint, anise, and cumin are due, and should be paid promptly, fully, and cheerfully; but these being done, there are other things which ought not to be left undone, — nay, there may be other things which should have been done first.

The letter is excellent where it belongs. It is a guide through a wilderness, the director, but not the source of strength. It is a watchword in battle, convenient, generally the sign of a friend, but not infallible. It is a body for the soul, a fit residence for the indwelling of the Holy Spirit; but when, instead of acting in the capacity of servant to the spirit, it gets the upper hand, — when, instead of being informed with the spirit's glow, it strikes in, till letter and spirit congeal together in one frozen mass, — then, indeed, the letter killeth.

Not long ago I read an anecdote, in which a certain faulty Mr. A. was rebuked. He was granted to be upright, benevolent, charitable, patient, — in fact, he seemed to be endowed with nearly all the Christian virtues, while the sole *per contra* was, that he never talked to people about personal religion, never conversed with them upon their own salvation. If this were an isolated case, it would not be worth while to animadvert upon it; but the same disposition is so often manifested, the same tendency to regard a constitutional quality as a fatal sin or a cardinal virtue, that it is worthy of a moment's attention.

First, the man who has professed Christ before men, and who subsequently leads an upright, pure, and blameless life, is daily and hourly and momently preaching Christ and him crucified with a silent power, with a persistent working force, which there is no agency in earth or hell strong enough to withstand. And, furthermore, if all Christians would lead such lives, it would almost seem that not one word would need to be spoken for Christ, — that the glory of God would be so revealed in his Church, that men would flock to it as clouds, and as doves to their window, — that this city set on a hill would be seen to be a city of refuge, whereunto the weary and the heavy-laden would flee, and find eternal rest.

"Pure religion and undefiled before God and the Father is this, To visit the fatherless and the widow in their affliction, and to keep himself unspotted from the world." Can anything be more explicit? And if one professing to be Christ's disciple fulfils these conditions, who shall dare preach any other Gospel or set up any other standard?

Secondly, religion develops, but does not create faculties. If a sinner is a confirmed tailor, he will not turn poet when he becomes a saint. He may become a better tailor, but he will be a tailor still. If he is a shoemaker by nature, he will not be a sculptor by grace. If he has been witty, he will not suddenly discover a capacity for dul ness; and if he has been stupid, he will not imme diately astonish you with his brilliancy. If he was a sociable man before his conversion, he will be sociable after it; and if he was reserved be- fore, reserved he will continue. There may be exceptions, but this is the rule. It follows, then, that the man who is most fluent and ready in exhortation and prayer is not necessarily the man who lives nearest to God. He may be, but we cannot from such facts alone infer that he is. I once heard of a woman whose Lares and Pe- nates were disorder and uncleanliness; whose husband and children were squalid and repul- sive from sheer neglect; but who descanted with unctuous fervor on religious topics, and when asked by a modest and admiring matron how it was that she could do this, " It's grace," she replied, complacently, — " it's grace that enables me to do it." One can but think that, if it were grace, it was a great pity that grace had not taken another turn, and set her to mending her family's clothes, and making their home decent. In my opinion, however, it was not grace, but some-

thing quite different. Of course I do not mean
to say that a clean floor in your own house is
of more importance than a soul saved in your
neighbor's ; but Christ, whether his favor is sought
for yourself or others, is always to be sought in
the way of duty, never out of it ; and as it is a
wife's unquestionable duty to attend to the affairs
of her household, she cannot systematically neglect
that duty without incurring grave suspicions as to
her Christian character.

This is not said in any captious spirit towards
those who have the gift of tongues. They may
be the very best Christians in the Church. Their
power may have received an additional impulse
from religion. Its owner may have cultivated it
all the more assiduously for Christ's sake ; and if
so, he has done well, and he shall not lose his reward. I only wish that effects shall be attributed
to their proper causes, that the gifts of nature and
the gifts of grace shall not be confounded. Nor
will this involve any derogation from the latter.
Nature is just as truly from God as grace. Grace
and nature work harmoniously together, if we can
but ward off prurient fingers. Nature furnishes
the foundation, and grace rears the superstructure.
This is the point I aim particularly to impress, —
that when religion permeates the soul, it elevates,
refines, strengthens, and sharpens the powers we
possess, and not the powers we do not possess ;
that some are naturally orators, and that others

are not; that while some can preach the truth
with their lips, others can preach it only with
their lives; that this distinction is not superficial, but has its basis deep down in the human
heart; that a recognition of it will facilitate the
working of the Divine economy, and that a non-
recognition of it occasions great friction, waste,
and trouble.

I have heard

> "Men whose life, learning, faith, and pure intent
> Would have been held in high esteem with Paul,"

and women whose whole prayerful, loving, beautiful lives were a constant gospel, lament their own
inefficiency, and gaze with self-reproachful admiration upon those who had this gift of tongues.
Dear friend, there are, it may be, so many kinds
of voices in the world, and none of them is without signification. The fair temple that crowns
the summit of Mount Moriah went up without
sound of hammer or axe, but the glory of the
Lord dwelt therein.

In a great machine there are many wheels and
pulleys and weights and frames and bands. Some
move swiftly, some slowly; some with a ceaseless
click, some with a heavy thud, some in unbroken
silence : but all are parts of the same machine ; all
combine harmoniously to the same end.

Undue self-reproach on the part of silent toilers
is not the only or the chief evil resulting from a

want of discrimination. By it, the strength of
the Church is diminished, her working power
wasted, and the coming of Christ's kingdom delayed.

For example : there is a deficiency of teachers in
the Sabbath school. An appeal is at once made to
the Church. The low state of Zion is lamented.
The activity and zeal of Christians in their worldly
calling are contrasted with their backwardness in
the Lord's service. Men and women are urged to
press forward, to come up to the help of the Lord
against the mighty, to stand in the breach, to
work in the vineyard, — all of which for the time
means to come into the Sunday school. No stress
is laid upon qualification. On the contrary, disqualification does not seem to be taken into the
account. In fact, nothing but impiety seems to be
recognized as a disqualification. If a man has the
love of God in his soul, it is presupposed that he
can assume and successfully maintain one of the
most difficult positions in the world ; and if he
should be reluctant to assume it, it is more than
hinted that his faith needs inspection. The consequence is, that some good man, of tender conscience, but no great breadth of views, — desirous
above all things that the world should be reformed
and renewed, but with a rather vague idea of the
modus operandi, — ignorant of the science and inexperienced in the art of teaching, but fearful of
grieving the Holy Spirit and discouraging his min-

ister, — mistakes the voice of God in his soul for
the temptings of the Devil, and takes upon himself
the charge of eight or nine bright-eyed, wide-
awake, fun-loving boys. He enters upon his duties
with painstaking devotion. He prepares his lessons
carefully. He prays over them. He is punctual
and constant in his attendance ; but, in spite of all
his efforts, his boys harass his very soul. Sometimes the spirit of unrest enters into them, and they
are full of " quips and cranks and wanton wiles."
Again, they seem to undergo a transformation the
moment they enter the class, and, from intelligent,
lively lads, become mute, heavy, stolid lumps. It
is a pitiable sight. Both sides are to be pitied,
neither blamed. Human nature is particularly
strong in boys, and they cannot be interested unless there is something to interest them ; but human nature is also strong in teachers, and they cannot interest if they have not the power. The boys
and the man were not meant for class and teacher.
The two parts do not tally. The wheels move in
opposite directions, and the works are at a stand-
still. This is not the way to do things. The Jes-
uits knew better than to squander power thus.
They recognized the eternal fitness of things.
They selected the man for the place, and the place
for the man. Let us do the same. There is no
good, there is infinite harm, in attempting to put
all upon a dead level. It is a fact that a man needs
certain qualifications to be a teacher, just as much

as he does to be a doctor or a lawyer. The teacher is born, and not made. All the learning of the colleges, all the training of the normal schools, I might add, all the piety of the churches, will not supply the place of — *knack.* Without this, one may command the respect of men, but he cannot secure the attention of boys ; and to be a good teacher, a man must not only secure the attention of his scholars, he must possess himself of them body and soul.

True, the greatest genius is often obscured by over-sensitiveness, and belief in one's own inability is not infallible. Those who have been most successful in a great work have often shrunk from entering upon it. That, however, only makes vigilance the more necessary on the part of those who select workers in any department. It does not countenance an indiscriminate demand upon all for all departments, or for any department.

True, also, that out of the mouths of babes and sucklings God perfects praise, but that is no manner of reason why we should set up babes and sucklings for our preachers and teachers. They perfect praise where God has placed them, in the nursery ; and many a woman will perfect praise in her household, and many a man in his counting-room, when, if you wrest them from their appropriate spheres, and plant them in a lecture-room before fifty or five hundred people, or in a Sunday school in front of a dozen children, they will perfect only platitudes.

B

I know that God chooses the weak things of this world to confound the things that are mighty, but that is no reason why we should. He knows what he is doing. He has a broader horizon than we. He sees farther and clearer. Strong and weak are earthly terms. In the apparently feeblest engine there are hidden forces, — hidden from us, but palpable to the eye of Omniscience, and only waiting his command to leap into mightiest action. This one thing is certain. He never fails. He never chooses agents too weak to accomplish his purposes. His causes are always proportioned to his designed effects. His means are always exactly adapted to his ends. That is all one desires the Church to do, — as nearly as may be to adapt means to ends. But so long as we are human, and therefore forced to judge from appearances, let us strive to balance weight with power. Let us elect the brawniest arm to strike down the stubbornest foe, and the softest hand to bind up the sorest wound.

> " God moves in a mysterious way,
>   His wonders to perform."

Mysterious to us, but doubtless perfectly logical to him. Let us be logical too, and see that our premises are correct before we confidently anticipate a conclusion. Trust in God is a nullity, if the powder is not dry.

I know that men and women whose bodily presence is weak, and whose speech contemptible, have

consecrated alike their weakness and their strength
to God, have taken up the cross in Sabbath school
and conference-room, and have brought down blessings on themselves and their neighbors. So your
little girl comes to you, " Papa, Mamy has made
you a purse to put your cents in " ; and she holds
up to your eyes an astonishing specimen of needle-
work, a bit of brown cambric with sprawling, zigzag white stitches of variable lengths and independent directions, twisted into an indescribable shape,
but with a palpable hole in the corner where the
cents are to go in. You take the little sewing-
machine in your arms, smother her with caresses,
and say : " Yes, it is a beautiful purse. Papa must
kiss every one of the little fingers that made it.
Just see the cents go in. There now, papa will
put it in this drawer, and when he wants any cents
he will find them in the little purse that Mamy
made " ; — and Mamy jumps down and runs away,
her little heart just as brimful of happiness as if
she had indeed bestowed upon you the purse of
Fortunatus.

Just so, I think God, our Father, in his infinite
love to us, in his boundless, sympathizing tenderness, receives the work of our hands, according to
the love which prompted, and not according to the
skill that wrought. Blessed be his name for ever
and ever that he does so ; otherwise where should
we appear ? And if the sole result desired were
the beneficent effect produced upon specific in-

dividuals, perhaps this kind of cross would sometimes be as effectual as any. But there is a
work to be done. Growth in grace is not the
only object of life. A soul's salvation is the salvation of but one soul, and there are millions. Let
us economize our forces, — economize, I say, not
squander or hoard, not cast before swine nor
hide under a bushel. There are mountains to be
levelled, ravines to be bridged, valleys to be filled
up, rivers to be spanned, causeways to be built,
before the way is prepared for Christ's coming, —
and we are to do it. Surely it can best be done
by giving to each man what he can do best. Let
one have the commissariat, one disburse the funds,
one collect the revenue, one arrange the work, one
instruct the ignorant, one wield the spade, one smite
the anvil; and when each one thus does with his
might the real work which his hand has found to
do, then shall the cry go up consistently, heartily,
effectually, "Come, Lord Jesus, come quickly."

Personal conversation on religious topics, or, to
be more specific, personal appeals to those who do
not profess to be Christians, is a matter of so much
importance and so much difficulty, that I may be
pardoned for following it a little further. I have
been already asked, whether I do not think professing Christians are greatly deficient in the matter of making "personal appeals," and whether I
should not regret giving comfort to the Christian who goes on from week to week, and from

month to month, and from year to year, without once speaking of his own love to Christ, or commending his religion by word, as well as by example, to those around him.

If common sense were brought to bear on this matter, I should answer both questions in the affirmative far more unhesitatingly than I am now able to do; but, so far as I have observed, common sense is very largely dispensed with. What I mean is, that we do not talk about religion as we talk about politics, literature, or art. Religious conversation, as a great many of us conduct it, *is* formidable, and the wonder to me is, not that so many shrink from it, but that so many can be found who dare to grasp so unwieldy a weapon. Observe a party of us, — sound orthodox people, in a bright, cheerful parlor. We are merry, gay, social, piquant, lively; till a "revival" is broached, or the state of the Church, or something else of the kind, when immediately a change ensues. We look steadfastly solemn; our faces elongate; our voices assume an indescribable tone, — something between a sigh and a moan. All vivacity, sprightliness, originality, die out. A stranger would take Christianity to be a very doleful affair.

Why should we do so? Why, becoming religious, should we cease to be natural? Why should we walk in a treadmill of set words and phrases, — forms which were indeed instinct with life to those who originated them, but to us, too often, meaningless and cold, — the dead husk without the kernel? Let us adopt a more excellent way; let us talk of religion as we talk of other things, — naturally, heartily, vigorously, — saying what we mean in our own tongue wherein we were born. Let us not set up a bugbear, and then blame timid people for being scared.

You have seen little children play at being grown up. You know what demure airs they put on; nothing can equal the sobriety, the gravity, the unmitigated sternness, the unbending severity, of their deportment. We laugh, not because they are such clever imitations, but such charmingly ridiculous caricatures, of ourselves. Just so, it seems, the angels must have many a laugh at our expense; for, ceasing to be human, we do not become angelic, any more than the little ones become men and women when they cease to be children. Putting off the natural, we do not put on the supernatural, but rather a nondescript garment suited neither to heaven nor earth, — a decided and measured mournfulness, that would be ridiculous if it were not harmful. It was all very well for the morning stars to sing together, and all the sons of God to shout for joy; but you find no such irregular proceeding among New England Puritan Pilgrim-Father Orthodox Christians.

I suppose we shall all be considerably surprised, when we get to heaven, at finding things there different from what we expected; but it seems to me that some will be a good deal more surprised than others.

We ought at all times, but especially when we are conversing on religious topics, to banish the cast-iron, daguerrotype look from our faces. We sometimes fancy that, because God looks at the heart, he does not look at anything else. We have positive proof that he does. The question to Cain was not only, " Why art thou wroth ? " but, " Why is thy countenance fallen ? " A proud look is an abomination to the Lord, as well as a lying tongue. Moreover, the heart not only gives expression to the face, but the expression of the face reacts on the heart. Try to scold with a smile on your lips, or kiss your baby with a frown on your brow, and you will be convinced. It is almost impossible to feel cross while you are looking pleasant, or disconsolate while you are looking cheerful. So with the voice ; let it be natural, soft, not pitched on a high key, nor whining, nor melancholy. There is nothing in the Bible which requires Christians to be sad. The religion of Jesus wears no sombre hue. On the contrary, the Scriptures continually teach us, by precepts and examples, to rejoice evermore, to joy in God through our Lord Jesus Christ. Who, indeed, shall be happy, if not those who have placed all their hope and their faith, all their present and all their future, in the hands of Omnipotent Love ?

There will of course be occasions when the utmost solemnity of voice and look is alone fitting. I deprecate the flippancy and thoughtlessness with which the most terrible denunciations of the New Testament are sometimes uttered, as much as I do the lugubrious cadences with which its sweetest and tenderest promises are pronounced. What is objectionable is the one aspect put on for all occasions, whether warning the careless, or directing the inquiring, or comforting the desponding, or instructing the ignorant, or congratulating each other on the wonderful works of God. What is desirable is, that the tone and manner and expression shall be dictated by the love or faith or fear or hope or sorrow of the heart, and not by an outside conventionality.

Another suggestion is, that we should not draw so exact a boundary line between religious and secular topics. We fence off our Christianity, and deem it meet to drape ourselves in ghostly garb when we enter the sacred enclosure. Of course, young Christians, and old Christians too, judge that there must be something very grand and awful to demand all this pomp and circumstance, and they exceedingly fear and quake. It is not so. Religion is not a thing that must be veiled from vulgar gaze, and watched and guarded lest it be profaned. It is itself a purifier, consecrating everything that is brought into contact with it. It is not a garment to be worn carefully lest it be soon destroyed. Rather is it the living skin, constantly renewed, growing with the growth of bone and muscle and nerve. It is not a tank whose waters must be economized lest the supply fail, but a fountain springing the purer from being drawn for all humble, daily uses. It is no electri fied manikin, shrivelling at a touch into insensate shapelessness. It is itself the very electric principle that vitalizes and animates all. It is a vigorous, hardy growth, not a frail house-plant; therefore bring it out into the air. From shade and shine, from storm and rain, from dew and frost, it will only gather strength. Let the winds rock it; it will strike its roots deeper into the earth. Let the sun beat upon it; it will only robe itself in denser green, and bourgeon in gayer hues. Time can but toughen its fibres, broaden its branches, circle its sturdy trunk with signal rings, till the tender shoot is become a worshipful oak, and singing birds lodge in the branches thereof, and men sit under its shadow with great delight.

Therefore *use* your religion. Use it

> " without stint or spare,
> As men use common things, with more behind ;
> And in this ever should be more behind."

Strive to get acquainted with God. Be reverently familiar with him. Do not confine your knowledge of him to his aspect as God the Judge, or God the Saviour, though that may be the grandest of all, and may receive your highest

2

adoration and your warmest love. Study his
ways in the continuous revelation of his works,
as well as in the crystallized revelation of his
word. See God the artist, in the sunsets that
gild the evening sky; God the machinist, in the
mechanism of your own body; God the benefactor,
in the wonderful laws of ice; God the chemist, in
the laboratories of earth and air; God the historian, in the record of the rocks; God the builder,
in the mountains which he has piled up to heaven.
See God, too, in the thousand little happinesses
that cluster about your daily life. It is God who
makes the outgoing of your morning and your
evening to rejoice, just as truly as it is God who
spake the world into being. It is God who folds
you in happy sleep at night, just as much as it is
God who sent his Son to die for you. God speaks
to you in the song that trembles into your heart
from the lips you love, just as truly as he speaks
to you in the voice of his thunders. Warning the
impenitent is our chief idea of religious conversation, whereas it is only one topic in a worldful.
Let it have its due place, and it will be less
dreaded. Let us talk to our little ones of God
just as we talk to them of their father. Let
Christ-love and mother-love grow up together in
their hearts. Learn to think God. Be full of
God; and out of the abundance of the heart the
mouth will speak. One reason why we find it
so hard to talk of God is that we live so far from

him. We worship him, but it is a great way off; and he would be nigh, even at our own doors. He *is* there. Recognize him. Not only before the gate of the sinner does Christ stand waiting. It is at your door, O my brother, that he knocks. Open it and let him in. Take him to your heart. Believe in him. Crown him King there, at the centre of your life, and all the outposts are his.

There will always, probably, be more or less reluctance, hesitation, diffidence, in conversing about matters which pertain to the inner life. Facts are easily discussed, but feelings are evasive. Many a man can give you a full, clear, and accurate account of the state of his business, who, if set to work to develop the state of his mind and heart, will stammer, repeat, blunder, and finally fail altogether of his end. You have, I dare say, often heard of people who " could talk about anything but religion," or about religion in its external and organic aspects, such as churches, benevolent societies, councils, etc., but as soon as you began to speak of experimental religion, their mouths were shut ; and this fact is generally stated in a manner that implies reproof, — implies that the reason why they say nothing is because they have nothing to say. It is a subject upon which they have no thoughts and in which they feel no interest.

This may be true. Undoubtedly it often is true ; but let us hope and believe that it is not always so. There are whited sepulchres, fair in outward seeming, — within, full of dead men's bones and all uncleanness ; but there are also noble houses, reared by wealth and art, beautiful without, but more beautiful within for the love and faith and trust, the thousand household virtues, the manifold nameless tendernesses, that make of every hearth an altar, of every home a heaven. There are mirages which reveal to the eye of the thirsty traveller the sparkle of waters that he shall never reach, — the greenness of trees under whose shade his weary limbs shall never rest ; but there are also oases where the stately palm yields her fatness, and living springs gush forth healing and strength.

So there may be men in the Church, but not of it, who adhere to the organization, obey its laws, · contribute to its support, frequent its sanctuaries, and call its members brethren, who yet can never speak of the love of God, because, deceiving or deceived, their dry, dead bones have never been vitalized by that love ; but may there not also be men, just as exemplary in conduct, just as chary of words, who *have* in their secret souls that well of water which shall spring up into everlasting life ?

For religion is of the spirit. True, it spreads its broad and fruitful branches over the whole life ; but its roots go deep down into the heart, there, in silence and darkness, unheard, unseen, to suck in the vital juices which are to supply its nourishment and further its growth. It may develop itself in churches and charities and exhortations and prayers, but its spring is in the heart. There it works in loving tenderness, in sweet repentance, in saintly sorrow, in heaven-born aspirations, — and a stranger intermeddleth not with its joy.

Is it not so? Can it not be so? Must silence always indicate vacuity? How do we judge in other cases? When a man loves a woman with a love that conquers life, does he tell her of it in well-turned periods? Is he ready and fluent whenever occasion offers or does not offer? Does he not rather deal in broken sentences and delicious silences? Do you not even go so far as to suspect the love that harangues in elegant metaphors, with faultless rhetoric, — that always has the right word in the right place? And if lips are sometimes sealed when a human love is strong, can you not believe, and, since it is your brother whom you are judging, will you not believe, that Christ-love may also consist therewith, — that the silence may come solely from the reluctance of the heart to discover its own secret workings? This may be only one of many causes that contribute to the same result; but if it is one, it ought not to be left out of the account.

Since this sensitiveness is a natural quality, we cannot destroy it if we would, and we would not if we could. It may hinder and sometimes prevent free communion, but it has its work to do. It is, therefore, to be managed, not defied, or overborne. It follows that real interchange of feeling on religious topics obeys the same laws that interchange of feeling on other topics does. In its outward manifestations, in its practical and wise benevolences, the Church can band together. In all social and kindly offices, its members should prove to themselves and show to the world how Christians love one another. They are baptized into one name, moved by a common love, bound by a common vow. They should be real "brothers in unity." But further than this they are not required to go. Friendship, confidential outpourings, the exosmose and endosmose of souls, is a matter of magnetism, not of morals or religion. Respect is awarded to worth ; excellence wins esteem ; but

> " Our likings and dislikings
> Have their own instinctive laws."

Church-members, like others, will group themselves unconsciously, according to hidden organism. Money or learning or " high birth " does not decide it, but internal construction. One man is indifferent to circumstances, and can unbosom himself without regard to time or place. Another must enter into his closet and shut the door. That closet may indeed be the solitude of his own study, ·or the circle of his chosen friends, or the place where heavy-laden souls cry out for weariness, or Christian hands, prayer-burdened, lay hold on God;

but wherever it is, it must be in the atmosphere where alone his soul can live, and move, and have its being. It is useless to demand or expect otherwise, and he who does so knows little of human nature.

Therefore, if a brother is silent when you would fain have him moved to speech, think it not always because he is not a Christian, but sometimes simply because he is not you. You choose your own time and place. Grant him the same liberty.

This sensitiveness works in two ways. It not only restricts Christian intercourse, but it renders necessary the utmost watchfulness in dealing with those who are not Christians. Here, alas! we often fail. We are not delicate and wise in our modes of operation. It does not hurt a drum to be beaten, but a harp gives up its soul of sweetness to the touch of dimpled fingers. Some hearts are all out-doors, and some are a labyrinth in which, unless you get a clew-thread, you may grope forever without discovering the secret chamber where the Presence sits enthroned. Therefore be wary, be vigilant, be wise. Feel your way. Do not fire your shots at random. Your object is not — ought not to be — to discharge or exhibit your revolver, or to show that you can pull a trigger. It is to do execution, — to bring down the foe that is leading a soul captive. Take aim before you shoot; otherwise your charge may go crashing in among heart-strings, and still their quivering forever.

" Be instant in season and out of season," is an injunction that has been sadly misunderstood and misapplied. There are good people — the Lord reward their unselfish seeking, and not visit their blunders upon the heads of their victims! — who fancy it to mean that " personal appeals " are always in order. I knew a woman, bearing now, I doubt not, a new name among the angels, who, feeling it her duty to admonish her neighbors of theirs, and not being endowed with a nice sense of the fitness of things, used to startle her friends by the most unexpected forays. If, at a social gathering, she saw a person in whose salvation she was interested, the presence of one, two, or a dozen others was no obstacle to exhortation. " Dear Mr. A., *won't* you seek religion? Promise me that you will seek religion." I have heard a person, whose own heart was full of love to the Saviour, ask a young lady sitting next him, at a dinner-party, if she did not find great consolation in the doctrine of the resurrection of the body. It is unnecessary to multiply instances. All the way along, we more or less waste our strength by smiting when the iron is cold. Yet we might learn a better lesson every day. The children of this world are wiser in their generation than the children of light ; and the children of light are often wiser about everything else than about the light itself. When your little three-year old trips, nightgowned and barefooted, into your room in the

morning, and climbs up into your bed, and begins
forthwith to plan and execute surprising excursions,
planting his heel upon your throat, and his fist on
your nose, plumping himself down at irregular intervals, entirely oblivious of paternal sensations,
you hardly undertake then to imbue his mind with
quiet, loving, religious thoughts.   His little soul,
fresh from long, dreamless sleep, is wide awake.
Every nerve and fibre of his body is quivering with
life, and harnessed for action.   So, if you are sensible, you tumble him over, and roll him about,
and punch him, and knead him, and tickle him,
till he screams with delighted laughter.   But when
he has danced away the summer day, and goes to
his mother, tired, happy, and subdued, she takes
him in her arms, and tells him

> " That sweet story of old,
> How Jesus appeared among men,"

and with the music of divine love murmured into
his ear from lips that are only not divine, the blue
eyes film, the silken lashes droop, and the child-
soul wanders off into the land of sleep; but the
human and divine, woven together in his heart
forevermore shall, through all the years that are to
come, preserve his eyes from tears, his feet from
falling, and his soul from death.

If you do not learn it from your course towards
your child, you may learn it from his towards you;
and I often think that children have a certain

2 *   c

fresh, instinctive knowledge of human nature that after years incrust and destroy. When you are waiting in your half-warmed breakfast-room, impatient of delay, and anxious to be gone to your office, your boy amuses himself as best he can ; it is when you sit by your evening fire in dressing-gown and slippers, in happy quietude, that he wriggles up your knee, sits astride your lap, and says confidently, " *Now*, papa, tell me a story."

All the way from infancy to old age, if we wish to make an impression on hearts, we must take hearts when they are open to impression. I do not attempt to give, and I do not think there is, any specific rule. Every man is constructed upon a different basis, and must work and be worked after his kind. Some it may be well to meet breastwise, with full front, breaking in upon their absorbing business, or pleasure, or madness, with a " Thus saith the Lord." Others will be moved by a loving word, a tender inquiry, a gentle suggestion, as you walk home with them on a summer evening. You must be the judge of where and how, but *judge*. Do not follow a blind impression that you are to make home-thrusts right and left, without regard to time or place. Do not fancy, as an excellent woman whom I knew seemed to do, that your social, religious duty is discharged when you have put to every person you meet the question, " How do you feel in your mind " ? The human heart remains ever an unsolved and in-

solvable problem. Only by careful study and unceasing prayer — self-work and God-help — can
you begin to take its measurement. The cure
of souls is no trifling matter, to be entered upon
as impulse may direct. The bow drawn at a
venture may send an arrow quivering in between
the joints of the armor, felling a foe to earth ; but
also it may drain the life-blood of a friend. Your
random "appeal" may be the savor of life unto
life ; but unless you have made it judiciously,
you have no right to expect it to be anything
but of death unto death. Of course I do not
mean anything so absurd as that you must never
speak to a friend on matters that pertain to personal religion, unless you have carefully weighed
beforehand all the circumstances, and deliberately chosen to do it thus and so. I would have
you, rather, like the skilful general, who, indeed,
plans his campaign beforehand with painful care,
but is guided in carrying out its details by the
movements of the enemy, marching and counter-
marching, as best he may baffle his wary foe.
The unpremeditated onset is often the most brilliant and successful ; but its very brilliancy and
success are due, in large measure, to the skill
that watched and the patience that waited.

Grasp the opportunity. Make one if you can ;
but be a little careful that it *is* an opportunity.
Watch. It will not be long. " God's occasions "
are constantly " drifting by."

Do you say that I have put lions in the way?
Not at all. They were there before. I have only
tried to point out one or two, that you may be on
your guard. It *is* a fearful thing to live. We do
not half enough feel it. We walk lightly among
eternities. We lie down and rise. up, we go out
and come in, we smile or frown, we utter a brief
good morning, we look a look of love, we smile a
smile of hope, we breathe a word of prayer, we
pass by on the other side, and a soul plumes its
wings for heaven, or plunges into the depths, and
we know it not.

Who is sufficient for these things? God. With
him our weakness is strength. Without him our
strength is weakness. We are instruments in his ·
hands. It is for him to use us. It is for us to lend
ourselves to his uses, — joyfully, jubilantly, entirely,
with infinite blessing to ourselves, or reluctantly,
grudgingly, lazily, to our final and infinite dismay.

It is far more trouble to think and plan and
contrive how best we may serve God, by most
wisely directing lost and wandering souls back to
him, than it is to push thoughtlessly forward without reflection, or investigation, or ever going below
the surface of things. But what else are you living for? What would your farm and your merchandise avail you, if your only son, the heir of
your name and fame and fortune, were doomed
to hopeless captivity? What shall it profit a man
if he gain the whole world and let slip his brother's

soul ?   For if a man love not his brother whom he
hath seen, how shall he love God whom he hath
not seen ?   And what lazy love is this that will
throw out a rope to his sinking brother, but will
not take the trouble to see whether it be long
enough to reach him, or strong enough to bear
him ?

By using a little tact in the " cure of souls," our
work becomes not only more agreeable, but more
pleasant.   If you talk to a man at a fitting time
and in a natural way, not with routine and for-
mality, not simply from a cold sense of duty, not
with a desire to proselyte him, nor pharisaically, —
but out of the depths of a loving heart, yearning
over the spirits that are in prison, longing to loose
the bands of the oppressor, and to guide the wanderer to Christ, — in ninety-nine cases out of a
hundred, you will, I believe, meet not only courtesy and kindness, but the sincerest gratitude.   This,
indeed, is not essential, but it is pleasant.   Duty
ought to be followed up to the mouth of the cannon
that has powder and a chain-shot inside, and a
fusee scattering sparks outside ; but it is neither
religion nor morality nor courage to go there
from sheer love of the heads, trunks, and limbs
out of which glory is inferred by the historian.   A
duty is not to be shirked because it is disagreeable :
but if it can be made agreeable, by all means make
it so.   It is a fine thing to be persecuted for righteousness' sake.   It strengthens and toughens and

develops the soul. We reverence the heroism that
would be sawn asunder, slain with the sword, wander about in sheep-skins and goat-skins, in deserts
and mountains and dens and in caves of the earth,
yet, strong in faith, would not deny the Lord. But
we have very little of that kind of persecution ;
ours comes in a mild form, and we rather enjoy it. In fact, except among sound orthodox
Christians, there is not much persecution in these
latter times. We like to flatter ourselves that
there is. We like to fancy ourselves bearing a
cross, because it enables us to claim the crown.
Young people, who have just begun to think upon
their ways and to turn their feet to the testimonies of the Lord, read of the cruel mockings and
scourgings recorded in the New Testament, and,
forgetting that they are not living in Rome in the
days of Nero, exhort each other to courage and
constancy after the manner of Paul and the early
Christians. If you bring them to the point, — in-
sisting that they explain definitely what they mean,
— they will probably conclude that they refer to
the scorn, ridicule, contumely, or coldness " of
the world." Even of this, however, there is
very little in New England. I dare say a good
many of my young readers will be considerably
shocked at hearing it; but it is true. Religion
here walks in silver slippers. It is, on the whole,
appreciably more respectable to be within than
without the pale of the Church. I have been

amused to hear young men counsel each other at
prayer-meetings not to fear the jeers of the world,
when their world was composed of an overwhelming majority of at least nominal Christians, —
when their certificate of church-membership was,
if not a passport, at least a recommendation to the
" best society " and the most lucrative clerkships.
It would be very strange if it were otherwise. Our
young people, and our old people too, make the
mistake of applying to our own state of society
facts which are true only of other and far different
ones. Would it not be singular, if the descendants
of the Puritans had thus early so far cast off the
faith and practice of their fathers, as that society
generally should hold in contempt all that they held
in reverence ? We may have degenerated, but not
with such rapid strides. We have softened the
harsher outlines of a stern belief, rendering it, we
hope, more effective ; but we have as yet by no
means discarded it, substituting therefor devices
of our own. Many foreign influences are at
work, and many foreign elements have been introduced, — some for good, some for evil ; but the
basis is unchanged. There may be places —
cities, towns, villages — where religion is despised,
but I have never seen them. The great mass
of intelligent people in our land — which is the
great mass of the people — treat Christianity
with outward respect. I can go further, and
say that I never knew a truly humble, devout,

sensible, consistent Christian ridiculed on account of his Christianity, except in a few religious newspapers and Sunday-school books. I have been surprised to see the respect paid to religion by those who made no pretensions to it themselves.

It is true that inconsistent Christians do get a good many hard hits ; and as most of us are more or less inconsistent, it follows that most of us have to wince occasionally, but we have no right to complain. It may not be kind or chivalrous in the hitter, but, if we present a vulnerable point to the foe, we must expect him to take advantage of it. We flatter our self-love that we are following the footsteps of the martyrs, when we are but stumbling along by-paths of our own. It is not our Christianity, but our inconsistency, that is laughed at, as it richly deserves, and may consider itself let off lightly at that. When our efforts for others are received with ridicule, ten to one it is because we go to work in a ridiculous way. I do not say this harshly or reproachfully. It is a simple statement of fact. Some of us are naturally absurd. We take hold of things in general the wrong way. Some of us are only partially absurd. Let us acknowledge the fact good-naturedly, and if we fail where we earnestly hoped to succeed, let us consider whether it may not be due to the outcropping of our absurdity, as well as of another's total depravity. When we enter the portals of the

church, we take our bundle of peculiarities with us.
So far as they are stumbling-blocks in other peo-
ples' paths, we ought to do all that we can to remove them ; which being done, we are guiltless.
But do not let us magnify them into religion, and
think the cause of Christ bound up in them. They
may be our fault ; they may be our misfortune.
In either case they are not our glory.

We confound incident with essence ; and the result is harmful. It is wrong, and wrong is always
harmful. It is unjust, and injustice works woe.
People are bad enough ; it does not conduce to
God's glory or their own good to make them out
any worse than they are. They have a sufficient •
alacrity in sinning; do not let us call that a sin
which is only a difference of taste. I once saw a
pious woman seem as much distressed because her
brother spoke lightly of the preaching faculty of a
certain minister, as if he had told a lie ; when the
fact was, that the minister, although the very salt
of the earth for goodness, — a burning and shining
light for all moral virtues and Christian graces, —
was an intolerable proser in the pulpit. Famine
itself could hardly obtain meat off the dry bones
of his theological disquisitions. Do you not see
that such a confounding of facts must have a tendency to make a man desperate ? If you visit
upon mere difference of taste, or an acute sense of
the ridiculous, the reprobation which belongs only
to moral obliquity, — if you identify your weak-

nesses with Christ's strength, and consider a dart
aimed at one to be also and inevitably aimed at the
other, — you must not be surprised if he whom you
wish to serve and save, following your example,
falls into the same mistake, and the name of Christ
thereby suffers reproach.

Be careful, therefore, not to confound men with
principles, the religion of Christ with your ex-
emplification of it, the susceptibility of the mind
to various emotions with the " opposition of the
natural heart " to truth. Make the cause of Christ
always yours ; but do not suppose that your cause
must invariably be the cause of Christ. The shell-
fish and sea-weed that cling to the ship's keel are
not the ship. They are only obstacles to its progress. The heavy blows, the burning and scraping
and scouring, are only to clear them off. Nobody
is going to scuttle the ship.

In the world ye shall have tribulation, but the
tribulation of New England Christians in the year
1860 is from within rather than from without, —
it arises from our own sins rather than from the
sins of others.

Whoever wishes to work effectually for Christ
must put his armor on. It is no work for lazy
people. It needs the wisdom of the serpent, the
harmlessness of the dove, and the strength of the
lion. Let us *watch* for souls, as those that must
give account.

III.

ORDINANCES.

"Let no man therefore judge you in meat, or in drink, or in respect of an holyday, or of the new moon, or of the Sabbath days : which are a shadow of things to come; but the body is of Christ." — Col. ii. 16, 17.

E who are Congregationalists have small reverence for the Apostolic succession. We can hardly believe that·virtue has been conducted over an unbroken line of fingers eighteen centuries long, and we are rather surprised at the credulity of our Episcopal brethren. Yet we sometimes pay ourselves, and demand from others, as great a reverence for certain forms, as if those forms had been intrusted to our keeping by the great Head of the Church. We are as inconsistent as we fancy " Churchmen " to be credulous. They logically require reverence for what they believe to be a true apostolic succession. We illogically demand equal reverence for that for which we claim only human origin.

I suppose the whole Protestant world is a unit

as regards the necessity and propriety of assembling together on the first day of the week for the purpose of worshipping God in a direct and especial manner. The teaching of Scripture, both by precept and example, and the experience of the Christian world, have shown that the social element of man's religious nature needs this for its adequate sustenance and generous growth. But as to the particular manner in which this worship shall be conducted, or the number of times that we shall assemble ourselves together on Sunday, the Scriptures do not give a distinct intimation, and we acknowledge no other authority, — nor is there, in fact, any unanimity of custom in the matter. Many a New England village has, however, settled the question as succinctly and definitely as if it had consulted Urim and Thummim and received response. Extemporaneous prayers uttered by the clergyman alone, written sermons, and choir-singing, — for quality, two church services and Sunday school in the day-time, and prayer-meeting in the evening, — for quantity. The question of quality I do not now propose to discuss, but let us examine a little this question of quantity.

I have no right to reproach you for going to church only once on Sunday, and you have no right to reproach me for going four times. By your one attendance you express your approbation of, and your respect for, the institution, and by the

four, I express just as much, and no more. You
uphold the ordinance just as powerfully as I.
The man who goes to a theatre twice a year expresses his opinion that the theatre is not a sin
per se, or confesses that, although a sin, it holds
out to him a temptation too strong to be resisted,
just as truly as he who goes to the theatre every
night. So the man who goes to church once on
Sunday, lifts up his voice in favor of church-going
just as loudly as he who goes four times. Thus
far they stand on the same ground. But the difference between them is this. The latter shows
by his repeated attendance that the kind of food
which he there receives is best adapted to his soul.
He can worship God better in the great congregation than elsewhere. He can, for the time,
pray better with other men's lips than with his
own. He can praise better if other men "join
voices" in his praise. His soul can better grasp a
truth which has passed through the alembic of
another man's soul, than one that presents itself
to him at first hand. His social nature is largely
developed. He craves companionship. His fervor is not spontaneous, but communicated. His
heart strikes fire only when smitten by the thought
or feeling of another heart. His heat is developed
by friction. All this is natural to him, and right.
The church and the prayer-meeting are to him the
house of God and the very gate of heaven. There
he sees the angels ascending and descending.

There his faith and hope and love, wakened to
new life, bridge for him the finite and the infinite,
the present and the future, earth and heaven.
The communion of saints fills him with holy joy,
and as his reluctant feet turn lingeringly away, he
exclaims with rapture, " How amiable are thy
tabernacles, O Lord of Hosts ! "

The former shows with equal clearness that he
possesses a different organization.   Other conditions are more favorable to his growth in grace.
The savory meat that his soul loves cannot be
furnished him by the bow and quiver of Esau,
even though he be a mighty hunter before the
Lord.   It comes to him in " saintly solitude."
From between the covers of musty books, the old
truths, ever fresh and ever young, spring up to
meet him.   Dry leaves exhale for him the sweetest odors.   Old-time thoughts, still glowing with
the piety that conceived them, fragrant with aroma
caught from the thousands of hearts which they
visited with healing as they passed down the ages,
have for him a charm, a pungency, a power, which
the words of no living preacher possess.   The
wisdom of the past girds him with wisdom for the
future.   Among the heroes and martyrs of other
days he finds his fitting panoply.   He puts the
new wine to his lips, but he feels that the old is
better.   Or it may be that he finds Christ in field
and grove.   He hears the voice of the Lord walking in the garden.   A bird of the air carries the

message of love to him. The brooks ripple it.
The winds murmur it. The waves sparkle it.
"Rock and tree and flowing water" are God's
messengers to him. Every harebell that swings
its purple cup to the summer breeze, every lily
that opens its white bosom to the evening dew,
every blade of grass that wrests a homely but vigorous life from the uncareful soil, are ministers of
God to him. He finds a gospel in the hum of the
bees, in the chirr of insects, in the busy, unconscious happiness that stirs around him. God's
wisdom, God's providence, God's fatherliness,
meet him everywhere. Earth and sea and sky
are to him a harp of a thousand strings. Touched
by his tuneful hand they quiver into melody, and
every creature which is in heaven, and on the
earth, and under the earth, join the song, — the
voice of a great multitude, the voice of many
waters, the voice of mighty thunderings, saying,
Alleluia! The Lord God omnipotent reigneth.
Blessing and honor and glory and power be
unto him that sitteth on the throne, and unto
the Lamb, forever and ever.

So far all is right; but when number one turns
on number two, or number two turns on number
one, and begins to rebuke him for his mode of
spending the Sabbath, all becomes wrong again.
Every man must decide as to the kind of food his
soul needs. His liberty is not to be judged of
another man's conscience. The gay canary-bird

pecks a dainty breakfast from its little cup of seeds, and rings out full-throated thanks on the morning air. The meek-eyed oxen crop the purple clover, and in its strength patiently bear the burden and heat of the day. The oxen would starve on the canary-seed, and all the clover in the world would not supply to the bird the place of its one little cup.

It is often true, I sorrowfully admit, that many people who stop away from church are actuated by no right motive. They not only do not worship God at church, but they do not worship him anywhere. They are simply lazy and indifferent. Their idea of rest is lounging. They doze away the Sabbath day in profitless, and therefore harmful idleness.

But also there are many constant attendants on religious services whose course is guided by nothing higher than habit. They have been brought up in a certain way from infancy, and they never think of doing otherwise. Others go for excitement. Some will marvel at this, but when a man has been digging potatoes or hoeing corn or mending shoes for six days, it is a pleasant change for him to put on his best coat and go to meeting thrice on Sunday, and he feels as if he can hardly get too much of it. Others do it for the sociality of the thing. In the country villages, for a considerable part of the year, it is the principal opportunity that friends have of meeting each other, exchanging kindly greetings, and displaying the fine clothes which their own skill or industry has procured. I do not say that these are wrong motives. I do not think they are. It is quite innocent to take pleasure even in wearing a pretty bonnet to church ; but it is only innocent. It is not virtuous. It is not devout. It is not holy. If it is not combined with some higher motive, there is a sin of omission, and the act of going to church is no more religious than the act of eating breakfast. Yet that such cases often occur, does in no wise militate against church-going, nor disprove the fact that there are devout worshippers in every sanctuary, — men and women who go there to call upon the name of the Lord. Just so does the indifference and irreligion found in the other class not prove that a man may not, in the exercise of an enlightened judgment, absent himself from the morning, afternoon, or evening service, and yet be a man after God's own heart.

So far, I have only desired to show that staying away from a portion of the church services is not of itself a sin, and ought not to be considered a presumption of irreligion or indifference.

I now go further, and suggest whether this wholesale church-going be not a hinderance to our upward progress. Is it not sometimes allowed to usurp the place of other duties ? If we went to church less, could we not serve God more ? Do

we not make a kind of salve for our consciences,
soothing ourselves for the neglect of other duties
by the punctual performance of this ?   Is it not,
sometimes, a device of the enemy to take away
our attention from the real sin that is undermining
the foundations of our faith ?   I would be very far
from wishing, even had I the power, to strike at
the root, or at the smallest opening bud, of any tree
whose leaves are for the healing of the nations ;
but there may be straggling or withered branches
that ought to be lopped off, and which no one hand
is strong enough to do.   It must be the work of
many, — all feeble, it may be, yet powerful in
union, and impelled by hearts that would fain gain
strength for themselves by helping other hearts to
bear their burdens.   So I would speak of such a
matter with great diffidence, — rather in the form
of suggestion than of advice.   I would not lift up
a rash, presumptuous hand against anything which
has contributed to the happiness and received the
sanction of millions.   An old-time custom has always in itself somewhat venerable.   The simple
fact that it *is* a custom, commends it to respect.
Anything that indicates and moulds character is
entitled, at least, to serious attention.   Even if
wholly bad, we cannot forget that it emanated
from, and reacted upon, responsible immortal beings, and we

> " walk backward with averted gaze,
> And hide its shame."

If it be good, we recognize and cherish it as a mighty engine for truth. If it have outgrown the occasion which gave it birth, or if it be, as is very common, partly good and partly evil, we lay it aside reverently, or strive so to modify it that it shall conduce only to highest ends. But we ought not to let our reverence so far mislead our judgment as to refuse to see the evil, or, seeing it, to remove it. *Nam consuetudo sine veritate vetustas erroris est,* "Custom without truth is the old age of error." If it is best for us all to spend the greater part of Sunday in public religious services, let us all do it. If it is best only for a part, let a part only do it. If it is asserted that there is a more excellent way, let us, as we love God and our brother, examine that way before we decide for or against it. Let us prove all things, holding fast only that which is good.

It seems to me that we put Sabbath-keeping generally on too low ground. We call it duty when it should be privilege. The Sabbath is a feast, and not a fast. It is less a command than a boon. It is granted to us, above and beyond being imposed upon us. It is our great rest-day, given us that we may not faint from overmuch weariness. After a week's toil of body, or mind, or both, God, in his fatherly love and tender care, presses upon us this great gift that our souls may live. He stays the sweeping tide that we may take our soundings, reckon our latitude and lon-

gitude, find where we are and whither we are
steering. In the dizzying whirl of life we need
— O how greatly do we need, and how sorely
do we suffer without it!— this regularly recurring
interval of quiet, that we may look gratefully back
over all the way which the Lord our God hath
led us, and trustfully forward through all the
future till the end come.

But often we baffle these designs. We spend
our Sunday in what I can call nothing but religious dissipation. We scarcely commune with
ourselves at all. We leave no time for it. We
live in public. We flit from service to service.
We listen with more or less attention to one, two,
three sermons, besides spending an hour or so in
Sunday schools. We fast during the week, gorg-
ing ourselves on Sunday. It seems to me nothing
more or less than a kind of theological cramming.
The result is, and must inevitably be, a spiritual
dyspepsia. The food we receive is ill-timed and
ill-measured, and nourishes a morbid or partial
growth. It goes but in small proportion to blood
and bone and sinew, — to strength and symmetry
and life. Much of it is as water spilt upon the
ground. The waste is immense. So our religion
lacks a well-proportioned development. It has a
tendency to go off into all manner of side issues,
instead of meeting the world, the flesh, and the
devil face to face, and putting them all to flight.
It runs to prayer-meetings and technicalities rather

than to right living. It is more concerned to keep
heretics out of the Church than to bring sinners
into Christ's fold. It sticks on to the outside of
our life instead of penetrating to the centre, purifying the heart. We set our religion here, and
our business there, stirring them together a little
occasionally ; whereas they should chemically
combine, forming a third substance, which is
neither the one nor the other, but infinitely better than either, — namely, a Christian life. Paul
gives the recipe and the result. " Not slothful in
business. Fervent in spirit." This is " serving
the Lord."

The Sabbath is a rest-day, but change is rest.
We are just as much rested by standing after we
have been sitting a long while, as we are by
sitting after we have been standing. It is the
duty of every man to keep the Sabbath holy, but
the best way for him to keep it depends somewhat
on circumstances. Whether a certain course of
action will give him rest or not, depends upon
whether it will give him change. He must be the
judge. Every man must do that which is right
in his own eyes, subject to the "higher law." If
his business during the week is such as occupies
the body rather than the mind, then it will be not
only harmless, but beneficial, for him to keep
his mind at work on Sunday. The Sabbath-
school and prayer-meeting will give scope to faculties that might otherwise languish from inaction.

The well-thought (whether or not well-written) sermon will give him something to take hold of. If it is a little knotty, abstruse, or unusual, so much the better, provided it be tangible and portable. Behind the plough, on the bench, over the anvil, he will straighten the tangled doctrine and clear up the clouded truth. It is the quiet, meditative tenor of his daily life that enables him to spend his Sabbath in profitable activity.

If, on the contrary, his business engrosses all his energies, physical and mental, he needs quiet on Sunday, — the song of praise to soothe, — the voice of prayer to elevate, — the sermon to direct his attention to other matters than his business, or to his business from a different and a higher standpoint. The home circle, too, the society of wife and child,

> " The graces and the loves that make
> The music of the march of life,"

all have their ministry of salvation to him. They soften and spiritualize the heart that would otherwise grow hard from the very anxiety of its affection.

We have, unhappily, yet not without reason, contracted a distrust of natural religion, or the religion that God reveals through nature. We are afraid of it as if it were some insidious monster, that must be strangled in its innocent-seeming infancy, lest it attack and destroy our Christian faith. I have heard young people warned against it as a kind of hidden heresy and infidelity; whereas, it seems to me that natural religion is just as good as revealed religion, as far as it goes. It does not, to be sure, go a long way. We have something which goes a great deal farther. Yet many nations in many ages have had nothing else. It is not absolutely necessary to our salvation, because we have a more sure word of prophecy. Yet it is a help whereunto we shall do well to take heed. It would be very wicked and very weak — a crime and a blunder — for us to turn away from the revelation of the Bible, which is definite and explicit, to the revelation of nature, which is in a degree vague and indistinct; but it is not only wise — it is the highest wisdom — to take the two together, to bring each to the interpretation of the other. It would be extremely stupid for a man to go down cellar to live because he had bought a pound of tallow candles. It would also be somewhat stupid for him to refuse ever to light his candles, because God has furnished a sun. The only sensible way is to take in with utmost grasp the rich, full, all-pervading sunshine, but, if thereby the ends of charity and cheer can be better promoted, not to despise the farthing candle at evening hour.

Natural religion is not Pantheism, — at least, not the Pantheism that abrogates God, — not the Pantheism that makes the creature coequal and coextensive with the Creator, — that confounds the work and the worker. There is a true Pantheism, — to see God in all. That which would fain have us take the vessel for Him that made it, is a false Pantheism, if, indeed, it be not Atheism. The blind and base confusion of the one is as far removed from the enlightened adoration of the other, as darkness is from light. The one is a positive truth ; the other, a negative falsehood. But because we reject the falsehood, we need not reject the truth. We are not to worship Nature, since she is only God's handiwork ; but we ought to revere her because she *is* his handiwork. What God thought it worth his while to make, it is certainly worth our while to examine. We are losers if we do not. The Land and the Book complement each other. The light of the Bible thrown full upon the face of Nature brings out a hidden loveliness that her priests and prophets, groping without it, never saw; and when earth and sea and sky shall have given up the secrets which are in them, the holy words that are now but a faint nebula of light will shine out full, distinct, and clear, each

> " A spotless star, a fixed, central sun
> In the mind's heaven, unchangeable and one."

Yet we, learned and unlearned, are very heathen in this matter. On the one side, we too often put science in the place of God. We attribute events to causes, forgetting the great First Cause. We go back one step, and stand exulting in our knowl-

edge, as if we had gone back to that divinely
simple, yet inconceivable and fearful "in the
beginning." An apple falls, and we call it gravitation, and glory in the grand discovery, and
plume ourselves on our acuteness and our wisdom.
—as if we knew anything about gravitation, except
that it is. One puny little star in the grand and
awful universe, we sweep around in our appointed
cycle. Infinite mysteries are about us and beneath
us, in which we have neither hand nor voice. No
influence of ours can hasten or retard, or in any
way disturb, the earth in her swift career. Impelled by an unseen force, guided by inexorable
law, she wheels through the circling heavens.
We sit perched on her surface for a few days,
turning our little glasses upon the worlds that go
flashing by, — shrinking now and then with sudden fear, as some unknown messenger seems to
threaten destruction to our frail chariot. We
delve a few feet down among the granite records,
striving with dim eyes and feeble hands to wrest
their secrets from the rocks. Painfully and labori-
ously, generation after generation, shred by shred,
we gather a few facts, and then a " giant intellect " arises, and compels admiration by the an-
nouncement of some "great law," which is only
the general statement of assorted facts. So in
the lapse of ages we discover here and there
gleams of the vast system by which God governs the universe. We play at hide and seek

3 *

with the truths of space and time. Right, if
we do it right, — and productive only of good.
Wrong, if we do it wrong, — and conducive only
to evil.

It needs not to wage war with science. That
would be the blindest, and, fortunately, the most
useless stupidity. Science is the handmaid of religion. Every step we take in the knowledge of
mind or matter brings us intellectually, and should
bring us morally, nearer to God. Our very mistakes are fruitful of good, since every error ex-
posed diminishes, by so much, our distance from
the truth. There is, there can be, no contradiction
between the truths of science and the truths of
the Bible, for truth is always at one with itself.
What contradiction exists, lies between seeming
truths, or our conceptions of them. As we increase in wisdom, all discrepancies will disappear.
True theology and true geology will dovetail into
each other. If it could be otherwise, — if the
Bible needed to be shielded from the light of
advancing knowledge, lest its own light should be
quenched or dimmed, it would be no Bible at all.
A revelation that needs to be propped up is a
sorry kind of revelation. If, when science is
rounded to completion, it shall contradict the
Bible, let the Bible go. We do not want it. It
will have done its work. Let it be gathered to
the Korans, and the Eddas, and the Shasters.
But it will not! Science and theology are both

in their infancy. They have not yet put off their swaddling-clothes. We only look through a glass darkly. When the full glory is revealed, we shall see how, along the world's dark ages not yet closed, both have been working together for good. Meanwhile, let us be modest. Let us be reverent. Let us remember that a law is only God's mode of action. Science is recreant to her trust if she makes us satisfied with anything short of God. Better that we should look upon the fearful sights and great signs in the heavens, — upon plague and pestilence and famine as the direct scourges of God, than that we should say "gravitation," "electricity," "malaria," and put God out of all our thoughts. All that we can do as regards other worlds, and the most we can do in this, is to discover what *is*. We say the planets revolve round the sun, and the sun around its sun. Nitrogen destroys life, and oxygen destroys life, but nitrogen and oxygen together support life. We can neither explain nor alter the facts. We cannot add one cubit to our stature, nor make one hair of our heads white or black. How worse than useless, then, for us to attempt to divorce science and religion. How thousand-fold orphaned should we be, if we could cut loose from God. How senseless is it for us to construct our little theories from our fragmentary facts, — houses of straw, which a breath from the next generation may blow away, — and then stand off and exclaim, "Is

not this great Babylon that *I* have built?" O
fools and slow of heart! He that sitteth in the
heavens shall laugh! The Lord shall have us
in derision.

But, on the other side, who is it that is working
this divorce of science and religion? Not the
"undevout astronomer," not the philosopher, who,
in the strength of his mighty intellect, refuses
to believe in the need or the fact of revelation,
and scouts the idea of a miracle. To be sure,
he does what he can. He harnesses himself to
Satan's chariot, and drags with all his might and
main; but the Lord has taken off the wheels,
and it would be very up-hill work, if you, Christian brother, did not stand close in the rear and
push. One sinner destroys much good, but not
so much as the conscientious, narrow-minded,
bigoted Christian destroys. It is you who do the
mischief, — you, who refuse to recognize anything
as religious or devout or Christian unless it is
measured off by your yard-stick; you, who, with
unskilful hands, build fences high and wide, and
with presumptuous lips cry aloud, "The temple
of the Lord, the temple of the Lord, the temple
of the Lord are these"; you, who denounce those
who are seeking the pearl of great price because
they do not push their search in your domains;
you, who lay upon the necks of disciples a burden
which neither our fathers nor we were able to
bear; you who distrust the discoveries and dis-

courage the advances of science because they trench upon your crude, preconceived notions of truth; you, who seem to fancy that in the "march of mind" the ark will topple over unless you put forth unsanctified hands to steady it; you, who wantonly or ignorantly confound looking at God through nature, with looking at nature as God, — him who strengthens his faith by studying the wonderful works of God, with him who first wrests them from their author, and then substitutes them for faith, changing the beauty of ear-rings and bracelets into the hideousness of a golden calf, and then falling down and worshipping it.

Do not, by any possibility, misunderstand me to advocate that namby-pambyism that rejects the creeds which it has not strength enough to grasp; keeps itself afloat in a weak solution of feeble sentiment, second-hand poetry, borrowed metaphysics, and stolen Christianity; proves its independence of thought by not thinking at all; its elevation above the atmosphere of belief, by exploding in perpetual vacuum; reviles the intellect which it cannot fathom; pelts with mud the dead lions whose living roar would have imparted to its heels a vigor never possessed by its head; mocks at the Samsons, blind and chained, grinding in the prison-houses of error, from whose little finger, when free, it would have shrunk in shuddering dismay; and, decrying the ministry of the word, is itself a perpetual sermon on the text, "Vanity of vanities." A creed is but the expression of belief, and though the wisest man probably believes something that is not true, the very worst of creeds is better than no creed at all. Nothing is so fatal as indifference. In the snow-country it is better to go in the wrong road than to stop going altogether. The man. who has no belief, would better sell all that he has and buy one.

The natural religion that I mean is referred to in the sixty-fifth Psalm. The old Hebrews, half-civilized as they were, if not rather half-savage, were wiser in this thing than we. To them it was the voice of the Lord that broke the cedars of Lebanon. It was the Lord that sat upon the flood. They saw his mercy in the heavens and his faithfulness reaching unto the clouds. It was he who prepared rain for the earth, and made the grass to grow upon the mountains, who gave to the beast his food, and to the young ravens which cried, who filled them with the finest wheat, scattered the hoar-frost like ashes, called forth his ice like morsels, caused his wind to blow and the waters to flow, brought out the hosts of the stars by number, and called them all by name.

Well will it be for us when the unlearned seek wisdom, and the learned humility; when the fool on the one side and the philosopher on the other, — the child in knowledge and he that is a

hundred years old, — shall alike call not only upon
his angels to praise the Lord, but " Praise ye him,
sun and moon : praise ye him, all ye stars of light.
Praise him, ye heaven of heavens, and ye waters
that be above the heavens. Fire, and hail ; snow,
and vapor ; stormy wind, fulfilling his word ;
mountains, and all hills ; fruitful trees, and all
cedars ; beasts, and all cattle ; creeping things,
and flying fowl ; praise the name of the Lord :
for He commanded, and they were created. His
name alone is excellent ; his glory is above the
earth and heaven."

Assembling together for prayer and praise is rather the festival of our religion than its practice. The
work, the duty, the struggle, the thick and brunt of
the battle, come in the week-days. We meet to
eat the bread and drink the waters of life. During the week these ought to enter into the system,
becoming blood and brain and nerve and sinew.
If a man stays away from the banquet, he has his
share of all the sorrow and suffering appointed
to men ; yet rejects the consolation which the
gentle ministrations of the Gospel afford. The
curse that was pronounced upon Adam falls just
as heavily on him ; yet he closes his ear to the
soothing voice that would fain make him forget
the burden, and rejects the outstretched hand that
would help him bear it. His path is steep and
difficult, like all paths, but he will not take the
proffered cup that would "medicine his weariness."

If it is his ignorance, he is surely to be pitied ; shall
he be any the less pitied if it is his sin? Is not
sin the saddest of all sorrows ? It was over wild
and wicked men — a fierce and violent rabble —
that Christ's heart melted in infinite compassion.
" O Jerusalem, Jerusalem, *thou that killest the
prophets, and stonest them which are sent unto thee.*"
It is this Divine pity that we need, — this godlike
yearning over sin-sick souls. We are too apt to
be wanting in charity, tenderness, consideration.
We try to drive where we should seek to win.
We remember Christ's " O serpents, generation
of vipers ! " and forget his " that ye love one
another." We are more ready to follow him
with the scourge of small cords in our hands, than
with his new commandment in our hearts. If
God saw as man sees, scarcely could the righteous
be saved. *He* knoweth our frame; He remembereth that we are dust. Man, often ignorant of
the one, is often forgetful of the other. We can
hardly be too severe in judging ourselves, or too
lenient in judging others. Generally he who
is most just toward himself is most charitable
toward his neighbors.

There is not a little self-indulgence mingled
with our church-going. The meeting-house is
not always the post of duty. A father goes in
the morning with his older children, and leaves
his wife with a fretful, sickly baby in her arms.
All day long she nurses the suffering child. Not

a moment of rest, not a chapter from her Bible, does the Sabbath bring to her. It is one long weariness and anxiety. I think that man would serve God a great deal more effectually by staying at home and minding the baby awhile, so that the mother can get a little quiet out of her Sunday, than by going to church and listening complacently to two or three excellent sermons.

Fathers and mothers often forget the wants of their little ones. The poor things are too young to understand or enjoy Sabbath services, and not young enough to be kept at home and amused, — *particularly if there is no servant.* So the time which should be a holiday for the body, and a holy day for the soul, drags wearily on for them. They nestle restlessly, or sleep mercifully, through the long sermons, and employ themselves at home as best they can. The legitimate channels through which their life flows being cut off, their exuberance is continually carving for itself new and illegitimate ones. Happy, both for themselves and their parents, is the hour that sees their little feet pattering bedward. It ought not to be so. Sunday cannot be too early made the bright day of childhood. All that is beautiful and pleasant and sunshiny, as well as all that is holy, ought to be entwined with their Sunday memories.

This cannot be done without self-sacrifice. Children must have something to do; otherwise

E

they will make something, and that something will
generally be mischief. They are active, and not
passive. Their spirits should not be repressed,
but guided. It is not enough that they be kept
out of danger ; they should be instructed, amused,
and made happy, — not by servile petting, but by
wise training. The nursery can be wrapped in
Sunday surroundings. It needs no formidable
preparation. A few books and pictures by the
father's or mother's eye and hand and voice can
be invested with attraction. Love is fertile in
expedients.

Yet it is true that it cannot be done without
time and trouble. But if one of the reasons why
children are born is not to discipline their parents
by trouble, why were they not born all grown up?
It would be far easier for the father and mother to
leave their children to the care or the carelessness
of a hired nurse and enjoy themselves in church, —
or, if there be no nurse, to take the young unfor-
tunates with them, to sleep or wriggle or sit out
in dumb, sad patience what seems to them an in-
terminable sermon, — than it would be to stay at
home and provide for the wants of these eager
young souls, just dancing on the threshold of life ;
but there is no trouble like the trouble with which
a child's folly, sin, and shame bring his father's
gray hairs to the grave. If the day should ever
come when your house is left unto you desolate,
your hopes shattered, and your heart broken,

through a son's misdoing, you will look with bitter
and unavailing regret on the time when his guileless soul, his loving, plastic nature, and every innocent charm of childhood, called to you to cherish
and save, and you would not hear. There is that
withholdeth more than is meet, but it tendeth to
poverty.

Devote at least a part of your day to the moral
needs of your dependent little ones. Let them go
to church, even if they do not understand. They
need discipline as well as their parents, and they
also need to form habits of church-going. But
do not keep them at it longer than they are able
to bear. Let pleasure share with duty the opportunity to interest and the power to teach.

As men live in communities, it is often necessary to ask, " What will be the influence of my
action ? what would be the consequence if every
one should do as I do ? " in order to answer the
question, " Am I doing right ? " The fact that
we sometimes lay too great stress on this point is
not a reason why we should lay on it no stress at
all. While it is true that a right action is always
to be done, and a wrong action always to be
shunned, be the consequences what they may, it
is also true that there are actions whose character
is determined by the consequences which are designed, or which may be expected to flow from
them. If a boy goes to college, or a girl takes a
daily walk, because it is what he or she likes to do

better than anything else, it is simply innocent; if they do it against their inclination, but cheerfully because their father wishes it and they desire to obey and please him, it becomes virtuous; if beyond this they are actuated by the desire to do right, — to please God by obeying their father, — it is religion. The motive of action often lifts the action out of the slough of sin, or off the plane of innocence, to the higher planes of virtue and religion. The Paul who withstood Peter to the face because he was to be blamed, was the same Paul who would eat no meat while the world standeth, lest he make his brother to offend. It was the motive alone which made the first act bravery and not brawling; and the second, consideration and not cowardice. The boldness with which he bearded Peter was no more praiseworthy, and certainly I think less rare, than the liberality and courtesy which induced him to abstain from meat.

Inextricably woven together as the lives and destinies of men are, the greatest good of the greatest number seems to be the direct object of that course of action whose ultimate end is to glorify God and enjoy him forever. So far as individual happiness may consist therewith, it is to be consulted; but if the two clash, individual happiness must give way. Now it often happens that the two do clash. The highest real good of the many can be obtained only by sacrificing the highest apparent good of the few. Yet does this

in no wise affect the duty of all — not excepting
the sufferers themselves — to work for the highest
general good. Common law recognizes this. A
butcher, is not allowed to place his slaughter-house
wherever it may be most convenient to himself;
nor a farmer to dam up, for his own purposes, in
his own field, a brook, whose stoppage would diminish the value of his neighbor's field. If, then,
a man is not suffered by law to benefit his purse
at the expense of his neighbor's, he certainly ought
not to be allowed by religion to benefit his soul at
the expense of his neighbor's. As a matter of fact
I do not suppose this can ever happen. Material
and spiritual laws differ so far, that the good which
he might obtain from his liberty would be over-
balanced by the evil which he would suffer from
his selfishness.

Attendance and non-attendance upon church-
services are not, therefore, to be decided solely by
their effects upon individuals, but upon the community. A man may believe that he should receive more benefit by stopping away from church
altogether; yet, unless he thinks it would be better on the whole for every one to do the same,
and Sabbath services, therefore, to be discontin-
ued, it would not be right for him to do it. Eventually he would not suffer, since, as I have before
intimated, his loss in one direction would be more
than compensated by his gain in another. But a
conscientious and wise man would not probably

consider a difference of opinion or of taste between
himself and his pastor or his fellow-worshippers
sufficient to justify such a course of action. Nothing would be enough except a conviction that his
attendance would be a connivance at wrong, — in
which case, he would think it right for every man
to do the same.

A man might, indeed, say that he would have
every one imitate himself in so far as that he should
judge for himself, and go, or refrain from going,
as he chose ; and when the Millennium comes, I
have no doubt this is precisely what we shall do ;
but for a few years more, probably, we shall have
to act, not simply with reference to the true, the
thoughtful, the wise, and the good, whose sole
object is to find the right path, and to walk therein, but to the careless, the frivolous, the unthinking, the selfish, who need to be coaxed and tempted
and drawn and driven into the kingdom of heaven.
We will not, however, dwell on this part of the
subject, but consider the consequences that would
ensue if every one should adopt the plan of going
to church once or twice on Sunday, instead of
twice or thrice.

I shall suppose that a plan is to be *adopted*, —
intelligently, conscientiously, from principle, — and
not that a habit is to be fallen into carelessly, from
indifference or laziness. And here let me say, my
irreligious friend, that you can, if you choose,
wrest my words, as the words of better and

wiser persons than I have been wrested, to your own destruction, but I disclaim responsibility for any such consequences. I shall express my views as clearly as I can ; and if lukewarm piety in any of its thousand-fold manifestations shall be aided or abetted by any word of mine, it will be because I have not the intellectual power to express my opinions and convictions in intelligible language. What I wish and design is, not to smooth the broad way, but to knock as many stumbling-blocks as possible out of the narrow way. I address myself particularly to the conscientious, to Christians, to those who would count all things but loss if they might so win souls to Christ, to men who for the truth's sake would march to the stake, who would willingly prove all things in order that they might hold fast that which is good, but who, in pursuit of noblest ends, do not employ the wisest means. I address them not for their own sakes merely, but for the sake of the lost souls who wander up and down, poor and miserable and blind and naked, to whom the light of God's Word is dimmed by the imperfections of the glass through which, almost alone, it darkly shines on them. If there are Christians who are perfectly satisfied with the present state of things, — who think that everything is doing that can be done to Christianize the world, — who believe that all future changes in modes of operation must be of degree, not of kind, — I do not speak to them; but to those who believe in a moral as well as in a material progression, — who believe that in grasping truth we have not attained all truth, — who would gladly receive from any quarter, however humble, any suggestion, however faint, which professes to endeavor to show how " one more unfortunate" may be brought in from the highways and hedges to the feast of the Lord.

The first obvious result would be irregular, and often small audiences, which would embarrass and discourage the minister. This, however, is an evil not without remedy. The minister, being a sensible man, as well as a devout Christian, has only to proportion the number of his services to the number of his hearers. If a large part of his congregation prefer no afternoon sermon, why should he not omit the afternoon sermon? In every place where there is more than one Evangelical church, the ministers could preach in their own churches in the morning, and have preaching by turns in each other's churches in the afternoon. This would give those who wish to go all day an opportunity to do so, while it would also be convenient for those who may be detained in the morning. The father and mother or nurse could take turns in minding the little ones at home, and at the same time feel that they were reaping the full benefit of the pastor's ripest thought. For (as a second result) any man's one sermon a week would probably be better than the best of his two a week, on an average ; while he who addresses a congregation gathered from two or three churches would be excited by that circumstance to do his best, and his best would be better than if he were obliged to write two or three sermons every week. There may be objections to this plan. The mother who stays at home with the baby in the morning, might choose to hear her own minister in the afternoon rather than be obliged to have recourse to a stranger. This, however, is only one of several disadvantages that arise naturally from babies, and must be compensated from domestic resources. Arrangements can be made so that she can hear her own pastor once a fortnight at least, and a good sermon once a fortnight is better than a poor one once a week. The deficiency must be made up by considerations of the general good, — assuming, of course, that the general good would thereby be increased. Another objection is, that, unfortunately, the relations of Christian congregations are sometimes such as to preclude the possibility of any such fraternal commingling. Such congregations can only be recommended to give up preaching altogether, and fast and pray themselves into a better state of mind. The petty feuds and jealousies and bickerings which sometimes exist between neighboring congregations are a disgrace to our Christianity, and make the " See how these Christians love one another ! " a burning and bitter sarcasm.

4

A better plan still, and one that seems to me to combine every excellence and exclude every defect, is that which has already been adopted by some churches, namely, to have preaching in the morning and Sabbath school in the afternoon. This can be done equally well whether there be one or more churches in a town. But in any society it should be universal ; that is, the Sabbath school should not be considered as established for the young only, but for all, just as much as the preaching is for all. All the intellect, all the available force of the congregation, should be brought in and used, either in the way of teaching or learning. It should be no superficial thing, — a half-hour or an hour spent in languidly trifling over a portion of Scripture with wandering eyes, divided attention, and ill-concealed weariness. It should be taken hold of by all — both teachers and scholars — as a work to be done. The most vigorous minds should be enlisted, the most powerful brains aroused, the deepest thought stirred. Rough minds will gain polish, and polished minds will gain strength. The Bible should be looked upon, not as a nosegay to be gracefully carried and daintily held ; but as a mine to be explored with fixed faith in its treasured gold. The whole congregation can be put on the quest of one truth. The child and the man can investigate the same subject. The former will, of course, only take its more obvious bearings ; the latter will explore its inner workings; and between the two will be every grade of interest and discovery. The people will become the active searchers for truth, instead of its passive recipients. Yet while their efficiency will be increased, their receptivity will be increased in proportion. The pastor's sermons will be far better understood and appreciated, and far more effectual, because the soil will have been broken up and made ready for the seed, instead of being hard and sun-baked as it often is. His close contact with his people will give point to his sermons. The Sabbath school will be a band of union. Pastor and people will stand on common ground. He will get at hearts. He will learn the difficulties that beset common minds. He will strike out ideas. New trains of thought will be suggested to him. He will be continually taking new stand-points. He will know the needs, the redundancies and the deficiencies, of his people. He will learn their spiritual and intellectual peculiarities, and where the most effective blows are to be struck. The energies of the Church will be brought out and developed. It will be a power instead of a weight, a hive instead of a sepulchre, a vineyard of the Lord instead of a valley of dry bones.

Instead of one preacher, there will be fifty preachers. Every pastor will be the leader of a host, and every church a magazine of weapons mighty through God to the pulling down of strongholds.

The benefit of some such arrangement to clergymen, and — since whatever benefits the pastor benefits the people — to the people, would be incalculable. Not only would it give him a broader sweep, but a clearer vision. It is in the nature of things impossible that a man should write three sermons a week, year in and year out, without a deterioration in the quality both of his sermons and of his mind ; not that his last sermons grow worse than his first, but worse than they would have been if he wrote fewer of them. The reason of this is not, as many suppose, that he writes himself empty, that the fountain runs dry, that he has nothing to say, and, being forced to say something, must utter platitudes. On the contrary, I suspect that ministers scarcely ever catch up with their note-books. There is a great deal of wickedness in the world, and a great deal of holiness in the Bible. It is the business of the minister to bring the two into contact; to transfix man's falsehood with God's truth ; to dissipate the mists of sin and stupidity with the clear shining of the Sun of Righteousness ; to stab every brazen-faced vice with the sword of the Spirit ; to bring the lamp of the word to bear upon all the hidden things of darkness, and reveal their loathsomeness. Whether this can be done with or without observation, it is equally his duty to it. We must reason of righteousness, temperance, and judgment to come, whether Fe-

lix scoff or tremble ; and until there remains on
earth no sin to be rebuked, no ignorance to be
taught, no soul to be saved, the minister will
hardly lack themes.

But to their successful treatment time is necessary ;—time to compare, to infer, to illustrate,
and to present; time to observe and collate facts,
and to deduce conclusions ; time to investigate
the past, to comprehend the present, and to shape
the future.   Can any minister, who at all appre-
ciates his calling, save time enough from his
family, social, and parochial duties to bring all
his forces to bear on the elucidation of three, or
even two, separate subjects every week, in such
a manner that the presentation of his views shall
be in every case the very best that it is possible
for him to make ?   This is, I think, what every
minister should aim at, what every people have
a right to expect, and what they should endeavor
by every means in their power to help him do.
If the same amount of study, research, and
thought that is spread over three sermons were
concentrated on one, the one subject would be so
much better managed, the one truth would be
presented with so much more deftness, point, and
pungency, that the Gospel would seem to start
up into new life.   The very consciousness that he
could give his whole thought and strength to one
thing, would deepen the one and increase the
other.   He could throw himself into it unreserv-

edly, distracted by no misgivings as to what was to become of the second sermon. There would be a unity of design, a skill in execution, and a completeness of effect, which would not only give him pleasure in the present, but would nerve him to new exertions in the future, — while his other duties, having a reasonable time allotted to their performance, would refresh instead of wearying him, — would return him to his study eager to grapple with his theme, instead of hurried, nervous, conscious of being unable to do anything as it should be done, and worried by that consciousness into still greater inability.

To the people, also, it seems to me that, apart from every other consideration, one sermon would do just as much good as two. A thorough exposition of one doctrine will give them food enough for thought, — a forcible inculcation of one duty will give them opportunity enough for practice until the next Sunday comes. In fact, the impression of one sermon is likely to be deeper than that of two. If it is good, it may be better left to work its own way undisturbed. If it is poor, the second will probably be poorer. A good sermon following close upon the heels of a good sermon, distracts the attention, annuls the effects of the first, and prevents a practical application of either. A poor sermon following a good one, acts like damp air on an electrical machine.

"But *is* going to church too much one of the crying sins of the age?" it has been asked. Is it not a waste of ammunition to fire away at what is at most only an error of judgment, and that in the right direction, when so many grievous sins spring up in deadly luxuriance around us? Very true, church-going is *not* a crying sin, and, if it stopped with itself, might well be let alone; but when one has a headache, you put mustard-poultices on his feet. Why do you do it? His feet are well enough; it is his head that is disordered. Why not poultice that? Because you know that the best way, or at least one of the ways, to get at his head, is through his feet. The head and the feet and the limbs are not separate individualities, but members of one body; and whether one member suffer, all the members suffer with it; or one member be honored, all the members rejoice with it. If the feet are too swift, whether to evil or to good, it is not the feet only that presently falter, but the whole head is sick and the whole heart faint. So also is Christ. Ye are the body of Christ, and members in particular. Wrong in one may produce wrong, either the same or different, in another; and even error may produce wrong. Consumption in one generation gives asthma to the next. The mother's scrofula distorts the child's spine. The drunkard's blear eyes come out in the son's bloodless lips. Is it not possible that there may be a closer connection than you think between your multiplication of new moons and sacrifices, and the mournful companies that are going down to the chamber of death? If they be not the "crying sin," may they not be one of the causes that produce it? Or, if they do not actually produce it, do they tend to prevent its immediate removal? No crime is so small that we can afford to commit it, no mistake so slight that we can afford to make it. A single misplaced figure in the calculation sends a ship plunging upon the pitiless rocks, and the waters sweep over it forever.

That people sin is no reason why we should go on blundering. Our brother's faults are no excuse for our foibles. Because men cheat each other, shall we lie in bed in the morning? Shall we pursue a course of action not the best, because it is not the worst?

Man's chief end is to glorify God. But there are two ways of glorifying him; one is to worship him, the other is to work with and for him. In the one, we meet to call upon his name, to praise his excellences, to discover his will; in the other, we strive, or ought to strive, to get his Gospel into the heart, and bring it out in the life, of Smith the merchant, and Brown the farmer, and Jones the pickpocket, and Jenkins the politician. If a great sin stands in the way of Christ, and prevents his advance, by all means slay the great sin; but if a little error retards his approach, do not hesitate to remove that, even if the sin be not slain. Whatsoever thy hand finds to do, do it with thy might.

I do not consider that those who stop at home in the morning because it is cloudy, in the afternoon because it is warm, in the evening because it is foggy, — who saunter lazily, or ride aimlessly, or read indiscriminately, or doze listlessly through the Sabbath hours, — have solved the problem. While I do not desire to see the Sabbath become a Jewish rite on the one hand, neither do I desire to see it become a German holiday on the other, but a Christian festival. It should be a day of rest; but indolence and negligence are not rest; nor is a mere ceasing from labor the highest kind of rest.

The Sabbath was made for *us.* Let us neither abuse nor neglect, but use it. Let it be the servant of our souls; not the slave either of our prejudice or our folly. I claim and desire no liberty but that wherewith Christ hath made us free. That I want in largest measure.

O for the tender, loving, considerate spirit of Christ, who, by a new consecration, gave the Sabbath doubly to man, — to be alike the servant of his humblest needs and his highest aspirations!

IV.

CHURCH-SITTINGS.

NOTWITHSTANDING the high esti-
mation in which we hold public worship, we keep back a large part of the
community from joining in public
worship. While with one hand we unduly press
men into the Church, with the other we unjustly
shut them out. This must be wrong. Any system must be wrong which prevents the poor from
hearing the Gospel. When the disciples of John
would know from Christ's own lips whether he
was indeed the Messiah, the Deliverer, he gave
them certain signs whereby they should be able
to judge for themselves. One of these signs was
"the poor have the Gospel preached unto them."
If that was a criterion in the days of Christ, I
know no reason why it should not be a criterion
now. But if it is, there are many churches whose
creed may be profoundly orthodox, yet whose
practice in this respect would not entitle them to
be called Christian churches.

Magnificent church edifices are not objectionable, if rightly come by. Nothing is too rich, too beautiful, too grand, for the temple of the Most High ; but if, when these structures are built, they are accessible only to the rich, they are not the temples of the Lord, but the temples of the money that built them. I do not see how they can be anything but an abomination to the Lord. A majority of Christians profess to believe that the ordinances of the Sabbath day are an especial and paramount " means of grace." If, then, Christians build costly churches, and cause that " every door is barred with gold, and opens but to golden keys," what are they doing but practically and effectually, on their own showing, shutting poor people out from the means of grace ? Combining the doctrines and the customs of some churches, we can but arrive at the conclusion, that it is easier for a camel to go through the eye of a needle than for a poor man to enter into the kingdom of Heaven. Why should we send money to convert the heathen abroad, and shut church-doors in the faces of poor Christians at home ? We do it. Pew-rents in several — I think in many — of the churches in our large cities are such as to render it impossible, not only for the impoverished, but wellnigh impossible for any but the rich, to obtain seats. A mechanic, moving into the city from a country village, with a family to support, a clerk with a salary of a thousand dollars, a young merchant struggling for existence, cannot take a pew and go to church with his family. And if he stays at home, and gradually loses the distinctiveness of Sunday, — if his children grow up without any church home, or any of the influences and associations that often do, and always should, cluster around a church home, — am I my brother's keeper?

How must these things look to those who are thus shut out? The industrious and respectable mechanic, who has been trained under religious influences, though he has not wholly yielded to them, and who, coming from the social and homelike country into the city, naturally seeks among the first requisites a place where his family may weekly worship according to their wont, — what does he think, how does he feel, as he turns away from one and another church because the expense will not permit him to enter? The poverty-stricken, squalid, houseless, friendless poor, — do such customs tend to induce the belief in their hearts that Christianity is the common blessing of all mankind? How long shall the right hand baffle the left? How long shall we declare that the Gospel is to be the redemption of all, that the good tidings of great joy shall be to all people, and then stall up the very place where that Gospel is dispensed, the very place where those good tidings are proclaimed, as closely and exclusively as if salvation were the prerogative of moneyed men? How long will it take to "convert" Boston, New York, Baltimore, at this rate?

I have heard of churches where the pews are locked, and only their owners are suffered to enter them. May they stay locked to all Christian men! O my soul, come not thou into their secrets! Unto such assemblies, mine honor, be not thou united! These pew-owners, it must be concluded, expect to get into heaven through a private entrance. They have made a gravel-path outside the strait and narrow way, along which they may walk with stretched-forth necks and wanton eyes, walking and mincing as they go, and so be happily apart from vulgar travellers toward the celestial city. There is a postern-gate remote from the thronged portals, which opens only to their touch. They have rented beforehand the stateliest of the many mansions, and will meet only their own set in the golden streets. Is it religion or is it travesty?

I suppose there must be some justification, some cause, for this thing. If there is, I wish it could be brought forward. I am utterly at a loss even to conjecture it. To me it looks eminently and only unchristian, — directly and sharply opposed to the whole spirit of the Gospel.

It is said that provision is made for the poor, that chapels are built in which they are invited to worship without any expense. But, God be thanked! the great majority of honest, hard-working Northerners have too much dignity and self-respect to accept alms. They have a sensitiveness as delicate as that of the millionnaire. They will not live upon his charity any more willingly than he will live upon theirs. And this feeling—call it pride, or what you will — is both a beneficial and an honorable one. It is a bulwark against evil, and he intends mischief who would do anything to pull it down. A great majority of these people would choose to stay away from church altogether, rather than become the recipients of charity; and who can blame them ? Moreover, even if they were willing to go to the churches provided for them, the defect would not be remedied. We do not want — the world does not want — one church for the rich and one for the poor. We want a church where the rich and the poor meet together; the Lord is the Maker of them all. In other respects there may, and often must, be distinctions; but here every man stands, a naked soul before God. Christ died for all alike, Heaven beckons to all. Alas ! is not Hell from beneath moved for all to meet them at their coming ? In this matter, neither circumcision availeth anything nor uncircumcision ; but whosoever is athirst, let him come and drink freely, without money and without price. Learning, leisure, wit, wealth, may be the boon of the few, but the Gospel is the legacy of humanity. Christianity cannot be broken into grades by earthly distinctions without detriment.

At the feast of the Passover, the master and the slave alike partook : is Christianity more exclusive than Judaism ? Is the salvation of the world a less powerful solvent than the salvation of the first-born of the families of Israel ? If Christ could wash the feet of his disciples, cannot those disciples tolerate each other's presence ?

I believe in the very utmost levelling, the thorough radical democracy of the Bible. The only degrees it knows are degrees of holiness. Among them that are born of women, there may be none greater than John the Baptist ; yet he that is least in the kingdom of Heaven is greater than he. I do not believe religion will be aggressive in any community when it is not allowed free course to run and be glorified.

Our system — the system of building churches, and selling or renting the pews — is selfish even in its appearance. The idea of personal property is prominent. Surely every church ought to beacon to every wayfarer. Surely there should be no self intruding into social worship. As it is now, if a stranger moves into your parish, you cannot invite him to your church, and your church hospitalities, without laying yourself open to the suspicion of catering for your own interests. You want to help out your society ; you want his money to pay the expenses of the parish. Your hands may be ever so clean, but they will not look clean to a wicked and perverse generation.

Why cannot the whole matter of church taxes be abolished, and the church rest entirely upon free-will offerings? Why not let every man be accountable to God alone for what he shall do to — shall I use that common phrase? — "support the Gospel"? No; for wrong words, even if they do not spring from wrong ideas, tend to originate and perpetuate them. People do not support the Gospel; the Gospel supports them. The Gospel will live, whether they do or do not pay their five or fifty or five hundred dollars to uphold it. The Gospel will live, whether they attack, neglect, or cherish it; but without the Gospel, the good tidings, there is for them no life, "neither in this world, neither in the world to come." Our work is, not to support the Gospel, but to spread the Gospel and drive it home. The Gospel is no pauper, but a king. We are not to dole out to it a fitful pittance, but march under its banners, conquering and to conquer.

I would have the whole matter of church-rates taken out of mercantile, and put upon missionary ground. A Christian community has built a costly church. If that costly church is open only to those who can afford to buy a pew in it, it would much better have been a pine shanty, or even a canvas tent. If the mission of a church is to be subordinate to its architecture, then architecture is a device of the Adversary. Let a community build a church, and then throw its doors wide open to everybody, — yes, to everybody, native and for-eign, black and white, beggar, brigand, pick-pocket, — the worse the better, — and then archi-tecture may become the handmaiden of the Lord. Make your church beautiful, if so you may better express your love to God, — your appreciation of, and your gratitude for, the beauty which he has lavished; make it attractive, if so you may better lure outcasts into the fold: but let not ostentation or rivalry or ambition reign where only devotion should dwell; for so you shall have no cherubim, with outstretched wings, hovering over the mercy-seat, but only a golden calf.

Do you say that the by-way people will not come to church, even if there is one? Do you get the church ready, do you open the doors, then go out into the highways and hedges and compel them to come in; meet them at the porch-door with smiles, and warm words, and hearty hand-shakings; give them good seats, not in a corner by themselves, but among your own friends, with your own family, or by your own self; show, if possible, a little interest in them during the week; and, if they still continue stiff-necked and rebel-lious, think how much harder must be the work of the missionaries, who go thousands of miles to meet the heathen in their strongholds, than yours, who find your heathen under the droppings of your own sanctuary!

And if the outcasts do not come, there is another class who will, — the poor who live, not by shifts, but by honest and persistent industry, — men and women whose days are given over to severe and unintermitting toil; who have money scarcely beyond the utmost needs of life; whose ingenuity expends itself in making a cent do the work of a dime, and a dime the work of a dollar; the men and women who cannot incur the expense of church-sittings, yet who pre-eminently need the comfort and strength of church-service. These people ought to be in the church. They need the church, and the church needs them. They ought to be in it, not as mendicants, not by patronage or permission, but as children of one Father, disciples of one Christ, members of one flock bound together by a common need and a common hope. They ought to stand, rich and poor, on one level, interchanging friendly greetings, conversant with each other's views and fears and feelings, — joint students of the Bible, joint servants of the Lord. It is not necessary nor possible nor desirable that all should move on one social plane. Tastes and occupations must decide that. But if religion is not strong enough to rise above social distinctions, to create friendliness between different classes, to make the rich kindly and genial to the poor, and not patronizing or scornful, — to make the poor trustful and serviceable toward the rich, and not servile or haughty, — so that each class shall be reckoned the friend of the others, — so that he

that is greatest and he that is least shall alike be
the servant of all, — then religion has not done
the work which it was appointed to do. With a
church free, — free, not with inferences and conditions that encroach upon self-respect, but absolutely free, — I feel sure that many, many more
of these classes would find their way into the
courts of the sanctuary, and that it would be
much more a sanctuary than it is now.

But how shall the church be paid for? The
warmest missionary *feeling* does not pay a debt
which is represented by coin. Very well. A
community that is able to build a church, and sell
pews, is able to build a church without selling the
pews. If you are rich enough to build a church
for yourself, you are rich enough to build it for
your neighbors. If you are able to own a pew,
you are able to give it away. I do not mean that
you can do both, but you can do one as well as
the other. Churches are now built mainly by
voluntary contributions. Let them still be built
by voluntary contributions; only, when they are
built, let them be churches, and not ecclesiastical
drawing-rooms. Make your church as fine as
you will, only not too fine to be trodden by dusty
feet. Let it be just as good as you can afford to
give away in the name of the Lord, and no better;
for, beyond this, sin lieth at the door.

But, besides the original outlay, come the continuous expenses of preaching, and all the minor

details. What of these? I would have every
one of you, upon the first day of the week, lay by
him in store as God hath prospered him. Let the
"contribution-box" be carried around on Sunday,
and every man decide for himself and between
himself and God alone. Then the rich man may
give of his abundance, and the poor man of his
poverty, and both out of the love of their hearts.
Then the poor man may feel that he is doing his
part toward bearing the good tidings to a sorrowful world; and if he cannot bring a lamb
without blemish, nor yet a turtle-dove, nor two
young pigeons, his tenth part of an ephah of fine
flour shall be a sin-offering holy and acceptable
to God.

Would this give but a precarious support to a
pastor? Not so precarious as that of his Master,
who had not where to lay his head, — not so precarious as that of Elijah, for whom the ravens were
butcher and baker, and whose drink was the brook
by the way, — not so precarious even as it is now.
The minister would not only have just as much
money as he now has, but it would not come to
him, as it too often does, grinding, grating, scraping out of rusty purses, with a noise of friction that
puts every nerve to the torture; it would leap out
warm from the heart, shining with a love-light
brighter than any gleam of gold, and so have to
him a worth that no mere money can represent.
As ministers receive their salaries now, it is nei-

ther one thing nor another. It is not a tax which
people must pay or go to prison, and it is not a
gift which blesseth him that gives and him that
takes. It has neither the inexorableness of the
one, nor the spontaneity of the other. It has free-
will enough to admit of grumbling, and not enough
to excite gratitude. It is a miserable half-and-half
thing, all that I have ever seen of it. I do not
mean that every man of a parish makes his " minister's tax " a disagreeable matter; but there is
more or less — generally more — disagreeableness
to contend with in every parish. The very term
" minister's tax " is harsh. It does state exactly
what many people mean. It is not a free-will
offering to help spread the Gospel. It is not a
man's part to support the government. It is simply and solely the *minister's tax;* and it is not, and
never will be, pleasant to have a man take you
by the throat, and exclaim, " Pay me that thou
owest." It is far too often that this sum is paid
as if it were a personal charity to the minister. A
grumbles because he is called on to subscribe thir-
ty-five, while B, who is worth twice as much as
he, only pays thirty, and C " signs off " from the
parish, and pays nothing at all, and it is a burden
everywhere. By having a system of free offerings,
all this would be abrogated. Every man would
be his own guide, and antagonisms would be
soothed away. He that pays, pays unto the Lord,
and he that pays not, unto the Lord he doth not

pay it, and himself is the only judge. He knows
his own circumstances better than another, and
upon each returning Sabbath he gives as God has
prospered him. He is not mulcted in a fine, but
to the Saviour who died for him he brings a thank-
offering, grateful. It is the helping hand which
Jesus permits him to reach forth to save the world.
It is the effort he can make to cause that Christ
shall not have died in vain.

Why appeal to the lower part of man's nature,
when there is a higher open to appeal? Why
insist that that shall be only a duty which might
just as well be a delight? All men are generous,
if you but approach them generously; or rather
all men have a capacity for generosity, and, if it be
not developed, it ought to be gently and genially
educated into development. If it do not unfold·
in the kindly sunshine, there is surely no good in
trying to split it open with a hammer. Men will
sometimes pay the " minister's tax " loath, but the
Gospel suffers more harm than it receives good
from their money. " Of every man that giveth
it willingly with his heart, ye shall take my offering," commanded Jehovah to Moses. What was
the result? " They spake unto Moses, saying,
The people bring much more than enough for
the service of the work. . . . . And Moses gave
commandment, ... saying, Let neither man nor
woman make any more work for the offering of
the sanctuary. . . . . For the stuff they had was

sufficient, and *too much*." Just so I believe it
would be if we would have more faith in God
and in the better parts of human nature, and less
dependence on taxes and securities. Ministers
would not only have a "support" for the body,
but for the heart and soul, and, perhaps not at
first, but after the whole system was in full play,
there would be large surplusages to be disposed
of. And whatsoever shall seem good to thee and
to thy brethren to do with the rest of the silver
and gold, that do after the will of your God.

Another objection urged against church com-
munism is, that it destroys the sweet and tender
associations which cluster around the family pew.
But does it of necessity? Things in general have
a wonderful tendency to fall into grooves. In a
certain part of Massachusetts there are commons
extending some eight miles. As you approach
them from the city a sign-board entreats, "Don't
rut the roads." Seeing that travellers have the
whole pasture-land before them, one would suppose it to be easy to comply with this request;
but, in spite of broad commons and supplicating
sign-board, right along in the same track goes
carriage after carriage, wearing deeper and deeper
ruts into the sandy soil, till it is already become
harder for a light wagon to get off the track than
it seems to be for many steam-carriages. Would
not the same principle obtain in churches? Would
not families naturally fall into the same places?

and, especially if they wished to do it, would they not find it easy of accomplishment? Are there not in our chapels and vestries at evening meetings certain seats where you always expect to find certain people? Do you not know precisely where to look for Deacon Smith and his wife? Are not 'Squire Jones and his family always here, and Dr. Brown and his sister always there, or thereabouts, and all without any quarrelling or *lobbying?* And if, instead of chapel and occasional meetings, it were church and regular service, would not the tendency be still stronger? I rather think affairs would arrange themselves so that a family which would fill a pew would be allowed to occupy a pew just as regularly as if it had a quitclaim deed to it ; and, of course, the longer a family occupies one pew, the stronger becomes its claim to it. Is not this enough for association? It surely will not be said that ownership is necessary. Nobody will maintain that a pair of lovers ·can have no tender reminiscences of moonlit walks by summer seas because they do not hold the ocean in fee simple.

But supposing it were true that associations would be somewhat disturbed, or even forestalled, would that be really a conclusive fact? The church is pre-eminently for social worship. The associations appropriate to it belong to the great family of Christ. There, God is our Father, Jesus our elder brother, and all who love him and all who seek him are his children. All kinship of the flesh ought to be subordinate to this kinship of spirit. At the family altar you offer your family worship. By the very act of going to church your family yields, for the time, its family life, throwing it into the commonwealth, and becoming a part of the great congregation; and the great congregation becomes, or should become, one in Christ Jesus our Lord. What, then, have any one's personal associations to do against the utmost freedom of admittance? Between memories and a blank, one would of course choose memories; but between my memories and my brother's life is there any room for choice? Shall the poor man's children, for whom Christ died, be excluded from the sanctuary, that your children may look back in their maturity to some particular place in it with a soft sadness and love? Shall the doors be closed to his children, that the walls may be more attractive to yours? Shall the poor man be shut out of the church, that the rich man may be shut into a pew?

If churches were filled under the present management, the principle would remain the same, though the practice would lose the most superfluous of its odious features. It would still be invidious for the rich to enjoy a Gospel which was not available to the poor. But the offset would be that a rich man's soul is worth just as much as a poor man's soul; and whether you pay for a pew

5   G

five hundred dollars or nothing, a church can be no more than filled, and, having filled all, the duty would be to build others. But how many churches are there where full ranks are the rule, and vacancies the exception, — where, morning or evening, there is no opportunity to say, "And yet there is room"?

A man, poor in money, but rich in mental and moral treasures, tried to obtain a seat for himself and his family in one of the Boston churches, — one to which he was drawn by the peculiar adaptation of the pastor's preaching to his own spiritual wants. He was willing to take the lowest seat in the synagogue; but even that he found, upon inquiry, to be utterly beyond his means. So he goes roaming about the city, now at this church, now at that, now at none, belonging nowhere, nowhere at home. I went one afternoon to the one at whose door he had knocked in vain. I judged at least one half the seats to be empty. Do you think I did not long to go up into that pulpit and preach a sermon at which both the ears of every one that heard it should tingle? Woe unto you, Scribes and Pharisees, hypocrites! for ye shut up the kingdom of Heaven against men; for ye neither go in yourselves, neither suffer ye them that are entering to go in.

A courteous and Christian writer, quoting certain remarks regarding pew-locking in the first part of this article, while putting in a gentle and

partial defence of the custom, thinks the remarks
are too sweeping, and that there is in them nothing of the sweet spirit of the Gospel. Perhaps
not, but the Gospel has other spirits than the sweet
one ; and I submit that, when one stands face to
face with a custom which openly and systematically causes that the poor have not the Gospel
preached unto them, it is no time for the exercise
or the display of such a spirit. It was not the
sweet spirit of the Gospel which the Pharisees
heard in Christ's indignant thunders. It was
rather the strong, yet such a strong as brings forth
sweetness. Nay, I may almost say it was the sweet
spirit, but revealing itself in another guise. It was
the same Divine love and pity that shone in his
tenderest words, — love for the poor, the ignorant,
the oppressed, — which fired his lips against those
who misled and oppressed them. And when, now,
after the Gospel has had free course to run and be
glorified for these eighteen hundred years, whole
communities name themselves with Christ's name,
and then, in order to receive the benefits of that
Gospel whose own proof of its divinity is that it is
to be preached unto the poor, form themselves into
a close corporation which none can enter but by
payment of a fee that is entirely beyond the means
of a large majority of the people, it seems to me a
spectacle that would have received the severest
denunciations of Christ, and should receive the
severest reprobation of Christians.

To the law and to the testimony.   If the Bible
sanctions this practice, it is right.   If the Bible
discourages it, it is wrong.   But if it is not directly opposed to all the tendencies of Bible teachings,
then Bible teachings are not plain enough to be
understood by a common mind.   If it is opposed
to the Bible, then the men who advocate and uphold it are bound to show cause for their action.
The burden of proof lies with them, and not with
those who point out the discrepancy.   Slavery is
the mother of abominations.   It is not for the
assailants of slavery to stay their hands out of regard to the possible virtue of many slaveholders.
It is for the virtuous slaveholders to come forth
and demonstrate their virtue.   I will not say that
the people who lock pews and monopolize preaching are not Christians.   Sanctification is a grad-
ual process, and a man may be sanctified to the
degree of going to church himself, and not to the
degree of going out into the highways and alleys
and inviting his brother to come to church.   But
a general view cannot take in individual virtues,
and the general view shows the great majority
without a church-home, or any means to provide
one, and the small minority sitting in state in their
splendid waste-places; this is not Christianity, but
thoughtlessness, selfishness, stupidity, pride, making a great gap between the supply and demand
of the bread of life; and this wickedness, as disas-
trous in its reflex as in its direct influence, and the

people who, professing to be guided by the teachings of Christ, cherish or permit this wickedness,
cannot fail to receive, in this respect, the unquali-
fied censure of those who believe that " inasmuch
as ye did it not to the least of these, my brethren,
ye did it not to me."

When it is asked, " If I am able to do thus
and so, if I am able to hire a $5,000 man and a
$300 pew to hear him in, have I not a perfect
right to do it, — just as much as I have a right to
send my children to expensive schools beyond my
neighbor's reach?" No, I answer emphatically,
you have no such right, if there is any truth in
the Bible, — if a Christ ever lived and died. You
have a right, but it is a pagan right, a legal right,
a right under the code of Justinian, not under the
code of Jesus. Under the Law, every man looketh
to the things of his own; but under the Gospel, to
the things of his neighbor. There needed no crucified Saviour to tell us that we might secure for
ourselves the best things possible. We should have
known that without the cross. But Christ died,
the just for the unjust, and placed us forever under
the most solemn bonds to love our neighbor as
ourselves. Where our tastes conflict with our
neighbor's life, we have no right to indulge them.
Unless the world is to be saved by some other
foolishness than that of preaching, we have no
right to keep preaching away from the world. If
you think the Gospel is not necessary to men, or

if you think church services are not the best way,
or not a good way, to present the Gospel to men,
that is another question. But if you think church
services, at least at present, are pre-eminently the
" means of grace," — so pre-eminently that those
who are brought to Christ from beyond the limits of
church influences are rare and remarkable exceptions, — then you have no right to indulge in church
luxuries whose effect is to remove from your brother church necessities. You shall not spread for
yourself a feast of fat things, while Christ's little
ones all around you are famishing for bread.

It is said that a free-church system is impracticable. What does *impracticable* mean ? Everything is impracticable till it is put in practice. I
am told that there are already several churches
conducted on this plan. A slight sketch of the
origin and history of such a church might be more
useful than a great deal of theoretical talk. But
the success or failure of any single enterprise of
this nature does not settle the question, any more
than the success or failure of any one attempt at
congregational singing settles the question of cho-
ral or congregational music. So many circumstances come in to complicate matters, that one
needs large induction.

The experiment may be tried in bad faith, in a
manner so hasty, injudicious, and half-and-half,
that no good result shall follow. Begin without
harmony, understanding, sagacity, confidence, en-

thusiasm, or tact, and of course it will fail. Anything would fail under such circumstances. Grasp
it so that you can have *purchase* before a failure
shall be considered final. Let people be interested. Let them feel the matter to be of as great
importance as if they had embarked in it their
whole fortune. Let them be determined to succeed. The Hindoos and Siamese are not made to
pay "minister's tax," nor pew-rent; and if it is
possible to send a free Gospel all around the globe,
shall it be easily considered impossible to dispense
it to the heathen and the half-Christianized — and
these two classes very nearly exhaust the population — at our own doors? Let the children of
light be as wise in their generation as the children
of this world, let Christian men organize as saga-
ciously for Christ as politicians organize for politics, let it be felt to be as essential to bring people
to church on Sunday as it is to bring voters to
the polls on election-day, and many an impracti-
cability would pass into an accomplishment.

To give money to build a church in a poverty-stricken locality, to support it by contributions, and occasional attendance from neighboring
churches, and make it a kind of pet charity, may
be a Christian deed; but it is not establishing, and
scarcely is it trying, the free-church system. To
retain personal possession of the pews in a church,
and all the appurtenances of church-ownership,
while saying that the church is glad to have all

come who choose, is not a fair, adequate, and honorable experiment of the free-church system ; and
unless the experiment is fairly tried, it is not tried
at all.   To drag along after an idea, is not to test
its practicability.   Gather into your hand all the
elements, and give it a body and an arena, and
then it may prove its powers.   Let there be dis-
cussions, deliberations, votes, and whatever legal
formalities may be necessary to furnish a firm foundation.   If a church is to be formed, or one already existing as a monopoly is to be thrown open
to all, let it be done intelligently.   Let its position
be first clearly seen, and then clearly shown, its
plans and purposes laid before the public, and all
— families, individuals, transient visitors, residents
— invited to form, for the time, one church.   It is
true, as has been alleged, that this would bring in
a great number who would not be the poor and
devout, but mere curiosity-seekers.   But this, so
far from being an objection, is an inducement.
Nothing innocent is an objection which brings
responsible beings into a church.   That alone is
objectionable which keeps them out.   If the church
is what it ought to be, it will ignore a man's motives in coming.   No matter what he came for,
satisfied that it has him there, let it go to work
and improve the time.   Does the Spirit of God act
only upon those who decorously pray for him ?   Do
regeneration and sanctification come only to those
who deliberately seek them in their careless days ?

Paul had a worse motive than curiosity in going to Damascus. He was breathing out threatenings and slaughter against the disciples of the Lord, but suddenly there shined round about him a light from Heaven. The motives which take a man to the house of God lie between himself and his Maker. The only facts which concern us are by any honorable means to get him there, and then build him up in the nurture and admonition of the Lord. If he be worldly, indifferent, attracted only by novelty or a name, drifting, unprincipled, so much the more is his casual presence in the church to be desired. If he will not go from principle, how fortunate that he will go from whim! There, truth has him at an advantage, and may hope to conquer the evil spirit. The opportunity may never come again, but this once you have drawn him out of his fortifications. You can force him to do battle on your own ground. It may be that, in the midst of his carelessness and curiosity, suddenly a light from Heaven shall shine round about him. And he which converteth a sinner from the error of his ways — whether he be a citizen or a stranger — saves a soul from death.

Do you say that this filling of churches with a flitting audience will still preclude the poor from attendance on the sanctuary? Fly swiftly round, ye wheels of time, and bring the happy day when there are not churches enough for the people who wish to worship!

5 *

How terrible would be our daily walks, if our streets were filled with the

"Friendless bodies of unburied men"!

How dreadful to go on our errands of business or pleasure, if at every step we were forced to touch, with shuddering feet, the lifeless tabernacles of departed souls, — stumbling here against a prostrate body, turning aside to avoid another there, looking down upon them lying in heaps under our parlor windows, and, in spite of every effort, brought continually in contact with crumbling clay! We take good care that this shall not happen. We make no question here of wealth or poverty. A man may be ever so poor, but once let the breath leave his body, and he is immediately taken care of. Once ceasing to be a man, and becoming a thing, church and state both come in; solemn rites are said, prayer and psalm and funeral hymn are not wanting. Decently, reverently, — whether the past has known the rags of a pauper or the purple of a king, — the carbon and hydrogen and phosphorus that have been honored with the presence of a soul are laid back in the bosom of the great mother, — earth to earth, ashes to ashes, dust to dust.

But a decaying body is not so pernicious as a decaying soul. The soul that has lost its principle of life, not only passes on to its own destruction, but it taints whatever it touches. The souls that go to and fro in the market-places, unsanctified, unholy, unloving, thinking of no beauty, caring for no purity, having no hope and without God in the world, — are not only eating away their own life, but they are corroding society. An evil soul is not only an evil substance, but an evil influence. It preys upon itself, and upon all around it. It is a missionary, as much more successful than ordained evangelists, as the line of its operations lies with, and not against, the current. It pollutes the earth, and vitiates the air. It is at once the nucleus and stimulus of evil. When it shall have fled, wailing, from the body which it has degraded, you will bestir yourself, giving to the suffering slave an attention which you denied to the far more deeply suffering master. But why can you not open to souls your church, as well as to bodies your churchyards? You will have your dead buried out of your sight. Be equally faithful to have the sin-smitten soul buried with Christ in baptism, to rise with him in newness of life.

I am loath to leave this subject. I am so sure that nothing will come of what I have said. The thing which has been is that which shall be. One little boat cleaves the ocean-wave, but the ocean closes again, and there is no change. Yet I pray you do not pass carelessly by. If what I have said is not well said, do you say it better. If it is not truly said, utter you the truth. If this is not a good way to bring the Gospel to the poor,

show a good way. If it is not the best, show a
better. It is not a matter that can be let alone
safely, — either for the world or for yourself. We
are each his brother's keeper, and we shall surely be inquired of one day concerning the trust.
We can hardly yet render a satisfactory account.
What I see is church edifices half filled, church
organizations half torpid, and cities eager and
crowded ; the Gospel not reaching the tenth part
of the people, and the people every one of them
going on inexorably into life, going down inevitably to death. What I want to see is every church
made the glowing centre of all moral, intellectual,
and social life ; a city of refuge for all who are in
any trouble of mind, body, or estate ; a city of rejoicing for all who are rich and increased in goods,
and have need of nothing ; the dread and rebuke
of unrepentant evil-doers, the counsellor and com-
forter of repentant ; the dispenser of solace, the
promoter of joy, the home of the homeless, the
friend of the friendless ; warm in love, wise in
action, quick in sympathy, sagacious in council ;
the house of God, the very gate of heaven. To
bring about this most Christian end, I know no
better means than that thou shouldst keep the feast
unto the Lord thy God with a tribute of a free-will
offering of thine hand, which thou shalt give unto
the Lord thy God, according as the Lord thy God
hath blessed thee ; and thou shalt rejoice before the
Lord thy God, thou, and thy son, and thy daughter,

and thy man-servant, and thy maid-servant, and the Levite that is within thy gates, and the stranger, and the fatherless, and the widow that are among you, in the place which the Lord thy God hath chosen to place his name there.

V.

A VIEW FROM THE PEWS.

WHEN a new thing is to be introduced to the public, machinery must be used. A missionary, going to preach Christ among a people that never heard of him, must probably have recourse to measures which he would not need to employ with a nominally Christian people. The latter know all that it is necessary to know *about* Christianity. What they need is to learn Christianity itself. They are to be led to church and to religion by the true service of the one and the inherent excellence of the other. There is very little use in exhorting them to go to church, and there is no use at all in upbraiding them after they get there for not going. The first is like repairing a deranged clock by setting the pendulum a-going with your finger. It makes a few oscillations and stops, for the trouble lies above among the wheels. By outside influences you may induce a feeble swing between house and church, but you will never make a vigorous vibration till you go in among the cords and cogs and put the vital mechanism in order. Nor is clerical remonstrance any more effective than lay effort. It is not objectionable on the ground of lawfulness, but of expediency. I have not an overweening admiration of that bland serenity which never speaks a severe word. As a freak of nature it is curious and pleasant to contemplate, especially where circumstances are so arranged that there is no call for severity; but as things usually are, a good plain rebuke, rare but thorough, not fringing off into sullenness and pouting, but sharp at the edges and solid in the middle and well set in sunshine, clears the air and accomplishes purposes; yet in the pulpit it does not accomplish the purpose desired, because the people who feel it are the people who do not deserve it, and because it has not generally a good basis. It is not surprising if ministers often feel moved to administer it, nor that they often do administer it. But it will not effect much, for it is not striking at the root of the matter. Lions, it is well known, do not write history, and consequently do not make any great figure in history. In our ecclesiastical dramas the congregations play the part of the lions, and the clergy are the historians. The minister has " centralization," the habit of writing and speaking, and the pulpit. The congregation is heterogeneous, unorganized,

unaccustomed to making periods. The minister
has presented his story very fully, and no doubt
very truly ; but we have seldom, if ever, been
called to look at the truth from the " congregation
side." But why should a minister think himself
justified in complaining of his small audience, any
more than a lawyer of his few clients, or a physician of his few patients, or a shop-keeper of his
few patrons ? There may be especial obstacles in
especial cases, but, as a general thing, if a doctor
is skilful, people find it out, and employ him. If
the grocer has good coffee and spices, he will have
good customers. But if the minister fails of hearers, it is because people are cold and dead. Perhaps so, but is it not his own hand that killed
them ? Men want spiritual food much more than
they want sugar and coffee ; and if a minister can
discover and provide the thing which they need,
why must we suppose that they would not follow
natural laws and apply to him ? Why are people
in the one case simply acting after their kind, and
in the other case giving themselves over to the
god of this world ? Because the doctor and the
lawyer have to do with this world's interests,
while the minister treats only of spiritual things.
But spiritual things belong to the world as much
as physical things, nay, more. Godliness is as
profitable for the life that now is, as for that which
is to come. Ministers often plant themselves on
the fact that they preach the Gospel, as if that

were the conclusion of the whole matter. Audiences may be small, faith feeble, thermometers low, but they preach the Gospel whether men will hear or forbear. But it is not the Gospel that men go to church to get. They have at home as much Gospel as there is. What they need in church is to have the Gospel explained, applied, enforced. The Gospel may be in a way preached without any real explanation, application, or impression. The mere fact that a man preaches the Gospel, is not conclusive as to the nature of the work which he is doing. Men ought to be aroused, stimulated, impelled. Their attention must be commanded, if not by duties, then by devices. But this is "sensation" preaching. Well, all preaching is sensation preaching. You cannot sit still and hear a man talk for half an hour or an hour without some kind of a sensation. The only question is as to what kind. Shall it be a sensation of interest, or indifference ? Of resolution, or weariness ? Of repentance, or disgust ? There is much unnecessary alarm in this respect, — unnecessary, if one looks at it from the pews, however it may seem from the pulpit. A correspondent of the Congregationalist, in the early part of the war, was troubled because a daily journal advertised a series of sermons on the Military Heroes of the Bible, to be concluded by one on " Jesus, the Captain of our Salvation." I must confess I cannot see the smallest objection,

H

either to preaching the sermons, or announcing
that you are going to do so. I should think that
very apt and excellent discourses might be written
on that theme. There are military heroes in the
Bible, — witness Abraham, Joshua, David, — and
there are valuable lessons for us in their career
and character. At that juncture of affairs, the
lessons afforded by the military portion of their
lives were peculiarly apposite. We have Scriptural authority for calling Christ the Captain of
our salvation, and the term has now for us a
stronger meaning than ever before. All military
character and experience are invested with new
interest. Why not, then, strike while the iron is
hot ? I should think it was just the thing to do.
If ministers find that they can induce people to
come to church by adopting some such " cry,"
they are surely justified in doing it. Would they
be justified in not doing it ? True, the intelligent,
devout Christian may not need any such stimu-
lant, and, if he have a cultivated mind and delicate
taste, may rather dislike it. But the intelligent,
devout Christian is not to be taken into the account here, because he knows the way to the
Saviour. He is in the right road, and may be left
to himself. Christ came not to call the righteous,
but sinners, to repentance. It is the worldly, the
careless, the frivolous, the reckless, who need to
be lured to God ; and if their weakness and wickedness can be touched by catch-words, let us use

them. Paul was a thoroughly orthodox and a tolerably able and successful preacher, and he tells us his manner of working: " Unto the Jews I became as a Jew, that I might gain the Jews ; to them that are under the law, as under the law, that I might gain them that are under the law ; to them that are without law, as without law, that I might gain them that are without law. *To the weak became I as weak, that I might gain the weak ; I am made all things to all men, that I might by all means save some.*" " Even as I please all men in all things. " If the services of the sanctuary are helps to heaven, if men are more likely to be led to Christ by going to church than by staying away, we can hardly be too eager to gather them in ; and to seize our military fever at its height, and make it an instrument of moral improvement, was a clever stratagem, a tripping of Satan in his own net, which should call forth admiration rather than censure. And if it is right to do it, it is right to say you are going to do it, and to say it in the most public manner. It would be very delightful if everybody belonged to some church, and walked in all its ordinances blameless. We should then need only the notice from the pulpit, and each man would wend his orderly way to his own church ; but while there are so many who flit from place to place, perhaps to church, perhaps to concert, possibly to club, we will not only make them a feast of fat things in our church-

es, but we will go out into the highways and
hedges with our invitations, and compel them to
come in, that the house may be full. When every
man has his own plot of ground in Zion, and can
sit under his own vine and fig-tree, we will all
stay at home and cultivate our own farms with
gladness and singleness of heart; but while the
sad earth spreads out her waste places, blessed are
ye that sow beside *all* waters.

It is objected, that all this savors of the theatre,
and conceals the pure word of God with a mere-
tricious glow. But it is right to learn even of an
enemy. You may go to a theatre night after
night, and find it filled with attentive crowds;
while in the same city the churches yawn with
empty pews. May not the secret of this large
audience and this rapt attention be seized by the
children of light? Is there not something in
the mastery which the actor obtains over the
assembly — something apart from the nature of
the entertainment — of which the minister may
legitimately possess himself, and which, if he be
wise in his generation, he may use with more than
an actor's power? A clergyman of eminent parts
and position went once into a newsboy's theatre
for the express purpose of seeing " how it was
done "; and, said he, " I learned more about
preaching there than I ever did at a meeting. I
was a good deal more insighted into human nature
when I came out than when I went in." So far

as a theatre understands and applies natural laws,
let our churches be theatrical.

Yet, " What are we coming to? " ask good
men despondingly, in view of such innovations.
Would that one could reassure them by answering,
" Nothing in particular." From a lay point of
view, it seems impossible to believe that the mischief which lies in this direction is worthy to be
compared to the mischief which lies in the opposite direction. The prejudice against " sensation
preachers " appears much more unreasonable than
any success which they may have attained. Let
the " Reverend Graphic " alone. He is doing a
good work. He that is not against us is on our
part. The point is to cast out devils. If he succeeds in that, let us not forbid him, though he
followeth not us. There is no man that can cast
out devils in Christ's name that can lightly speak
evil of him. Is this a begging of the question?
But can it be proved that the Reverend Graphic
really accomplishes less good than the Reverend
Prosy? May be he cannot cast out your particular devil; may be not mine; but their name is
Legion, and it shall go hard but some will get a
wound. What seems rhodomontade in a quiet
country village, may seem chaste and correct
discourse in a fast and furious city. What seems
rough to the cultivated hearer, may be but natural to the uncultivated. What would be startling
and incongruous to you, might only tempt the

palled appetite of another. If an angel from heaven preach any other than the true Gospel, let him be accursed; but if he preach the true Gospel, let him have free course, whether he preach it with drums beating and colors flying, or with the still, small voice. Let all things be done decently and in order, and, as far as possible, with elegance; but there are, it may be, so many kinds of voices in the world, and none of them is without signification. If a little engineering, a little stir, a little show, a little craft (of the Pauline kind), a little melodramatism, can draw men to the courts of the Lord, let no one shrink from the sacrifice of his own tastes, if by any means — *by any means* — he may save some. What said Paul? Some in his day preached Christ even of envy and strife, to say nothing of " sensation " and vainglory; some of contention, not sincerely, supposing to add affliction to his bonds. What then? Notwithstanding, every way, whether in pretence or in truth, Christ was preached; "And I therein do rejoice," cried the glorious, great-hearted man, " yea, and will rejoice."

The fear of anything unusual, or not conformed to the canons of correct taste, sometimes goes so far that one might almost think an attractive pulpit were presumptive evidence of an heretical pulpit. To enliven and adorn it is to depreciate it. Men admire, in a minister, agreeable manners, a cultivated voice, apt and elegant language, rich

and forcible illustration, and are immediately reminded of " one that hath a pleasant voice, and
can play well on an instrument." How many
and many times have I heard that quoted by
clergy and laity, and almost invariably misquoted.
One would suppose, from its application, that
God's people in old time turned away from the
true prophet, who spoke somewhat roughly, to
listen to the false prophet with the pleasant voice
and the skilful hand. On the contrary, it was the
true prophet who spoke sweetly. The Lord said
unto Ezekiel, " *Thou* art unto them as a very
lovely song of one that hath a pleasant voice, and
can play well on an instrument." Instead of
making against these accomplishments, it makes
strongly in their favor. The man whom the Lord
made a watchman unto the house of Israel went
out on his errand, not only fired with the zeal of
the prophet, but clothed with the graces of the
orator. He ate the roll as he was commanded,
but it was in his mouth as honey for sweetness.
True, neither the roll nor the honey turned a
rebellious people from the error of its ways. Men
heard the lovely song and the pleasant voice, but
gave no heed to its teachings. Yet a prophet was
among them, as they presently came to know. It
is not to be supposed that in our days, any more
than in Ezekiel's, a pastor's skill or culture can
redeem his people. Even though a Paul plant,
even though an Apollos water, God must give

the increase. But if Paul understands the chemistry of soils, and the nature of seeds, if he draws a straight furrow and holds a steady hand, if he observes times and seasons, making hay while the sun shines, and mending tools on rainy days, his fields will be much more likely to yield increase, and will be far finer to look at when they have increased, than if he contents himself with scattering seed, hit or miss, and pays no regard to conditions.

Again, people who are in search of a minister recount their list of requisites, and are met by the sarcastic advice to repair to heaven for their prodigy, or by a disquisition on the unreasonableness of people who expect all the gifts and graces for eight hundred dollars a year. But the people are not always so unreasonable as is supposed. They sometimes make great demands, because they do not understand what it is that they want. Girls talk in heroic verse of the virtues which their suitors must possess; but by and by they marry men who are not taller by the breadth of my nail than any of their contemporaries, and live happy ever after. They have precisely the strength and support and companionship which they need, and never discover that the superlative qualities which they demanded exist in the positive degree, or discover it only to make merry over their own girlish folly. They are not troubled, because they are suited, and that is better than ideal Bayards.

Just so people talk of clerical perfections; they know that they want something which they have not, and they get at it as near as they can. But let a man go among them, never heeding their fine words, but with skill to discern their real needs and power to supply them, and their phantom of perfection quickly fades away before the face of the mere man, who breaks for them, not in word only but in truth, the bread of life. He who gives them what they need may dispense with many of the things they talk about. A very warm friend and parishioner of one of the most popular preachers in the country, admitted that he scarcely ever heard a sermon from his pastor in which there was not something to offend the taste. But the fire of his nature consumed all minor defects. His people passed over all the dross, and treasured the fine gold. Arbuthnot was a man of pleasing manners and agreeable exterior. Abernethy was, in popular parlance, "a bear"; but the "lovely song" of the one did not turn his science and skill into dilettanteism, nor did the gruff rudeness of the other give him in his anterooms one crowd the less. It is not true that people are more unreasonable regarding their minister than they are regarding other classes of servants. They do not expect the village doctor to manage the complicated and difficult cases; but they do expect him to take their children comfortably through the mumps and measles. They do not go to the "Cheap Cash

6

Store " for silks and broadcloth, but they expect
to find there good sheeting at a fair price. They
do not complain if their lawyer is not paid three
thousand dollars as a retaining fee, but they will
not long employ him if there are flaws in his title-
deeds. In point of fact, people bear deficiencies
in their pastor with far more patience than in any
other case that I recollect, except, perhaps, that
of teachers. It is partly because they do not
know any better. They do not know what a good
minister or a good teacher is, and might do, and
they plod on ; but of the fact, I think there can
be no question. A doctor and a lawyer are much
more dependent on their professional skill than the
minister. People do not apply to the former on
the strength of their being excellent men, genial,
benevolent, kind-hearted ; but the latter is retained, respected, and defended against outside
detractors, on that very plea.   .

Attractiveness is not the prerogative of depravity. The beauty of holiness is winsome. Very
few have so distorted their nature by sin as not
to be able to see the loveliness of religion. Also,
the word of God is positive, aggressive, radical.
A minister, then, has to present that which is
beautiful to a race which, however degraded, has
still an appreciation of the beautiful, and that
which is calculated to arouse thought, to a race
capable of thinking. Besides this, the minister
has other advantages. He holds the key of all

hearts in his hand. His position allows him, without the faintest suggestion of impertinence, to
inquire into the secret hopes, fears, and feelings
of his people. If he does this with tenderness
and tact, he will not only not be repulsed, but his
face will seem to them, as it were, the face of an
angel. He will bind them to himself by everlasting cords. In every family circle he will be the
honored and thrice welcome visitor, the sharer of
intimate interests, a revered, a confidential, I had
almost said, a sacred friend. The opportunity is
before him. Nothing lacks but himself. If he
have but the innate wisdom, he may fling repub-
licanism to the winds, and become such an auto-
crat as never Eastern despot dreamed of being.
Moreover, he has his pulpit. His people have
voluntarily made him their leader. They have
put themselves in the attitude of learners, listen-
ers, followers. The iron is ready before him;
there needs but the arm to smite, strong and sure.
In country villages he has still other advantages.
The people have few, if any, concerts, lectures,
addresses, wherewithal to amuse themselves.
Books and pictures are scarce, and time to con-
sult them, limited. The minister, therefore, represents other departments as well as his own. He
is not only Paul, but Cicero and Socrates. He
is religion, and also literature and the fine arts.
His people look to him for guidance in most things
that do not pertain to their own employments.

What right, then, has a sermon to be dull, or a minister to lose his audience? If, with all his advantages, he does not command his people, whose fault is it? He may, indeed, require time. It may take months, perhaps years, for his harvest to ripen ; but if, when sun and shower have done their work, the seed still remains in the ground and there is no fruit, it is possibly not wholly the fault of the ground, but of the farmer who did not till it aright.

I think it is as much a minister's duty to make sermons interesting as it is to make sermons. A sermon that does not interest an audience is nothing to them. I do not say that it must please them, but it must fix them. If a man cannot do that, then, so far as preaching is essential, he ought not to be a minister. The truths with which he has to deal are the most important in the world, and, if he cannot present them forcibly enough to secure attention, he should make way for some one who can. I am not advocating extravagance either of word or gesture. Fury and pounding and shouting and starting may startle, but they excite mere animal attention. You can stop a canary-bird's song by hallooing at him. One of the ablest ministers I know — a man whose church is filled every Sunday — is a quiet man. His voice seems not to be raised above the tones of common conversation. He stands in his pulpit a gentleman, dignified, affable, cour-

teous. Sometimes his words are roses, and sometimes they are cannon-balls. If roses, they have
the fragrance of June ; if cannon-balls, they speed
straight to the mark. In both cases the characteristic of the attention he secures is not so much
excitement as fixedness : if this attention depends
at all upon his manner, it is manner so impalpable
that you see nothing but the man and the matter
in their apparently spontaneous expression.

I hardly know how to say what I wish to say
in words that shall, on the one hand, do justice to
the unquestionable importance of the subject, and,
on the other hand, not do injustice to the real
excellence against which no word should be
spoken. It is at the best an ungracious task to
speak of fault or flaw, and the greater the excellence in which the flaw is found, the more unwel-
come the duty of pointing it out. But I am the
more emboldened to speak, because I am confident that, as the people often do wrong ignorantly,
because they have never been warned by their
pastor, so the pastor often fails to reach the people
from the sheer ignorance of the road. Confident
also that the dearest wish of the pastor is to save
his people from their sins, I feel sure that many
will gladly listen to statements which, whatever
may be their intrinsic worth, have at least the
value of being honest testimony.

My testimony is this : so far as the real exigencies of life are concerned, so far as people get any

help for the week-days from Sunday's sermon, a
man might just as well have gone up into the pulpit and talked in the Old Frisic through the half-
hour, as to have preached nine out of ten of all the
sermons that I ever heard. They may be excellent theological essays, but they are slender helps
to right living. In truth, I do not see how it is possible for men who are alive and in the world, and
see men and women all around them full of faults,
full of virtues, full of weaknesses and meannesses
and capacities and peculiarities, and then have
a chance to speak, and not say anything about
it all. How can a living man have free course
for half an hour, and not come in contact with any
one either to help or to hurt? How can a man
fire into a crowd for half an hour, and hit nobody?
It must be that the minister does not stand on the
same plane with his people. They are congre-
gated on the earth. He is groping or charging
among the clouds. Like the soldiers at Bunker
Hill, he fires over their heads, and, like their offi-
cer, one feels moved to cry out, "Shin 'em, boys,
shin 'em!" The people are groaning and trav-
ailing in pain, they are bewildered in the laby-
rinths of life, they are overwhelmed in the tide of
worldliness and ignorance and selfishness and passion, and their minister comes to them with his
emasculated abstractions. The people crave
bread, and they get — theology. But scorn theology, the science of sciences, the central truth?

Nay, verily. Absorb in your seminaries as much science as you can, but do not transmit it to us raw science. Assimilate and transmute it into the sincere milk of the word, that we may grow thereby. What we, the people want, is not theology theological, but theology vital. We do not care for oxygen and nitrogen; we want air.

Preach doctrinal sermons, not skeletons, but living organisms, clothed with nerve and sinew and muscle. Preach practical sermons, but let them smell of the soil. There is no gulf between the two. Doctrine and practice are not two things, but two parts of the same thing, — root and fruit of one tree. There is no doctrine that has not man's welfare for its end; there is no practice that bears on any other object. Juice will not be found in the doctrinal sermons of him whose practical sermons are sapless. How did Christ preach the Gospel? He forbade family quarrels. He warned his hearers against the evil practices of the Scribes and Pharisees. He bade no one dare to come up to the temple to worship until he had paid his just debts. He not only enjoined upon them not to commit adultery, but told them what the first step in adultery was, that they might shun it. He talked to them about their families, and their lawsuits, and their habit of borrowing. He told them how they should accost people in the street; what they should give away and how they should give it; how they

should pray and how they should keep fast-day.
He told them just how religion bore upon their
business and their associations.   He bade them
not to backbite or slander.   He warned them
against preachers who came preaching false doctrine.   Common things he discussed in common
language, enlivening his discourse with pungent
questioning, illustrating it by numerous stories,
and garnishing it with vivid and beautiful pictures
drawn from the summer fields and humble homes
around him.   Through it all rang the tender un-
dertone of love, — pity for the suffering, strength
for the weak, trust and comfort for the poor.
O, no wonder the people were astonished at his
doctrines, and that when he came down from the
mountain great multitudes followed him !   A writer in the Congregationalist says that a clergyman
once preached on the text, " Thou shalt not
steal," and on Monday morning the streets were
full of people carrying home books and tools
which they had borrowed.   As soon as they were
told what to do, they did it.   But so rare is it to
hear a sermon that gives one any definite thing to
do, or points out any special fault to correct, that an
audience sometimes looks with something like suspicion on such a sermon when it does come.   They
do not exactly know what to make of it.   They
are not quite sure it is religion at all, but rather
think it is morality; and, as Unitarians are supposed to be given over to morality, the minister

needs to have years and experience, or his creed
may be called in question. Ministers have so
narrowed the prerogatives of the Gospel that the
people do not know how broad is its domain. The
pastor is the educator of his people. Not only their
religion, but their morals, their manners, their
habits, their politics, are his province. Whatever
may be the impression to the contrary, they will
not be restive under his rule if he but hold the
sceptre wisely. If he but have moral strength, he
will surely have moral force. Trouble is the result of undue assumption. Position will not give
him force, but it will do much to utilize it. Suggestions and inculcations that would be resented
from a layman are received respectfully from a
clergyman. What would be meddlesome interference in the former, is duty in the latter; and if
the duty be deftly done, people will recognize it.
If a man takes hold of his work by the blade instead of by the handle, he must expect to cut his
fingers, and if he was born blind and cannot tell
which is which, he ought not to choose an occupation that requires edge-tools.

I know a man who, in the midst of a community hostile to his views, preaches to a church many
of whose members are his political opponents.
He lays down his principles in plain terms, and
inculcates them with great earnestness, yet with
so much grace, tact, and courtesy that even those
whose convictions do not yield to his arguments

6 *   I

have a profound respect for his character, and a warm affection for himself. Undoubtedly a people may become, by a long course of false or feeble teaching, so depraved that they will not bear the true light; but surely the greater part of the churches of New England, in the nineteenth century, will bear all the light which a minister can throw upon them. And at the worst, it is better to be thrust out of the synagogue for speaking the truth, than to keep one's place within by suppressing it.

This tact is no less necessary to the minister out of the pulpit than in it. The position of a minister has a tendency to isolate him, in a measure, from lay humanity. M. Robert Haudin tells us, that dipping his hands into water enabled him to plunge them, without injury, into masses of molten metal. The water changes into a vapor, which interposes between the skin and the fiery mass, and there is no real contact. So we have seen ministers walking about among their people; life throbs and glows and seethes and rages around them, but they are enveloped in an impalpable, professional atmosphere of their own creating. They hear the dash of the waves; they see unhappy souls struggling in their pitiless embrace, and O how gladly, how eagerly would they reach out a hand to save! but the impalpable atmosphere rolls between, and they cannot come nigh them.

It is not so in other professions. The lawyer *must* possess himself of the facts of the case before he undertakes its charge; or the reputation and purse, both of himself and his client, will be endangered. The doctor must know the symptoms, the delicate sensations, the sharp pains and the dull aches of his case, or his prescriptions are at fault, and his patient dies out of his hands. Client and patient are well aware of this, and need little coaxing to unburden themselves of facts and feelings. But that part of a man which comes under the minister's jurisdiction is neither purse nor pulse; it is only the soul, — the immortal principle which underlies, overtops, and permeates this life, and all future life; and men are chary of it. Partly from indifference, the result of wilful shortsightedness and ignorance; partly from a natural timidity and disinclination to bring to light the hidden things of the heart; partly from actual inability to embody shadowy, half-defined, and not half-understood ideas in words, — men are backward in revealing the symptoms of their diseased souls to him who would gladly help them to a cure. The spiritual physician must feel his way along. He must walk by sympathy, not by sight or sound. He needs a sixth sense to interpret to his heart what his eyes and ears have brought to his brain. He must not content himself with taking a bird's-eye view of the surface of things; he must drop his line into the deeps and shallows to find out whither the currents tend, where the undertow lurks, and where the eddies play. He must be on the alert to find out what those influences are which make the cheek flush and the heart throb ; and having found them, he must know when to use them, and when to refrain from using them. He should study to insert the right word in the right place ; to have the power of putting himself, in a moment, in the position of the person whom he wishes to benefit. In fact, I consider this power indispensable in a minister. If he has it not, he has mistaken his calling. It is not possible to be a good pastor, and I do not believe it is possible to be a good preacher, without it. A man may write disquisitions, full of sound doctrine, right reasoning, careful learning, instructive to the reader, and perhaps also to the hearer, valuable contributions to the ecclesiastical literature of his age; but he cannot thrill along the heart-strings of his people one day in the week, if he rides over them rough-shod the six remaining days.

To illustrate, in part, what I mean: I once knew a minister — one of the excellent of the earth, humble, devoted, and untiring, willing to spend and be spent in the service of the Lord — who used to strike out after this fashion. He would make a call; have the whole family assembled, from the father down to the little girl nine years old, and, beginning at the head, pounce upon each in turn, put to them individually the most point-blank questions, express to them in a most decided manner, and with the utmost freedom, his opinion of their character and prospects, give a little wholesale advise, pointed with a warning, finish off with a prayer, then mount his horse and ride away. But can any man of common sense suppose that it will do any good to talk to a father of his sins in the listening presence of three or four half-grown up children ? If a man is beginning to think upon his ways, if he has compunctions of conscience, if he has doubts or fears or hopes which his pastor's hand may do much to remove or strengthen, is this a good opportunity to bring them forward ? Will he be likely to converse freely, — to show the wounded place whereon the balm of Gilead should be laid ? Will a sensitive, shrinking, timid girl be disposed to lay bare her secret heart in the presence of her merry, romping, careless brothers ? Will she unveil to half a dozen pairs of eyes, the hidden thoughts which are scarcely revealed to her own ? How *can* a minister be so blind, so ignorant of human nature, as to expect to accomplish anything in this way ?

I know another case, where a girl of sixteen was propounded for admission to the church. Her pastor visited her a few days before the appointed Sabbath. Several members of her own family and several visitors were assembled in the parlor. The talk was light and discursive. He sat on one side of the room, she on the other. Presently there came a lull in the conversation, of which he took advantage. Turning to her he began, in that peculiar tone which, if never heard, cannot be imagined, and, if once heard, need never be described, "You are about to take a very important step."

Of course, this remark, being dropped suddenly into the current of conversation, had the effect of a breakwater. Everything was in confusion for a moment. The visitors did not know what it meant. The family, who did, could not, in politeness, *rush* to the rescue, while the silent victim certainly did not look as if she were capable of taking any step at all.

Now this good man, and many other good men, would not " needlessly set foot upon a worm," yet day after day they walk, all unconsciously, over quivering nerves.

Ministers are apt to forget that, to every heart, its own experiences are new and fresh. They know that as in water face answereth to face, so doth the heart of man to man. They have seen the same doubts agitating, the same fears terrifying, the same contradictions perplexing, the same hopes dawning, the same promises comforting, the same faith glowing, for ten, twenty, thirty years. They have acquired a professional familiarity with spiritual phenomena, and they forget that these are inwoven with the innermost life of individuals, — that to bring them suddenly into the day is exquisite torture. It is true that the two-edged sword of Divine truth does sometimes cleave its way down into the heart so deep, so unerring, that the stricken soul seems for a time to lose consciousness of all external things, and cries aloud, " Lord, save or I perish ! " The world recedes ! The sinner stands face to face with his sin, and it is too dreadful for him ! In such a case, circumstances are little heeded. But oftener the Spirit descends gently, like the dew of Hermon, softening the parched soil and preparing it for heavenly seed. Then, whoever would work in this garden of the Lord should have a skilful hand, a delicate touch. Without it, he breaks the bruised reed. He wounds when he sought only to heal. He meets silence and apparent coldness, where he would fain find warmth and confidence. He marvels that the ways of Zion mourn, that few come to her solemn feasts.

But do not always think,

> " Because the song hath ceased,
> The soul of song hath fled."

True, the harp is still ; and it may be because music has died out of its chords ; — but may it not also be because your untutored fingers have no power to wake its tone ?

Again ; what weapons do ministers furnish their young people against infidelity ? How many of their church-members are ready to give a satisfactory answer to the Cappadocians and Bithynians

who might ask them a reason of the hope that is
in them? How many women who have grown
up in a Christian congregation can show any but
the most superficial cause why they are Congregationalists and not Episcopalians? How many men
can tell where truth and falsehood meet in " Essays and Reviews," or Renan's " Life of Jesus " ?
Essays and Reviews? I should be glad if boys
and girls generally could repeat the Ten Commandments in order, or know what part of the Bible is prose and what is poetry. Do you say that
belongs to parents? Say it to the parents, then.
Sermons are preached to fathers and mothers, in
which they are admonished to bring up their children in the nurture and admonition of the Lord;
but from which a young mother could not gather
a single hint to guide her in managing her baby.
It is the eager desire of parents to do that very
thing, and they would gladly welcome instruction;
but to be good for anything, it must be definite.
It must be like, in kind, to certain papers on that
topic by the Rev. John Todd, printed in the Congregationalist. You may not agree with everything he says, but the man who sets one thinking
and observing for one's self, is more helpful than
he who never excites thought enough for agreement or disagreement.

I spoke of " Essays and Reviews." They are a
foreign growth, but they scatter seed, and there is
plenty of ground ready to receive it. It will surely

spring up, and bear fruit, unless supplanted by a better crop. "Spiritualism" sprang from our own soil, and grew up like Jonah's gourd. For a time, scarcely a community existed in which some uneasy table could not be found. I have heard a doctor of divinity, in preaching against it, use arguments which seemed to satisfy himself, and which perhaps might satisfy any one who knew nothing about the matter, but which a man, who had given a particle of honest attention to real occurrences, might sweep away with one pen-stroke. The absurdity of the refutation was only equalled by the absurdity of the thing refuted. I do not say *the* great mass of sermons, but *a* great mass of sermons, are like the bodies of which we sometimes read, which, exhumed after having been a long time dead, preserve the form and fulness of life, but, brought out into the light of day and touched by vital air, crumble at once into ashes and nothingness. It is better not to touch these things than to touch them weakly: but men need to be clad in the whole armor of God.

Besides the quality of preaching, there is surely an abundant room for improvement in the manner. The number of good readers, good elocutionists, good orators, among ministers, is surprisingly small. Not only are the young men, fresh from theological schools, in a crude state, but the strong probability is, that they will never ripen. They may grow in grace and in the knowledge of

our Lord and Saviour Jesus Christ. Their views
may broaden, their sympathies deepen. Their
certainties may waver into hypotheses, and their
doubts change into belief. They may grow charitable, tolerant, catholic, genial. And they may
not; for there are those who, if they deepen at all,
deepen only in the one rut wherein they started, —
men whose weaknesses and errors time petrifies
instead of removing. But, often, while the man
and the minister goes on from strength to strength,
the orator preserves a masterly inactivity. He
does not purpose to do otherwise. Some, as I have
intimated, frown down any attempt to adorn and
beautify their oratory. They call it extolling the
little at the expense of the great. It is toying,
trifling, frivolity. It is frittering away on shadows
what should be spent on substance. So they scorn
" rhetoric." Grace of style, smoothness of diction,
correctness of pronunciation, beauty of modulation,
sweetness of voice, ease of manner, appropriateness of gesture, — what are these where souls are
to be saved ? It is Unitarianism. It is Lyceum-
izing the Church. Your Orthodox minister is not
going to be caught, nor to catch you, by such
chaff. He proclaims from his pulpit that he does
not expect or endeavor to charm you by eloquence. He does not aim to be "popular." He
does not seek to please you by figures of speech
and poetical periods and smooth doctrine. Let
others cater to your tastes : he gives you the

word of God. If you do not like his preaching, it is because your natural heart revolts against the unadulterated Gospel ; it is because you want to be amused and entertained, rather than warned and instructed.

But, while righteousness, temperance, and judgment to come are not to be abandoned on account of any reluctance to accept them, or any preference for something else, there are other things which ought not to be neglected. These things ought ye to have done, and not to have left the others undone. Anything that attracts men ought not to be considered unworthy of the minister's notice. If certain qualities will induce men to listen to the truth, he ought to cultivate such qualities, if by any means he may . save some. He should be content with nothing lower than the highest. If men, for the sake of gaining the applause of their fellows, will labor to make themselves attractive, shall not he, so much the more, for the sake of gaining souls ? Let it be remembered, that to be popular is not to be shallow, that to be interesting is not to be weak, that to be nice is not to be finical, that rhetoric is not incompatible with religion. If a man has a message from God, let him not fear to clothe it in language too beautiful, or to present it in a manner too winning. Let him not disguise it, and make it repulsive. The Gospel is sometimes presented so uncouthly or so indifferently or so unfeelingly that men are repelled rather than drawn; and the minister who repels them will talk of the opposition of the natural heart, and sincerely believe that it is his plainness of speech, his fearless utterance of the truth, or fearless rebuke of sin, that is distasteful. It is well for a minister to be so simple that the most ignorant can understand him, so well educated that the most learned can respect him, so refined that the most fastidious need not be offended. It is not required that he shall know more about everything than any one else; but he ought either to be great in his own line, or respectable in all. If a geologist knows more about geology than any other man living, he will have the respect of the community, even if he is not well versed in literature; but if he is only a mediocre geologist, he needs to have a good deal of other knowledge to keep him afloat. Just so with ministers. Very few are so great in their special department that they can afford to be small in others. Very few wield a logic so powerful that rhetoric can give no further strength. Genius itself is improved by culture, but ordinary endowments are nothing without it. Everything that might increase influence should receive close attention, not to the neglect, but to the greater effectiveness, of weightier matters.

Many a sermon, which evidently might do good, is spoiled by being badly delivered. Words are mumbled. Sentences are hurried through. Emphasis is set at defiance. Our finest hymns are ruthlessly murdered. Some hymns are bad enough of themselves, but good and bad are ground in the same mill, and come out alike, sheer doggerel. We shall not soon forget the impression produced by such a reading of the line

"Faith, set upon a world to come."

Instead of making a slight pause after " Faith," as the sense required, and bringing out the true idea of Faith, with steadfast eye fixed upon a future world, the minister rather scanned the verse, bringing the pause after " upon " and the emphasis upon it, thus :

"Faith set upón — a world to come,"

as if faith were a hare set upon by a pack of hounds. It really needed reflection to select the real meaning from the possible ones into which the barbarous accents of this excellent man had translated it.

It is rather worse to disfigure hymns in this way than sermons. The sermon is a man's own, and his own reputation alone suffers ; but the author of the unfortunate hymn is dead, or absent, and cannot help himself. On the other hand, however, the sermon is to instruct, admonish, and enlighten the people ; and if, by carelessness or wilfulness, it is badly written or badly spoken, it is *not* the man's reputation alone that suffers, but the welfare of the people, which is of infinitely more

importance. The most excellent .way is for a man
to learn to read before he begins to preach, — then
he can read anything. If, unfortunately, he has
already begun to preach without knowing how to
read, " it is never too late to mend."

A great many sermons are preached in a lifeless,
professional tone, as if the minister were preaching because it is his business, not because he has
something to say. He receives so much money,
and gives so much sermon in return. For value
received he promises to pay, and he is paying, —
like the honest man he is. He does not love you,
his hearer, but he does not hate you ; in fact, he
is not thinking about you at all. He is not thinking about anything in particular. He has nothing
in view. He has written a sermon, and is there to
preach it ; the rest is none of his business. If you
listen to it, or like it, or do not, it is all one to him.
Ministers may not often feel so ; but it often looks
as if they did. There is no mark by which you
shall judge that they heartily believe what they
are saying, or heartily wish you to believe it, or
think it to be of paramount importance that you
should believe it, or that their hearts are in the
thing at all. If this is not a fault, it is a great
misfortune. A man must be himself, but he may
make improvements. He cannot change, but he
can work up his raw material. Some naturally
have more action and animation than others ; but
if ministers asked women to marry them with no

more apparent earnestness than many of them preach the Gospel, priestly celibacy would not be a peculiarity of the Romish Church. Action need not be violent or vulgar, and quietude need not become monotonous and tiresome.

Some ministers are so unfortunate as to have contracted an indignant, vituperative way of preaching. They launch the denunciations of the Gospel at our heads with an air that seems to say, "Good enough for you!" They look upon gentle words, winning persuasions, encouragement, and consolation askant, as "smooth doctrine." Objurgation is their forte. Fire and brimstone are more available with them than the milk and honey of the promised land. It is a thousand pities. Nothing hardens people like continued fault-finding. If their minister always rebukes them for sin as if he were angry with them, they will be flinty to his touch; but if they see his heart melting with compassion and sorrow and tenderness for them, even while he abhors their sin, there is not one in twenty that can withstand it.

I wish, too, our clergymen would look a little more carefully to their language and pronunciation. In these things they should be an ensample to their flock. "If gold ruste, what shuld iren do?" Yet they often help to vitiate rather than preserve or purify the good old well of English undefiled. How often is "taught him" transformed and deformed into "taught 'im." "And

yet " does duty as " an' jit." " Made use of "
would hardly be recognized if spelt as it is sound-
ed, — " may juice of." " Blessed union " is flat-
tened out into " blessy junion." How many ministers are there who, at first sight, will correctly
pronounce

Invariable,	Treasure,	Hope,	Therefore,
Occasionally,	Measure,	Whole,	Often,
Superintend,	Vital,	Coat,	Rise, (noun,)
Innumerable,	Testimony,	Soon,	Humor,
Extraordinary,	Consumed,	Worldly,	*View*, —

words which I have far oftener heard mispro-
nounced than pronounced in the pulpit. How
can we go right, if our leaders do not lead in the
right way ?

Was an Orthodox minister ever known to use the
word " wife " in the pulpit ? From the manner in
which he steers around it, one might suppose that
its utterance was under a ban. Your " consort,"
" companion," the " partner of your joys," or
" sorrows," or " bosom," is recognized, but nobody
ever prays for your " wife." Why is it not just
as well to say that Mr. A. will preach in the *afternoon*, as in the " after part of the day " ? Why
not say that the man whose life you are sketching
was *married* at such an age, rather than that he
" entered into the married relation " ? Why shall
we not hear in the pulpit our own tongue in which
we were born ? If dignity cannot stand Anglo-
Saxon, so much the worse for dignity. Good,

simple, common, honest, racy, idiomatic words and phrases are not only the strongest, but often the most eloquent. The cumbrous euphuisms of a pulpit *patois* are neither pleasant to the taste, nor good for food. Doubtless many sermons which seem dry would be found to be really succulent if they could only be translated (though others, indeed, might suffer from such a process) ; but they are given in a language and in tones which no one ever hears at his table, or in his parlor, or in a railway car ; and it is difficult to believe that a person who has anything to say would talk in such a fashion. Paul was as argumentative, as abstract, as learned, as theological, as any one need be, but his words were concrete and cleaving. I do not always understand him, but I feel confident that he understood himself. The line of his arguments sometimes seems to run zigzag, but you can see that he is in deadly earnest. He was so interested that he became interesting. Sympathy makes up for sense. Through all these eighteen hundred years his dead lips speak with a fire and fervor, his silent voice rings out with a clearness and power, that many a living voice and living lips do not attain.

It is a mistake to suppose that sermons on every-day life in every-day language require less study and thought than others. They require more. When you come down to matters which every one touches at some point, every one is plaintiff, defendant, advocate, and judge. A clergyman can write the learned lore of the schoolmen, and we are so little interested and know so little what he is aiming at, that he has things pretty much his own way. A man may build us a pantheon or a pagoda, and we cannot swear that it is not the one nor the other. But if he undertakes to build us a house to live in, we shall know whether he succeeds, and he must hit the nail on the head, or he will bruise his hands, besides driving the nail awry. Nor does the use of common language mean the use of vulgar language. Colloquialisms sometimes will illustrate truth, but they should be used only in a state of fusion. To go out of one's way to use them, is to abuse them. Vulgarity is always inadmissible. No fancied benefit can atone for the employment of such words and phrases as " scamp," " turn up your nose," etc., which I have heard used in Orthodox pulpits. A minister should be the last to countenance terms which are unbecoming in a gentleman.

Do these things seem trivial ? But God, in ordaining his priesthood, would not be ministered unto by a man who had a flat nose. How much less shall one serve in his sanctuary with unclean lips !

I am afraid that I may seem to be making out the people to be a kind of injured innocent, and the pastor an ogre preying upon it. Not so. The people have faults and to spare. With the wisest manipulation, there will doubtless always be some fault. But a people is not all fault. That is the point I wish to bring into prominence. If I have made it too prominent, it will only balance undue depression, and the average altitude will not be far wrong.

It may be said, also, Why seek to bring people to church, if church services are so deficient? Why? Because half a loaf is better than no bread. Because God commands us not to forsake the assembling of ourselves together. Because experience shows that a community without a church is very likely to become a community without God. Because you always expect a church-going people to be more respectable, virtuous, and benevolent than one that is not, and you are seldom disappointed. But when you look at the other side, so appalling is the extent of practical heathendom, so shallow is the depth of practical Christianity, that it almost seems as if everything still remains to be done. We are as good as we are, because our ministers are so good; we are as bad as we are, because they are no better. Like people, like priest. A people must be as low as its lowest; it can be no higher than its highest.

I have not drawn any fanciful picture of parochial bliss. It is from ministers themselves that I have learned what ministers may be. It is in the light of the pulpit that pulpit shadows deepen. If I had not known the influence which ministers may exert over people, if I had not known the love and respect which people may feel towards ministers, I should not have dreamed what that influence and that deference may be. I have mentioned no defect which has not fallen under my own observation. I have painted no grace which is not from the life. If the standard is set too high, it is not my hand that bore it. I have but pointed to its folds, floating far up in the clear, pure air, not without a hope that the sight may do somewhat towards inspiring the fervent battle-cry, " Forward! All forward! "

VI.

PRAYER-MEETINGS.

THEN they that feared the Lord spake often one to another, and the Lord hearkened and heard it." But if the Lord hearkens to everything that is said at our prayer-meetings, and if, beneath the words, he discovers the underlying motive and feeling, I sometimes fear that his book of remembrance will receive its largest accession of names from other quarters.

Prayer-meetings, — meetings for prayer, — yet how little real praying, — for that matter, how little praying of any kind. By way of illustration, let me mention one instance. At the instigation of certain missionaries, a prayer-meeting was to be held a short time ago, for several nights in succession, simultaneously throughout Christendom. At one of these meetings, which lasted three hours, there were two, possibly three prayers; not more. The rest of the time was consumed

in talking. It was said that no one was to occupy more than ten minutes. When a man has
but ten minutes to talk, it is obvious he ought to
talk fast and concisely, and not waste time in apologies, — if he has anything to say ; if he has not,
he ought not to speak at all. The first speaker at
this meeting was at least five minutes in really
beginning, and then he became so entangled
in his metaphors and similes, that he did not
clear himself for half an hour. In a parlor, this
would have been a gross impertinence. What
was it in a chapel ? No matter how well he might
have talked, no matter if he had spoken with the
tongues of men and of angels, every well-bred person must have felt that he was thrusting himself
in where he did not belong, that he was occupying
time which was due to other people. The second
man, who had evidently been "reading up" for the
occasion, brought out, for another half-hour, the
biography of two good men, whose memoirs are
in every one's hands, and if they were not, there
was no appropriateness in supplying the deficiency
on such an occasion. A third occupied himself
in mourning over the low state of piety in the
Church. And so it went on for three hours, — a
prayer-meeting for the conversion of the heathen,
and not one tenth of the time devoted to praying,
and the heathen left out altogether. Many Christian hearts may have been edified, but it certainly
seems to me that the world can be converted in a
far more economical way than that.

This was, perhaps, an extreme case, but is it exceptional to have a prayer-meeting made the vehicle of crude reflection, shallow emotion, superficial experience, monotonous exhortations, vain babblings, — much of self, little of God, — much of vain repetition, little of soul-wrestling, — too much of the Pharisee in the temple, too little of Jacob at Penuel?

Would it not be well if church-members, instead of lamenting that the ways of Zion mourn, and few come to her solemn feasts, would seriously set themselves to inquiring whether the feasts are worth coming to. If, when we invite people to a feast of fat things full of marrow, of wines on the lees well refined, we furnish forth our tables with dry bones and brackish water, ought we to complain if they are shy of accepting our hospitality? Were a man ever so fond of bread, he would hardly relish a meal of stones; how much less when his appetite has become so vitiated that he has lost his desire for the bread of life, and needs to be lured by all innocent devices!

It is not the want of cultivation and education that makes the empty benches at our prayer-meetings. True, there are solecisms, rhetorical redundancies, awkwardness of posture, and uncouthness of gesture, which are not sweet to eye or ear; nor am I of the number who believe it sacrilege to take exception to anything that occurs in religious meetings. The ark was holy unto the Lord, so that Uzzah, putting forth a presumptuous hand to it, was smitten for his error and died ; but the ark went up from Kirjath-jearim in an ox-cart.

So long as men are influenced by extraneous things, we ought to make extraneous things appropriate. Our best is not too good for the Lord's service. He does not want the poor and the lame and the sick for an offering, but the firstlings of the flock, without spot or blemish. The old woman's principle was correct, though we may perhaps demur at her application of it, when she poured the contents of her molasses jug into her terrified pastor's tea-cup, with the affectionate declaration, " can't be too sweet for the minister ! " It is absurd to suppose that, because a man is religious, he need not be intelligent, — that piety is to be a shield for ignorance, — that any kind of grammar will do for a prayer. Of course it is better to pray blunderingly than not to pray at all ; but better than either is it to pray without blunders. This world's language, in its most cultivated state, is not too good for the courts of heaven.

I make these remarks, first, because there are men who seem rather to glory in their ignorance, who speak of their want of " book-learning " as a praiseworthy thing, who boast that they have none of the graces of oratory, and who go on hammering out their disconnected sentences with a self-complacence at once ridiculous and disgusting.

Of all forms of pride, this is the most intolerable. Pride of birth, pride of wealth, pride of beauty, have some excuse in the intrinsic value of the thing possessed ; but pride of ignorance and stupidity and vulgarity has no shadow of palliation. An ignorant man unconscious of his ignorance is a pitiable object. An ignorant man conscious of his ignorance, striving every day to remove it, and modest in the consciousness, commands not only sympathy, but respect. An ignorant man, glorying in his ignorance, is a nuisance that ought to be abated. We admire sense and energy and worth that have struggled up to prominence and influence, though the garment be coarse and the dialect harsh ; but it is not the coarseness and harshness that we respect, but the manhood that we discern in spite of them. Much as we value the man with them, we should value him still more without them. The energy that quarried the marble was wonderful ; if it could have polished it too, it would have been still more wonderful ; but it would be ineffable stupidity for a rickety beer-cask to waddle up beside the marble shaft, and claim fellowship on the score of a common ugliness. A diamond in the rough is a treasure for a king's ransom ; but the rough without the diamond is mere rubbish ; and even the diamond must be cut into brilliancy before it is worthy to be set in the king's diadem.

Above all things, let us not bring our ignorance

7 *

as a sacrifice unto the Lord, well pleasing. No thought can be too beautiful, no language too chaste, for his service. When we speak directly to him, his glory often overshadows us so that we can only bow our heads in reverence, and humbly say, " Lord be merciful to me a sinner"; and even when we look away from him, and would fain speak of his excellences, his grandeur, and might, and majesty, his loving-kindness and tender mercy beam upon us with such refulgence that we can only exclaim, " The Lord, he is the God; the Lord, he is the God." But when we are moved to speech, earth and sea and sky can furnish nothing too rare and precious to adorn it.

The ark went up in an ox-cart; but it was no battered, disjointed, rattling vehicle. It was a " new cart." Christ rode into Jerusalem on an ass, but it was a fresh young animal, whereon never man sat. Let us take to God the strongest and the fairest and the best, and continually strive to make the best better.

I have said thus much, secondly, because so many draw a line around all religious services, and consider everything within it as without the pale of legitimate criticism ; but when one speaks of a wicked man digging a ditch, which shall fall on his own head, can one help reflecting what a remarkable ditch it must be, even if it was found in a prayer ? When a man uses the same verb fifteen times in three minutes, can one help wishing he would leave it out twelve or thirteen times? But if you should say so, you have, doubtless, many excellent friends, who would look upon you with a kind of holy horror, as a modified species of heathen. There are men who seem to think it irreverent to address the Deity in natural tones, and pitch their voices in prayer on a most unearthly key. There are others who seem to lose their breath in pronouncing the name of the Lord; but these things must never be noticed. Everything that happens "in meeting" must be taken without wincing. This seems to me unwise and uncandid, — uncandid, because little absurdities do occur; why should we not frankly admit it? Is not our religion strong enough to bear it? Unwise, because it helps men cherish little foibles, which hinder their usefulness, which they ought to get rid of, and which a very little kindness in others, and pains on their own part, would enable them to remove. We have the treasure in earthen vessels, and earthen vessels are liable to mould in the damp, and to crack in the frost, and to have bits nicked out from unexplained causes. If we refuse to have them examined and cared for because they contain a sacred treasure, we may find, to our sorrow, that a part of the treasure has escaped through a treacherous hole in the bottom of the jar.

Suppose David had found the ark in a dilapidated old cart, and had called out his thirty thousand chosen men with harps and psalteries and timbrels and cornets and cymbals, to give it a triumphal entry into the city; would there not, very likely, have been men here and there who would have discovered and announced that the paint was worn dingy, that the shafts were broken, that the tire was springing from the wheel, and the linchpin was coming out? And if David had tried to silence them by saying, " Hold ye your peace ! it is the ark of the Lord," would they not have justly replied: " Not so. It is not the ark of the Lord. It is nothing but an old cart; but because it does carry the ark of the Lord, it should be the very best that the land can furnish. Go to, let us cast aside the miserable thing, and build a better, even a worthier."

To ridicule the honest efforts of shrinking modesty requires a weak head and a bad heart. He who can feel, not to say express, a sentiment approaching to mockery at the mistakes which sensitiveness and agitation will often make, has a coarse-fibred as well as a depraved mind. The finest natures often make the worst figures in public. Real delicacy feels a sympathy with the embarrassment so strong, and a respect for the courage so profound, as to preclude every other emotion; but these feelings are not called out by the objectionable habits into which men fall through carelessness or ignorance.

Still, as I was about to say, these things are only circumstances; they are not essences. They do in no wise account for the leanness that often presides at our spiritual feasts. The bodily presence may be weak, and the speech contemptible; but if the fire of Divine Love be kindled in the heart, there will flash through all disguises an eloquence which is not of the earth, earthy; which is of the Lord from heaven. The faltering words of a hesitating soul trembling between fear of man and love of God have often cloven the armor of a selfish, worldly nature, piercing even to the dividing asunder of soul and spirit. The angel of the Lord lays the live coal alike upon the lips of learned and unlearned, and speeds them on heavenly errands.

There are in prayer-meetings more serious defects than these, — defects which admit of no palliation, — defects which every one ought to deprecate, condemn, and, as far as possible, root out. I mean the mockery of holy things; the cant which, under the name of piety, wearies the Lord with its words; the Pharisaism which would pass for Christianity; the wholesale slander which covers itself with the mantle of religious zeal; the censoriousness which assumes the garb of faithfulness; the heartlessness which handles the denunciations of God as a child handles its playthings. Such displays are not common. Shame that they should ever occur! Shame that the way to heaven should ever be turned into a way to death !

Not so bad as this, yet radically wrong, both as a fact and as a sign, are the paucity of thought and the shallowness of feeling so commonly exhibited at prayer-meetings. Our exhortations and prayers are too often the result of an outward necessity, not of an inward prompting. We speak, not because our hearts burn within us, — not because we feel that, if we should hold our peace, the very stones would cry out, — but because the meeting must be kept up. Instead of definiteness, conciseness, and pith, — "infinite riches in a little room," — we have abstractions and dilutions and doublings and painful egotisms. It is routine and duty and treadmill. This must be, just so long as our *lives* furnish nothing higher. If we put God out of our thoughts on Monday and Tuesday, we cannot have any new thought of God wherewith to strengthen our brother's soul on Tuesday evening. No harvest can spring up where no seed is sown. You cannot be warm and filled because you are bidden to be. You cannot feel interested simply because you ought to feel so. You cannot have something to say because you are called upon to say something. A thought must be wrought out in your soul before it can pass through your lips. We can gather ourselves together and multiply words, but unless we are *charged* with love to God and love to man, heart meets heart to little purpose; brain flashes no light on brain.

It is not that worshippers are to be startled into attention and interest by news, novelty, eccentricities, conceits, and far-fetched combinations, nor that prayer-meetings are to be turned into exchanges, where people are to meet in order to tell or to hear some new thing. It is the grand *old* truths that the world wants perversely to forget, and of which it needs to be forever reminded, but in love, not hate or scorn or pride. It is the same old carol words chanted by Moses when time was young, — harped for all ages by Israel's shepherd-king, — swelling in fuller strains as the heavenly host gathered over the hills of Judæa, — that man needs to have forever sung to him in new notes and chords and concords, that shall witch back his flagging interest, and charm away his indifference "ere he is aware."

What we want is more of the spirit of Christ in our hearts. Our chapels can never become the gate of heaven till there is more of heaven in ourselves. "The kingdom of God is within you." The life of the prayer-meeting depends on the life of the shop, the office, the farm, the dairy, the kitchen, the closet.

This meagreness of life is often painfully indicated by the avidity with which unusual incidents are seized and spun out and wrought into moral reflections and practical applications. An immense

quantity of nondescript rhetoric is evolved in the
attempt to " improve " a " providence." Undoubtedly there is such a thing as a providence,
and there is such a thing as improving it ; but
providences are always happening, and we are
not always improving them when we think we
are.

Providences (as the word is colloquially used)
are always happening. To the man whose eyes the
Lord hath opened no day passes without bringing
fresh proof of God's love or wisdom or power; but
many of us walk with blind eyes and deaf ears
to the beauty that breathes and the music that
rings all along our daily paths. Only when we
receive a great shock, when something breaks in
upon the selfish, stolid monotone of our lives and
forces our notice, are we startled into wonder,
admiration, and awe, and exclaim, " Surely the
Lord is in this place, and I knew it not." Then,
with honest purpose, with, no doubt, sincere desire to learn and to teach the lesson which it bears,
we begin to expound and warn and infer and admonish, till the theme is " done to death." Waked
suddenly from our slothful inertia, we lay about
us right and left with eager but awkward strokes.
By as much as we have been remiss before, by so
much we now overdo. This is, indeed, better
than the inertia. Agitation, be it ever so violent
and irregular, is better than stagnation. But
better than either is the quiet, healthful flow of

the life-giving river rolling through green meadows and purple vineyards to the peaceful sea. Our lives should be more equable. If our religion permeated all the root-fibres and branch-tendrils of our souls, it would bud and blossom in perpetual spring; whereas it too often lies long dormant, and then shoots up into spasmodic and short-lived growth. If God were to us an own familiar friend in whom we trusted; if we could learn to look with serious, yet not sad eyes, upon the eternal side of all living, and entwine the practical, the present, the homely, and the humble with the grand, the unseen and eternal; if we could look upon the shop, the field, the kitchen, the parlor, not simply as the servants of the body, but as the ministers of the soul, — we should not need to fasten upon any one incident to furnish the staple for our prayer-meetings; we should be embarrassed only by the multitude which from all sides would call upon our souls to praise the name of the Lord. We should be continually improving providences, — speaking often one to another of the wonderful works of God.

On a certain Sabbath morning, several years ago, an earthquake set one of our New England cities a-trembling for a few minutes, and then went on its way; but throughout the day, and I know not how long after, the religious services were saturated with earthquake. It was served up in the pulpit and the Sabbath school and the prayer-

K

meeting, by clergy and laity, till one could not help feeling that the good people handled the poor earthquake a great deal more severely than the earthquake handled them. Do not misunderstand me. Do not suppose that I object to drawing moral lessons from physical or other occurrences. Object? It is the very thing which I think we ought to do, — only we ought to do a great deal more of it — and a great deal less; more in some directions, less, relatively, in others; more on ordinary, less, relatively, on extraordinary occasions. From every such occurrence it is meet, right, and our bounden duty, to draw all the good it has to give; but having pumped it dry, what is the use of jerking the handle up and down, especially when thousands of living springs are welling through the verdure under our feet, and all around us?

It is, indeed, but natural that rare events should excite more attention than common ones. Although an earthquake no more exhibits and illustrates God's power and presence than the daily returning sun, yet it will, from its very infrequence, produce a deeper and more solemn impression of his power. This is all right. It is not that one event goes too deep, but that the many do not go deep enough. The one impression need not be diminished, but the other needs to be increased. We shall never attain the measure of the stature of the fulness of Christ till we get into equilibrium, till we better understand the relations of things. We need to remember that God numbers the hairs of our heads, and watches the young sparrows as they fly, and calls the stars by name, and showers new mercies every morning, and fresh blessings every evening. If we will but assign to these every-day events their true place in the Divine economy, we shall not exhaust ourselves and others with convulsive efforts to wrench from some startling and unusual event the lesson which every sunrise would gladly teach. He who can express the strength-giving juice from all fruits, need not cling to the dry rind of any. If we would see God's providence, his wise and careful and benevolent foresight, as displayed wherever we choose to look, we should not harp upon any single exhibition of it. But we forget the undulations which make the landscape so rich, so varied, and so beautiful, and notice only the mountains that lift their hoar heads to the clouds. Thereby we lose much ; for though the mountains are grand, and speak grand words, — of passion soothed into repose, and strength ministering to humanity, and vigor waiting upon beauty, — yet the mountains are few and far, accessible only to individuals, and require toilsome journeyings and waitings and watchings ; while the hills swell everywhere, clothed with greenness and crowned with flowers. The thunder-cloud sweeps over the sky, and flings its impetuous abundance to the earth, that drinks it in with thirsty lips ; but the life that wakes in maple-buds, and pierces the brown soil in tender herbage, and breathes in the first sweet scents of snowdrop and hyacinth and arbutus, is the child of gentle spring showers and silent summer dews.

We have all heard of· the man who was gratefully narrating the mercy of God in preserving him unhurt when his horse stumbled and threw him upon the rocks. " But I," said his friend, " have still greater reason to be thankful ; for my horse did not stumble at all."

This is the key to the whole matter. This is the way to make life fruitful of gratitude. Thus not only will deep call unto deep, but we shall see the loving-kindness of the Lord in the day-time, and in the night his song shall be with us. When we go to the house of God, it will be with the multitude, with the voice of joy and praise. Seven men shall no longer, in leanness of soul, lay hold of one theme ; but every man shall see the Lord under his own vine and fig-tree, and his mouth shall be filled with laughter and his tongue with singing, till out of the abundance of his heart he cannot choose but speak.

The quality of our moral reflections is often defective, as well as the quantity. When death wrenches a vigorous young soul from its palpitating body ; or when a gray head lies down peacefully in the grave ; or when the little children go up to Jesus from mothers' arms that would fain press them forever to mothers' hearts, God speaks. He that hath ears to hear, let him hear. But what is the message ? A good deacon rises in the prayer-meeting and reminds the young people of the uncertainty of life, — warns them that youth may be cut down as well as age, — and exhorts them to be prepared. All true and right, but not to the point ; because the young people have heard their mothers say that their friend's death was the result of a cold caught by carelessly sitting on the door-step with bare shoulders, through a damp summer evening, and they resolve — that it is an imprudent and dangerous indulgence, and that they will avoid it. It admonishes them less of the uncertainty of life, than of the danger of damp evenings. It was a mysterious Providence that smote down the strong man, blotting out his sun from heaven at its zenith, and shrouding his hearth-stone in darkness ; but not so very mysterious to the strong men who stand around his bier and remember that warm August day, four weeks ago, when he went home tired, heated, and hungry, ate an inordinate quantity of heavy food and unripe fruit, and drank large draughts of cold water, thereby throwing upon his system a burden which, in its exhausted state, it could not bear ; and they resolve — to be temperate. The lesson to them is less of the uncertainty of life than of the necessity of prudence and moderation. When the little baby lies in its tiny coffin with strange, wan cheeks, and unbabylike, thin hands, the tender-hearted mothers bend over it and weep with those that weep ; but they mentally resolve not to keep their own babies shut up in the close air of the nursery, as this baby was, and not to nauseate them with food when they are already suffering from surfeit. And the mothers and the strong men and the young people are right, though the good deacons are not wrong. They are right, because a very large proportion of deaths are untimely, and the lesson which they ought to teach is less of the uncertainty of life than of the certainty of law, — the inexorable sequence of effect and cause, — the fixedness of our organization, — the absolute impossibility of sinning against our constitution without suffering the penalty. This is a lesson which should be learned, and this the time when hearts are often most ready to learn it. They have begun to point the moral themselves ; if their leader has a sharper eye and a stronger hand than theirs, let him complete the work. Where they are slow to learn, let him be swift to teach. But would it not be considered rather below the dignity of the occasion to derive such a conclusion from such an event ? *Is* it below the dignity of the occasion ? Has God, or has he not, given our health and our life in large measure to our own keeping ? Is it according to his eternal purpose that babies and young men and maidens shall die, or that they shall do the world's work, and go down to the grave like a shock of corn *in its season*, fully ripe? Does he intend that we shall violate the laws of our being, either through ignorance or carelessness, and then resign ourselves piously to the dispensations of Providence? *Is* it a dispensation of Providence? Is it not rather a dispensation of improvidence?

I know there are many cases where death comes prematurely and unaccountably, but there are more cases than we heed where it comes prematurely and accountably; and the very fact that there are sorrows which no foresight can prevent is an additional reason why we should guard against unnecessary sorrow.

I know that the innocent often suffer from the transgressions of the guilty. When a young man dies from his over-bold deed, his mother, who would have given her life to save him, goes down to her grave mourning. When a reckless engineer drives his engine headlong to destruction, — when an ill-built factory crumbles to shapeless ruin, — the guilty and the guiltless, the responsible and the irresponsible, perish in a common death, and their mourners go about the streets. Healing balm for their stricken spirits, — oil and wine, and tenderest ministrations. But the question comes back, What is the whole lesson to be derived for all from every death? And in each case, what is the whole lesson to be derived from this man's death? What is the moral which this event chiefly points?

For it cannot be said that, even when death is self-invoked, prudence, carefulness, caution, is the only lesson taught. Every soul that parts the veil between this and the unseen world, no matter under what circumstances, lets in a ray of light from that world, which our heavy eyes often fail to see ; and whoever strikes off the scales so that we can take in the heavenly vision does God service by bringing heaven to earth.

But what I mean is this : if there is a right and a wrong in this matter ; if there is a *sin,* the wages of which is death ; that is, if death be the direct result of culpable carelessness or ignorance, we ought not to let the lesson which it directly teaches go unlearned, and point out only the one which it teaches indirectly ; we ought not to confine ourselves to one aspect of the case, — the uncertainty of life and the certainty of death, — and warn and admonish from that stand-point only. When a man dies, let us see whether it be not an admonition for us to live. It may say, "Set thine house in order, for thou shalt die " ; and it may say, "Set thine house in order *or* thou shalt die."

We make a mistake. We do not appreciate life. We do not rise to the height of its dignity. We exalt death and degrade life, when we should exalt life and degrade death. Death is a penalty, — " the mark of our shame, the seal of our sorrow," — the deep dishonor of our race, — the yoke

under which we must all bend our captive heads.
In death itself, there can be nothing noble, for
death is involuntary and inevitable. Death passes
upon all, for that all have sinned. Death is repulsive. It works woe to strength and beauty.
It changes the likeness of God into dust and
desolation.

But life is glorious. Life is the time to serve
the Lord. Life is fruitful of great deeds. Life
carves the soul into Divine symmetry, if we will
but grasp it nobly. Life is the battle-ground;
the hosts of sin are marshalled on the one side,
the hosts 'of holiness on the other; man can
choose on which side he will serve, and there
is no greater victory than the victory over sin.
From the beginning to the end of life, the stal-
wart arm can always find a sturdy foe; and every
blow struck is a blow for suffering humanity, and
for the Christ that died to redeem it; and every
blow struck is sure to be successful.

What is death to this? Death is only an incident; life is the essence. Death is passive; life
is active. Death is shrinking; life is aggressive.
Death is but for a moment; life is forever. Death
is the blot of time; life is the radiance of eternity.

When we talk about preparation for death, then,
what do we mean? Is there any way of preparing for death except living rightly? Since death
is not a thing to be done, but to be endured; not
heaven, but the passage into heaven; not the

8

judgment, but an antecedent of the judgment;
not even a putting off, but a falling off, — while
all the good and all the glory are to be got from
life, — shall we not bend all our forces to living?
Since it is not a poetic fancy, but an eternal truth,
that

> " There is no death, — what seems so is transition "

from corruptible to incorruption, from mortal to im-
mortality, — shall we not cry out with the tranced
poet and the rapt Christian :

> " O Life, O Beyond,
> Thou art strange, thou art sweet ! " .

Blessed be God for giving us the boon of a life
so flooded with glory that its light stretches across
the very valley of the shadow of death, to where
the shining ones stand on the other side to receive
the eager soul, — for the boon of a life so heroic
that it ennobles even death, throwing its mantle
over that ghastly Terror, and so wrapping it in
the folds of love and faith and courage and constancy, and all the grand, sweet virtues of martyrdom, that men rush to its embrace as a friend,
and Death, disarmed of his sting, and conquered
by Almighty power,

> " Kisses them into slumbers like a bride."

" The present, the present, is all thou hast for
thy sure possessing." We know that we can
serve the Lord to-day, but we know not what
shall be on the morrow. The possible grave hid-

den in its mysterious folds may be, for one,
shrouded in thick darkness; for another, haloed
with light; but to all it is indistinct. This we
know, that if we serve the Lord to-day, whether
by worshipping him in the great congregation, or
by giving a cup of cold water to one of his little
ones, he will not fail us.

Christ, laid hold of in faith to-day, will sustain
us in the overflowing of the waters to-morrow.
Though now, in the full flush of youth and health
and strength, every nerve instinct with vitality,
we cannot look at death without pain and shuddering, let us not fear. Dying grace will come
with dying. God, who hath so loved us, will not
leave us then. A father does not caress his child
through the long summer day, to abandon him at
nightfall. Darkness may veil him from the little
one's sight, or slumber lull him to temporary forgetfulness; but his loving-kindness wraps his child
about in the still hours, and a fatherly presence
is in the house for good. More loving than this,
an eye that never slumbers, and to which no darkness is a veil, watches over us in all our weary
wanderings, and will surely not lose sight of us
when the dark river heaves its cold billows at our
feet. More than this, as a father precedes his
frightened child along rocky ways, removing all
obstructions, encouraging him with friendly words,
and holding out sustaining arms in the gloom, so
God came from Teman, the Holy One from Mount

Paran, and passed through the valley of shadows, wresting from death his sting, from the grave his victory, making the crooked places straight, and the rough places plain, that we, his weak, fearful, trembling children, may come off, not unharmed only, but conquerors and more than conquerors, — may have, not only a safe deliverance, but a triumphant entrance into the city of our God, to go no more out forever. O love of Christ, which passeth knowledge! Unutterable love, from which neither principalities, nor powers, nor things present, nor things to come, nor height, nor depth, nor any other creature, shall be able to separate us! Shall we fear to trust it? Shall we, through fear of death, be all our lifetime subject to bondage? Nay, rather let us walk joyfully before him till the end come, and then lie down as joyfully in the arms of everlasting love; for so he giveth his beloved sleep.

Again, there are too many meetings, — not too many, perhaps, in the aggregate, but they are not equally distributed, and there are too many in spots. In sparsely-settled villages circumstances may prevent the evil, but in many of our large cities gregariousness is rampant. The clergyman in a city church on last Sunday morning gave out the following notices: "Morning Union Prayer-meeting every morning at nine, and Evening at five o'clock. Church prayer-meeting on Monday evening. Stated prayer-meeting on Tuesday evening. Church meeting on Wednesday evening, and lecture on Thursday evening."

To the mental vigor, moral power, and general effectiveness of the pastor, if he attends all or half the meetings, such a round of services must be ruinous. No resources can supply so continuous a demand. He must offer to his people the dry rind of other men's grapes, instead of the richness of his own purple vintage. Thought and feeling are wrought up by palpable endeavor to the proper pitch, instead of coming down by simple force of gravity from a cataractic height of inward life so vast, that every drop of water weighs a pound, — not because it is hurled hard, but because it cannot help it. Christian individuality is endangered by this prevailing tendency to association. The type of character is less strong, vigorous, independent, than it should be. Religion is more conventional and less personal. It fastens on to the tongue, but does not strike in. Temptation comes to a man alone ; so come strength and firmness and integrity. Through the unexplored solitudes of the heart the whisper of the tempter steals, and the still, small voice of conscience speaks. There the battle is fought and — lost to sin and shame and sorrow, or won for truth and right and God ; and where the battle-ground is, there should the man be at home. The way to keep a foe from a disputed territory is to overrun it with your own armies. If you would not

have the Devil march into your own heart, and
stake it off and take possession, you must pre-empt
the ground yourself in the name of the Most High
God. Satan is a great coward. He dares not
attack us in the broad day, when we are surrounded by the good, and hedged in by good influences,
but he steals upon our aloneness, — if it may be,
unawares. Let him find that we have been there
before him, — that Christ is lodged in every most
hidden depth of the soul, and every remotest
wilderness, — that every avenue is barred, every
pass guarded, every barricade bristling with guns,
— and he will call off his force with slight attack.
Resist the Devil and he will flee from you.

It is not in the woods, surrounded by its mates,
sheltered from the full fury of the storm, and de-
prived of the full glory of the sun, that the tree
attains its grandest growth. It is alone in the
fields that its real might and majesty are seen ;
for there the North wind sweeps down in un-
checked madness, and every root thrusts out its
fibrous fingers in unrelaxing grasp upon the sturdy soil, and every slender twig exerts its utmost
strength to wrench itself from the icy embrace.

There are people who seem to find the one
Mediator between God and man, the man Christ
Jesus, insufficient. They can have no communion
with God unless there is a corporation between
him and them. They cannot find any house of
God unless there is a multitude going up with

them. They are not easy until they have all things common. They seem not to have any, or at least they have a very feeble, conception of a rivulet whose course can be marked only by the deeper tint of violets, and the fresher green of the upspringing grass. Unless they see the foaming, and hear the roaring, they do not believe there is any water there. By active piety, they understand a readiness to take part in prayer-meetings and exhortations. The more a man talks, the better and brighter Christian he is. They cannot conceive how any one who has tasted and seen that the Lord is gracious, can prefer to stay at home of an evening, rather than go to the chapel or vestry. They are omnivorous and voracious. Any kind of a meeting, so that it is a meeting, suits them. They are shy about waiting upon the Lord alone. Whenever they present themselves to him, they seem to want a retinue. Such piety is suspicious.

Association is a very good thing in its place, but when it destroys or diminishes the sense of personal responsibility; when it substitutes the temporary enthusiasm arising from contiguity of place, for the serene and steady flame of love towards God; when it hides individual weakness with collective strength in cases where the former will, in the long run, not only ruin the individual, but the mass, — then association is a very poor thing, or, which amounts to the same, a good

thing out of place. Its evil effects are continually seen. How often do we hear of Eastern
church-members leaving their homes, settling in
the West, and then forgetting their principles,
neglecting their duties, and living without God and
without hope in the world. Yet the moral almost
invariably drawn is, that churches must be established, and ministers sent there, in order to prevent
such grievous relapses, — which is a very different
moral from what I should draw. Undoubtedly the
men ought to go, and the churches ought to be
formed ; but I do not infer it from such facts. I
infer that our mode of operation needs to be over-
hauled at the East, rather than established at the
West. I should say that the trouble arose from
what happened before the man left his old home,
rather than from what happened after he reached
the new. His course there is the natural result
of his course here. He withers like the mown
grass, and for the same reason ; because he is
severed from the source of nourishment. Shall
we not then supply the nourishment again ? Not
at all. Such nourishment is factitious. "All my
springs are in Thee ! " The ordinances of religion are but pipes for the better conveyance of the
water of life to thirsty souls. He mistook them
for the fountain itself, and when they were severed, instead of repairing directly to that, he
faded as a leaf, — he died of thirst.

There is no reason why a man who has once

been born into grace should not go on growing in it, — whatever his circumstances may be. A man who owns a Bible has the very best of facilities for learning God's will, though he has not all. But the trouble is, men do not accustom themselves to standing alone at home, and consequently they are weak in the knees when they go abroad. They band together, and sway together, and hold each other doubtfully up. All well enough if it were possible to stay together always, and man's chief end were to keep his feet; but since circumstances necessitate frequent separations, and it is the duty of every individual to attain and exert the greatest strength possible to him, this dependence on others proves to be poor preparation for the coming contest. It relaxes the muscles that should be tensely tightened, and the nerves that should be firmly strung. So, when the man goes off into the wilderness by himself, he shivers and shakes and falls. To remedy this defect by multiplying churches, is like trying to strengthen a baby's legs by tying them up in splinters. They will not give way while the splinters are on, but the moment the splinters are removed, down they fall as weak as before. This is not the way mothers do. They strengthen the weak hands and confirm the feeble knees with generous supplies of wholesome, nutritious food. They teach and guide, and leave the little feet to totter on alone at the risk of a few falls.

8 *   L

A faith that lays hold on God, and strikes its roots into God, and derives its sustenance from God, may be shaken, but cannot be sundered. A faith that faints and dies must have had its source this side of God, and needs not to be renewed, but to be thrown off, to make room for a better. Every young Christian should be trained to stand, and walk, and fight alone. Out of weakness he should be made so strong that his single arm can subdue kingdoms, stop the mouths of lions, and turn to flight the armies of aliens. It should be an established fact that a man is to be just as active and efficient a Christian single-handed in the midst of a wicked and perverse generation, as if he stood in the assemblies of saints. The Church militant is not precisely like the World militant; for whereas, in the latter, superior numbers will conquer inferior, in the former, one can chase a thousand, and two put ten thousand to flight, — and yet they are, perhaps, not so different after all, for in both it is quality, not quantity, that wins the day. A regiment of well-trained soldiers will disperse a mob of angry thousands, and one valiant, able-bodied, well-armed Christian is more than a match for the snares of the crowded city or the squatter's wilderness.

I have no faith in a religion that cannot stand fire. Of what earthly use is it, in a world where temptations are the order of the day, where your adversary, the Devil, walketh about like a roaring lion, seeking whom he may devour? If a man cannot be a good Christian without the countenance of associates, he will not be much of a Christian with. Understand, this does in no wise militate against the ordinances of religion, any more than Abraham Lincoln's present position indicates that colleges are useless, and splitting rails is the royal road to greatness. When a man neglects an opportunity to avail himself of such helps to learning as a college affords, the chances are ninety-nine in a hundred that he has no desire to learn. The Church is the Christian's college. If he can, he will gladly improve its advantages. If he cannot, he will by no means sink into stupidity and sloth, but rub along as best he may, and come out strong in the end. Too many undergraduates make that the end which should be the means, and when they come to be weighed in the balance, they are found wanting. They have not strength to resist unto blood, striving against sin.

We shall be judged singly, and not in squads. The Church and the World must appear before God by individuals, and every man give an account of *himself*. If thou art wise, thou art wise for thyself. If thou scornest, thou alone shalt bear it.

VII.

THE PROOF OF YOUR LOVE.

HE ministry of the word at the present day, in the pulpit, in the prayer-meeting, in private conversation, and in our religious literature, fails to make all the impression of which the truth is capable,— fails to bring men up to the mark for•the prize of their high calling, — fails to wield most effectively the two-edged sword of Divine power, — nay, sometimes blunts its edge and destroys its temper, because of the subjectivity to which it appeals for tests of Christian character. "Am I, are you, is he, a Christian?" is the anxious question that arises in every hoping, trembling, awakened heart, — hoping and trembling for itself or for the weal of some dearer life than its own. How shall an answer be obtained? How *is* it obtained? The inquirer is urged to observe the state of his mind as to the plan of salvation, — his views of his character in the sight of God, — his

clear exercise of faith in Christ, — his sense of
pardon and acceptance, — his reception of Christ
as the only redemption, etc., — all orthodox and
therefore unobjectionable, — all subjective, and
therefore, in a measure, useless; for the weakness of man is that he can in no wise thread
the labyrinth of his own mind; and the misery
of man is that, though his heart is deceitful and
desperately wicked, all the light that travels to
his soul must pass through it. Even if we could
take out of man all his sin, whether original or
acquired, — leaving him just as he is, only pure,
— still he would be ignorant of the workings of
his own mind. He would know effects, but
would be little skilled in causes. The how and
the why and the wherefore would be, for the
greater part, a sealed book to him. How much
more, when the heart has become warped and
clouded and untuned by sin, so that when we
demand just judgment, we receive the verdict
of prejudice and inclination and passion; when
we look through it, we see but dimly; when we
strike it, it gives an uncertain sound.

How many of us know from what our ideas are
derived, whence our conclusions are drawn, or
whither our opinions tend? I am brave: is it
because I came of a race of mountaineers, or because I have never been in circumstances of real
danger, or because I am surrounded by ample
protection, or because I have never met the pre-

cise object suited to call forth my peculiar latent
cowardice? I am moved to indignation by the
corruption that pervades our land: is it the innate
nobility of my soul, or the Puritan church spire
whose shadow fell athwart the path of my young
years, or a sordid, fixed, yet perhaps vague conviction, that, in the long run, honesty is the best
policy, or the dull delight of a half-unconscious
revenge for the disappointment of my youthful
hopes of political prominence, — any or all of
these? The emotion in a man's mind may be
love to God and repentance unto salvation, or it
may be the influence of an earnest, faithful, beloved minister's mind upon his own, or it may be
that his heart, softened by the tears of some recent
affliction, can more readily receive the impress of
the Saviour's footsteps, or it may be the magnetism
of cognate life, or it may be all combined. The
workings of the mind are, from its very nature,
complex and hard to be understood; but when the
element of sin is thrown into the calculation, who
can make the crooked paths straight and the rough
places plain? "Is thy servant a dog that he
should do this thing?" cried the astonished and
indignant Hazael: for looking into his own heart
he did not see ambition, avarice, tyranny, oppression, cruelty, treachery, murder, — *couchant* lions
in covert lairs, biding their time; yet they were
there, and the prophet's eye, divinely keen, penetrated their lurking-places, and an hour came

when they rose in their strength and wrought a fell work.

Deeply and sadly impressed with the deceitfulness of this uncertain heart, another prophet cries out, " Who shall know it ? " and from the heaven of heavens comes the calm response, " I the Lord search the heart," — implying, as plainly as words can imply anything, that only the Lord is sufficient for these things. Yet, be it remembered, through this abyss of wickedness which no line of ours can fathom, must the beams of the Sun of Righteousness shine upon us. Surely, then, it cannot be wise to trust so largely to its representations. It cannot be wise to make so much account of the interpretations of an organ which has so often played us false that it has, in a measure, lost the power of truth-telling, — nay, even of discerning between truth and falsehood ; for it is not only a deceiving, but a deceived heart, that turns us aside so that we cannot deliver our souls, or say whether or not there is a lie in our right hands.

Real self-examination being, then, so difficult — not to say impossible — for many, for most people, that they can make little headway in it, a great deal of the advice which inculcates it must be misplaced and injudicious. The self-examination which does amount to anything is generally incidental and involuntary. Ordinarily, set a man down to put himself, in cold blood, through a course of self-examination, and he is out at sea without compass or star or sun. His thoughts go flying off in a tangent towards all quarters of the globe. The last thing in the world that he can concentrate himself on, is himself. Some are conscious of this ; some are not ; but that does not affect the result. A boy sincerely believes that he has been studying his lesson, when he has only been poring over his book ; but his lesson is no more learned than if he knew he had been idling all the while.

Frames of mind, by which we set so much store in making up an inventory of Christian possessions, are comparatively of small value. A large proportion of the copious extracts from private diaries, which enter so largely into our religious memoirs, are not only tiresome and useless, but positively pernicious. As a general thing, they would better never have been written ; but to drag them into print is a harm to the world. Morbid anatomists may find pleasure in it, and nerveless organisms may feel no pain ; but a healthy, sensitive soul can be only shocked. They prove nothing, — nothing, at least, which they were designed to prove ; for frames of mind are largely dependent on frames of body. Given a feeling of despondency ; it may be a sense of sin that overwhelms the soul, or it may be the dyspepsia. Digestion is a great aid to devotion. Serenity is the natural concomitant of a well-ordered dinner ; while a man who is suffering the horrors of clammy bread,

or an unmasticated dumpling, or a midnight mince-
pie, can hardly help viewing himself as altogether
vile, — and will not be far out of the way, either.
If we feel called upon to write out in our journals
a description of our raptures and our despondencies,
we should prefix to every one the bill of fare for
the day, the hour of rising and retiring, the amount
and quality of exercise taken and work performed.
Thus the recital may be of service to physiology,
and, since physiology, like every other true science,
is the handmaid of religion, — to religion. This
is not, as some seem to suppose, making religion
wait upon the appetite, degrading it into a mere
camp-follower of the stomach, and projecting into
our theology a gross materialism. It is, on the
contrary, a thrusting back of the material, which
is always insolently attempting to encroach upon
the spiritual. It is branding the criminal, that all
men may see and shun him, or defend themselves
against him. It is the soul saying to the body:
" Hitherto you have rioted with impunity, but you
shall go no further. You have masked your evil
deeds under a penitential sorrow, and, through
ignorance or negligence, you have escaped scot-
free. You have indulged your inclinations, and I
have paid the penalty. You have run up the
score, and I have footed the bills. Now we will
have a settlement and a readjustment. I will
condescend to your weaknesses, but I will not be
responsible for them. They must be my sorrow,

but they shall not be my sin,—least of all, my glory."

Such transcripts are, I think, injurious for two reasons; first, they emit a flavor of vanity and hypocrisy. If it was a strictly private diary, its privacy should still be respected. If it was not strictly private, its value as a faithful transcriber— which is its sole value—is gone. Secondly, they often raise a false standard. They are apt to be held up for our example, and young people are taught to believe that they ought to have a similar experience. The probability is that they ought to have no such thing. One man's feelings are no sort of criterion for another man's feelings. Hold up God in his thousand-fold manifestations, and duty in its thousand forms, and let every man originate his own feelings. Love to God and faith in Christ are called forth by something outside of us, not by anything within us. Looking unto Jesus, not looking unto ourselves, is the true way to grow in grace.

Plant divine truth, loosen the soil around it, water it, and weed it, and let it alone. Do not be continually digging up the seed to see if it has sprouted.

It was human weakness endowed with heavenly wisdom that cried, "Search me, O God, and know my heart; try me, and know my thoughts, and see if there be any wicked way in me, and lead me in the way everlasting."

In morals — in anything except mathematics —
there can be no mathematical certainty. The full
assurance of faith is — the full assurance of *faith*,
not of positive, demonstrable knowledge ; and faith
is the substance of things *hoped for*, the evidence
of things *not seen.*

It is said that, outside of mathematics, every
statement is but the balance of probabilities. If
this is true of matter, cognizable by the senses and
with balances external to us so that we can examine them, how much more is it true of mind,
wherein is no lens to annihilate distance or to
magnify minuteness. The mind's eye unassisted
must examine the whole. With naked arms we
go down into the soul's arena to wrestle with her
concerning fate. Vaguely we question her of her
conditions.

To ask a sick man what is the matter with him,
and to rely upon his answer, would be the stupidity of a quack. The man of science questions him
of his symptoms, it is true, and the patient describes them with what accuracy he may. Sometimes clearly, sometimes perforce obscurely ; but
in all cases the object is that he, the doctor, may
judge, from the patient's feelings and from his own
observations, what the real state of the case is ; he
knows that certain sensations which the sick man
describes refer to sources of which the sufferer is
ignorant. But in all spiritual diseases the sick
man is his own physician. No man, no being

save the Omniscient, knows the motives of his conduct, the conditions under which these motives became his, the particular points, in short, which make him different from other men.

And still the question remains unanswered. Still the

> " . . . . . point I long to know, —
> Oft it causes anxious thought, —
> Do I love the Lord or no ?
> Am I his or am I not ? "

And still it will remain unanswered till we look for it in the direction of " how do I live ? " as well as, and rather than, in the direction of " how do I feel ? "

Men grope for something tangible. Reaching out after their feelings while their feelings elude their grasp, or yield only to mislead and deceive, longing for a real consciousness, a full assurance, which they do not find because the test of character does not come within the scope of their certain knowledge of themselves, they set up other tests. The minister says, truly, Scripturally, and often eloquently : " You must repent of your sins, and forsake them. You must take up the cross and follow Christ. You must deny all ungodliness, and every worldly lust, and live soberly, righteously, and godly. You must fear God and keep his commandments, and walk circumspectly before him." And the weary, heavy-laden, sin-sick heart says : " Yes, I will do all this. I will repent of my sins and turn to Jesus. I will take up my cross

and join the church. I will be baptized by the
minister, or confirmed by the bishop. I will go
to church, to the Sabbath school, to the prayer-
meeting, and the conference. I will take part
whenever I am called upon. I will speak to the
unconverted, warning them of their danger, and
trying to lead them to Jesus. I will maintain
family and private prayer." All right things to
do, only they are not Christianity, but a part of it.
Unless complemented by other weights, we have
a false balance, which is an abomination to the
Lord.

To preach the Gospel is, as I understand it, first
to explain it, secondly to enforce its obligations.
The first is theology theoretical; the second is
theology practical. They dovetail into each other.
The first without the second is useless; the second without the first is inconsequent, — besides
being weary, stale, flat, and unprofitable. They
react upon each other. The first makes the second intelligent; the second informs the first with
vitality. The first alone is a dead faith; the second alone is a dead morality, — both fit only to be
cast out and to be trodden under foot of men. An
enlightened brain will regulate the heart, and a
devout heart will interpret many hard sayings to
the baffled brain. Seeking to learn God is grander
than the possession of all other knowledge; and
there is no commentary upon the Holy Scriptures
like a holy life.

Now when the obligations of the Gospel are enforced, I would have the tests of character brought down into the pews, scattered along the benches of the chapel, disseminated through memoirs and all religious literature, in a manner that can be comprehended and applied by learned and unlearned, and which learned and unlearned alike need. Thus: Which of you who profess to be Christ's disciples has this day, for his sake, manifested or felt any interest in his little ones? Which of you, for the welfare or happiness of any human being, or of any creature dependent on your care and tenderness, or coming into any sort of relation with you, has made — or has entertained the wish or design, if opportunity offered, to make — any sacrifice of time, inclination, money, or courtesy?

If you wish to know whether you are a Christian, inquire of yourself whether, in and for the love of God, you seek to make happy those about you by smiles and pleasant sayings? Is it a matter of concernment, when you sit down to your breakfast, to say a bright word of sympathy or endearment or playfulness or cheer to your wife, your son, your daughter? Do you give Tommy a preliminary toss as you place him in his high chair, or do you praise Kitty's first awkward attempt to smooth her own hair? Do you notice the little arrangements that have been made for your comfort and convenience? Do you compliment the cook on the nice coffee, or the light buckwheat

cakes, or the beautifully brown toast which she sets
before you, — particularly if the cook bears your
own name? When the cat puts up her soft paw
to remind you that she is there, does your hand
slide down to rub her fur, and thus make her happier for your thought of her, — or, if a law of the
Medes and Persians forbids her the dining-room,
do you throw her a bit of bread to console her exile? Is the faithful dog rewarded by his share,
not only of food, but of favoritism? If you have
yourself an unconquerable aversion to cats and
dogs, do you still see to it that their lives are not
a burden to them? If you meet a child crying in
the street, do you endeavor to console him? Do
you ever buy a penny's worth of candy for the
ragged boy who is looking at it with eager eyes
through the shop-window on Christmas eve? Do
you take pains now and then to speak a cheery
word to the widow whose only son has gone on a
long sea-voyage? As your sons and daughters approach maturity, does their obedience and affection
increase or diminish? Do they go out from your
house as from a prison or from a home, — with
eager feet indeed, but with a tender lingering at
the last? When you come into the house, do you
bring sunshine with you? If there is a cloud on
your brow, do your family seem more anxious to
dissipate it, or to get out of your way? If your
sons see you on the other side of the street, do they
run over to join you, or do they turn down an alley

to avoid you, or keep on their own side till they
are obliged to cross? Do the clerks in your ware-
house, the carpenters who are building your house,
the Irishmen who are laying your pipes, the plough-
man who is furrowing your land, the gardener who
is pruning your trees, like to have you pass by, for
the pleasantness of your manner in commending
their labor, or the courteousness with which you
listen to their complaints or requests, or the quiet
consideration with which you suggest alterations
and improvements? Do mothers like to have
their sons work on your farm during the summer
months, and do the boys like to come? In short,
are you a comfortable person to live with? Are
you pleasant to have about?

We often have in the columns of religious newspapers sketches of eminent Christians. I read one
lately of a farmer's wife who used to delight in
prayer-meetings, celebrated her children's birth-
days by prayer, and spent whole days in praying.
All these are favorable signs, but before I pronounce her an eminent Christian, I should like
to know whether, previous to her withdrawal from
the family circle to pray all day, she made any
provision for the extra labor that her absence
would devolve on others, or whether Bridget had
to skim the milk and wash the pans, besides her
cooking, sweeping, and dusting, or whether the
work was let go till the next day; and if so,
whether the next day went smoothly. I should

like to know whether, when a little restless, chubby hand upset the gravy-boat on the clean table-cloth, she bound herself over to keep the peace,— whether in her house cleanliness was made subservient to comfort, or comfort to cleanliness, — whether she ever laid down her sewing and took into her arms the half-sick and wholly cross, fretful, and miserable four-year-old boy, to charm away his unhappiness with a fairy story, or any kind of story, or song, or simple talk, — whether she gave her heretical neighbor credit for as much candor, sincerity, truthfulness, earnestness, and unselfishness in his religion as he developed and she recognized in his character of citizen, neighbor, and father, — whether the delicious green-pea soup that she sent in to the sick woman next door was the result of an extra amount made for the purpose, or whether the Irish girl dined per force, that day, off cold boiled pork and potatoes, — whether she was generally ready to step into the wagon when it came to the door on Sunday mornings, or whether she provoked her husband to wrath by keeping them all waiting.

> " The world is wide, these things are small."

But it was a pebble's edge that ordained the course of two mighty rivers, —

> " One to long darkness and the frozen tide,
> One to the Peaceful Sea."

The trouble is, that, when you present things in

9   M

this light, so many people look upon it as a substitution of morality for religion, — works for faith. It is nothing of the sort. It is bringing one alongside the other, in which position only are they of any use in the world. The black knight swore that the shield was gold; the white knight as stoutly maintained that it was silver; but they shivered their lances for a half-truth, — for it was gold on one side and silver on the other. It is true that mere morality does not make a perfect man, for we are justified by faith; but wilt thou not also know, O vain man, that faith without works is dead, and, of the two, by far the worse off? for good works may benefit others, though they have no beneficial reflex influence, but a dead faith cheereth the heart of neither God nor man. Faith and works are like the two blades of a pair of scissors. They must be riveted together in order to accomplish anything for their possessor. Separated, one is worth as much as the other, — both good for nothing. Truth is many-sided, though always integral. God alone can see its sublime integrity,— we contemplate it in phases. From too long gazing on one, we forget another, and our religion becomes one-sided. " Just as if works were anything! " a young girl was overheard to say, coming out of a prayer-meeting. " Just as if ploughing and hoeing and planting and weeding are anything! " the farmer might as well say; " it is rain from heaven and dew and sunshine that I want."

Very true, but rain and dew and sunshine may
fall on the plain a thousand years, and never once
shall his fields wave their silken tassels to the
breeze, or his barns overflow with garnered grain.
The sunshine floods in vain the soil that is not prepared to receive it. No rain can germinate the
seed that has never been planted. That the one
is vain without the other, is no truer than that the
other is vain without the one. Paul presented
one side of the shield to the Roman disciples, and
they shut their eyes to the other, — wresting his
words to their own destruction. But James, just
as truly inspired as Paul, held up to view the side
which they ignored, and, with a sturdy common
sense that scarcely needed any higher wisdom,
rounded their theory to completion. " What doth
it profit, my brethren, though a man say he hath
faith, and have not works ? can faith save him ?
If a brother or sister be naked, and destitute of
daily food, and one of you say unto them, Depart
in peace, be ye warmed and filled ; notwithstanding ye give them not those things which are needful to the body ; what doth it profit ? Even so
faith, if it hath not works, is dead, being alone.
Yea, a man may say, Thou hast faith, and I have
works ; show me thy faith without thy works, and
I will show thee my faith by my works. . . . . By
works was faith made perfect. . . . . By works a
man is justified, and not by faith only." " Believe in the Lord Jesus Christ, and thou shalt be

saved," said Paul, presenting that phase of the
truth that was best fitted to those whom he addressed. " The devils also believe and tremble,"
follows up James, throwing himself once more
into the breach, and driving back the formalism,
selfishness, and malice that would march under
the banner of Paul's succinct words.

So the Bible balances itself, — repentance unto
salvation bringing forth fruits meet for repentance.
It is ours to keep the balance true, but we do not
do it. I cannot, of course, speak of the Church
as a whole, but, so far as it has fallen under my
observation, I should say that its religion was
ahead of its morality, — that church-members, as
a class, perform their distinctively religious duties
better than the duties which are not distinctively
religious ; while it seems to me to be of the first
importance that the morality of the Church should
keep pace with its religion, — that its duties in
the world, as citizens — merchants, farmers, lawyers, mechanics — should be as scrupulously performed as its duties to itself. If the Church were
true to her divine calling, the gates of hell should
not prevail against her. It is because she is false
to her trust that her chariot-wheels drive heavily.

Every now and then, some sharp-sighted, keen-
scented hound sniffs a heresy, and anon the hunts-
man puts the bugle to his lips, and all the faithful
are summoned to hunt down the game ; but as I
read history I find that in every age the world has

been growing heretical, and that, while some of its heresies were heresies indeed, others have been the peaceable fruits of righteousness, so that the cry has ceased to inspire terror. The name is no longer formidable. The manner in which Paul worshipped the God of his fathers was heresy to the tithe-paying, stiff-necked, hard-hearted Jews, and Tertullus, arraigning him before Felix, with self-complacent eloquence could find no meeter characterization than that "pestilent fellow," the "ringleader of the sect of the Nazarenes." To the pampered ecclesiastics of the sixteenth century, the right of private judgment was a most damnable heresy; and even Sir Thomas More, a man of clean hands and a pure heart, who himself dared to die for a principle, could earnestly advocate that Tyndale be burnt at the stake for the well-being of Christ and the Church. For eighteen hundred years, the Devil has been crying "Wolf!" and there have never been found wanting a great multitude of foolish, and a small sprinkling of wise men, who, untaught by the past, would leave their pleasant firesides and rush pell-mell to the rescue; but when the confusion is over, and we come at length to the conclusion that we have been imposed upon, and that the death-dealing wolf was nothing but a harmless little ewe-lamb, and return, somewhat crestfallen, to our homes, we find that our crests must fall lower yet, — that we are the victims of a double deception, — that while we were flourishing our shillalahs, and wrenching our arms with random blows, right and left, at nothing, Satan has walked in at the back door, and helped himself, — helped himself to our probity, our courtesy, our self-command, our uprightness and honor and manhood.

Brethren, these things ought not so to be. "We have been stunned long enough with the cry of 'Gospel, Gospel!' we want Gospel manners," — and what Erasmus wanted, we want to-day. Half of the heresies would die out of themselves, if let alone, and a holy life is the best bulwark against them all. The worst heresies that I know of — those that lay hold of the strength of the Church, that tie her hands, and paralyze her tongue, and poison her atmosphere — are lying and stealing and avarice and selfishness. It is they which eat out the heart of Christianity, making that which should be the temple of the Lord, wherein all who desire to behold his beauty shall inquire, a sepulchre full of dead men's bones and all uncleanness.

Of a surety the Church has a work to do, and how shall she be straitened till it be accomplished! All who hinder the completion of the work, all who weaken the power of the Church, are fighting against God. But the weakeners of her power are from within, not from without. She gets a few pricks and scratches from her foes, but she receives her severest wounds in the house of her friends. Freedom and slavery, activity

and stagnation, the Bible and priestcraft, drew
their swords on the soil of Spain three hundred years ago; kingly power and monkish des-
potism combined to crush out the young truth
with a success to which three centuries of degra-
dation bear sorrowful witness. But it is not so
with us. Our fathers fought the battle, and won
the victory, before we were born, and we enter
into their labors. Now, the Church has only to
arise and shine. The puny adversaries that attack
her now are not worthy to be compared with the
giants that were on the earth in those days. If
she had on the whole armor of God, all the isms
that hurtle against her would make no more impression than a child's dimpled fingers on the
granite shaft of Bunker Hill. She herself furnishes her enemies with their most effective weapons. The battering-rams of Satan would thunder
at her gates in vain, if traitors within did not sap
the walls. She would not only hold her own, but
she would carry the war into the enemy's camp, —
aggressive, energetic, victorious, — if her rank and
file were trusty. If you believe Unitarianism or
Parkerism or Spiritualism to be not of God, show
by your purer and more benevolent life, by your
greater truthfulness, your sweeter temper, your
larger charity, and your stricter honesty, that the
word of God has freer course to run and be glorified in your creed than in the other. You may be
slow of speech and slow of tongue, but nothing

can withstand the logic of a manly, blameless, beneficent life. Heresies can be lived down a thousand times more effectually than they can be hunted down. Let every one be able to give a reason for the hope that is in him, and then let him show out of a good conversation his works with meekness of wisdom.

It cannot be too deeply impressed on our minds that it is the good people that do the mischief. If villany could only be confined to villains, we should not find it so hard to set the world right. When a highway robber plunders a man, or a notorious liar tells a lie, or a confirmed miser passes by on the other side of suffering, want, and unhappiness, we do not feel that Christ has been struck at. There is harm done; sin is committed; but Christianity is not impeached. Rather her hands are strengthened. We feel more deeply the need of some such influence to restrain us from evil. It is the sober, loyal, industrious, Sabbath-keeping, sound-principled, respectable church-member whose weaknesses and wickednesses spring up and bear fruit an hundred-fold. Every church-member who indulges in dishonesty, petulance, niggardliness, falsehood, wilful ignorance, quarrelsomeness, or selfishness, is an active missionary of the Devil, and a missionary laboring with every advantage.

When light is suddenly let in upon the life of a blood-stained pirate, the world shudders, — catching a glimpse at the abyss into which man, left of his Maker, may fall, and crime becomes more hateful than before. But when a statesman, covered with years and honors, or a clergyman, who has long broken the bread of life to his people, goes over to wrong-doing, or to wrong-suffering, morality and religion are stabbed; for not only will multitudes be led to go and do likewise, but other multitudes, standing afar off, will attribute to Christianity the weakness of its professors, and so the Son of God is crucified afresh, and put to an open shame. When Satan comes with horns and hoof, unmitigated and hideous, we are shocked, and flee from him; but when he puts on his robes of light, we take him to our hearths and hearts — the dear, benevolent, large-brained one — and entertain him sumptuously unawares.

This ought not to be so, but it is so. Men ought to judge justly, but they will not. Because a church-member is obstinate, stiff-necked, and rebellious, men ought not to think that the spirit which the Gospel inculcates is not gentle and easy to be entreated, but they do. The sin of doing it is theirs, but the sin of giving them occasion to do it is ours, and no small sin is it, — if any sin can be small, — either in its extent or its consequences. Practical infidelity in the Church sows theoretical infidelity broadcast over the world, — the hideous dragon's teeth spring up into strong-armed men against the law and the Gospel.

It would seem as if this truth would be patent to

9 *

the most unthinking ; but if it is, why is there so
much defect in our holiest things ?   If we know
that, while there is a sense in which every sin of
the "unregenerate" is a preacher of Christianity,
there is no sense in which the sins of the "regen-
erate" are not a grievous and deadly wound, — if
we know that, while every sin committed by the
confessedly unprincipled throws into greater relief
the purity of the Gospel, and increases our sense
of its need, every sin committed by the professedly
principled tends to directly the opposite, — how is
it that we who profess to have taken Christ into our
hearts, and to follow those sacred feet through all
our way, can, not simply fall into sin, but walk
into it in broad daylight, with both eyes open, and
stay in it and revel there ?   How can we forget
that the shadow of our sin falls athwart religion,
and dims the light that should shine upon those
that sit in darkness ?   With what force would not
the minister's words fall upon the ears of the unrepentant, if he could point to his church and say,
" Behold Israelites indeed, in whom is no guile ! "

I remember reading a sketch of a young girl
who, for a long time, resisted almost sullenly the
advances of her Sabbath-school teacher and friends,
seemed proof against the influence of the Gospel,
and, indeed, doubted its genuineness and authentici-
ty.   Years afterward, when she had been brought
under its power, it was ascertained that the stum-
bling-block in her way had been the selfishness

and worldliness of an aunt who professed the religion of Christ, but whose life was not conformed to
its principles. So the young girl judged — not
alone from hardness of heart, but naturally and
logically — that religion was an imposture. Her
reasoning was quite correct, only her premises
were not true, though they had sufficiently the
appearance of truth to deceive an older and wiser
head than hers. By their fruits ye shall know —
them. By the fruits which religion shows in one
man, we know the power of religion in one man.
But she, and many others with her, make the
mistake of translating Christ to mean, by *their*
fruits ye shall know *it,* that is religion. Now, if
we were in the habit of taking enlarged views, of
judging justly, of deducing universal conclusions
only from universal premises, there would be less
responsibility on individual Christians. The history of Christianity, in its inception and progress,
proves its divine origin and its perfect adequacy ;
but nineteen men out of twenty never take a comprehensive view of anything. They know little
or nothing of the working or the spread of Christianity. They judge it from what they see of it
in their grocer and butcher and shoemaker, and
others with whom they have dealings. True,
they can and ought to judge it from their Bibles ;
but the question is not what they ought to do,
but what they do, and as long as they form their
opinions from the grocer's life, the grocer is under

double bonds to give a true rendering of its principles.

Here is a member of an Orthodox church "in good and regular standing." His place at church is seldom vacant. His attendance on prayer-meetings is prompt and constant. He lifts up his voice in prayer and exhortation, tells what the Lord has done for him, would on no account walk or ride on Sunday, except from necessity, scarcely even from mercy, has an acute sense of moral responsibility, and professes to desire to speak and write only what will be for the glory of God and the good of souls. Near by lives a woman, a widowed wife, who, in the abandonment of her sorrow, has neglected to perform a usual courtesy towards him, — which omission, by vigorous effort, may be twisted into a culpable indifference to religion, but which has really no more connection with religion than has the rising of the sun or the falling of the dew. There are several things which he can do. He can say, "This woman is crushed by grief and overwhelmed by cares to which she is unaccustomed. It would be unworthy in me at such a time to notice so slight a matter." Or he might say, "This is too important a thing to be allowed to pass silently. I will ascertain whether my suspicions be correct, and if so, I will, at a fitting time, gently advise, and suggest whether duty do not point out a different course." Not so. He does what looks very much like soothing his

wounded and inordinate self-love with the idea of
doing God service, assumes the worst possible motives for the trivial act, so turning a sorrowful,
momentary forgetfulness towards himself into a
deliberate sin against God, and smites with cruel
reproaches, harder in her condition to bear than
blows, one whom God has already sorely smitten.

Here is another man who is not a Christian.
He scarcely believes in moral accountability. He
seldom goes to meeting unless there is a prospect
of unusually fine singing. He generally stops at
home on Sunday, writes letters, reads the newspapers, has a jovial dinner, drives a span of fine
horses, smokes half a dozen cigars or so, and loun-
ges generally. He is too gentlemanly to swear,
unless he is very much excited. He drinks wine,
but seldom loses in it his self-control, — becomes
animated, but not boisterous. He is waited on one
day by a man of noble character, but wanting in
what we Yankees call "faculty." This man's affairs are entangled beyond his own power to extri-
cate them. An able but unscrupulous person is
attempting, with every prospect of success, to wrest
from him his little property, and he, being acciden-
tally thrown in with my pleasant pagan friend,
applies to him for counsel. My friend is not a
lawyer. His profession, which is active and exacting, removes him entirely from that sphere of
life; but he is clear-headed, — a man of great
practical sagacity, great common-sense. He is

moved by the calamity that threatens an innocent, brave, though "incapable" man. He knows that a lawyer's fee would exhaust a large portion of the poor man's estate. He sees the direction in which steps ought to be taken. He leaves his own business to his own hurt. He takes up the cause of the poor man, heads off his opponent, clears away the rubbish, works through a whole summer till the poor man's rights are triumphantly established, and his small property restored to him beyond danger of alienation, and then goes home without one cent of fee, with no reward save the gratitude of the man and his family who have been saved from penury, and takes up again the broken thread of his own business.

In the light of the Divine precept, " Bear ye one another's burdens, and *so* fulfil the law of Christ," which of these men went down to his house justified?

We, who are large-minded and wise, are not deceived in this thing. We know that, though religion may adorn and illuminate a one-story house, it can never make it a two-story house. We know that the first man was essentially narrow-minded and petty, and that religion may have expanded him, though it had not made him great. We know that the leaven of love may have been in his heart, though it had not yet leavened the whole lump; that his short-comings may not have been because the good work was not begun

in him, but because it was not finished, and that
this particular short-coming was in a quarter that
the Gospel had not reached; that he was not necessarily, nor even probably, utterly hypocritical
in his prayers, praises, and professions, because he
had showed himself in this respect utterly selfish;
that religion is not an imposition because here it
had left him in the lurch. We know, too, that
the second man started in advance. He was or-
ganized with a larger heart. He had by nature
what the other will hardly attain by grace, and,
even with that advantage, his generosity would
never have attained so rich a growth had it not
struck root in a soil mellowed through no in-
tervention of his, by the culture of eighteen centuries, and opened in the reflected beams of the
Sun of Righteousness, which shines alike upon the
evil and the good. We know that his natural
kindliness has been fostered by the genial atmosphere that wrapped him about unconscious, and
that it would have borne still fairer fruit had he
but suffered the dews of Divine love to penetrate
to the roots. We know all this, and are in no
danger of deeming religion a deception on the one
side or a superfluity on the other.

But your clerk, who is an observant, though
necessarily from his years an inexperienced young
man, does not think of all this. He sees only the
expressed premise, and he judges therefrom. He
sees the irreligious man fulfilling the law of Christ,

and the religious man breaking it. He sees the one performing an act which commands his highest admiration, and the other guilty of a meanness which excites his severest contempt; nor does the religious indifference of the one, or the religious zeal of the other, seem to be at all affected by it, or in any way related to it. What shall he infer? What will he probably, or at any rate, what is there danger that he will infer?

I am aware that I am not on the highest ground, but it is not low. To lead an upright life because our neighbors are looking at us, is less noble than to do it because God wills it. The latter is a sufficient reason for the practice of every virtue; yet if the former, from its constant presence and definiteness, will stir us up by way of remembrance, when the latter is momentarily forgotten, we need not despise it from the heights of our loftiness. If, beyond this, we are incited by the desire to benefit our brother, to guide him to the right way by keeping our own light burning brightly, to win him to the Gospel by showing him into how fair a shape the Gospel has carved our own lives, — then, indeed, though we be not on the highest ground, we are but little lower than the angels.

Every one who subscribes with his hand unto the Lord ought to understand — and if he does not understand, his spiritual teachers should instruct him — that on his Mondays and Tuesdays and

Wednesdays and Thursdays and Fridays and Saturdays, on the market-days and quarter-days and holidays and baking-days and washing-days and sweeping-days, on the spring sales and the winter's sledding, on the fall sewing and the summer picnics, on the morning prayers and the evening parties, should be inscribed, Holiness unto the Lord !

Daniel purposed in his heart that he would not defile himself with the king's meat and wine, thinking that pulse was better, and they tried him for ten days with pulse. If at the end of that time he had exhibited shrunken cheeks, thin lips, cavernous eyes, and a general leanness in his bones, it would have furnished but a poor argument in favor of his vegetarian diet; but when, at the end of ten days, his countenance appeared fairer and fatter in flesh than all the children which did eat the portion of the king's meat, there was no more trouble about it. He had his pulse and welcome. His looks were an argument which nothing could gainsay or resist.

So, when the presidents and princes, moved with envy because Daniel had been preferred above them, sought to find occasion against him concerning the kingdom, they could find none occasion nor fault ; *forasmuch as he was faithful, neither was there any error or fault found in him :* and in despair they exclaimed, " We shall not find any occasion against this Daniel, except we find it

N

against him concerning the law of his God."
Daniel's courageous devotion would never have
been handed down for the world's admiration and
imitation, if the presidents and princes could have
discovered a flaw in Daniel's account-book, an
attempt to embezzle the funds, a neglect of the
material interests of the kingdom, or a conspiracy
against the king's life.

The religion that the world is dying for is not a
treasure, valued and cherished, indeed, but cherished under a glass case in the best room, carefully
dusted, and visible only on days of high festival.
We want a religion that is an atmosphere, wrapping us about above and below ; going down into
the lungs in deep-drawn inspirations, to purify and
energize ; filtering into the blood, to tint and
quicken ; spreading out in the skin, to protect
and adorn ; piercing noisome cellars to dispel the
noxious, death-dealing vapors ; mounting into the
parlors and bed-rooms and kitchens, to keep them
sweet and healthful ; permeating and interpene-
trating all things ; a savor of life unto life.

We want a religion that softens the step, and
tones the voice to melody, and fills the eye with
sunshine, and checks the impatient exclamation
and the harsh rebuke ; a religion that is polite,
deferential to superiors, courteous to inferiors, and
considerate of friends ; a religion that goes into
the family, and keeps the husband from being
spiteful when the dinner is late, and keeps the din-

ner from being late, — keeps the wife from fretting
when the husband tracks the newly washed floor
with his muddy boots, and makes the husband
mindful of the scraper and the door-mat, — keeps
the mother patient when the baby is cross, and
keeps the baby pleasant, — amuses the children as
well as instructs them, — wins as well as governs,
— cares for the servants, besides paying them
promptly, — projects the honey-moon into the har-
vest-moon, and makes the happy home like the
Eastern fig-tree, bearing in its bosom at once the
beauty of the tender blossom and the glory of the
ripened fruit; a religion that looks after the appren-
tice in the shop, and the clerk behind the counter,
and the student in the office, with a fatherly care
and a motherly love, — setting the solitary in families, introducing them to pleasant and wholesome
society, that their lonely feet may not be led into
temptation, forgiving occasional lapses while striving to prevent them, and to supply, so far as may
be, the place of the natural guardians by a vigilance that attracts without annoying.

We want a religion that shall interpose continually between the ruts and gullies and rocks of the
highway of life, and the sensitive souls that are
travelling over them.

We want a religion that bears heavily, not only
on the "exceeding sinfulness of sin," but on the
exceeding rascality of lying and stealing, — a religion that banishes short measures from the coun-

ters, small baskets from the stalls, pebbles from the
cotton-bags, clay from paper, sand from sugar,
chicory from coffee, otter from butter, flour from
cream of tartar, beet-juice from vinegar, alum from
bread, strychnine from wine, water from milk-cans,
and buttons from the contribution-box.   The religion that is to save the world will not put all the
big strawberries at the top, and all the bad ones
at the bottom.   It will sell raisins on stems, instead
of stems without raisins.   It will not offer more
baskets of foreign wines than the vineyards ever
produced bottles, and more barrels of Genesee flour
than all the wheat-fields of New York grow and
all her mills grind.   It will not make one half of
a pair of shoes of good leather, and the other of
poor leather, so that the first shall redound to the
maker's credit, and the second to his cash ; nor, if
the shoes have been promised on Thursday morning, will it let Thursday morning spin out till Saturday night.   It will not put Jouvin's stamp on
Jenkins's kid gloves ; nor make Paris bonnets in
the back room of a Boston milliner's shop ; nor let
a piece of velvet, that professes to measure twelve
yards, come to an untimely end in the tenth ; or a
spool of sewing-silk, that vouches for twenty yards,
be nipped in the bud at fourteen and a half ; nor
the cotton-thread spool break, to the yard-stick, fifty
of the two hundred yards of promise that was given
to the eye ; nor yard-wide cloth measure less than
thirty-six inches from selvage to selvage ; nor

all-wool delaines and all-linen handkerchiefs be amalgamated with clandestine cotton; nor water-proof cloaks be soaked through in an hour; nor coats made of old woollen rags pressed together be sold to an unsuspecting public for legal broadcloth. It does not put bricks at five dollars per thousand into chimneys which it contracted to build of seven-dollar materials; nor smuggle white pine into floors that have paid for hard pine; nor leave yawning cracks in closets where boards ought to join; nor daub ceilings that ought to be smoothly plastered; nor make window-blinds with slats that cannot stand the wind, and paint that cannot stand the sun, and fastenings that may be looked at, but are on no account to be touched. It does not send the little boy, who has come for the daily quart of milk, into the barn-yard to see the calf, and seize the opportunity to skim off the cream; nor does it surround stale butter with fresh, and sell the whole for good; nor pass off the slack-baked bread upon the stable-boy; nor dust the pepper; nor "deacon" the apples. It does not put cotton gathering-threads into the skirt, to succumb on the slightest provocation; nor content itself with fastening seams at the beginning and the end, trusting to Providence for the security of the in-termediate stages.

The religion that is to sanctify the world pays its debts. It does not borrow money with little or no prospect of repayment, but concealing or glossing over the fact. It does not consider that forty cents returned for one hundred cents given is according to Gospel, though it may be according to law. It looks upon a man who has failed in trade, and who continues to live in luxury, as a thief. It looks upon a man who promises to pay fifty dollars on demand with interest, and who neglects to pay it on demand with or without interest, as a liar.

I believe more sin has been committed by non-payment or tardy payment of debts than by any heresy that the world ever heard of. The indifference of some professing Christians on this subject is astonishing. It would seem as if they did not recognize any moral obligation whatever in respect of their debts. There are, of course, many different classes of non-paying debtors. There are, doubtless, men who take advantage of " the times " to cheat. Under cover of money pressure they stop payment to their creditors when the state of their business does not demand it. They trust that their individual short-comings will be attributed to the universal panic ; and the money which of right belongs to their clerks, or other *employés* or creditors, is devoted to that interesting tonsorial operation known as " shaving notes." There are others who seem to " fail " systematically. It is a regular, periodical part of their business arrangement, and by long practice they attain a " strange alacrity in sinking." Of such I do not speak. The Spirit of the Lord can probably touch the

men who have turned their consciences into a com-
mercial barometer, a bank-note detector, and who
worship a golden calf; but they certainly present
a very discouraging field for human effort. Nor
do I refer to those who nobly struggle and bravely
fall,—who, in their counting-rooms and over their
ledgers, make as heroic a stand and as manly a
fight as any Leonidas at Thermopylæ, and who
fall at last, not through weakness or fear or treachery, but overpowered by the inexorable "logic of
events." I refer now to you, who are a member,
in good and regular standing, of the first or the
fiftieth Congregational Church in Boston, or elsewhere,—you who are liberal in your expenditures,
generous in your gifts, kind, genial, popular, and
well beloved. You are an excellent man in a general way, but I have somewhat against you. The
hire of the laborer which is of you kept back by
fraud, crieth. By fraud? Yes, by fraud. It is
a harsh word, but an honest. You take your family out to a sleigh-ride, and have never paid the
man who mended the sleigh after it was broken in
your previous ride. You have no account with
him. It was a mere trifle,—a trifle to you, and
perhaps a trifle to him; but the trifle is his, not
yours, and you retain it unjustly and unrighteous-
ly. He does not like to ask you for the sum, it is
so small, and you told him you had not the change
at the time, but you would make it all right. Why
do you not make it all right?

Why do you not, madam, pay the man who has been giving your daughter French and German lessons now these two quarters? He is an exile, a nobleman, a man of education and refinement (though that does not affect the fact of your indebtedness). He cannot bring himself to ask you for the money which is justly his due. But his wife and his little boys are to be provided for. His pupils are few, and he can with difficulty make both ends meet even when every link is in the chain; but when your link is missing, the case is indeed discouraging. Why do you not pay him? You have not the money by you? But you have everything you need, and a great many things that you do not need. If you cannot afford to pay him, why did you engage him? Can he afford to give lessons that you cannot afford to buy? Sell your watch, sell your bracelets, and pay him. Pay him now, if you'pay at all. It is his. From the moment the money was due him it was his, and every moment since that time you have been retaining another's property, and you are an extortioner and unjust. It is no matter whether you know that he stands in need of it or not, — or even whether he does stand in need of it. That is none of your business. You did not engage to pay him so much if he needed it; but so much. No person is so rich that he does not want to be paid what is due him, and when it is due. You have no right to assume that your creditor is richer than

you, or beyond want, and therefore you need not
be particular about promptness. You do not know
the actual state of the case, and if you did it is
nothing to the purpose. Pay what you owe. Did
you forget it? Then go at once and make everything square, beg his pardon, and pray to the Lord,
if perhaps the selfish thoughtlessness of your heart
may be forgiven you.

You, high-spirited friend, who are always a victim to the " laws of trade," you are the man.
You fancy yourself to be one of those lofty souls
who soar above the sordid many. You have no
accumulative faculty. You are perpetually in pecuniary trouble, simply because you have a proud
disdain, a sublime incapacity, for accounts. Your
generous indifference is the seal of your genius.
Do you know that you are intolerably mean?
Your grand scorn of money brings you into straits,
to get out of which you do things which the nar-
row-souled, calculating Yankee neighbor, whom
you despise, would blush to think of. This is one
thing you did. When your friend asked you to get
his fifty-dollar check cashed for him at the bank,
you did so; but returned him only forty-five dollars,
remarking, in your careless, off-hand, jovial way,
that you had " retained a V for commission fee."
Here is another thing you did, — borrowed a dollar
of your seamstress to pay a little bill that was presented when she was by, and never returned it, —
and never will; and you do not call yourself mean!

10

That generosity which is generous to itself and its family, and forgetful of or unjust to others, is of a very suspicious and exasperating character. One man would like summer drives and holiday journeys as well as another. He would like to dress his children prettily, and give them toys at Christmas, and lighten his wife's labors, and relieve the poor, as well as another; and it cannot be pleasant to him to see the other doing all these fine things, and know the while that that other owes him money which he neglects to pay, and which, paid, would furnish him with more than one of these comforts which he is now forced to deny himself.   And though a sparkling wit, a bright smile, and a ready sympathy may hide or veil the meanness, the meanness is none the less there.   Selfishness will not take the trouble to be careful about little things, to deny itself pleasant things, to think of unattractive things, to plan about commonplace things, and so it rides gayly over its own duties, and wickedly lays on others' shoulders the burden which itself will not move with so much as one of its fingers.   Such high-mindedness " smells to heaven."

Men and brethren, pay your little debts.   If you will cheat, cheat sublimely, like Fowler and Floyd, but do not attempt to ride two horses at once, by sustaining on one side the character of a high-minded Christian citizen, and on the other that of a petty purloiner.

There is another sin, near of kin to the foregoing, which ought to lie more heavily than it does on the conscience of the Church, — not that the Church monopolizes the guilt, but she is stained by it, and deeply stained. I mean the non-fulfilment of engagements. You can scarcely offer a grosser insult to a person than to accuse him of falsehood, yet the chances that he will tell a falsehood are fearfully large. Not that society in general is wholly addicted to manufacturing stories " out of whole cloth." A very large proportion will adhere to facts with tolerable closeness in detailing their observation or experience ; but the number of whom, in making business arrangements, it can be said that their word is as good as their bond, is very small, — if their bond is good enough to be taken without a surety. It might be more gracious, and perhaps more correct, to put it a little differently, and say that the number of those whose word is not as good as their bond is very large.

It is strange that the interests of men, apart from moral considerations, should not make them more careful to keep their engagements. In some acceptations it is absolutely essential, and in all it must be profitable. The merchant, the railroad conductor, the expressman, the postmaster, would soon find their occupation gone, if they allowed it such " loose ends " as many others do. For example, your new house is to be ready for you by Thanksgiving; but if you get into it by New Year's, you will do well. It is true, unexpected hinderances arise. Contingencies which the builder could not foresee have prevented its completion, and he is not at fault. But the wonder is that unexpected contingencies arise with such a remarkable regularity that one scarcely *expects* his house to be done at the time agreed upon. Again, your little boy is anxiously waiting his first pair of boots. By special contract they are to be sent home on Wednesday, so that his half-holiday may be made glorious. But the half-holiday drags drearily by in old shoes, and when the boots will come home " God and the shoe-maker alone know," as a little boy once despairingly said, in such a case. Your little daughter's cloak is to be finished on Friday, to make sure of her having it for Sunday. Saturday morning you call and beg the dress-maker to report progress. It will be ready for you in the afternoon. At seven P. M. you call again, and by waiting two hours in your carriage, on a frosty night, you get it to bring home, with the seams yet rough, and the cape half sewed. The artist who furnishes the illustrations for your monthly magazine solemnly affirms that he will have them completed in time for a seasonable issue. By dogging him morning, noon, and night, you get your magazine out a week after the proper time, and after your table is loaded with letters informing you that the writer's February number has not been received, and begging to know why. You are going down to the annual meeting of the Tract Society to report the proceedings for your paper. You meet a friend who says he is going, and offers to report for you. That is the last you hear of him, and your paper goes to press without the report. A load of coal is to be brought on Tuesday, and it comes on Thursday. Your " country cousins " are to visit you " the first of next week," and you are kept at home from a pleasant party by their coming down upon you on Friday. Your friend is to call for you at half past six, and he comes lounging along at seven.

This is all wrong. A good business character and a good Christian character require that we should meet our engagements. Unnecessary failure is alike unthrifty and sinful. If we are so unfortunately constituted that we cannot recollect our promises, we ought not to make them. Say frankly, " I will do it if I do not forget ; but the chances are that I shall forget." Then make an effort to remember. A great deal of our memory, bad and good, has its seat in the heart. Love thy neighbor as thyself, and thou wilt not forget thy neighbor's parcel any sooner than thine own. It is selfishness that gnaws holes in our memories. We will not take the trouble to try to remember, and so we cause our friends great inconvenience, and injure our own souls. But many forget their own affairs with great regularity. They are as great a trouble to themselves as they are to others. To such, one can only recommend constant effort to overcome an inconvenient habit, and constant scrupulousness in making engagements. Let them always make it clearly understood that they are not to be depended on, and so avoid the appearance of evil. Let tradesmen promise less recklessly. If they have already engaged to finish by Saturday as much work as they can finish, let them not engage to do more. It is both a wrong and a bad policy. If they state their inability, the work may go to a rival establishment; but if they deceive, somebody will be, not only disappointed, but exasperated, and they will have a poor chance of a second job from the same quarter. Extraordinary skill in workmanship can stand such strains awhile, but the conscience suffers irremediably. If a carpenter does not know that, so far as his plans are concerned, he can begin a barn on the first of March, let him not engage to begin it then. If it is contingent on the completion of another job, let him mention such contingency. The carpenter may lose money, but the man will gain manhood. If it is doubtful whether the tailor can finish the coat in season, let him state the doubt. His neighbor may get the job, but he will keep his word.

Let the world do as it may, the Church should

free its skirts from such sins. If pecuniary interests are not strong enough to keep us in the right
path, religious interests should be. All these
things come within the scope of religion. The
Christian name should be a tower of strength. It
should stand for probity, integrity, truth, and
honor. But the matter rests with us.

Religion will do for us just what we will it to
do, and let it do. If we are content to be
furbished for Sundays with an additional coating
of respectability; if, when our names are en-
rolled on the church lists, we consider ourselves
booked for heaven, with nothing further to do
than show our tickets at the stations; if we look
upon religion as something to be adopted, and
whose adoption keeps us from going to balls and
theatres, reading immoral books, driving and walking on Sunday, and using profane language, then
religion will do this for us, and nothing more.
But if we stop here, we come sadly short of the
glory of God. Stop here we shall, unless we
press with determined purpose towards the mark
for the prize of a higher calling. Religion will
not come down into our lives, purifying, refining,
softening, elevating, making every day beautiful,
every house the gate of heaven, every body a
living sacrifice, holy and acceptable unto God,
unless we bring it down.

VIII.

CONTROVERSIES.

IT is not religion that gets into religious newspapers now and then, and looks and acts so much like slander, spite, hatred, envy, malice, and all uncharitableness, that, if we did not know, we should certainly christen it by such names; nor is it religion that creeps into the churches, and sows seeds of dissension, which spring up and bear fruit a thousand-fold, in *ex parte* councils, seceding cliques, angry minorities, insolent majorities, degrading rivalries, heart-burnings, and jealousies. Examining some issues of the " religious press," and observing the charges and refutations, the criminations and recriminations of religious men and religious bodies, one feels constrained to cry out imploringly :

> " Let dogs delight to bark and bite,
> For God hath made them so :
> Let bears and lions growl and fight,
> For 't is their nature, too :

" But children, you should never let
Your angry passions rise ;
Your little hands were never made
To tear each other's eyes."

The acerbity and violence of religious controversies, both in respect of doctrine and of fact,
are proverbial, and no wonder ; but should it be
so ? Is the thing inevitable ? Is it essential to
the preservation of the truth in its purity ? Stagnant waters are indeed apt to be muddy, but does
stirring them up with a pole, necessarily cleanse
them ? Is it any excuse to allege that religion
is of paramount importance, and therefore men
ought to understand it right, and therefore, if they
will not comprehend it by fair means, they shall
by foul, and therefore we will

" Prove our doctrines Orthodox
By apostolic blows and knocks " ?

Shall a man take his theology as the homesick
alligator at the Aquarial Gardens was forced to
take his food, — by having it rammed down his
throat ? We should scarcely attempt to proselyte
our Universalist neighbors by going to the school-
house where they are assembled to worship, and
breaking the windows. We know very well that
those are not the kind of stones in which men
look to find sermons. Nor do we consider the
Mohammedan method of propagating religion, by
fire and sword, as altogether unexceptionable ;
yet there are words harder than stone, fiercer than

10 *   o

fire, sharper than a sword, — and we too often use them with unsparing hand, instead of putting on the breastplate of love, and walking in wisdom towards them that are without.

The worst feature of religious controversies is the undignified, unmanly, and unchristian personalities in which opponents sometimes indulge. Very angry small boys, being afraid to attack the big boys who have roused their indignation, will occasionally take refuge in distance, and find consolation in "making faces" at the enemy. So we, being unhappily debarred from the privilege of burning our antagonists at the stake, stretching them on the rack, or breaking them on the wheel, betake ourselves to the newspapers, and call names. What good does it do anybody? We are like children, pounding the stone that made us stumble and fall. Our fists tingle and redden and smart, but the stone bears it with great equanimity. It does not require genius, or wit, or character, or eminent piety, to make and string epithets, though it does require all these to apply them in all cases justly. A blind fit of anger will manufacture them in unlimited quantity, and anger is not careful to ascertain whether they fit or not. Personalities, so far from strengthening a cause, almost invariably indicate and increase weakness. Luther did not thrust the table-cloth in the face of his opponent till he had exhausted his arguments. It was the Epicureans and Stoics, standing on the crumbling ruins of an effete superstition, that rudely asked, "What will this *babbler* say?" but Paul's address to the gay Athenians was a model of high-bred courtesy. His feet were on the Rock of Ages, and he could afford to maintain intact

"The grand old name of gentleman."

Nay, even Michael the archangel, when, contending with the Devil, he disputed about the body of Moses, durst not bring a railing accusation, though, if the character of the parties concerned would ever justify it, that would certainly seem to have been the time. In one respect, at least, religious controversialists would do well to copy political. Parliamentary courtesy confines itself to acts. It forbids inquiry into motives. A Representative in Congress, who would not hesitate to accuse his colleague of constructive treason, would by no means yield to the temptation of asserting or intimating that he had inaugurated a measure, or introduced a bill, or advocated a reform, for the sake of making himself popular at home, and securing votes at the next election. But theological and ecclesiastical courtesy is less scrupulous, and many disputants rush in where statesmen fear to tread. Motives are attributed with a lavish generosity. Facts are asserted to have been suppressed, quotations garbled, insignificant and impromptu opinions lifted into undue and deceptive prominence, for the sake of making out a case. Yet it can easily be seen that the rule of parliamentary courtesy is based on common-sense grounds, — has its foundations in human nature. We *must* be ignorant of motives in a great degree. We cannot know, however strongly we may suspect, or however logically we may infer, the reason why a man goes to the right instead of the left. The probabilities are generally so arranged that we can judge with sufficient accuracy for all ordinary purposes ; and as things go, we are forced in our daily life to act with reference to motives whose existence we can only assume. Yet when we come to the point, so inexplicable is the human heart, so intricate are its workings, and so momentous the issues involved, that etiquette does well to step in and diminish the mischief which Christianity is not allowed to prevent. Surely politeness should not be suffered to do for statesmen more than Christianity does for Christians.

I see no irreverence, but rather an appreciation of the truest, noblest, and holiest meaning of a most ill-used word, in the often quoted lines of the old dramatist Dekker, who, speaking of Christ, says :

> " The best of men
> That e'er wore earth about him was a sufferer :
> A soft, meek, patient, humble, tranquil spirit,
> The first true gentleman that ever breathed."

In many of the accusations, concerning both motive and action, which we bring against our brethren, I do not think we can be at heart sincere. The allegations are so grievous, that, if we believed them as thoroughly as our statements indicate, and as we perhaps think we do, we could hardly help putting on sackcloth and sitting in ashes.

There is a peculiar liberty wherewith members of Congress make themselves free. In their deliberations you shall hear such words as *liar, murderer, incendiary, assassin,* applied with a frequency, pointedness, and enthusiasm very terrifying to Northerners, who have been accustomed to understand the word murderer to mean one who has killed a man with malice aforethought; assassin, one who has murdered in the dark; liar, one who tells lies; incendiary, one who sets buildings on fire. If, however, you bring these wordy warriors to the point, you will find that their words have a certain derived, political, Pickwickian sense, entirely beyond the scope of unpolitical understandings, and are used merely to illustrate an argument, to enforce a principle, and quite probably simply to adorn a tale. Your contemptible scoundrel, your black-hearted traitor, is a quiet, respectable man, — a colonel, a lawyer, perhaps even an ex-Governor, — a man who is thought a good deal of by his neighbors and townsmen, whose wife dotes on him, who goes out in broad daylight, unarmed, fearless of policemen, and next whom you have yourself sat at dinner, chatting agreeably, without a suspicion that his vile soul was insecurely linked to one questionable virtue, and indissolubly riveted to a thousand fearful crimes.

So we sometimes see religious newspapers charging each other with acts which should exclude the perpetrators from the fraternity of honest men ; or, through the medium of religious newspapers, one church, or one fraction of a church, or one ecclesiastical body, or one member of it, accuses another of an act, or a course of action, which, in sober truth, amounts to nothing more or less than obvious, persistent deception, dishonesty, trickery. Though we do not, like our Congressional contemporaries, speak the names of these various sins and crimes, we just as really attribute them to our brethren.   Translate out of the language of the church into the language of the world, — substitute invoices, notes, and stocks for platforms, resolutions, and contributions, — and you have as fine a list of state-prison offences as is often seen outside of a court-room.

Can such be correct transcripts of facts ?   Is it true that a church, or any body corporate, whose very existence as such is professedly to cultivate and disseminate the principles of sound morality and true religion, does fall so far short of the faith delivered to the saints, — does so far forget its origin, and pervert its aims, — as to violate common law and common honesty, and persist in its violation, deliberately, against repeated remonstrances, by sheer force? Yet we see no convulsion in the community. Nothing intimates that a great grief is fallen upon Israel. Everybody eats, drinks, and sleeps as usual. The pulpits still stand, and the law and the Gospel are appealed to from that vantage-ground. The sacramental cup is still raised to devout lips. The gray heads of the culprits still go in and out among the people with no diminishing of honor. No odium is attached to their persons; no stigma to their names. What a state of things does this argue! A whole church plunges into darkness, and the

> " majestic heaven
> Shines not the less for that one vanished star."

Can we wonder that the world will not let itself be converted? To what should it be converted if it were willing? Would it be an advance for a community that sends its thieves to prison when it catches them, to merge itself in a community that is content to print a few columns of *exposé* on the subject? If the stream where you wish to drink is muddy, you will scarcely find clear waters by descending. You want to go up, not down; up on the high lands, where threads of crystal cleave the gray old rocks, and gather purity from the earth's deep bosom and the sky's clear blue.

If it is not so, if the acts only appear dishonest because we are looking at one side, why do we not say so, or why do we say anything about it?

Every man is to be held innocent till he is proved guilty. If there is any stand-point from which we can view our opponent's position, and find it not dishonest, we ought to mention it. We have no right to look at him from *a* stand-point, and hold him up to view as a criminal, and ignore another, from which he may be seen as simply mistaken, or deceived, or blameless. Still less have we a right to take innocent facts and construct upon them a guilty hypothesis to suit our foregone conclusion. A right to do it? It is sin. It is more than murder. It may rob a man of what is more precious to him than his life. It attempts to take away from a man what, taken, would leave him stripped of his manhood, and a man's manhood is worth more to him and his friends than his bone and muscle. I just now heard one Christian man say that he did not believe another Christian man would do a certain thing. He had asserted that he would do it. He had induced others to change their course of action by the assertion. He would defraud scores of people by not doing it. He had given, as was confessed, no slightest sign that he would not do it. The time appointed for the fulfilment of his engagement was far off. He was a man who, though cordially disliked by some, was as cordially loved by others, — a man who stood high in the esteem of intellectual men and eminent Christians. A neglect to perform his promise would make him what the world calls a rogue, a swindler, a rascal. Yet lightly, able to assign no single reason, a Christian man could and did imply all this against him. He probably did not mean all this, but his words meant it, and so any uninterested and casual listener could hardly help understanding them to mean.

A little incident fell under my notice a few days ago, which may be worth recording, not on its own account, but as an illustration of the way things happen.

Two women were chatting together of pies, puddings, and preserves, as is the manner of women, and presently fell to comparing notes as to tomatoes, — both were fond of them, — " excellent preserves," — " How much sugar do you use ? " " After all, I like them best raw, sliced, with pepper and vinegar." " Why *I* never heard of any one's eating them that way." " O, it's very common. Did you have any difficulty in planting them ? " " No, we put them right in with the corn, and had enough for ourselves and all the neighbors." And so on till the topic was exhausted, and then, after a short pause, one of them remarked, " There 's one thing I don't like, and that is tomatoes ! " The second woman looked up in astonishment, evidently hesitating whether to let it pass or not, but finally, curiosity prevailing over politeness, she quietly asked, " Pray, what have we just been talking about ? " " Why, citrons,

have n't we ? "   "*I* have n't ; you said tomatoes."
" Well, I *meant* citrons, and was thinking of
citrons all the time," — and so it passed off with a
laugh.

This slight incident vividly impressed on my
mind the danger in which we all are of being
held responsible for opinions which we never
entertained, and of attributing to others false-
hoods of which they are entirely innocent. The
case in question was one of no importance in
itself; but such mistakes are just as likely to be
made in cases where passions, prejudices, and interests are concerned ; and when the little discovery that is to set things right does not happen to
be made, one will believe, to his dying day, that
the other told a downright lie, and the other will
believe just as long, and just as sincerely, that
one has circulated a slander. A great many people would never in this world be convinced that
such a mistake could arise — if passions were enlisted ·on either side. Yet, undoubtedly, a great
many of those remarkable things which nobody
can explain come about in just as guiltless a way
as this. Misunderstanding is so common a cause
of quarrel, that the very word has come to signify
a quarrel ; but misunderstanding is not the only
cause of misunderstandings. Misstatements make
trouble, and are not so easily detected. A little
girl, being asked how many chickens she had,
answered promptly, " A hundred hens and a hun-

dred chickens." Apart from a certain balance
and finish of the numbers which do not generally
belong to things in this world, and the undue
proportion between parents and offspring, which
gave an air of intrinsic improbability to the statement, it would have passed muster very well;
certainly nothing was further from her design
than to tell a lie; but the hens and chickens
that came at call were countless to a child, and
hundred was a number expressive to a child's
mind of infinity, — so the two infinites were
brought together, and a very pretty falsehood set
going. Have you never yourself begun a sentence, and before you got through forgotten what
you were talking about, and, with your mind a
thousand miles off, finished it quite at random,
and, of course, with utter disregard of truth?
But you are not an habitual liar. You have a
very firm belief that you would not tell one wilful lie. There are very, very few who have
not demonstrated human fallibility with their own
mouths. What large-hearted charity, then, should
we exercise towards others! What generous margin should we leave for mistakes and whimsical
mental action! How positive the proof, how overwhelming the presumptive evidence, before we
can be prepared to believe evil of men, — especially if we have known them upright!

There was great excitement among the children
of Israel when the news came that the tribes be-

yond Jordan had built an altar and set up for themselves. It was a secession which could not be tolerated. God had ordained *one* altar, and there all
offerings must be brought. They remembered
how the whole nation had suffered for the sin of
one man, when Achan had coveted the accursed
thing, and how much more should the defection of
two and a half tribes draw down upon them the
Divine displeasure? No, it must not be allowed.
The whole congregation of the children of Israel
gathered themselves together at Shiloh, to go up to
war against them. Before proceeding to extremi-
ties, however, they appointed a committee, chosen
from the first families of the nation, to prepare and
present a remonstrance to avert, if possible, the
shedding of blood, and bring back the wanderers
to the worship of the true God. The delegation
departed, came to their brethren, and laid the
case before them in terms of spirited and indignant remonstrance. " What trespass is this that
ye have committed against the God of Israel,"
urge these Protestants, " to turn away this day
from following the Lord, in that ye have builded
you an altar, that ye might rebel this day
against the Lord? " They bring up the mischief
that followed the sin of Baal-peor. They insist on
the essential oneness of the nation, and the impossibility of one part's sinning without all parts suffering in consequence. They refer to Achan as
example and warning. They offer, in case their

brethren are dissatisfied with their bargain, to give them possessions among themselves, even at this late day. It is an admirable address. It lacks only one thing. That, however, chances to be the thing on which everything else hinges, namely, an inquiry into the facts. The only ground of their action is rumor. " The children of Israel *heard say* " so and so, and, instead of sending to investigate the rumors, assumed the rumors to be true, and sent to punish the sin. It is a wonder, indeed, that they did not fight first, and despatch their messengers afterwards. As it was, this conference finished the matter. One word from the supposed offenders quashed the whole proceedings. They repelled the charge with the most impetuous eagerness, and declared that they abhorred such a sin as much as anybody. " The Lord God of gods, the Lord God of gods, he knoweth, and Israel he shall know; if it be in rebellion, or if in transgression against the Lord, (save us not this day,) that we have built us an altar to turn from following the Lord, let the Lord himself require it." They go on to show that, so far from desiring to separate themselves from their brethren, and turn away from the worship of the true God, they have built the altar expressly to keep him and them in remembrance, to " be a witness between us and you, and our generations after us, that your children may not say to our children in time to come, Ye have no part in the Lord "; for this altar, the pattern of the true altar, should be a perpetual witness of their unity.

The committee were extremely delighted that the mountain had not brought forth even a mouse. Probably they were too simple even to feel a little crestfallen, as we should almost think they would; and the children of Israel seem to have received with unmitigated satisfaction the tidings that they had made much ado about nothing, and to have disbanded their forces, and blessed God, and gone home in a very satisfactory frame of mind.

"And the children of Reuben and the children of Gad called the altar Ed; for it shall be a witness between us that the Lord is God."

Guilt, sin, crime, are things so terrible, that we can hardly be too cautious how we ascribe them either to individuals or to corporations. These things are not done in a corner. Smithville and Joneston would each, perhaps, give scarcely more than a vote apiece, if it were to divide its votes equally among the Presidential candidates for the coming election, and whether the Presbyterian Church of Smithville overpowers, overreaches, and swallows up the Congregational Church of Joneston, or whether Joneston carries the day over Smithville, is, as a business matter, of little importance to the people of the United States; but we are, or profess to be, the body of Christ, and members in particular. We form ourselves into churches expressly to cultivate and propagate the religion whose rule is love. If we cannot keep ourselves together without wrangling, how can we bind up the world with us in the bundle of life ? How can we strike hands against the enemy, if we fall out and chide and fight among ourselves ? If our religion has not vitality enough to allow us to disagree peacefully, how can it have enough to be aggressive ? What inducement shall the world have to adopt it, if it cannot keep the churches sweet ?

When we combat a man's opinions, let us be sure that we combat his opinions, and not a garbled mockery of them. We cannot be too careful against misrepresentations. Few things are more exasperating than to see one's views caricatured, and then held up for judgment, and few things are more common in the discussion of opinions. Our Arminian friend alleges that the Calvinist denies free agency, — an absurdity at which the Calvinist would laugh, if it did not involve consequences too serious for laughter ; but our Calvinist friend affirms that the Unitarian believes Christ to be a mere man, — an assertion which shocks the pious Unitarian almost as much as it does the pious Trinitarian. You think too many novels will destroy the mind's balance, and your friend replies, " Ah ! you don't believe in cultivating the imagination," — as if you do not approve of raising hay unless you lay your whole farm down to grass. You defend novels, believing them capable of being vehicles of truth, and most potent preachers of righteousness, and are surprised to hear yourself quoted by the inveterate and wholesale devourer of " yellow-covered literature " in defence of his course. You recommend travelling to the hollow-eyed student, and are gravely informed that a rolling stone gathers no moss. You hint to your peripatetic friend, that a little closer acquaintance with the philosophers would aid him in his profession, and you are met with

" All work and no play
Makes Jack a dull boy."

The feelings awakened are such as would be aroused, if, while you were endeavoring to make parents feel the necessity of pure air, warmer clothing, simpler food, and healthier and more obedient habits for their children, some one should take your boy, and shave his head, and slit his ears, and paint his rosy cheeks blue, and put rings in his nose, and take him around the neighborhood as a specimen of the result of your system of physiology. " Here is Mr. Such-a-one's boy! This is the kind of child his method turns out. This is the system, fellow-citizens, that he wants us to adopt. Can't we do better than this with our present one?" Do you think you should feel that you had been quite fairly dealt by? But thoughts, opinions, sentiments, are the children of the brain and the heart; should not their integrity be just as scrupulously respected? Besides, if you undertake to maletreat a child, he can scream and writhe and kick, and give you a deal of trouble; but a thought, a sentence, lies passive under your pen-point. You can mar and mutilate and murder, and send it out to the world, and silence is its only protest.

All such misrepresentations must have originated somewhere, and it is difficult to believe that they all arose from sheer misapprehension. While many who repeat them doubtless believe them sincerely, it seems hardly possible but that some have repeated them who do not believe them. Unquestionably many of our Southern brethren really fear that the triumph of Republican principles will inaugurate fire and sword and general ruin; but is it possible that those who have stood nearest to the Republican party, and had every opportunity to inform themselves of its character, have fallen into such a delusion from want of simple apprehension? We do not severely blame the masses for not knowing, for such knowledge is with them subordinate, but we do blame the politicians, for it is their business to know. So in theology; the shoemaker, and the tailor, and the milliner, do not generally — and it is not essential that they should — investigate for themselves the doctrines of the different sects. They derive their impressions largely from their theological teachers, and if their impressions are wrong, they are

11   P

scarcely to be blamed. It is the ministers, who are expected to be conversant with such things,—the speakers and writers, who ought to know whereof they affirm before they affirm it,—with whom the blame chiefly rests. It is no fault in a clergyman not to be aware that a gridiron is not a toasting-fork ; nor is it necessarily a fault in his cook to think Universalists and infidels the same thing. Neither is responsible for the knowledge that belongs to the other's department, but ignorance in his own is a folly and shame to him. Worse still is it to palm off his ignorance upon others for wisdom. It is not only folly, but sin. Educated men have, in the first place, no right to be so narrow-minded. You excuse it in those whose horizon has been limited ; but colleges are built, and tutors appointed, and boys introduced to the wise men of old days and new, for the express purpose of taking broad views,—of becoming liberal, catholic, comprehensive. If, however, notwithstanding all this, they are narrow-minded, let them, if possible, keep it to themselves. Do not let them preach their narrowness to others, calling it orthodoxy or piety. It is bad enough for a man to pluck out his eyes. It is worse for him to pretend that he can see, to a man born blind, and so lead him with himself into the ditch.

Language is often ambiguous. Misunderstanding is often honest. Clear understanding is sometimes next to impossible. With the utmost care, and with conscientious intent, we do not always arrive at the undisguised idea. If a man wishes to be stupid, he has every opportunity. If he chooses to believe that his opponent maintains that black is white, it is altogether probable that he will be able to believe so. But language is not so ambiguous but that, if we try with sincere purpose and fixed attention to get at what a man means, we shall in the main succeed, — at least enough for all practical purposes. Intelligence is more under the control of the will than many suspect. Will to see clearly. Determine to understand quickly and correctly. Make a point of apprehending other people's views. Be sure you are right before you go ahead. But if we are more intent on proving our own zeal, displaying our own keenness, building up our own cause, than we are at getting at the truth, we shall do harm, — and be verily guilty, not only concerning our brother, but concerning ourselves and God.

I do not mean to decry religious, theological, or ecclesiastical controversies. They are important elucidators of the truth. In the present state of religious knowledge, and probably for hundreds of years to come, a church without controversy will be a church without vitality. It is by sharp collision that the sparks of truth are struck out. Let us deal heavy blows and a good many of them, only let us bring down our sledge-hammers on the anvil where lies the truth that is to be shaped, and not aim them at each other's skulls, — which is neither pleasing to God nor edifying to man, nor favorable to the elimination of truth.

Let us also give more latitude to the brains of our brethren. We are very apt to attribute difference of opinion to the wrong source. We allot to the heart the responsibility that belongs only to the head. If a man thinks it is right to do what we think it is wrong to do, we call it self-indulgence. If he refrains from doing what we allow ourselves to do, we call it austerity. A good many of the rank and file of the Orthodox army, not to say a leader here and there, will hardly admit that Universalists and Unitarians have the glory of God and the welfare of man just as much at heart as have the Orthodox. There are still extant many Congregationalists who can by no means reconcile cards and piety. Christ has some very little ones who think dancing not quite so atrocious as murder in the first degree ; and there are who believe that he that doubteth any of the Five Points or the Thirty-nine Articles is about as good as damned. Hear what the Apostle Paul saith : —

" Who art thou that judgest another man's servant ? To his own master he standeth or falleth. Yea, he shall be holden up; for God is able to make him stand. . . . .   .

" But why dost thou judge thy brother ? Or why dost thou set at naught thy brother ? For we shall all stand before the judgment-seat of Christ. . . . . So, then, every one of us shall give account of himself to God. Let us not, therefore, judge one another any more."

The Apostle cannot mean that we are to form no opinion of our neighbor, for it is not in the nature of things that a man should walk in and out before a community ten, twenty, thirty years, without leaving an impression.

What, then, does he mean?

If we turn to the fourteenth chapter of Romans we shall find that he is talking about difference of opinion in minor matters. One believes that the ritual, Mosaic law is still in force, and he is accordingly observant of days and meats. Another believes it to be abrogated, and considers all days alike, and all meats clean; but the Apostle, with characteristic liberality, defends both sides. "If you think it is wrong to eat meat, eat it not, only do not call him who does eat, a pagan. If you think it is right to eat it, eat, but do not call him who abstains a stickler. Look somewhat behind deeds to motives, and know that in certain regards the truest piety is consistent with opposite beliefs and actions."

We need Paul's large-hearted wisdom quite as much as did those old Romans.

Shibboleth is a very good test-word, if you only want to find out whether a man is an Ephraimite; but it does not help to distinguish between Jew and Gentile.

"Believe on the Lord Jesus Christ and thou shalt be saved," is the simple and succinct theory of the Christian religion. "Pure religion and undefiled before God and the Father is this, to visit the fatherless and the widow in their affliction, and to keep himself unspotted from the world," are the two lines of its practice,—charity and purity. Eighteen hundred years ago a voice was heard crying in the wilderness of Judæa, "Bring forth fruits worthy of repentance"; and when the people, ignorant, asked, "What shall we do?" the voice replied, "He that hath two coats, let him impart to him that hath none; and he that hath meat, let him do likewise." And the publicans said, "What shall we do?" And the voice replied, "Exact no more than that which is appointed you." And the soldiers asked, "What shall we do?" And the reply was, "Do violence to no man, neither accuse any falsely; and be content with your wages." So everywhere throughout the New Testament, shades of doctrine, forms of worship, are of less account than the deeds of every-day life. In the twelfth chapter of Romans we have a beautiful presentation of the sacrifice which is pleasing in the sight of God. There is a sketch, limned by a Divine hand, of a true Christian community. Yet we greatly fear that it is a study, and not a portrait.

Theology, the science of GOD, is a sublime and infinite thing. Earth serves for a beginning, but eternity can give no end. Yet with incredible self-confidence we lay down our propositions, affirm our belief therein, and drag up our brethren to the mark. Now God has revealed to us certain great facts and principles — quite enough for our guidance in this world, quite enough for our entrance into a happier — in letters of living light, which all may read; but after all, great is the mystery of godliness. The Bible is the perfect work of an Infinite Being; but we bring to it the imperfect strength of finite minds. We may study facts and draw inferences, but theological science is not susceptible of mathematical demonstration. He who brings to the investigation humility, thirst for knowledge, love to God and man, will eventually find the hidden truth, the pearl of great price; and he who brings haughtiness, a belief full-formed, a prejudiced mind, and seeks only confirmation, will also find what he seeks, — confirmation. Truth will " not unsought be won," nor will she be wooed by proxy. It would have been just as easy for God to reveal everything, as to reveal a part, — to reveal it beyond the possibility of misconception, as to reveal it as it is. As it is, the best men in all ages have differed regarding some of its teachings; and this fact indicates that the Bible is a part of the machinery of God's moral government. By the way in which we receive and study it shall our disposition towards him, in part, be judged. Let us, therefore, be charitable towards those who differ from us. Original structure, education, surroundings, give to every mind its own individuality. Through its own peculiar atmosphere God shines upon every heart. To one, clouds and darkness are round about Him; to another, He dwells " never but in unapproached light."

All young people who do their own thinking, or any considerable part of it, are liable to be more or less troubled with doubts. They pass through an attack of heresies almost as regularly as through the measles; in fact, the one bears about the same relation to the soul that the other does to the body; neither being dangerous, if well treated, both capable of causing the greatest injury if carelessly or ignorantly managed.

There are two kinds of doubters among the young; one the bright, active, " smart fellow," who wishes it to be distinctly understood that he is not going to believe that two and two make four simply because his father did. He insists on a demonstration of it to his own satisfaction, and, if you cannot demonstrate it to him, and there is evidence that two and two make five, he will believe that two and two make five, notwithstanding the arithmetics. For that matter, the very fact that all arithmetics have hitherto made and maintained this assertion, is rather a reason to him why he should not believe it, — at least, it gives him a lively desire not to believe it. He wishes the world and posterity to be aware that his is an original mind, looking at things as they are, and not at things as " old fogies " see them. His doubts are consequently brought forward promiscuously, publicly, on the slightest provocation. It gratifies him to have an opportunity — or to make one — to show the investigating, independent, fearless turn of his mind. Not that he is not a very fine young person. He may be really promising and superior. It is a more hopeful sign in a young man to be too stirring, than too stagnant. It is natural for old men to err on the side of conservatism, for young, on the side of radicalism ; and it is unnatural for them to change places. When college, or contact with men and affairs, has taken the conceit out of our young friend, and the furnace of affliction has purified him, and time has enlarged his vision and matured his judgment, he will be an excellent citizen, one of the pillars of the Church, — if he is but decently well manipulated.

The second doubter is quieter, graver, more reticent. You may live a year with him, and not discover that he does not go along your highway, but strikes out into little by-paths of his own. His differences from your opinion are modestly and hesitatingly spoken, generally unpremeditated, or divulged by accident, or perhaps timidly suggested to you in half-way hints, with a vague hope that you may come to the rescue. They almost sadden him. It is a sacrifice to him to be obliged to go

11 *

contrary to the traditions of the elders. He wishes that he could believe implicitly everything which he has been taught. His doubts are real difficulties.

In both these cases, it is of the utmost importance, though for different reasons, that the person or persons to whom such doubts are expressed, should not seem nor be shocked, nor startled, nor surprised. In the first place, it is just what the first young person wants. Nothing would please him better than to thow a shell into the orthodox camp, and see it burst and scatter the orthodox in all directions. Nothing will take the wind out of his sails more effectually, than to have you go up to his tremendous shell and turn it over, and roll it about playfully, and demonstrate that, after all, it is only a harmless football, — you have seen scores of them in your day, — in fact, patronized them yourself, when you were young. Finding that he does not make a sensation will presently cure him of trying to make sensations, and the desire to make them will die out altogether before long.

It is absolutely essential, however, that you receive the second young person with an unruffled deportment. You are not to be shocked, first, because if you are, you will repulse him, and secondly, because there really is nothing shocking about it. The Christian religion is full of mysteries. The Bible is a quarry of truth, in

which men have been digging for centuries, and
have brought up many a massive block, most of
which are, as yet, but blocks, irregular and uncouth. Comparatively few have been carved into
shapely statues, that can delight the eye and satisfy the soul. One looks farther into the future
than another. You see the Apollo hidden in the
marble, but your young friend sees only a jagged
fragment; and there is nothing that need surprise
you in his limited vision. To be shocked, and to
let him see that you think him on the high road
to Infidelity and Atheism because he cannot look
upon this, that, and the other as you do, — because
he cannot reconcile seeming discrepancies, nor
prevent their troubling him, — is the sure way to
drive him headlong into the very slough of Infidelity. He knows that he is sincerely seeking the
truth. He knows that he is not only willing, but
anxious, to believe in the Bible; and to have you
start back in horror at his explorations, and hint
of rationalism and free-thinking and shipwreck,
not only disgusts him, but has a strong tendency
to throw discredit on a Bible which cannot stand
the test of sound reasoning and careful inquiry;
and so his mole-hills are magnified into mountains
of difficulty. To be sure, it is you that are weak
in the faith, not the Bible; but he, as well as
many who are older and wiser than he, is very apt
to confound a cause with its supporters, and to
make the weakness of the latter an indication of

the weakness of the former. He will, perhaps, never again mention the subject to you, but, kept back in the recesses of his own mind, it will loom up a hideous monster, while, if you had brought it out into the light, it would have roared him as gently as a sucking dove.

The true way is to receive him kindly, and draw out his thoughts freely and fully. If he has difficulties which you can explain thoroughly, explain them, but do not attempt to do so unless, before you begin, you are quite sure that you can finish. An explanation that does not explain, is a thousand times worse than none; while few things will give him more confidence in himself and you and the Bible than for you frankly to say, " That point is indeed hard to be understood. I do not fully comprehend it myself, but it does not trouble me. I have put it aside as one of those things that we know not now, but shall know hereafter." Lay it down at the outset that nobody is responsible for the Bible. Nobody is under bonds to make its different parts adjust themselves. It is God's book, and its harmony is his affair, not ours. Our business is to study and practise it. If any one chooses to harmonize Geology and Genesis, or the Law and the Gospel, very well. It will doubtless do much good in the way of removing stumbling-blocks, and, as a missionary work, is well worth while. But to do it for the Bible's sake, is absurd, — and there is a great deal of that sort of

thing done. One would think that the Bible was
gotten up by a conspiracy of Christians, who felt
bound to sustain it, and that if all its crooked places were not made straight, it would go by the
board. Do not you fall into this mistake with
your ingenuous and doubting friend. Let him
see that you, for one, believe in the Bible thoroughly, — believe in its Divine origin and self-sus-
taining power, and that it will go on a year or two
longer, even if you cannot put everything right.
Your confidence will be contagious. He will instinctively feel that a cause which gives its friends
so little anxiety, must have an inward strength.
Teach him also how to take his reckonings, by
showing him that our opinions generally are but
the balance of probabilities, and that we believe
the Bible, notwithstanding its obscurities and apparent discrepancies, just as we believe a great
many other things, because it is far easier to
believe than to disbelieve; but do not for a moment suppose that you are advancing the cause
of truth by denying that it is beset with difficulties, or by ridiculing or repelling those who cannot
fail to discern them.

I do not admit that it is of no consequence what
a man's belief is, if he is only sincere in it. So far
as a man's belief affects his character and conduct,
it is of the utmost importance that he believe
right, as I shall presently attempt to show; and a
belief that does not affect the character and con-

duct needs to be looked into at once. There is a
definite boundary-line between truth and falsehood, and he who stops short of it, or goes beyond
it, is in danger. Particularly in matters that directly pertain to our eternal well-being should we
see to it that we do not build on the sand; but
this does not justify us in breaking our neighbor's
windows, or calling our neighbor hard names every
time we see him at the front door, even if he has
chosen a sand rather than a rock foundation ; and
especially is this true if, as is often the case, we
have never seen his underpinning, but only know
it by hearsay, or inferentially.

Moreover, it is unquestionably true that the
reason why many of us have no doubts, is because
we have no thoughts. We hold the truth in our
hands. We call it ours. We toss it playfully
hither and thither. It is to us an heirloom trans-
mitted with the family name ; but we have never
penetrated the crust of words, to the idea that lives
and glows and throbs beneath; while our doubting, wavering brother, on whom we look coldly
and distrustfully, more earnest and searching than
we, has rent off the casings, and the iron has entered into his soul, fierce, burning, scarifying.
Shall we scorn ?   Shall we not rather reverence ?

For him who speaks flippantly of commonly held
beliefs, — who carelessly flings out doubts, and
affects indifference or contempt of them, — for the
sake of an appearance of greater independence and

free-thinking, but who is equally a stranger to conscientious belief and conscientious doubt, one has small sympathy, — yet pity even for him. But for the serious mind, struggling in mists and darkness, though the darkness be his own sins rising up like a cloud between his soul and God, we cannot have too great a liberality, too warm a tenderness. We cannot roll the cloud away, but we can give him a helping hand; or, if he refuse the proffered hand, we can still pray to Him to whom the darkness and the light are both alike.

Particularly let us be careful how we bandy epithets. Let us beware that we give no opprobrious name to one who, loving God, and striving continually to serve him, is overwhelmed by a host of Satan's legions, — cast down, but not destroyed. Far more justly should we reproach him who, professing to sit in the full glory of the holy of holies, has only reproach and contumely for those who are still groping in the valley of the shadow of death.

Standing on the hill-top, bathed in the full splendor of God the Creator, of Christ the Sufferer and the Saviour, of the Holy Spirit, the Mediator and Intercessor, our souls are wafted up into the region of faith and rapture, and we shout, exultant, "Lord, I believe!" but down in the valley, among the dry, dead bones, delving in the deep recesses of our own hearts, awed by the evil that broods, gloomy and shadowy, over the world, our highest effort is to cry, with tear-streaming eyes and quivering lips, " Help thou mine unbelief ! "

It is unspeakably pleasant to know that, amid all the clash and clangor, one clear song of victory pours continually up to God. With a thousand hesitations and blunders, with all the bickering of evil passions, there is a steady progress towards the heights of Christian concord.

" It *does* move though," was the indignant protest of Galileo's unconquered and unconquerable conviction, when Galileo's timorous lips had weakly renounced the new-born truth. Ignorance would have remanded the world back to its pristine immobility, and swept the sun around it as aforetime ; but the elastic and invincible truth sprang up from beneath the weight of priestcraft and tyranny, and asserted itself in unshorn strength.

The world *does* move. All along the road, in the World and in the Church, are way-marks of its progress. Old hypotheses that were the husks of truths or refuges of errors, old hatred that a closer acquaintance has cast off, old inventions that were but the first essays of genius, scattered broadcast, mark its grand, triumphal march. Retrogressions there are, and weary wanderings in wildernesses, and many a sluggish halt, but the Lord has spoken to the children of men, and they go forward.

Some thirty or forty years before a star guided the wise men to the cradle of the baby-Christ, there was living in Rome a gay, generous young gentleman, whose name is still held in pleasant remembrance. Possessed of an ample fortune, a part of the year was spent in town, and a part in the retirement of his Sabine farm; but whether amid the gayeties of the metropolis, or by the murmur of the Bandusian spring, or at the frequented baths of Baiæ on the shore of the many-sounding sea, his wit, his education, his accomplishments, and his elegance drew around him the most fashionable, intellectual, and cultivated society of Italy; and to this day he keeps his place in the front rank of lyric poets.

Yet this scholar and gentleman, so polished, so refined, on the occasion of the departure to Greece of a gentleman whom he perhaps justly disliked, published a poem in which he begged the winds to remember to lash the sides of his foe's ship with frightful waves, to snap his ropes and break his oars, and hide with cloud every friendly star. He gloats over the fruitless toil of that foe's sailors, the deadly pallor of his face, and his unmanly wailings and prayers for succor, and closes by vowing a thank-offering to the gods, if the man shall perish shipwrecked on a hostile shore! And nobody seems to have taken exception to it. Suppose Longfellow, or Lowell, or Whittier, should write such a poem to a political or personal enemy, what measure would they receive from "our best society"?

Sixteen hundred years later, Milton, a man whose fame no words can illustrate, in his political controversies indulged in a fierceness and coarseness of invective, which are banished now to the very purlieus of civilization.   In his answer to Salmasius, epithets of opprobrium and scorn are heaped up page after page.   "So little," he says, "do we fear, you slug you, any war or danger through your silly rhetoric."   "You, in the mean time, you silly loggerhead, deserve to have your bones well thrashed with a fool's staff."   "Meddle with your own matters, you runagate, and be ashamed of your actions, since the Church is ashamed of you."   "Speak out, you wretch, and never mince the matter."   "And when they have been an Œdipus to you, by my consent you shall be a Sphinx to them in good earnest, and throw yourself headlong from some precipice or other, and break your neck."   "I am weary of mentioning your lies, and ashamed of them."   "You impudent liar, what mortal ever heard this whimsy before you invented it?"   "You rascal, was it not for this that you, a renegade grammarian, were so forward to intermeddle?"   "I think that the best course you can take will be, for this long book that you have writ, to take a halter and make one long letter of yourself."   And this silly loggerhead, and runagate, and rascal, and liar, was no malefactor, but Salmasius of Leyden, generally accounted the first scholar of his age. We have sharp political and theological controversies now, but nothing equal to this. The world does move. What was Piccadilly then, is Billingsgate now. The leaven has worked, refining our language, softening our manners, and, may we not say? elevating our hearts.

IX.

AMUSEMENTS.

 YOUNG lady once remarked, that she should like to be a Christian, but she did not think she could give up balls.

This is an indication of the reason why many do not set about becoming Christians. They draw a line. On one side is religion; on the other side happiness. If they take religion, they take safety for the next world, but a cheerless kind of happiness for the remainder of this. If they take happiness, they take a gay, pleasant, agreeable life for this world, but run a risk for the next. A bird in the hand is worth two in the bush, and they, naturally enough, decide to make sure of this life at any rate, and sufficient unto the next life are the evils thereof. They do not know much about that future world, but they do know the present. They will keep what they get, and get what they can; and in a measure they are right.

Certain present happiness is better than uncertain future happiness. It stands to reason that the present, actual world, the world we were born into, the world we are now living in, is the world with which we are chiefly concerned. The future world will have its own conditions, its own duties; but they will not devolve upon us till we get through with this. It is our business to do the duties of this world, and it is our right to enjoy its pleasures. I, for one, should very much mistrust any man who should put heaven's work in place of earth's work; or who should promise happiness in the next world only at the sacrifice of happiness in this.

But it is not so. These people make a mistake. The beauty of true, Evangelical, Gospel religion — of Christ-religion — is that it is a religion for this world, — this busy, gay, social, active, living, present world. Not that it is confined to this. By no means. It lights up the dim aisles of the past and of the future, revealing to us all we know of the glory that has been, and promising us a glory yet to be revealed, such as eye hath not seen, nor ear heard, nor heart of man conceived. Glorious things it speaks to us for our comfort; — of a golden city, clear as crystal, unto which the kings of the earth shall bring their glory and their honor; of many mansions prepared for us therein by the Lord of light; of a life into which shall no more enter anything that defileth, nor any sorrow, or crying, or pain, or death. All this it promises us for an incitement, and the loss of all this for a warning; yet its present, its great, I had almost said its chief value, is not in the future, but in what it is doing for us every day. It is of inestimable price in this life, as well as in that which is to come. It is good for us in this world, even if there were no other. The virtues which it enjoins fit us not only for heaven, but for earth. They are not only pure, but profitable. They are due not only to Christianity, but to humanity. Whatever a man ought to do because he is a Christian, he ought to do because he is a man. Whatever wrongs his Christianity wrongs his manhood. Everything that is unchristian is impolitic. Sin is not only sinful, but it does not pay. Any act that transgresses God's moral law is a poor business calculation. Whatever increases a man's value in the Church, increases his value in the World. The better the Christian, the better the citizen. In proportion as bankers and brokers and merchants become true Christians, will business be put on a sure footing. Christian principles are the best possible basis for a business character.

So with the happiness of religion. It will take us to heaven, but we shall not have to wait till we get to heaven before we get any pleasure out of it. It pays as it goes. It is a comfort and a blessing all the way along. It is the one pleasure that never fails, that brings no after-pains. If it displaces old joys, it brings in new and better ones to fill their places. It is the very fountain of happiness, — not only spreading out into a placid lake at our journey's end, — a sea of glass mingled with fire, whereon they that have gotten the victory shall stand with the harps of God, — but all the way through the wilderness its waters break out, and its streams in the desert, so that even the parched ground becomes a pool, and the thirsty land springs of water. It is eminently and pre-eminently the religion of *now*.

But all this cannot, of course, be known by those who have not tasted that the Lord is gracious. They cannot forget those things that are behind, because they do not see in their true light the things which are before, and there is no beauty for them to desire. In all such cases two courses may be pursued. We may say, " You then love amusement better than life. You will sacrifice heaven to an evening's enjoyment. You will barter an eternity of bliss for a lifetime of uncertain and certainly fleeting pleasures. You will take gayety in exchange for your soul. Here is the choice : here, worldly pleasures ; there, heavenly. Choose this day whether you will serve the god of this world, or the God of all worlds."

This may be the wise course, but I do not think it is. The opportunity of choice is of no value unless we are acquainted with the character of the things to be chosen. Solomon's wisdom and

Enoch's goodness would be of small service when your little boy comes to you with his hands behind him, and says, " Which will you have, the right, or the left ? " In asking a person to choose between earthly and heavenly pleasures, you ask him to choose between what he knows and what he does not know. You ask him to give up something which he knows he likes, for something which he not only does not know that he likes, but rather thinks he does not like. Is it altogether to be expected that he will do it ? It is of no use to say that worldly pleasures, so called, are not real pleasures; because it is not true. They are real. There is pleasure in dancing, gambling, and horse-racing, — in fine clothes, theatres, and wine suppers. Every one who has tried it knows there is pleasure in it, and when you say there is not, you contradict the facts of his consciousness. Think a moment, — if there were no pleasure in it, why do so many do it ? Nobody ever cut off his hand for the pleasure of the thing. Nobody ever drank a friend's health in assafœtida. True such life does not bring the highest kind of happiness, but neither do ripe pears, nor tight roofs, nor well-tilled farms, nor well-ordered houses ; yet we do not despise them on that account, much less condemn them. A great deal that goes to make life comfortable springs from inferior sources. We cannot afford to slight the brook that ripples through our garden, because it was not born amid the snow-crested summits of the Rocky Mountains. True such pleasures may be dearly paid for in wasted time, ruined health, and shattered souls; but footing up bills is a quite different matter from running up bills. It does not come till afterwards, and may be very disagreeable without preventing the other from being just the opposite. Moreover, there are many worldly pleasures which are not offset by palpable, immediate disadvantages, and many more that have no disadvantages to affect them, — being not only harmless, but in their place useful. The man who has a pleasant home, a lucrative business, and the respect of his fellows, and who thinks he is enjoying himself, will hardly credit you when you inform him that he is not. Knowing nothing of that higher happiness which you hold up to him, and not having yet weighed his own in the balance to find it wanting, it is not entirely illogical that he should be contented as he is.

The trouble is, that you have precipitated the issue. Issues are always to be avoided, notwithstanding the fact that many, brought face to face with such issues, do choose the right to their everlasting joy; but laws are instituted for the protection of the weak, not of the strong. The feast which the Lord blessed was given to the poor, the maimed, the lame, and the blind. The test, the trial which strengthens one man, will kill another. Through thy knowledge shall thy weak brother perish for whom Christ died? When ye sin so

12

against thy brethren, and wound their weak conscience, ye sin against Christ. A wise parent will not plunge his child into a hand-to-hand conflict with disobedience, if he can help it. If the child is peevish and unhappy, and tending to insubordination, he will not immediately launch a command, though the command itself may be reasonable, and eminently fit to be obeyed. He will endeavor to soothe, to lead the troubled mind away from its troubles ; and when placidity is restored, and the little face is clothed with sunshine, the command will be cheerfully obeyed. Civilians, whose knowledge of battles is derived from Sallust and Gibbon, will be rampant for war, when experienced generals, who have seen fighting, who have been in the trenches, and heard the balls whistling around them, will be strenuous advocates of pacific measures. But though an issue is to be shunned, it is not to be shirked. By just as much as it is to be avoided, by just so much is it to be bravely met when it is unavoidable.

The old proverb says, " The Devil is old, and therefore knows many things," and if there is any one thing which he knows better than any other, it is human nature. Concerning God and the indwelling life and might of righteousness, he is short-sighted ; but how to mix truth and falsehood in such proportions that man shall accept it, how to combine truth enough to lull suspicion with falsehood enough to destroy the soul, he

knows to a charm. He is as well acquainted with
the laws of mind as we, and understands their
bearings, and how to use them for his own purposes, a great deal better than we. He knows that,
if men could clearly see what life with religion in
it is, they would choose it rather than life without
religion ; but this they cannot do, because religion
is of such a nature that one must possess it himself in order to get at any adequate conception of
its worth. He knows further, that if he can get
men to think they see the two, and to make choice
upon such vision, it will be a strong point gained.
To this end he holds up a nondescript article, —
something that has no existence in heaven, but is
of the earth, earthy, and of the Devil, devilish ;
something that is cold and negative and repulsive.
That he calls religion, and asks them to choose
that instead of their warm, sensuous, and real, if
short-lived pleasures ; knowing all the while — the
cunning schemer — that they will do nothing of
the sort. " Choose religion," he says, " religion
that will destroy all your pleasures, and give you
up body and soul to church-going, and psalm-sing-
ing, and prayer-meetings, and tract-societies, and
general solemnity." For this is undoubtedly what
religion means to a vast multitude of people, and
this invitation, recollect, he addresses to men who
have not yet got hold of the secret life which dwells
in church and psalm, wherever they are vital, and
to whom, therefore, psalms and hymns are but

sounding brass and tinkling cymbals. But little cares he whether they understand the terms of the bargain or not. Little cares he whether they know what they reject or not, so long as he knows what they accept. It is his aim to get them to turn away from God and cling to himself, and it is not in his nature to hold back, from conscientious scruples, when a little deception would serve his purpose. If he can make his proposal through the lips of some worthy and devout man, so that his victims shall not for a moment suspect that there is any cheating going on, so much the better.

There is another, and I think a more excellent way. Remembering that the person whom you are addressing is, as yet, totally unacquainted with the joys of religion, and knows it chiefly, if not wholly, by its duties and immunities, and even that but partially, — remembering also that a true idea is the very best lever with which to pry up a false idea, — would it not be better to dwell less upon the pleasures that are to be given up, and more upon those that are to be acquired, — to insist not so much that the longing soul shall abandon the leeks and onions of Egypt, as to set before him the milk and honey of the promised land ? Why not say to the gay girl who finds the ball-room an obstacle in the way to Christ, " Leave that question alone. Do not trouble yourself about it. Let it settle itself. The point now is to give your heart to God. You acknowledge that you owe allegiance to him. All that any Christian wants, or has any right to want of you, is that you should pay what you owe. In order to do this, look not upon the world which you fear to leave, but the God to whom you wish to go, — a God ready to pardon, forgiving iniquity, transgression, and sin, though he will by no means clear the guilty, — a God who is clothed with majesty, yet whose name is love, — a King omnipotent, yet a Father all-compassionate, — on whose side ranging yourself, you will be on the side of goodness, truth, right, against wickedness, falsehood, and oppression, — whose presence is fulness of joy, at whose right hand are pleasures forevermore, — whom having not seen we love, in whom only believing we rejoice with joy unspeakable and full of glory, and whom when we see we shall be like, changed into the same image from glory to glory."

From glory to glory, — such are the Christian's stepping-stones. Show them to those whose feet are almost gone. Show them that the religion of the Bible is not a religion of gloom and coldness and forlorn hopes and last resources, — a religion to be chosen as the least of two evils, — a religion for poor people and consumptive people and melancholy people, for sea-voyages and steam-carriages and thunder-storms; but a religion full, rich, vigorous, rounding itself to the most exuberant nature, adapted to the most active life, capable of filling the warmest heart, — a religion whose key-

note is love, whose banner over us is love, whose
precept is to rejoice evermore. Demonstrate to
them that there is not only righteousness, but peace
and joy, in the Holy Ghost. Set Christ before
them, the chief among ten thousand, the one altogether lovely. Bid them lay hold of his goodness,
clothe themselves in his strength, his beautiful
garments of purity and holiness and benevolence
and beneficence, and be called by his new name.

Shall we, then, leave out of sight the sacrifices
which God requires? Shall we hide the cross
beneath the crown till we have got people se-
curely into the Church, and then turn upon them
and bid them relinquish their former pleasures
upon pain of an evil name and public disfavor, and
so lay ourselves open to a prosecution for obtain-
ing converts under false pretences? Or shall they
indeed continue their dissipations and unworthy
amusements as things with which God is well
pleased? Shall they serve God and mammon?
Nay, verily. Thou shalt worship the Lord thy God,
and him only shalt thou serve. But having once
put a soul *en rapport* with its Maker, — having, as
far as in us lay, restored the broken links of the
chain that bound it to the Father, — we leave it to
make the reconciliation complete, the consecration
entire. Specific duty is a matter between every
soul and its God. If a man has really become a
child of God, God's will will henceforth be the rul-
ing principle of his life. He will desire nothing so

much as to find out what God wishes him to do, and then to do it. Loving God whom he hath not seen, he will love his brother whom he hath seen. He will no longer seek only his own, but his neighbor's good. Self will be deposed from the first place in his heart, and God will reign supreme. The dethroned monarch may set on foot many a rebellion, and the kingdom may, for a long time, have but little quiet, but the end will surely be peace, and he shall come whose right it is to reign. Balls and operas and gaming-houses, all the pleasures which the Christian world agrees in condemning, and all the pleasures which some condemn, and some connive at, and some justify, will appear before him in new lights as the sun of righteousness arises. He may not at first see everything in its real aspect. The glamour falls but slowly from his eyes, and men appear to him but as trees walking. He will need thought and reading and prayer, and the constant exercise of his reason. Christian counsel may cast away some of the stumbling-blocks from his path, but his own hand chiefly must lay the axe at the root of the trees ; and never fear but that he will eventually make straight in the desert of his soul a highway for the Son of God.

As for worldly pleasures, they will adjust themselves. Those which come between him and God it will be no sacrifice to relinquish, for he will have lost all relish for them. Those that do not thus

interfere, he need not relinquish at all. If he finds
that certain exercises leave him listless, indisposed
to action, unable to cope with the adversary, he
will instinctively shun them. Others that recre-
ate him from, and fit him for, the severer duties
of life, he will continue, — doing God service by
strengthening his soul for work. He will fall off
naturally from wrong amusements; he will not be
torn reluctantly away from them. Whatever
force is to be exerted will be exerted by his own
free will, not by any external power. From
what he sees to be deleterious, it will be a joy
to shake himself free. He is not to do anything
because it would be consistent, or refrain from
doing anything because it would be inconsistent.
The greatest villain in the world may lead a perfectly consistent life. It is absurd to do something to-day, because we did or said something
last year. We are older to-day than we were
last year, and our views should be broader. Last
year we may have been wrong. Let us to-day
be right. Let the dead bury their dead; let us
be concerned only to follow Jesus. We are to
stop away from the gaming-table, not because we
are church-members, but because we are men.
If it is not harmful for men to gamble, it is not
harmful for church-members. If it does not harm
a girl to go to balls before she joins the church,
it does not harm her afterwards. If dancing is
good for her womanhood, it is good for her Chris-

tianity. The Bible forbids to the Christian no
pleasure which is beneficial to the human being.
Christianity is simply the very highest state of
manhood. Indulgences that are injurious are injurious because they keep a man below his proper
level, not because he has signed a certain paper or
made a certain agreement. Drunkenness is wrong
because it debases the image of God, not because
it violates a pledge. Lust and avarice would en-
foul the soul if Christ had never died.

In a most thoughtful, elegant, and Christian
book, I lately read, "The sober Christian may
possibly feel a shock in finding Novalis describe
his faith as a foe to art, to science, even to enjoyment; yet does not his own daily experience
prove that the holding of the one thing needful
involves the letting go of many things lovely and
desirable, and that in thought as well as in action
he must go on 'ever narrowing his way, *avoiding
much*'?"

To all which I say emphatically, *no !* The holding of the one thing needful does not involve the
letting go of anything really lovely and desirable.
It not only makes it more lovely and more desirable, but more worthy of love and desire, and
therefore more worthy to be retained. Every
pleasure, every pursuit, which was simply innocent, puts on a new nature when the soul is fired
with religious fervor, and guided by religious principle, and becomes religious. Christianity acts

upon the occupations and recreations of life like a magnet upon iron-filings. Its strong current pours over the shapeless, incoherent dust, and sweeps the particles to their polar spheres. There is no longer listlessness and chaos. Every atom knows its place, and bends in unhesitating obedience to this new motive power ; so order is evoked from disorder. But pleasures, in becoming duties, do not cease to be pleasures. Eating and drinking to the glory of God is not only more beneficial, but more delightful, than eating and drinking to gluttony and drunkenness. Ambition, saturated with benevolence, and consecrated to God, not only brings forth fruit just as nutritive and just as plenteous, but a richer and more delicious fruit. Wisdom's ways are ways not only of profit, but of pleasantness. Religion organizes and symmetrizes life, but cramps nothing, annihilates nothing.

So it is impossible to believe with the same author, that " the rule of Christ is not only exclusive, but restrictive, and . . . . we need not look far into either literature or art to see to how many of their happiest energies this rule opposes itself." ·I believe that the rule of Christ, so far from opposing a single happy energy of literature or art, strengthens, .mobilizes, purifies, and vivifies them all. There is not a faculty, nor a power of the human soul, which is not utilized by being brought under the control of religion. They find their true sphere and scope only when Christ takes the lead, and trains all the faculties to heavenly purposes. The servants of sin never develop their inborn power till they become the servants of righteousness. We need to rid ourselves of the idea that Christianity is something extrinsic,— an afterthought put in after the man was finished,— a kind of free pass to heaven. We need to bear always in mind that it is rather the completion of an otherwise imperfect organization. It is the restoration of man to his original integrity. Without it he is only half made up. Religion does not naturalize a foreigner, but reinstate an heir. It does not take a man out of his hereditary place, and introduce him to one that is higher indeed, and safer, but unnatural. Religion is a rebinding of the soul to God, from whom it had cut loose. It is a restoration of the soul to its primal proximity to the Divine. There has been a fall. God made man upright. The Devil cast him down, he consenting. Christ seeks to set him once more erect, and when man, leaning on that strong arm, begins to lift himself out of the sloughs of sin, it is not a hand or a foot or a faculty that is lifted, but the whole man. Reason, judgment, imagination, wit, all gather themselves up from the miry clay, and begin to wash their robes and make them white in the blood of the Lamb. Everything that was noble is still farther ennobled. Everything that was ignoble enters upon a process of disintegration and destruction. A religion that should repress the energies of the soul would, from that circumstance alone, be suspicious. Religion broadens, heightens, deepens. It enlarges the domains of joy, and contracts the realms of sorrow. It robs grief of its sting, and gives zest and flavor to happiness. It turns calmness into delight, and content becomes exultation. Singing, writing, painting, planning, whatever ministered to ambition, pride, avarice, or any of the numerous retinue of selfishness, are wrenched away from the usurper, and marshalled, with acclamation, into the service of Christ. The author, further on, uses most just, judicious, and wise words in illustration of this, though they seem to contradict her former statements. " Such a life will seem less spiritual only because it has grown more natural ; the soul moves in an atmosphere which of itself brings it into contact with all great and enduring things, and it has only to draw in its breath to be filled and satisfied. I know not how to describe the grandeur and simplicity of the state that is no longer self-bounded, self-referring ; how great a thing to such a freed and rejoicing spirit the life in Christ Jesus seems."

Nor can we believe that " the print of the Master's footsteps, if tracked with any degree of faithfulness, will [necessarily] carry his own far out of the path of pleasure and distinction, and leave him amid scenes and among objects in which, save for this powerful attraction, he would have found nothing to delight in or to desire." God is not the

God of the poor, the ignorant, the obscure, any
more than he is of the rich, the learned, the distinguished. Christians are harder on this class
than is Christ. We can follow his footsteps to the
house of the Pharisee as well as of the publican.
Paul, the gentleman, the scholar, the aristocrat,
was not one whit behind the very chiefest of the
fishermen. The adaptation of Christianity to the
poor is brought out in the Bible with great force,
because that phase of it is the one most likely to
be hidden, and needs therefore to be held up to
continual prominence. But including the lowly is
not excluding the lofty. They that have riches
shall enter hardly, but they shall enter — through
Christ. We cannot serve God and mammon, but
we shall not serve God by giving up to mammon
the kingdom wherewith we have been intrusted,
and running away into the shelter of a monastery,
or a nunnery, or a clique. " Occupy till I come,"
was his command. We must keep in the world,
overcoming it, not overcome by it, — turning to
Christ's service all pleasure, all distinction, all intellect, all wealth, — despoiling mammon of his
treasures and adorning with them the temple of
God. That which has been is not that which
shall be. Behold, the former things are come to
pass, and new things do I declare. The pomp
and riches and glory of this world have been used
to illustrate the reign of Satan, but another day
shall dawn, to whose light the Gentiles shall come,

and kings to the brightness of its rising, — he shall come whose right it is to reign. Glorious in his apparel, travelling in the greatness of his strength, all that is beautiful and grand and mighty shall go out to meet him. All the kingdoms of the earth shall swell his triumphal train, yea, even the earth herself shall be a crown of glory in the hand of the Lord, and a royal diadem in the hand of our God.

That, therefore, is but a flimsy and suspicious kind of religion that works from without, inward; that keeps a man away from sinful pleasures, but does not keep him from wanting to go; that substitutes external restraints for internal promptings. It is probably better that a man should stop away from the gambling-houses because he is a church-member, than not to stop away at all. It is better that a woman should remain at home and go to bed at a seasonable hour, from fear of being called inconsistent, than that she should spend the night in dancing and wine-sipping. But if they look after the forbidden fruit with longing eyes, and wish the Church did *not* forbid them to pluck it, their religion cannot be anything worth mentioning. It certainly cannot be very comfortable. So far as its requirements are concerned, they might as well go as wish to go. Christ wants voluntary contribution, not forced taxation. I heard of a man once, who, when reproached for going to a pic-nic soon after his wife died, excused him-

self by saying that he asked his wife's mother if
she had any objection, and she said she had n't!
Such love is not worth much in the wear and
tear of life.

Therefore, also, the sacrifices which Christianity requires at the hands of its adherents are few
and small. Literally speaking, it requires none,
since it demands nothing that the noblest manhood does not demand ; but even in the ordinary acceptation of the term, its sacrifices are not
worthy to be compared with its privileges. The
followers of Christ sometimes make requisitions
which Christ himself does not. In blindness of
mind they call that common and unclean which
God hath cleansed, and insist that it be cast out
and trodden under foot. An old lady, speaking
of a merry young girl who had lately joined the
church, said : " Yes, I think she *is* a Christian.
I think there *is* a change, but Betsey will be
Betsey." Of course she will. Did Christ ever
require her to be anybody else ? But we, prurient meddlers, rushing in where angels fear to
tread, — we insist that the gay Betseys shall be
transformed into sedate Susans, which is just as
unnatural, unscriptural, and impossible as that the
sedate Susans shall effervesce into gay Betseys.
A great deal of the trouble arises from a misconception of the nature and ends of amusements.
There are those who think them a gross waste, if
not a misuse, of time. There are many more who

think anything like framing, planning, and arranging for amusements to be a frivolous occupation,
unworthy of a Christian, and indicative of a shallow, worldly mind. It takes away the·attention
from serious and important things, and fixes it on
those which are short-lived and trivial. So the
case was stated in a discourse by a learned, eloquent, and exemplary man, from none more than
from whom should one expect sound reasoning
and Gospel truth. He took, as he had a right to
take, high ground. He looked upon the question
of amusements in its relations to sin, — to man as
a sinner. " Here is a world lying in sin," was his
argument, — " estranged from God, and under his
wrath and curse. What mockery to God for
Christians to be planning *amusements* for such a
world ! " But this view of the subject, solemn as
it is, is far-reaching and comprehensive. It embraces, not the amusements only, but the occupations of life. ‸ It is whether the attention of Christians shall be given to any other matters than those
which pertain directly to the salvation of sinners.
It is whether Christian men shall give their time
and money to the construction of an ocean tele-
graph, while yet the day is far distant that shall
echo from pole to ˉpole the glad tidings of a Saviour's love. It is whether men shall build rail-
roads and steamboats, while millions upon millions
are rushing down the broad way that leads to destruction. It is whether they shall erect public

baths, providing for the cleanliness of the body, while the soul is a sepulchre full of dead men's bones and all uncleanness. It is whether they shall feed the hungry and clothe the naked, while so many are perishing for want of the heavenly manna and the robe of Christ's righteousness. It is, in short, whether men shall buy and sell and get gain, so long as any remain out of the ark of Christ.

It is useless to say that these, and other such schemes and occupations, have in view the health, life, or convenience of man, and are therefore essential, or at least useful and important. That is the very assertion made by those who believe it to be a Christian duty to provide amusements, and places the question at once on a different basis. They put amusements on precisely the same plane as professions and occupations. They say, and justly, that we must take men as they are, not as they might be, or as we should think best to have them. He who would benefit his kind must proceed on the premises God has given, not on hypothetical ones of his own. He must take into account that " all men are born babies," and for the most part stay babies all their lives, in a greater or less degree. The child is not only the father of the man, but he is the man in large measure. The earth is one great school-house, and men and women are the boys and girls, grown up indeed, but boys and girls still. Sometimes they are improvements on their juvenile selves. The passions have come more under control; the gentler affections have been cultivated; the mind has been nourished and trained; but too often a flimsy covering of false . politeness is thrown over radical defects. Mokanna's silver veil is used to hide features too hideous to be plainly revealed,·but which often show through in spite of Mokanna. Self-will has become obstinacy; zeal has become bigotry; lazy shirking has become positive chicanery. The average man is no better than he should be.

This is not a flattering picture. I would gladly be proved to be in the wrong, for the sake of believing that it is not a true one. But calling a man an angel does not make him an angel; and whether we do or do not believe in total depravity, we do not, as a general thing, lend our neighbor a hundred dollars without taking his note for it. A very able political newspaper remarks: "We have nothing to say of Original Sin as a theologic dogma; but in politics it is as solid as the multiplication-table." The first step in curing disease is to find out what the disease is. The first point in solving a problem is to have it correctly stated. Here we all agree that the disease is sin; the problem is to evolve from moral chaos a world of symmetry and beauty.

An old writer says, that he considers nothing human to be foreign to himself. If a heathen

could say this, so much more ought we to say it.
Whatever concerns humanity concerns us all.
Man is a triune being. He has a physical, intellectual, and moral nature. These are truisms,
but it seems necessary that they should be stated,
because we are apt to forget them, or to act as if
we did not know them. Man's physical nature
just as much needs to be provided for as his intellectual nature, and his intellectual as his moral
nature, and *vice versa.* Each has its inalienable
rights. No one is to be subordinated or sacrificed
to the other. The claim of no one is paramount.
It is just as wicked to cheat the body out of its
just dues as it is to cheat the soul, and the soul as
the body. The body has just as good claims to
consideration as the mind, and the mind as the
heart, and the heart as either of the others. The
body is just as necessary to the soul as the soul to
the body. Neither can exist in its present state
without the other. Both can exist separate, but it
will be no longer the same personality. The secession of either dissolves the union. The secession
of both does nothing more.

This complicates matters. If a man existed
in a state of pure intellect, he could be far more
easily managed. It would be a comparatively simple thing to minister to the mind diseased, if it
were not so mixed up with the body. But man
does not exist in a state of pure intellect, but of
intellect, and carbon, lime, and water. You cannot

lay your hand on a susceptibility of his soul that is not, or may not be, influenced by the susceptibilities of his body. All the emotions of his body so bear on the emotions of his soul, that it is often difficult to tell what is body and what is soul. He, then, who provides for the fullest symmetrical development of every bodily power, is so far fulfilling the chief end of man, according to the Westminster Catechism, though he that stops there stops short of the glory of God. It is, therefore, no more mockery to God to plan amusements, than to plan employments, because the former have, though perhaps a humbler, yet certainly just as important a place in the Divine economy. The nature and extent of man's amusements have just as much bearing on his immortal nature, as the nature and extent of his work. Amusements are just as necessary to his spiritual development as work or worship. Right amusements are just as beneficial to him as wrong amusements are deleterious. They do not directly tend to repentance or growth in grace, neither does work ; but as God is uniformly to be found in the way of duty, recreation being duty, he may be truly and acceptably served in recreation.

The question narrows itself down to this. To give attention to so-called secular pursuits is wrong, or it is not. If it is, the habits of the Christian world must undergo a vast change. If it is not, amusements, in their selection and arrangement, are entitled to the same kind of interest and attention as occupations.

A religious newspaper tells a story of a young man who " became anxious about his soul. He resolved to call on a.minister and ask his counsel. . . . . He found the minister standing in animated, not to say light conversation, with a couple of visitors, and arranging with them a visit to a gentleman in the country, who had a private ninepin-alley. The impression on the mind of the young man was very unhappy; he could not open his mind to the minister, and he retired without having derived any benefit from the interview. He, erelong, became a careless, and, in the end, an abandoned sinner."

Moral of the religious newspaper : " Things in themselves harmless are to be avoided, if they cause others to offend.".

Moral of ordinary observers: ministers must not engage in animated, particularly in light conversation, and must not visit gentlemen who keep bowling-alleys.

But do you really mean, religious newspaper, that ministers are to be uniformly grave and serious ? Does it not occur to you that the clergymen who are never light must be extremely heavy ? Is not the gravity of a man who is always grave nearly as worthless as the levity of a man who is always light ? Did not the Rev. Rowland Hill say that the man who is not a fool half the time is a fool all the time ? Is not too much nutritiveness just as bad a quality of food as too little, and did you never hear of people eating sawdust to restore the balance ? What kind of a picture would that be which was all shadows, and no lights, and what kind of people are they who would blot out the lights of the landscapes ? It is the Edmund Sparklers of society, you may be sure, who want men " with no nonsense about them." Did you ever hear a high-souled, whole-hearted, clear-brained, large-minded, cultivated Christian object to " animated conversation," not to say ninepins ?

And what kind of conversation would you recommend between a minister and his chance visitors ? Shall he inchoate a treatise on political economy ? Shall he entertain them with the differential calculus ? Shall he chat of fixed fate, free will, foreknowledge absolute ? Do you not very well know that, if you should make a friendly call upon your pastor, and he should take you up in this way, you would be exceedingly tired ? Do you not, you who have so much to do with ministers, — do you not know that many who are the very salt of the earth, first in every good word and work, are the many-sided men, — the men who touch life at many points, — the men of quick sympathies, who joy with the joyous, and sorrow with the sorrowful, — who neither laugh nor weep from a sense of duty, but because they cannot help it ? Are you not now thinking of individuals, tender of heart, strong of will, sound of mind, pure of purpose, who are as full of mirth as a nut is of meat? and would you have them abate one jot or tittle of that beautiful radiance that gleams over the surface of their lives, and lights up the dark paths around them, and so makes " a sunshine in a shady place," because —

Because what? Put the case as strongly as you can. Bring in St. Paul, as you certainly will. "If meat make my brother to offend, I will eat no meat while the world standeth, lest I make my brother to offend." Grant them to be parallel cases, — which they are not, for if St. Paul did deny himself the meat which had been offered to idols, he could get plenty more which had not, whereas our ministers are warned off from the whole thing, — but granting them to be parallel, — suppose by abstaining you make a great many more to offend than you do by partaking, what then? If a minister is himself, changing his moods according to his occupations, "from grave to gay, from lively to severe," he may, and probably will, run counter to some men's ideal of a minister, and so lose influence in certain quarters. But, on the other hand, if he puts a restraint on himself, checks the natural flow of his spirits, and flats out into a dead level of (falsely so called) dignity, he will, it seems to me, run counter to a great many more ideals, and lose a great deal more influence. He will practically give in to

the notion — I cannot dignify it with any higher
name — that when men become ministers they
cease to be men.   They turn into a kind of organic abstraction, a peripatetic sermon, — something that may lawfully eat, drink, and sleep, but
not clap, jest, or vote.   But why ministers should
unman themselves any more than doctors, or lawyers, or farmers, it is difficult to perceive.   If
it is right for lawyers to enjoy a joke, and to
make one if they can, why is it not right for ministers ?   Every man is responsible for all the good
which he is capable of doing, — no more, no less.
A lawyer is bound to fulfil every duty which de-
volves upon him.   Angels can no more.   The
greatest good is to be done by employing every
faculty in doing to its utmost relative extent.
God gave us none that is superfluous, none that
must be lopped off before we can serve him acceptably.   He does not demand the sacrifice of
any, but the consecration of every power.   If we
find people maintaining the contrary, we ought to
disabuse them of so mischievous an idea, — not
shape our course as if it were a correct one.   We
do not accept the rules of action which a worldly
man adopts for himself; why should we those
which he adopts for others ?   If he is not trustworthy to guide his own life, he certainly is not
trustworthy to guide ours.   What absurdity is it
for me to check my natural and innocent gayety,
because a man who has never begun to shape his

own life by Gospel precepts, and has never imbibed the Gospel spirit, sets up the idea that such gayety is inconsistent with religion? ·Why is my liberty judged of another man's conscience, especially when that conscience is an unenlightened one? If we do not give a man credence when he justifies his own course, why should we when he condemns ours? What kind of a rule is that which works only one way? What kind of evidence is that which is invalid against one man, but valid against another?

It is partly the fault of the Christian world, that the young man referred to went away disappointed. "Public opinion" should not be allowed to fall into such an error as that sprightly conversation should seem to be incompatible with the warmest piety. If the young man had been properly educated, he would have known that the minister could sympathize with his sadness none the less for having just sympathized with gladness. Nay, he would have considered it rather an indication of real sympathy. It is a little sentimental, but a very true saying, that

> " Hearts that vibrate sweetest pleasure
> Thrill the deepest notes of woe."

The soul that easily lays hold on joy lays easily hold on sorrow. Though the minister was not one to whom he could open his mind, it was not owing to the "animated conversation," nor to the bowling-alley, whatever he may have thought.

13   s

The minister may have been a frivolous, impious
man, a cumberer of the ground, a blind guide, a
shepherd whose sheep looked up and were not
fed; but that did not indicate it. The greatest
gravity of demeanor may coexist with the weakest
character and the pettiest ends; and of all frivolity, solemn frivolity is the most repulsive. It
not only pains, but exasperates. One is not only
annoyed by the littleness, but indignant at the
deception. Good sense is a good thing, and good
nonsense is a good thing, but nonsense setting up
to be sense is outrageous.

What punishment is severe enough for him
who would curtail "animated conversation"?
Who of us that has been dragged through weary
hours of "stale, flat, and unprofitable" common-
placeness would not have welcomed the advent of
any one, man or woman, who could have stirred
us up with a little animation, even though it
had been transferred bodily from the rhymes and
chimes of Mother Goose? Who of us that has
ever known the genial glow and happiness which
a royal mind brings when, leaving its cares, which
never are burdens, leaving its matters of state,
leaving all the insignia of its royalty, it comes
into the drawing-room of daily life, and draws
around it all grace and gladness, and sportive
fancy, and happy love, and wild winsomeness, by
a spontaneous outgush of the same blessed and
blessing qualities, — who that has ever basked in

the sunshine of such a presence, but must feel an
uprising of wrath against that prurient piety which
dares so much as lay a finger on the hem of its
beautiful garments ?

O the mischief that is done by this wanton,
wilful, wicked endeavor to curtail the sources of
happiness which our Creator has given us ! to dig
up and destroy the fair growths whose roots go
deep down into our nature ! It is a Sisyphean task.
It never can be done ; for it is a crime against nature, and nature breaks out in perpetual protest.
Its evil effects are everywhere visible. Young
people, unnaturally restrained, grow stunted and
narrow, or burst out into a license which is but
the travesty of liberty. The Word of God is
brought to bear on objects which do not come
within its range. The anathemas which are pertinent only to guilt are launched on innocence,
and moral distinctions are subverted. Look at
dancing, — one of the most healthful, the most
civil, the most delightful, and the most beautiful of
amusements, — singularly adapted to the vitality,
activity, and high spirits of the young, and greatly
conducive to ease of manner, grace of carriage,
and suavity of address ; yet put under ban by
whole communities, on the most frivolous pre-
texts. Some honestly think it wrong. Why ?
Not in its essence, — nobody thinks it is wrong
in itself, — but because " it leads to dissipation."
But it does not lead to dissipation. It leads away

from dissipation. There is whist,— a game that can find employment for the closest attention, the minutest observation, the strongest memory, and the soundest reasoning, yet of so wide a sweep that it can interest and delight a child of ten. Whole communities look upon this, too, as a snare of the Devil to entrap souls. Why? Not because it is wrong of itself, but "it leads to gambling." But it does not lead to gambling. It leads away from gambling. Let a family of children have an hour, or two, or three, in the evening, devoted to social amusement, and if they have all been working during the day, as they ought, this is none too much. Suppose them to engage in dancing. Some one goes to the piano, and the rest — father, mother, and all — take the floor. Occasionally their young friends are invited in to spend the evening, or such portion of it as they are allowed before sleep. Occasionally they spend the evening out, generally accompanied by father or mother, or both. Perhaps the little ones sit down with their parents to a game of whist, — the very youngest very eager to play his very best, that he may have a chance to play again. The evenings are varied ; sometimes it is checkers, or backgammon, or blind man's buff, or singing, or reading aloud, but every evening has in its bosom something pleasant for the children to look forward to, and back upon. The home is a little community, with its round of happiness as well as of tasks ; will dissipation be likely to invade such a home ? The haunts of vice are the haunts of restlessness, uneasiness, unhappiness ; what attractions have they for one who can find all their pleasures without their pains around his own hearth-stone ? Examine statistics, and see how many of the patrons and victims of gambling-saloons were accustomed in their youth to play cards around the evening table, and to dance before the evening fire, with fathers and mothers who loved them and prayed for them and watched over them.

Christians are verily guilty in this matter. Multitudes believe and avow that dancing is not wrong, but they will not countenance it because many do think it wrong, and the many who do think it wrong think it not wrong in itself, but dangerous in its associations and tendencies. It is an amusement in which the World indulges, and therefore the Church must give it up. Absurd ! Let Christian families adopt it, not covertly, apologetically, as many do, but honestly and openly, and its associations will very soon come round right. An innocent thing will not long be held disreputable after reputable people have taken it up. No matter if the World does talk about a " dancing Church " and a " card-playing Christian." The World does not decide questions of right and wrong for the Church, nor shall the World monopolize the best of anything. Let the World understand that the Church is not to be fended off from any occupation or amusement that she judges wholesome, because the World chooses to hoist the red flag of disease. Let the Church do a thing because it is right, not because the World will pat it on the shoulder, and say, " Good child, good child." Let the Church abstain from an act because it is wrong, not because, if she does it, the World will say, " Behold, thou art become as one of us." It is disgraceful bondage, — an insult to Christ. His cause does not want the patronage of the World. If it cannot stand on its own intrinsic value, let it fall at once. Moreover, the Christianity that can be distinguished from worldliness only by its acceptance or rejection of dancing, is a very insignificant article. Let your light so shine before men, that they, seeing your good works, may glorify your Father which is in heaven. Be so humble, so devout, so sincere, so honest, so helpful, so faithful a Christian, that the World, the flesh, and the Devil shall say, " Dancing cannot be wrong, for *he* dances." You can hardly read your title clear to mansions in the skies, you can have hardly begun to live the Divine life, if men say, " He cannot be much of a Christian, for he dances."

I acknowledge that the amusements in question have dangerous tendencies, but I should like to know if there is anything in the world that has not. They lead to dissipation and gambling; so eating leads to dyspepsia, and drinking leads to drunkenness, and a great many things lead to a great many others. But because men have been drowned in the sea, shall we never step into a bath-tub? Because a house is burned down, shall we never build a fire in the kitchen-stove? Because some people tell lies, shall other people not talk at all? Because one man has the heart-burn, and another delirium tremens, shall there be no more cakes and coffee? Nay, verily. This is not God's way of procedure. He gave Adam and Eve permission and desire to eat freely of every tree in the garden, with one exception, and that exception was within easy reach. He might have saved them and us from sin and suffering by placing all fruit beyond their reach, but he chose not. With a full knowledge that his gift would be abused, he yet did not withhold it. In like manner, he has given us all things richly to enjoy. We may abuse them, turning enjoyment into a sin, but that is not the fault of the giver or of the gift. The remedy for the abuse of a thing is not to destroy it, but to use it. Destruction should be reserved only for what is in itself wicked or useless. The remedy for dyspepsia is pure air, wholesome food, thorough mastication and salivation, regular and sufficient exercise, steady occupation, and ease of mind, — not starvation. Starvation is indeed a remedy, but it is a fearfully expensive one, and the dwarfed and misshapen natures of many of our young people, and old people too, show how fatally injudicious is the policy pursued in their cultivation. Amusements they must have, — pure, wholesome, lawful, graceful if you will; but if you will not, then impure, ruinous, disgraceful.

There is great disagreement of opinion and practice in the churches. There are many communities in which dancing is as innocent as kite-flying, and a great deal more common. There are many Christian families in which whist is an acknowledged and ordinary recreation. This fact should have its influence. It should lead those who disapprove to be modest. When any number of men, whose intelligence is respectable, and whose Christian character is unexceptionable, do something of which you disapprove, but which even you do not regard as a sin in itself, it becomes you to be measured in your disapproval. Because your friend is as good and as sensible as you, it does not follow that he is in the right and you in the wrong; but it does follow that there is so much basis for his differing opinion, that he need not be a knave or a fool for holding it. Because a dozen churches allow dancing, it does not follow that it is right, and your church must go to dancing forthwith; but it does follow that the opposition to your views is sufficiently respectable to suggest the possibility that you may be wrong; and there is a possibility, at least, that such opposition is founded on a need of nature, and not on total depravity. And another thing follows : when whole communities in a city hold such opinions, sporadic cases in villages should be treated with at least respect. It is hardly fair to hunt a man down for believing, in a country church, what scores and scores believe and practise in a city church, without the smallest remark, or even notice, from anybody. When there are two sides to a thing, and a man tells you he thinks it is right to take that side, you have nothing further to do. You may give him your own views as forcibly as you please, you may strive to enlighten his conscience by every means in your power, but you may not attempt to coerce him by any of those petty persecutions which you have so well at command. You can do it. If you are both by birth and education narrow-minded, it is not at all improbable that you will do it, and a good deal of mischief into the bargain ; but it will be the old Adam in you, and not the new, that will get the commission.

Let no man despise amusements. It is a subject which demands the most careful consideration. It should be just as truly a part of the Church economy as the sacraments. Mistakes here keep people out of the Church, and wound weak consciences, and confuse weak brains, and prevent growth of grace in the Church. Let our Christianity be comprehensive, symmetrical, well-developed.

13 *

Let our young people bring all their bounding
spirits, all the dew and freshness and gladness
of their youth, to the Lord, — assuredly knowing
that they are made in the very image of God;
that their mirthfulness came from him just as
much as their memories; that the ringing laugh
and the merry song, in their proper place, are acceptable to him, as well as the broken and contrite
heart, and the fervent and effectual prayer, in its
place. The Church wants all the elasticity, and
cheerfulness, and sprightliness, and wit, and humor,
that there is in the world, whether it belongs to
the young people or the old, and will find plenty
of work for it to do. God is not the God of the
dead, but of the living; not of the sorrowful only,
but of the rejoicing. Feasting and fasting can
and should be done alike to his glory. Jesus was
present not only at the tomb in Bethany, but at
the marriage in Cana. I know no reason why he
should not be present at merry-makings now, as
well as eighteen hundred years ago. He is the
same yesterday and to-day and forever. He does
not afflict the children of men because he likes to
do it. He rejoices in all innocent happiness. The
boy need not abate one jot or tittle of his love for
play, because of his love for God. The sudden
upspringing of the one, does not necessitate the
decrease of the other. The Christian ought, all
other things being equal, to be in school the
closest student; on the play-ground, the hardest

player; in the workshop, the nicest workman; behind the counter, the most valuable clerk; in the battle, the sturdiest fighter. Whatsoever things are true, whatsoever things are honest, whatsoever things are just, whatsoever things are pure, whatsoever things are lovely, whatsoever things are of good report,—all, all belong to Christianity.

Christ spoke the simple, literal truth, when he said that his yoke was easy, and his burden light. When the followers of Christ had to follow him to the rack, the stake, and the scaffold, to stripes, to the mouths of lions, to trials of cruel mockings and scourgings, to bonds and imprisonment, there was reason to speak of sacrifices. But, reluctant as we may be to confess it, the lines have fallen to us in pleasant places. The cup which our Father hath given us is sweet, as well as healthful, and it is no mysterious and hidden love which says, " Drink ye all of it."

X.

GOD'S WAY.

AND seeing the multitudes, he went up into a mountain : and when he was set, his disciples came unto him. And he opened his mouth, and taught them, saying,

"Blessed —— "

"*Blessed*," — fit beginning of the first recorded public discourse of Him whose life on earth was the blessing of the world.

In following those sacred feet over the hills of Judæa, we see that their constant errand was one of love. It was not alone that great, mysterious love wherewith he loved us before the world was, but the steadfast, human love, the love of the man-Christ, the tenderness which displayed itself constantly in every-day life, — which no coldness could chill, no stupidity tire, no perversity lessen, — a tenderness which it should be our strongest purpose to imitate, as it is our highest privilege to share.

And the common people heard him gladly. Great multitudes followed him. Populous Galilee, stranger Decapolis, Jerusalem, queen city of Judæa, and the Pagan countries that lay beyond Jordan, poured out their myriads to listen to the words of one who spake as never man spake. From lanes and alleys, from the purlieus of poverty and vice, from the Ann Streets, the Five Points, the St. Giles's of Palestine they came, the poor, famishing people, overborne in the great world-battle, over-weary with laboring up the Difficult hills; the obscure, ignorant, sad-eyed people, with whom life had been but a losing game, who, through weakness and wickedness had made little headway, — they came flocking around this new light whose soft shining had glimmered down even to them. They brought their sick to this wonderful Jesus, whom a vague rumor called the Christ, and he healed them. They brought their little children, and he laid loving hands upon their drooping heads, and blessed them. Strange words of cheer fell upon their sorrowful hearts, — tender, consoling, hopeful, helpful words. "That ye may be the children of your Father which is in heaven." Poor and miserable and blind and naked, — despised of the great ones of the earth, domineered over by the chief priests and Pharisees, could they be the children of the Lord of heaven? How sweetly on their anxious, care-worn hearts fall the affectionate words, "Take no thought for the morrow. Your Heavenly Father knoweth that ye have need of all these things." There are strong men standing before him, faint with the burden and heat of the day, and his loving heart bids them "Come unto me, all ye that labor and are heavy-laden, and I will give you rest." There is comfort and help for all. None are sent empty away. None are so insignificant that he passes them by. No service is so lowly that he will not glorify it. Only a cup of cold water to the least of these little ones shall have its reward, — shall be laid to the account of the King of kings. None are so great, so rich, so renowned, that he bids them trust to their greatness, their riches, their renown. When they come to him in trouble, he takes them just as readily to the arms of his loving-kindness. The outcast, loathsome leper feels a wild hope leap up in his heart, yet dares not ask the boon he craves, but, bowing, humbly worships the omnipotent Teacher. "Lord, if thou wilt, thou canst make me clean." "I will; be thou clean," is the instant response, and at one gentle touch the leper arises a new man. The ruler turns to Jesus, if perhaps his young daughter, lying already dead, may be restored to his arms, and Jesus takes the cold hand in his, and life pulses once more through the veins. Mind and body claim alike his care. A man of sorrows and acquainted with grief, he bears in his own the sorrow and the griefs of all other hearts. He says

to the palsied cripple, " Son, be of good cheer," —
to the long-suffering woman, " Daughter, be of
good comfort."

He never brake the bruised reed, nor quenched
the smoking flax. When his disciples, small in
wisdom, small as yet in faith, were terrified at his
miraculous approach, he did not even chide them
that their long intercourse with him had not given
them more confidence. He remembered that they
were dust, and hastened to reassure them. " Be
of good cheer. It is I, be not afraid." He knew
that the truth must be admitted little by little.
" All men cannot receive this saying." Even in
the hour of parting he repressed the throbbing of
his full heart in compassion for their weakness.
" I have many things to say to you, but ye cannot
bear them now." Where men saw nothing to
pity, he pitied. The disciples never dreamed that
it concerned them whether the multitudes who
hung upon their master's words were hungry or
not, but the Master had compassion on them because they had nothing to eat, and he would not
send them away fasting. Importunity did not vex
him. The blind men clamored so loudly and per-
sistently, that the crowd around were shocked at
the indecorum; but Jesus had compassion on them,
and touched their eyes. Hatred did not inflame
him. Even while pronouncing the death-doom of
the wicked city which had killed his prophets,
stoned his messengers, and should yet crucify him-

self, he wept over it, yearning with more than motherly love. Treachery could not alienate him. For Peter's shameful weakness, desertion, and denial there was only the earnest question, " Lovest thou me ? " Trouble could not move him to selfishness. In the last hours, when his soul was exceeding sorrowful, even unto death, and his human heart craved human sympathy and found it not, — even then his gentle reproach sighed itself into tender excusing, — " The spirit indeed is willing, but the flesh is weak." And notwithstanding all coldness, indifference, misunderstanding, betrayal, his last bequest was love. " Lo, I am with you alway, even unto the end of the world," — and while he blessed them, he was parted from them, and carried up into heaven.

Well might the common people hear him gladly, — him who made the lowliest among them kings and priests unto God. Well might they stand around him, a living breastwork against the hostile Pharisees. Well might they come unto him, and seek him, and stay him, that he should not depart from them. Well might they spread their garments in the way, and ring out his triumphant entry into the Beautiful City, " Hosanna to the Son of David ! blessed is he that cometh in the name of the Lord. Hosanna in the highest ! "

I see no reason why Christianity should not be advanced in the world in precisely the same ratio as Christian teachers follow the example of Christ:

and by Christian teachers I mean those who are
Christians at all; for every man is set to be a
preacher of Christ, apart from any laying on of
hands. Christ's mission, indeed, was not of consolation alone. It was of denunciation also. He
was a savor of death unto death, as well as of life
unto life. But salvation was the end, not destruction. Destruction was in full play already. He
came to seek and to save. Glad tidings of great
joy to all people, — Glory to God in the highest,
and on earth peace, good-will to men, — was the
birth-song of the Messiah. And it is to be observed that his severest wrath was visited, not
upon the people, however vile, but upon the leaders, the respectable Scribes and Pharisees, the
honorable men who dishonored the land; teachers
who perverted the right ways of the Lord; shepherds whose hungry sheep looked up and were not
fed; dogs in the manger, who would neither go
into the kingdom of heaven themselves nor suffer
others to go in. On them fell the weight of his
woes. For the people, blind, misled, ignorant, ful
of petty interest, petty ambitions, petty schemes
incapable of broad views, barren of high aspirations, treading the narrow circle of their narrow
lives with scarcely a look beyond, — for them
there was instruction, sympathy, encouragement;
a pointing to something higher, — to a future rest
for the weary, to many mansions for the homeless;
words that should lead them, but not too rapidly

T

or too suddenly, to the serene uplands that suburb the Heavenly City. " O earth, earth, earth, hear the word of the Lord." " Comfort ye, comfort ye my people, saith your God."

In all lives there is an under-current of sadness. In many lives there is more of shadow than of sun. The burden presses heavily. There are few homes in which disease and death have not made sad inroads. There are few hearts which do not bear the foot-prints of disappointment, — none which do not need the glad tidings of great joy, — the " Be of good cheer " with which Christ so often saluted the suffering believer when he was on earth. It is not that the Bible should be expurgated, — that milk and water should be substituted for meat, — but that the people should be comforted in sorrow and calmed in trouble, — that Christ should be shown, Saviour, Deliverer, Redeemer from sin and suffering, — that faint emotions should be recognized, feeble efforts encouraged, little leanings to good made the most of, knottiest points reserved for dexterous fingers, — that it should not be so continually dinged into men's ears that they are corrupt, as it should be whispered that Christ is holy. Is this preaching " smooth doctrine " ? Well, what of it ? Did not Christ come on purpose to make things smooth for us ? The world is surely rough enough. It bristles with thorns ; its brambles are continually rasping us. All along these four thousand years the way is tracked with

bloody feet. Let us have the smooth, sweet doctrines of the Gospel, oil of joy, and balm of consolation, grapes of Beulah, and honey of Canaan ;
for it is not the will of your Father which is in
heaven, that one of these little ones should perish.
Smooth doctrine! Is it not Christ's own doctrine?
And if it was not too smooth for the Jews, is it
too smooth for us? Is the American populace any
viler than the Hebrew populace ? Yet for one
word of rebuke to them the Master spoke a hundred of counsel and comfort. It was not " Shame
upon your pride ! " but " Blessed are the poor in
spirit ! " — not " Your cruelty is odious," but
" Blessed are the merciful ! " And who does not
know that people are a thousand times more likely
to be lured to virtue than shamed from vice ?

Now, of all times, let us learn what that mean-
eth, " I will have mercy, and not sacrifice." A
sound of battle is in the land, and there is sorrow
on the sea. The people may come up never so
bravely to the crisis, conscious of its magnitude,
and fired with sacred fury. But no enthusiasm of
victory, no heroism of sacrifice, can dazzle out the
agony. Aching hearts go up to the house of the
Lord on every Sabbath day, hearts wrung with the
pain of parting, heavy with fearful foreboding, —
anxious, sad, unrestful. It is not that they regret
their offering. They would not keep back their
precious things from the altar; but when the smoke
of sacrifice is gone up, and they sit silent in their

desolate homes, all the waves and the billows of sorrow rush over them.

O, if they could only see Jesus standing with outstretched arms! If they could only hear the Divine voice: " Let not your heart be troubled, neither let it be afraid." "My peace I give unto you." "I will not leave you comfortless." "In the world ye shall have tribulation, but be of good cheer ; I have overcome the world."

" Comfort ye, comfort ye my people, saith your God." Fathers and mothers, whose sons have gone to battle, whose sharpest pang at parting was lest it might be forever, who would have given up your beloved joyfully at your country's call had you but been assured that their eternal happiness was secure, — take comfort.

To the soul, time and space are not. The body knows them well, as foes to be killed, or friends to be enjoyed, advantages to be secured, or difficulties to be surmounted. But the soul cares for none of these things. With one bound she overleaps them all, and stands in the storied past, or the mystical future. She wanders, at her own sweet will, among the delights of Eden, or of the Millennium. The eye looks admiringly upon the soft gleam of the evening star in the glowing West, and anon the soul is there. The eye reads of the great white throne, and the soul bows before it. In all her motions she is impetuous. Thought, will, hope, despair, passion, require but a moment for the intensest action. A decision is instantaneous. A life-long purpose is formed while the pendulum swings once. Gratitude, love, and adoration may flood the heart at one throb, and fertilize it forever. The young hero who has just come back, pale and still, to the home he left "burning with high hope," went away from us in a moment. One moment the fatal bullet crashed in to the lair of life ; the next, the startled soul sped out into the great unknown. But before him to God went a prayer. From the already paling lips burst forth one sudden — who shall say unheard — cry, " My God ! "

" My God ! " What hope and love and trust, what awe and shock and terror have not those words embodied ! When calamity comes suddenly, and the soul is hurled from her routine, how quickly her earthliness and selfishness, even such as is innocent, fall off from her, and she turns, strong and straight, to her Maker ! In these eventful moments there needs no argument to prove, no inducement to persuade. Instinctively she recognizes her Author. True as the rivulet to the ocean, this life flows on toward the Infinite life. Repentance and love and faith unfeigned may be all compacted in a heart-beat. It has been quaintly said of a sailor to whom death came in a misstep among the shrouds :

> " Betwixt the mast-head and the ground
> God's mercy sought, is mercy found."

In her every-day life the soul is dainty and co-
quettish. She treads coyly. She advances with
retrogressions. Never so trivial a fear, or whim,
or fancy, shall suffice to keep her back from God ;
but in the awful presence of a great fact, or a haz-
ardous future, she rends away instantly all affecta-
tions, and lays hold on God with a strong, unrelaxing grapple ; and God, be sure, will not wrench
off the hand that clings to him. The soul that
flies to him in fear, and the soul that nestles to him
in love, shall alike find protection and consolation. It may be only at the close of a long life,
that the claims, or the attractiveness, or the
power of God is felt. Wrong, wrong! Yet, so
good is God, so long-suffering, so rich in mercy,
that even then he forgiveth iniquity, transgression,
and sin. Even at the eleventh hour his hand is
not shortened, nor his ear deaf; for his mercy en-
dureth forever. Let none despair for his loved
ones. The same love is around them now that has
been around them from the first moment that saw
them cradled in your arms. Commit your care
unto God, for he careth for you and for them.
Pray for them, be instant in season and out of season, and trust in God. Their hearts are tender
when they think of you, and God is very near a
heart that loves. The solemn exigencies of the
hour are messages from him. The danger that
impends and confronts is his agent for good ; and
as your boy walks his night-watch, or lies down

beneath the stars, or rises up for the inevitable conflict and the possible death, be sure the fatherly God, whom you worship, is not far off. Never to your ear may come his murmur of penitence and prayer. His soul may sigh itself out amid the smoke and thunder of battle. But Christ walks among the wounded and the dying, pouring in oil and wine, healing the broken in heart, and binding up their wounds. He hears their confession and petition or ever it be breathed, and long may be the bliss though short the shrift. Trust in God.

"My God!" it is the human heart bearing involuntary witness to the fatherliness of the Father. The brave boy, full of vigorous life, met death at the onset. The young heart that was so warm and true, that left behind, with thoughtful tenderness, its love and blessing, and last good-by, went not to an unknown God. How it had throbbed before, we do not know; but if, in that last, wild pulse, it claimed sonship and redemption, who shall say that, through Infinite love, it found not recognition?

And this God is our God for ever and ever. He will be our guide even unto death. We can never begin too early to love him. We do not know that *now* is ever too late.

The Old Testament has sometimes fallen into disrepute, because of the sternness and severity which it displays. The God of the Old Testa-

ment has been thought by some to be an aveng-
ing God, — strict to mark iniquity, — visiting
transgression and sin with his wrath and curse,
ordaining wars of extirpation, — revealing power
indeed, and inspiring awe, but not awakening
love, or exciting any of those warm emotions that
fill and flood the soul in that New Testament
wherein Christ records his behests.   It is true
that law is prominent in the Old, and Gospel in
the New Testament.   Sinai is not Calvary.   Yet,
scattered up and down those sacred pages are
countless and unfailing tokens of the loving-kindness of the Father.   The way is rocky and rough,
as needs must be, but fairest flowers spring all
along, and their fragrance pours on the air a perpetual sweetness.   From Genesis to Malachi, as
well as from Matthew to the final Revelation, witness after witness testifies that God is gracious and
long-suffering, slow to anger, and of great mercy.
The Father and the Son are one, and their name
is love.

We can see it in God's treatment of Elijah.
There seems to have been a time in the life of that
wise and pious prophet, when he was utterly dis-
couraged and dispirited.   He had shown himself
faithful and fearless.   He had dared to beard the
lion in his den.   He had dared to prophesy evil
to the atrocious Ahab.   Face to face, at peril
of his life, he hurled back Ahab's accusation, and
declared, "*I* have not troubled Israel, but thou

and thy father's house." He had dared, publicly, before the king and the people, to slay four hundred and fifty of the prophets of Baal. Then his courage failed him. The moment he found that Jezebel was on his track, he lost heart and hope. She was a woman whose ability was equalled only by her wickedness; and when a woman gives her mind to iniquity, she can generally do a great deal more in that line than a man. So, when he heard the oath that Jezebel had sworn against him, he immediately arose and went for his life; and reaching the wilderness, he sat down under a juniper-tree, and in bitterness of soul requested for himself that he might die. If God saw and spoke and acted like a man, Elijah would most likely have received a severe reprimand. "What is this?" an earthly Master would have said. "Why this sudden eclipse of faith? Whence this culpable and monstrous ingratitude? What ground have I ever given you for distrust? Have I not always protected you? Has a single hair of your head been harmed? When Israel was famishing and panting through the long years of drought, did I not feed you daily, pressing even the birds of the air into your service? Did I not restore a dead child to life at your prayer, and send down fire to consume your burnt-offering? Have I ever deserted you at a pinch? Have I not always honored you before the people? And now, through fear of one wicked woman, you are ready

14

to die! Die, then, since you are weak enough to desire it! Leave my service, if you have so little faith. I will choose a worthier man to be my servant."

God did not so. Our Father in heaven knew his fainting prophet's frame, and remembered that he was but dust. Elijah was, doubtless, over-weary from his headlong fright and flight. In the days of excitement that had preceded, probably his meals had been irregular, his sleep broken, and his health, in consequence, had become impaired. He had left his servant behind, and, unaccustomed himself to minister to his own personal wants, he doubtless experienced grave annoyance from that source. Uncertain of what lay before him, faint, perhaps, from lack of food, and weary with his rapid journey, the doors of his soul were wide open to the demons of despair, and Satan is always ready to enter in and take possession. His body acted on his soul, his soul reacted on his body, and altogether he was in a very melancholy way. But God knew all about it, and what did he do? Chide him and punish him, and so break the bruised reed? No; the first thing the angel did was to prepare him a nice warm supper, and make him eat. Blessed forerunner of those truly Christian ministers who make straight through the yearning stomachs of starving men a highway for the religion of Christ! And after Elijah had still fur-

ther been refreshed by sleep, the gentle touch of
the angel awoke him once more, and the heavenly
voice compassionately bade him eat because the
journey is too great. Not a syllable of chiding.
He was not yet strong enough to receive it. But
hiding in a cave among the mountains, the word
of the Lord came to him, " What doest thou here,
Elijah ? " Even then the reproach is more in the
accents than in the words. Lightning, and earthquake, and great, strong wind, were not hurled
against him, but the still, small voice melted into
his soul. More than this, his sympathizing Lord
gave him also Elisha for a disciple, companion, substitute, and successor, and comforted him with the
assurance that he was not the sole survivor of
God's worshippers, but that seven thousand were
left in Israel who had not bowed the knee to Baal.
We hear no more of Elijah's want of faith. God's
method with him was successful. When afterwards he was commanded to go down to Ahab,
he went straightway, and boldly charged him with
having wrought evil in the sight of the Lord.
Kings, or queens, or soldiers seem thenceforth to
have had no terrors for him ; and having fought a
good fight, the chariot of fire and the horses of
fire bore him to the heavenly city.

The story of Jonah is one at which people are
somewhat inclined to look askance. But, in judging of all narratives, you do not fasten upon one
incident to the exclusion of the rest. You look

upon the whole, and upon its bearings. Of all the books of the Old Testament, one we can least spare is Jonah. It is at once most human and most divine. It teaches, in the most gentle, delicate, and exquisite manner, a lesson which every one sorely needs, and it shows to us God, the God of the Old Testament, the God of Sinai, the God of justice, a God of fatherly tenderness, compassion, forbearance, — caring, loving, forgiving. We cannot give up Jonah for an improbability. We believe thousands of them every day. A generation that is credulous of Blitz, Anderson, and Houdin need not be incredulous of the Bible. If the skill of the created can give the lie to our senses, surely we need not try to shorten the hand of the Creator.

God chose Jonah to carry his message to Nineveh, — Jonah, an insubordinate, cowardly, narrow-minded, short-sighted, testy, hot-tempered, cruel, impulsive, insolent man, — not at all the person we should have suggested for such an embassy. But if Jonah had not been Jonah, where would our lesson be ?

God commanded Jonah to go to Nineveh. He straightway arose, and started for Tarshish. God told him to go one way, and he went another. When, however, shipwreck and ruin stared him in the face, a gleam of light shone out in his character. Frankness, courage, and something that looks like disinterested benevolence, appeared in his confession and direction: "I know that for my sake this great tempest is upon you. Take me up, and cast me forth into the sea; so shall the sea be calm unto you." When the generous-hearted sailors, after vainly striving to prevent so dreadful a fate, had reluctantly, and with many protests and prayers, sacrificed him, — one for many, — when the waters compassed him about, and he went down to the bottoms of the mountains, — his dormant faith awoke, and he remembered the Lord. With perverse ignorance, he had thought to escape from that Divine presence by going to Tarshish; but when the earth with her bars was about him forever, he looked again toward the holy temple, — and looked not in vain. God graciously accepted his repentance, and started him once more on his journey.

Up and down the streets of Nineveh walks the prophet, tolling the death-knell of the city. "Yet forty days, and Nineveh shall be overthrown." To that exceeding great city, full of silver and gold and pleasant furniture, full of gayety and wealth and fashion and splendor, that solemn voice must have come like the trump of the archangel. "Yet forty days, and Nineveh shall be overthrown." All the beauty and glory shall be swept away. For all the merchandise of gold, and silver, and precious stones, and pearls, and purple, and silk, and scarlet, — for the voice of harpers and musicians, and of pipers and trumpeters, for the voice of the bridegroom and of the bride, for the maiden behind her lattice, and the little children playing in the streets, — there shall be the abomination of desolation.   No wonder the stoutest heart quailed, and the boldest cheek blanched.

But things took a turn upon which Jonah had not calculated.   The people believed God.   A national fast was proclaimed, and most sacredly and solemnly kept.   From the king on the throne to the baby in the cradle, — yes, even to the horse in the stable, and the ox in his stall, — the nation clothed itself in sackcloth, and cried mightily unto God, and God heard their cry, and did not do the evil which he had threatened.

What was the effect upon Jonah ?   There came One after him, who wept over the approaching destruction of a great city.   " O Jerusalem, Jerusalem, thou that killest the prophets, and stonest them which are sent unto thee, how often would I have gathered thy children together, as a hen gathereth her chickens under her wings, and ye would not ! "   Nineveh had not stoned her prophet. She heeded his words, and humbled herself before his God.   Yet he took it as a personal grievance that she was not to be destroyed.   It was nothing to him that a whole population was not to be suddenly cut off from sweet life, — nothing to him that, where sin had abounded, grace should much more abound.   His own reputation loomed up before him larger than the life of a million souls.   His prophecy would not come true, and nothing was of any account compared with that. "Just as I said!" exclaims Jonah. "I knew God was gracious, and kind, and merciful, and would not do what he threatened. That was why I went to Tarshish. And now here I am, disgraced, and I might as well die as live." O bold, bad man! How dared he speak thus to the Most High God? How could he speak thus to the most loving Saviour? How wrest even infinite tenderness into bitter and insolent reproach? Why did not God smite him on the spot? But there is no thunderbolt, — only the gentle rebuke, "Doest thou well to be angry?" And Jonah, moody and sullen, takes up his station outside the city, to see if perhaps, after all, it may not be destroyed, and himself honored ; but even while sitting there, nursing his evil passions, the great God condescends to reason with him. A gourd springs up, sheltering him from the Southern sun, and his selfishness is exceeding glad. A blight destroys it, the sun beats upon his unprotected head once more, and he swings back again to the opposite extreme, and declares life not worth the living.

"Doest thou well to be angry for the gourd?" asks God, slow to anger.

"I do well to be angry, even unto death," is the fierce and passionate reply.

And then comes the application, — the lesson. "Thou hast had pity on the gourd, for the which thou hast not labored, neither madest it grow;

and should not I spare Nineveh, that great city,.
wherein are more than sixscore thousand persons
that cannot discern between their right hand and
their left hand, and also much cattle?"

Ah! Jonah, the lesson was not for you alone,
but for heady, reckless, selfish, obstinate human
nature everywhere.

If God were as strict to mark iniquity as man,
where should we appear? We often speak of His
justice, but God's justice is better than man's
mercy. Not a sparrow falleth to the ground without his notice. The little dimpled arms of the
Ninevite babies, stretching blindly out to him,
took hold of his strength, and held back the blow.
Nay, more than this, his loving kindness heard the
bleating of the sheep, and the low of the unconscious kine, and for

> "The young lambs bleating in the meadows,
>   The young birds chirping in the nest,
> The young fawns playing with the shadows,
>   The young flowers blooming toward the west,"

he repented him of the evil, and spared the city.

In old time, a test question was, "Are you willing to be damned for the glory of God?" One
rather inclines to ask some of our modern sons of
thunder, "Are you willing that men should be saved
for the glory of God?" It is difficult to believe
that all will eventually be redeemed to holiness
and happiness. So far as the Bible goes, if any
one thing is therein clearly taught, both directly

and by implication, it seems to be that there is a
limit to probation. But the more clearly this is
seen to be a fact, the more terrible does it become;
and when I hear the tone which is sometimes
adopted in speaking of, and with, those who hold
opposite opinions, I wish to ask, "Are you *willing*,
my Orthodox brother, that the world should be
saved? If, when you come to the gate of heav-
en, you should find the sacred portals flung wide
open to all, would you not feel a little disappointed? Would your heart give one great bound of
sudden and unlooked-for joy, or would your first
thought be, "Well, well! here is a pretty di-
lemma! Everybody pressing in, and what is to
become of my arguments and positions?" I suppose we are willing that men should go to heaven,
but we wish them to go our way. So far as one
may judge from appearances, if they will not go
our way, some will not feel much satisfaction at
seeing them there at all. We should be more
disconcerted at the sudden discomfiture of our
system, than we should be rejoiced at the accession of unlooked-for happiness. Jonah thought
himself extremely orthodox. Armed with a special
command, he felt quite secure in launching his denunciations right and left; and it did not in the
least agree with his idea of the way things ought
to be done, to have God strike in, and baffle all his
calculations.

Blessed be God that he does strike in. Jonahs

may fret and fume and pout and sulk, but he
will do of his own good pleasure. They cannot
hold him back from mercy, though that mercy dash
their theories to pieces. They cannot monopolize
truth, and force all purchasers to their stall. They
cannot barricade heaven, and refuse admittance
to all whose passports are not *viséd* at their office.
They may hew out turnpikes, and say to the Most
High, "This is the way, walk ye in it"; but He
that sitteth in the heavens is not confined by our
boundary-lines. His path is in the great waters.
His footsteps are not known. Are God's people
willing in the day of his power?

O that men would praise the Lord for his *goodness*, and speak and practise his loving-kindness!
As the mantle of Elijah fell upon Elisha, so may
the mantle of God's charity fall upon us, — making us more gentle, and considerate, and kind, and
thoughtful, and loving, — that we may win back
the wanderer, instead of driving him farther on
in the by-ways of sin, — console the downcast,
instead of adding to his despondency by harshness,
— and in all things follow Him whose feet are
beautiful upon the mountains, and whose messengers are anointed to preach good tidings unto the
meek, to bind up the broken-hearted, to comfort
all that mourn, to give unto them beauty for ashes,
the oil of joy for mourning, the garment of praise
for the spirit of heaviness.

XI.

THE LAW OF CHRIST.

E observed, not long since, a man endeavoring to drive a load of wood into a neighboring yard. The team consisted of a horse and a pair of oxen. The yard was up-hill, the load was heavy, the horse balky, and the man furious ; so, instead of " a long pull, a strong pull, and a pull altogether," they gave each a separate jerk in his own direction. The man passed from passion to profanity, the horse dashed right and left, the load grew palpably heavier, and the yard more and more up-hill. Meanwhile, the patient oxen were the chief sufferers. They pulled with all their might whenever they had a chance, but the wilful, selfish horse backed and twisted and pawed, and prevented their exertions ; and though all the drawing that was done was done by them, the long, fierce whip, in the hands of the enraged and indiscriminate driver, came down on the back of horse

and ox alike. It was a great pity. The task was
not intolerable. One strong, steady, continuous
effort would have accomplished it ; but the selfishness of one member of the firm, and the injudi-
ciousness of another, spoiled the whole. So the
man shouted, and the whip cracked, and there
was a great irritation, and the work was not done,
after all.

Then through the din and discord came softly
stealing the sweet words of Paul: " Bear ye one
another's burdens, and so fulfil the law of Christ."

" Bear ye one another's burdens." The way is
long, and a troop passes over it continually. There
is no point where we cannot find lamentation and
weeping and great mourning. There are weary
feet, feeble knees, bending shoulders, aching hearts.
There are broken hopes, disappointed ambition,
frustrated plans, mortified pride, wounded vanity,
slighted love, delayed success, detected guilt, misplaced confidence, shallow affection, loneliness,
poverty, shame, desolation, disease, death. All
these we can pass by with a sneer, with indifference, or contempt, or disgust, and so make the
burden heavier. It is in our power, if we will, or
if we are not careful to will otherwise, to give an
added bitterness to the cup that already overflows.
We can stand still, and keep back the helping
hand, the encouraging smile, the reassuring tone,
and thus make up-hill work for the struggling saint
or the returning sinner. We can go further, and,

by wanton neglect or a perverse rejection of our
own duties, add to those of our neighbor. The
burden which of right belongs to us, we can throw
upon our brother's shoulders, already overladen.

But on the other hand lies a glorious possibility. We can so walk that the road shall resound
with songs and thanksgiving. We can strengthen
the weak and confirm the feeble. We can offer
sympathy to the sorrowful, balm to the wounded,
comfort to the afflicted. We may draw back
shuddering from the sin, but we can hold out help
and hope to the sinner. If there is a palpable
germ of good, we can develop it, and if there is
not, we can dig for it. We can be on the watch
to discover whose burden bears heavily, and bend
our own necks to it. We can forbid the great
question of our life to be, " How shall I get on
best ? " and ask instead, " How can I best speed
others on the way ? "

How might this valley of the shadow of death
become the pleasant land of Beulah ! Our burdens would become light while we were striving
to lighten others. The chilled traveller saved his
own life in saving that of the perishing man, but
his fellow-traveller passed on, and was punished.
In the sorrows of others we forget our own. In
helping others we help ourselves. By keeping
our shoulders pertinaciously to our wheel, we shall
not any more than get out of the mire, while, if we
give a lift, here and there, when our brother is

stuck fast, we shall get to the end just as soon, and have a pleasant journey besides.

" The law of Christ." There are many points of doctrine hard to be understood. The Christian religion has mysteries which even the angels desire to look into, and which we cannot fathom. Through all our life we shall grope in the outer courts of many a truth, contenting ourselves perforce with the substance of things hoped for, the evidence of things not seen. But *this* law of Christ is one which we can fully know and promptly do. Simple, definite, explicit, he who runs may read, and he who runs the fastest may read the best. We need never be at a loss whether or not we are the children of God. We need not be over-anxious lest our calling and election be not sure. The test is always at hand. The law came from Sinai with thunderings and lightnings and earthquakes ; but the law comes from Christ in a still, small voice, and love is its fulfilment. Its precept is, " Whatsoever ye would that men should do to you, do ye even so to them." Judging ourselves by this rule, the best of us are none too good, and the most of us are intolerable — to our fellow-sinners ; — not intolerable to the long-suffering Father, not intolerable to the dear Redeemer, who knoweth our frame, who remembereth that we are dust, and so bears with us, and lets us live on, if perchance the earthly dust may one day " wear celestial glory."

Christian brethren, of whatever name, or sect, or nation, this is the seal of your apostleship. This is the essence of your creed. Do you fulfil the law of Christ by bearing one another's burdens?

When we look at what Christianity has done for the world, we thank God and take courage. When we look at what has not been done, at what remains to be done, we are ready to lose heart, and cry out, " Who is sufficient for these things?" When we see the nations that have been reclaimed from idolatry to the living God, the temples that have been reared to his worship, the houses that have been opened for the fatherless and widow, the diseased in body and mind, the afflicted and distressed of whatever name and nation, — when we see the kindly spirit of that tender religion that seeketh not its own, springing up around us in deeds of charity and love, — we can almost believe that our eyes have seen the salvation of the Lord But we turn the leaf, and another picture darkens before us. It is not that a great multitude do not go up to the house of the Lord, but that greater multitudes press down to the chambers of death. The charities well up sweetly still, but they well up in a desert, and the breath of the Simoon sweeps over them, and burning sand lies heaped around them, hot, arid, life-forbidding. The leaven is so little, and the lump so great, that faith can scarcely look forward to the time when the whole shall be leavened. It is eighteen hundred years since the song of peace on earth, goodwill to men, rang down from the skies of Judæa, and yet the tired earth finds no peace. For eighteen hundred years the religion of Christ, which, whether true or false, is conceded to be the best religion ever revealed by God, or devised by man, has been preached and prayed and sung and lived, and yet it has hardly begun to take hold of the life of the world. Not to mention the tribes of men who have never heard the name of Christ, nor the nations to whom the story of his birth and life and death seem but an idle tale, nor those who have adopted it but to wrest it to the destruction of judgment, reason, intellect, and manhood, we have but to look at our own country, state, town, church, heart, and we need not trouble ourselves about abstractions of total depravity, for we shall find on our hands more of the concrete article — total or otherwise — than we can readily manage. We are like a wide-reaching, thinly-settled country, over which a great army marches in victorious career. The old standards go down before it, and new ones are run up; but after the army is passed, there is not very much difference. A new banner streams on the air, but matters in general go on very much as they did before.

One of the points, and in truth the most common one, in which we come short of the glory of God, and of the duty which Christ enjoins, is a want of consideration for others. In a general way we doubtless desire to make other people happy, and to walk by the golden rule; but we make a rather bungling performance of it. The trouble lies in our application of the theory. The Bible says, " Thou shalt love thy neighbor as thyself"; we agree to it all, point out to our children the beautiful spirit of the Bible, and then go away, and do not love our neighbor as we do ourselves. We would not, perhaps, actually cheat him in a bargain, any more than we would cheat ourselves. We would not burn his house, any sooner than we would our own. We would make just as strenuous efforts to save his property if it were endangered. We do him a good turn when we can just as well as not, and even when it is positively inconvenient. But walking home from church with a vivid recollection of what you saw in the choir during the singing of the last hymn, you say, " What a bold, affected girl that Miss Smith is! The effect of her fine contralto voice is quite spoiled by her airs during singing." You would be very much displeased to have Mr. Smith say so about your daughter. " But," you answer, " if my daughter is affected, I expect people to say so, whether I like it or not. It might reach her ears, and cure her of her affectation. I would not go around decrying her to every one, but I consider it no harm to say to you what I think about her."

Perhaps not. There is scarcely more than a show of amiability, and not even a show of reason, in the dogma that one must never speak of a person unless one can say something good about him. It is quite right, and often edifying, to discuss people's faults and follies in the proper time and spirit, and with the proper persons. It resolves moral indistinctnesses, helps us to clearer views, shows us how such and such things appear to the eyes of our friends, and gives us thereby encouragement and warning to guide our own conduct; but in this very place there is great danger lest we do not leave a broad enough margin. We do not give elbow-room to modifying circumstances and to contrary possibilities. We take a view from our own stand-point, and pronounce judgment as if there were no other. Miss Smith, so far from being bold or affected, is in truth timid to a fault. It is positive torture to her to stand in that quartette-choir, confronting the congregation. It is only by the most earnest appeals that she has been induced to do it. The very boldness and affectation which you notice is only her native shyness, trying to hide itself, and overshooting the mark.

A mother, observing that the fruit-dish was prematurely empty, said to her little daughter, "Why, Lizzy, what has become of all the apples? Have you eaten them?" "No," answered Lizzy, "I have n't eaten one." Lizzy's mother had seen her eating more than one, and she was somewhat shocked at what she thought was Lizzy's false-hood ; but Lizzy persisted that she " had n't eaten one." After a great deal of questioning, it came out that Lizzy meant that there was one apple which she had not eaten, but her little stammer-ing tongue found a difficulty in conveying the idea.

"I don't believe Mrs. S. is very much of a lady," said one, of a new neighbor. " She was talking so loud this morning, that I heard her plainly as I went by the house, till I got clear up to the corner." After Mrs. S. had been in town awhile, it transpired that her mother, who lived with her, was very deaf, and the loud words were probably addressed to her.

A poor old woman who was never sensitive about her poverty, age, or ailments, used to cause much mirth in the minds of certain young people, because, though she pretended to be very lame from rheumatism, and seemed to walk with great difficulty when she first arose, yet, no sooner was she a few rods from the house, and partially out of sight, than she stepped off as sprightly as need be. The young people have now grown up into rheumatism themselves, and have ascertained from doleful experience that it was the nature of rheumatism, and not of " Aunt Harriet," which made her aged limbs stiff and unwieldy after long inaction, and gradually recover suppleness by ex-ercise.

You hear of a woman lecturing, or otherwise breaking through the ordinary routine of her sex, and you wrap the robes of your womanhood more closely around you, and congratulate yourself on your feminine delicacy, reserve, and modesty (that perhaps could not lecture if it tried), and deprecate female ambition, and discontent with one's allotted sphere, and neglect of appropriate duties,— while, if you could look into the lecturer's heart, you would see very likely no dream of fame, but of flannel petticoats for her little ones,* peace and rest of mind for an invalid husband, plenty for an aged and infirm mother, help for a struggling brother, salvation for a beloved sister.   You would see, perhaps, a delicacy and modesty as much greater than yours, as the intellect is stronger; battling with want and discouragement and adverse fate ; neglecting no duty, but forced by the pressure of many ; sighing for no broader arena than the household hearth, on which, alas ! the fire burns dim and low ; rising at last, weak indeed, but strong in the righteousness of its purpose ; conscious of being about to exile itself from the circle of sympathies in which it would delight to share, yet marching bravely to battle, though the most brilliant success must be defeat, — a martyr without the crown.   O women ! when a woman goes out from among you, be sure there is a cause.   Be sure that, whatever of

* See Mrs. Southworth's Autobiography.

vanity or weakness there may be in her character, her womanhood is stronger than it all. Be
sure she is drawn or driven by a power whose
might you do not see, and cannot measure. Be
sure there are lions in the way with which she
has grappled in a death-struggle, and by all the
gentleness and tenderness and love of your own
sheltered womanhood, by all your hope of future
good for the little ones who cluster about your
knee, and whose future paths you cannot trace
nor know what Fate may have in store for them,
deal gently, which is only justly, with these and
such as these.

> " The crowd, they only see the crown,
>   They only hear the hymn,
>   They mark not that the check is pale,
>   And that the eye is dim."

We go home from our shops and offices and
fields comfortable and tidy and well-to-do. On
our way we pass by our neighbor's house. The
fences are down, and the clapboards hanging, the
blinds broken, the panels loose, the paint worn
dingy, the door-step fallen in, the garden over-
grown with weeds, over-trampled by cows, over-
rooted by pigs ; and we condemn, in no measured
terms, the thriftless, shiftless, lazy owner, who
hangs around the tavern and the grocery, while
his health and house are going to ruin ; but we
do not see the thriftless, fretful, complaining wife,
whose whining voice, continued fault-finding, un-

washed floors, and ill-cooked food have undermined his strength, taken away all hope from his
heart and all spring from his life. Or, we pour
out the vials of our wrath upon her, knowing nothing of the invalid and half imbecile mother who
gave her child all the mind she had, and wore out
the remnant of her own weary life in a madhouse,
leaving her daughter to the untender mercies of
an ignorant, drunken father, without prop for her
weakness, or culture for any strength she might
possess. No, we know nothing of all this. We
can know nothing of it. All we see is the sin,
without the temptation ; the fault, without the
palliation ; the weakness, without the cause ; the
appearance, without the reality. We cannot tell
the difference between simple preoccupation and
haughtiness. A shrinking constitutional sensitiveness may look precisely like vanity. Bashfulness
masks itself under affectation. Misunderstanding
blunders into apparent untruthfulness. Shyness
protects itself behind the breastplate of pride.
Deep emotion blinds our eyes with the flash and
sparkle of levity. Life is a masquerade. Men
and women come and go in dominos, sometimes
of settled purpose, sometimes involuntarily, sometimes unconsciously.

Two inferences may be drawn ; one, that, since
we cannot know all the premises, we shall be
guiltless, even if we do arrive at wrong conclusions ; the other, that, since we do not know all

the premises, we should leave large margin for the unknown. Which of the two inferences we act upon will depend on whether our object is to justify ourselves or arrive at truth.

The persons towards whom we most need to exercise considerateness, are those with whom we come oftenest and most closely in contact; while the tendency is the other way. We are tolerably polite and considerate towards those whom we see only occasionally; and too apt to be thoughtless of the feelings, comfort, antecedents, and surroundings of those who sit by our own firesides.

There is a class of persons in our land, who, if common report be true, have appropriated to themselves an undue share of Adam's transgression. They not only fall into divers temptations unawares, but " have a strange alacrity in sinking." Like poor Edmund Sparkler, if there is any possibility of a mistake's being made, they are sure to make it. They do not, like the rest of the world, occasionally do a foolish thing, but they never " deviate into sense."

Editors of religious newspapers, city missionaries, evangelical preachers, and benevolent men generally, may be somewhat incredulous as to the existence of such a class ; but when I say that I refer to our Irish female servants, I am sure that American mistresses will rise *en masse*, and declare that, so far from exaggerating, the half has not been told. Cannot every housekeeper who reads

these words recall Bridgets and Ellens and Marys
by the dozen, whose moral memories were exceedingly treacherous on the score of collars and stock-
ings, who persisted in mopping the kitchen floor
with the dish-towel, or spicing the apple pies with
pepper, or plunging the knives into hot water?
Any lingering remains of scepticism may be dis-
sipated by observing with what fatal facility the
kitchen dynasties are overthrown, — the O'Fla-
hertys, the O'Mulligans, and the O'Bradys strut-
ting their little hour upon the stage, in brilliant
and rapid succession, and then seen no more.

The inefficiency of servants has been made the
topic of female conversation till it has become
proverbial, and no wonder. It is, perhaps, the
greatest evil with which the American housekeeper has to contend. Nerves, temper, health
itself, are worn out in the unceasing conflict with
blundering heads and awkward hands ; and after
Mrs. Jones has borne the burden and heat of the
day, she is surely entitled to whatever crumb of
comfort she can find in the fact that Mrs. Smith
is fighting, inch by inch, in the same good cause.
Mr. Jones may be somewhat tired of hearing the
changes rung on this one theme, but it is a safety-
valve which he will do well to think twice before
closing, either by petulance or ridicule.

To deny the existence or extent of the evil, is
useless. That there is a great wrong, or a great
many little wrongs, somewhere, is an obvious fact.

To charge home these wrongs to their authors would be, however, a difficult task. Many women consider themselves innocent martyrs to Irish incapacity, and would be shocked at the slightest insinuation of blame on their own part. Nevertheless, in many cases, the mistress is more at fault than the servant.

Under the old Jewish Theocracy, the rights of servants were recognized, their family membership acknowledged, and their comforts cared for. How much of this is true in our day? We complain that our servants render us mere eye-service, but do we deserve any other? Do we seek to establish any other relation than that of employer and employed? Do we remember that God hath made us of one blood, — that they are our brothers and sisters, influenced like ourselves by love and fear and hope, travelling with us to one judgment-seat, to be judged by one Lord, who was crucified alike for them and for us? Do we remember that by so much as we are superior to them in position, education, and character, by so much is their welfare in our care while our sphere intersects theirs, — that we are just as truly, if not just as far, responsible for them as for our children? We believe in the efficacy of prayer, yet many gather morning and evening in the pleasant parlor, and commend themselves, their wives, and their little ones to the care of the Heavenly Father, and pray for the prosperity of Zion and the coming of Christ's kingdom, while "the girl" plods on her wearisome way in the kitchen, beyond hearing, perhaps beyond thought. I know that the priests are said sometimes to forbid attendance on family worship; but let us at least ascertain that this is the case with our own particular servants, before we refuse or neglect to cast around them the shelter of our daily prayer.

Again, do we on the Sabbath day remember the commandment, Thou shalt do no work, thou, nor thy man-servant, nor thy maid-servant? Do we so arrange their duties that they can attend church at least half the day? We may believe that their faith is corrupt, but it is better than none. Not even a Romish priest so bars the doors of heaven that a humble, penitent soul cannot enter. Even if it were otherwise, we have no right to appropriate the time which God has given them for holy time. As far as in us lies, we should see that they keep the Sabbath holy, but at any rate we ought to be sure that they have a Sabbath to keep holy.

We complain of the gregarious habits of our servants. We dole out the weekly or semiweekly leave of absence, and wonder they can be so inconsiderate as to ask an occasional extra evening. We look suspiciously on their visitors, and sometimes go so far as to forbid them to receive their friends. It is true that they often do have a remarkable number of dead relatives, whose funeral rites they are called on to perform, and of burly "cousins" with filthy pipes and a rich brogue, — nor is it agreeable to have a "wake" in the kitchen every night. If our kitchen-girls were only cooking-machines, patented by " Wheeler and Wilson," wholesale restrictions would do very well. But as they are endowed with throbbing, yearning, hungry human hearts, the Gordian knot is not to be slashed in that way. Even people, with all the aid of books, music, games, family joys, and common interests, find an evening now and then hang heavily on their hands. How, then, can we condemn an ignorant girl, barren of mental resources, with small pleas-ure in the past, and small hope for the future, to a dreary, desolate solitude? " The pity of it, Iago, the pity of it." There is a golden mean between solitude and dissipation. A servant might give you the names and residences of half a dozen of her friends. If their character is good, let her receive their visits as often as their mistresses will allow them to come. She should understand, in this and in other matters, that you are acting for her interests as well as your own. This involves some trouble, to be sure, but it is in the end far less trouble to take the bull by the horns, than to be forever tossed on those horns.

If we wish our children to be happy at home, we try to make home attractive. Does the same principle obtain with servants ? Do we ever think of making a home at all for them ? Is a

room made pleasant for their reception ?   A few
yards of straw, matting, a few rolls of ninepenny
paper, a cotton table-cover, one or two engrav-
ings, a cheap vase, a whole looking-glass, a plain
rocking-chair, a pair of white curtains, do not
cost much, — the price of a fall bonnet will pay
for them all, — yet what a change would they
work in most "girls' rooms." When we complain
that our servants loiter over their work, dragging
through twelve hours what might as well be done
in six, we should do well to consider whether
we offer them any inducement to finish it earlier.
Have they anything pleasant to look forward to,
or must they simply sit down among the pots and
kettles over which they have been working all
day ? If they can read, do we take any pains to
provide them with books or papers suited to their
capacity, and thus incite them to despatch ? If
they cannot read, do we encourage them to learn,
or offer to teach them ? If their work is well
done, do we notice it, or do we confine our super-
intendence to reproving them when it is ill done ?

Before we accuse them of want of neatness,
have we furnished them with facilities for being
neat ? If we should recommend with voice and
water and towels and a temperate atmosphere
daily or weekly baths ; if we should notice or suggest a becoming arrangement of the hair, or the
improving effect of a collar ; if we should advise
in the choice of a dress ; in short, if we should

THE LAW OF CHRIST.

feel and show an interest in them as belonging to the same great family, I think we should be repaid a hundred fold.

The subject is one of greater importance than we are apt to suppose. The Irish form no inconsiderable part of our population, and a very large majority of the house-servants of New England belong to this soundly-abused class. They are in our families, mingling more or less with our children. They have a mighty, though indirect and silent power. If we do not influence them for good, they will surely influence us for evil. Surely they can be made a blessing both to us and to themselves. That they are here in such numbers, is a fact not without significance. They have an open-heartedness which is fascinating, — strong affections which are proof against neglect and abuse, — vivacity, versatility, sprightliness, wit, humor, and a certain eloquence, a graphic power of language, which goes down to the depth of our hearts, bringing up laughter and tears. They are capable of noble deeds, of heroic lives; but they come to us diamonds in the rough, with all their poverty, ignorance, and superstition clinging around them. Yet the Lord will surely require them at our hand, in the day when he shall make up his jewels.

Therefore should our lives be to them a constant gospel. Our superior education and refinement, and, more than all, our religion, should bring forth fruit in forbearance, benevolence, kindness, gentleness, and love.

Considerateness is indispensable, if the family wheels are to go smoothly. Without it there will be constant creaking. Yet a man will work all day, and come home and give all his money to his wife, and pride himself on her judgment in using it, and rejoice in her handsome dress and comfortable appointments, who will yet constantly annoy her by leaving a door open. A woman will devote herself to her husband with unwearied self-sacrifice in the way of consulting his tastes, keeping his clothes in order, tending him when he is sick, with a great deal more than the assiduity of a slave, and yet spoil everything, and throw him into a periodic fever, by having dinner ten or fifteen minutes late. It is on these little things that happiness hinges. Very few women run away from their husbands; very few men poison their wives, — few, that is, compared with those that do not, though a good many have been trying their hand at it in these latter days. It is the little foxes that get together and gnaw and gnaw till the beautiful vine that went up so bravely to meet the sun lies an unsightly wreck. Even one little fox can do a great deal of mischief, if he only keeps at it.

When a man and woman dwell in the same house, are called by the same name, and have the same interests, they seem to think that the laws of nature come to an end. Causes no longer produce effects, nor do effects flow from causes. Water will run up-hill, and chimneys will not smoke, though the flues be deranged, and corn will grow without being planted. They are no longer acquaintances and friends and human beings, with tastes that can be offended, and feelings that can be outraged, and sensitiveness that must be respected, and whims that are to be managed. They are a moral anomaly. They are lovers, and love is a self-made and self-perpetuating affair, with which they have nothing to do except to draw on it for every occasion. So, while the novelty lasts, and their oneness is something pretty to look at, and delightful to think of, and inexpressibly sweet in its freshness, they are thoughtful and polite ; but when that is well over, and the real wear and tear comes, and they need all the love they can possibly marshal to keep life from degenerating into " What shall we eat, what shall we drink, and wherewithal shall we be clothed ? " then they become careless about the small, sweet courtesies, let all the little pores through which love should filter be stopped up, and, passing through the valley of Baca, there are no wells.

It has sometimes seemed to me that, after all, there is not very much *love* between husbands and wives. I suppose that remark will be received with a howl of execration, and I hurry to compromise and conciliate by saying that undoubtedly there is a great deal, only it lies below the surface. I am quite sure, however, that if men and women showed to each other no more attention and tenderness and interest before marriage than some of them do after, they would not have been married at all. Before marriage, it would be coldness, and would result in separation ; afterwards, it is dormant love, and all right. Man is not, however, generally supposed to be a hibernating animal, and the ingenuous mind detects an inconsistency. As his hunger and thirst, his relish for books and business and society and honors and money, remain in active operation, it is difficult to see why his love should go into winter-quarters.

Women are less at fault in this matter than men. Their love does not generally become torpid so soon as that of men, and when it does, it is more easily awakened. This is attributable partly to nature, and partly to circumstance, as well as to some other things. Men are more selfish than women. The sphere in which they move has a tendency to make them so. The woman forgets herself in the little lives around her. She is occupied with the care of those who, but for her care, would die. She is in the midst of ignorant, innocent, unthinking little souls, who take no thought not only for the morrow, but for the to-day. They know nothing, and care nothing, about their own welfare ; and the mother's heart embraces them all, and lives in them all. The man is surrounded by men, strong, active, eager, keen, — all looking out for Number One. He must look out for Number One also, or Number One will not be looked out for. Other people have their hands full with their own interests. So he contracts a habit of making self prominent. It is true that wife and children are comprised in that self, but often in a latent way. If misfortune or disgrace meet him, the thought of wife and child makes it tenfold bitter; but ordinarily, as he occupies himself with his business from day to day, these home thoughts do not suggest themselves. He would probably be just as diligent in business, just as anxious to succeed, even if there were no home circle dependent on him.

Therefore, when he comes home at night, the day's habit comes with him. He will be likely to forget the changed atmosphere, and will go on looking out for the comfort, as he has been all day looking out for the interest, of Number One. If he remembers the change, he will remember it in the way of reflecting that he has been hard at work all day for his family, and now he wishes to be waited upon and to take his ease. He expects to be harried in his business, and lays out for it; but when he gets home, he desires peace and quiet, and to have everything suit him. He considers himself the Sir Oracle of the concern, and when he opes his mouth, he does not want any little dogs to bark in opposition.

This is the way he has a tendency to look at it, nor does it necessarily imply that he is totally depraved ; yet there is another side.

In point of real trial to temper, nerves, and patience, there is no comparison to be made between a woman's duties and a man's. As I sit, I hear the click of a shoemaker's hammer. From morning till night it seems never at rest. The shoemaker leads a laborious life, but how steadfast and calm! He drives the peg, and he knows it will go in. He made so many shoes yesterday, he will make so many to-day. At just such a time he will go home to dinner, with just such an amount of work accomplished. But his wife, busy in her kitchen, has a baby who is governed by no laws, and upsets all her calculations. If he sleeps through the morning, she will spring through her washing and ironing and boiling and baking ; but if he awakes, as he probably will at the most critical moment, everything has to give way. It is of no use to plan, for a chubby fist knocks down all her arrangements. Her baby is the most despotic of all tyrants ; he has not the slightest regard for public opinion. It is of no manner of importance to him whether the fire goes out, and the room is swept, or not. If he wishes to be rocked, he must be, regardless of consequences. Then very likely there are three or four more little ones who must be washed and dressed and fed, besides having dress and food prepared for them. If they

are all in the soundest health, they need constant
watchfulness; for children are unlike pegs. They
will not go where they belong. They are constantly making little lunges right and left, and getting
into mischief. Pluck them out of the sugar-firkin,
and they tumble straightway into the molasses-jug.
If there is a cistern on the premises, they will be
sure to plunge in sooner or later; and if there is
no cistern, it shall go hard but they will find
a tub of water, somewhere, large enough to sit
down in. Scissors and knives — everything that
has an edge to it — draw them as if they were
made of steel. A perverse prompting moves them
to pound everything that can be hurt by pounding,
and scratch and cut and tear according to the re-
spective sensibilities of the object. So it goes,
even when they are well; but when, besides this,
we think of the great army of measles, and scarlet-
fever, and chicken-pox, and mumps, and colic, and
cholera infantum, and inoculation, and teething,
that lie in wait for the young immortal and his
mother, the prospect is appalling; for the brunt
of it all comes on the mother. What is true of the
shoemaker and his wife is true of the blacksmith
and his wife, and the tailor and his wife. I know
that there are occupations which are more complex,
and demand the exercise of all the powers. But
the merchant and the lawyer, however absorbing
and perplexing may be their avocations, have to
do·with grown-up people. The merchant's clerks

are often quite as gentlemanlike and well educated
as himself.   His brother merchants are acute and
self-involved, but reasonable.   The lawyer's client
may be ignorant and stubborn, but he is an accountable being, and swayed by a homely, but
powerful logic ; but the wife is the mistress of servants inexperienced, even when well disposed, and
the mother of terrible infants.   Let a man try
to work with such tools, and such encumbrances,
and see how he succeeds.

It is true that a man's responsibilities are, in one
sense, greater.   If he makes a misstep, he brings
down with him partner, clerks, wife, and children,
sometimes shaking even church and society; while
the woman may let this, that, and the other duty
slip, and the sky does not fall.   But on the other
hand, it is the greatness of the matter at stake
which supports the man, and its littleness that
disheartens the woman.   She has the same round
— perpetually changing, yet perpetually the same
— of little cares and duties, which cannot be dispensed with, yet which never seem to amount to
anything.   It is all very well to cajole her with
" fashioning the young mind," and " training the
hand that is to guide the world," and " modelling
the greatness of the next age," but it is a long
way to the next age, and when the future statesman comes crying to his mother with Spalding's
Prepared Glue cleaving to his face and hair and
clean apron, and his fingers bleeding from the cuts

of the broken bottle, it is difficult to perceive that

> " The spirit that there lies sleeping now
> May rise like a giant, and make men bow,
> As to one heaven-chosen amongst his peers."

How, then, can a man who professes to be a Christian come home from his office, or shop, or field, to his nervous, hurried, anxious, care-worn wife, and harshly or coldly ask why dinner is n't ready, or what in the world she lets those children make such a noise for? Women are often exhorted to meet their husbands with a smile ; but what manner of value has a smile on the lips, if there be not a smile at the heart; and what manner of man is he who wishes his wife to crush back all her tears into her own bosom, and put on a mask for him? Is marriage to be a keeping up of appearances? Can love be retained only by a masquerade? Is a husband something that must be daintily fed, and gingerly managed, from whom the thorns must be hidden, and for whom the roses must blow, and, if they will not blow, wax flowers must be manufactured ? Surely not. At the basis of true marriage is truth. It is life, and not dilettanteism, that glows on the household hearth. If a man has manhood, he wants his wife just as she is, — whims, sorrows, vexations, and all. He does not want to be deceived by a papier-maché image, gotten up for the occasion. If things have gone smoothly, and she meets him with a smile, it is very charming. But if Johnny is threatened

with croup, and the baby is cross, and Bridget has
given notice of leaving next day, he is not selfish
enough to expect her to forget all this, or to wish
her to gloss it over and deceive him by pretending
to be happy when she is not. There are many
times when it will be better for him, and better for
her, that he should open his arms and let her have
" a good cry," and even if he is a little sentimental
and babyish, it will not cause any permanent harm.
This will soothe and calm her irritated nerves, and
they will talk it over, and so love will bridge the
chasm, and tunnel the mountain, and chain the
lions ; for the heart that loveth is not only willing,
but able. And the wifely tenderness will be made
so strong and grateful, that when the husband
comes home next day, in his turn irritated, de-
pressed, and savage, as "real good" husbands can
be, she will not heed his moodiness and surliness,
but will knead him, and mould him, and make him
over, so deftly that he will not know he has been
touched, till he finds himself sitting clothed and
in his right mind.

Waiting in a milliner's shop the other day, I noticed a nice little woman standing before one of
the counters, and a nice little baby, two or three
years old, perched upon it in front. The eager
mother was trying on, first one, and then another,
of the little pink and blue and white marvels of
hats, unable to decide which set off her darling's
blue eyes and fat cheeks best. It was a very pret-

ty sight. Her whole heart was in the work just
as much as General Scott's is in his, and the air
with which she would pick out the broad bows,
and give the hat a little pull and knock, and then
stand off to get the effect, bespoke an indescribable
self-satisfaction, or rather baby-satisfaction, — and
there, through all the pretty panorama of motherly
love of baby, and womanly love of bonnets, stood
her tall husband, looking as cross as could be.
Presently she held up one of the hats before him,
and said, half deprecatingly, " It 's three and a
half ! " And the moody fellow only answered,
" Get what you 're a mind to, *I* don't care ! " and
put his hands in his pockets, and sauntered to the
door.

If that man a year or two before his marriage
had been allowed to go into the same shop with
that woman, how different would have been his
demeanor ! How ignorantly interested he would
have been in every detail, how sweetly silly in his
suggestions, how slavishly acquiescent in hers !
" I don't care," indeed ! A refusal graciously
and Christianly given might have carried more
happiness than this surly permission.

A short time after, I happened to hear another
of the exemplary little wives with whom the
country is full say to her husband, " Charley, had
I better wear my rubbers ? " And the man had
the depravity to look up from his newspaper and
growl, " You know what the weather is, and you

know what kind of shoes you 've got. What is the use of asking me ? " But such a question before marriage would not have been referred back in that way. It is reasonable to conjecture that his reply would have expressed some fond, but entirely unnecessary alarm, supplemented by his own drawing on of the rubbers with a half playful, half tender remark about " the little feet," — if he did not descend into the lower depth of " footsey tootsey." I remember the dark eyes, the shining, abundant curls, the pure complexion, the graceful figure, the sprightly fancy, the vivacity and wit and kindness and generosity, — the countless charms and virtues of a brilliant and beautiful girl. She married a man of ability, education, wealth, and position. Shortly after her marriage, — only a little while, — a time that could scarcely be measured by years, — a gentleman who had known her in her glad maidenhood visited her ; and as he came out from the stately house, with all its luxurious appurtenances, he sighed gloomily, to himself :

> " They 've made her a grave too cold and damp
> For a soul so warm and true."

It is not poverty, or riches, or ease, or hardship, or health, or sickness, that makes women sad or glad.

It is neither desirable nor difficult to multiply examples. I only mention these because they are additional illustrations of the statement that men, a very large proportion of men, are much less careful to please their wives than they were to please their sweethearts ; and also because I have one more remark to make on the same subject. The remark is exclusively for men. No woman need read this article any further. If men are not guilty, what I shall say will do them no hurt. If they are guilty, I do not suppose it will do them much good ; but there are some things that will not rest till they are said.

The remark is this : Leaving out of view all question of religion, or chivalry, or decency, and looking from the lowest stand-point, it remains a fact that love, as well as honesty, is the best policy. If men were wise, they would see that the surest way to gain even their selfish ends is kindness. If a man's object is his own, and not his wife's happiness, the best way to get it is to do just what he would do if his wife's happiness were the object. In this case, as in many, perhaps in all others, utter selfishness and utter benevolence are at one in the means they employ. That is, the thing which will do the most good, on the whole, to others, will do the most good to one's self. A wife will keep her husband's house, and train his children, if he is indifferent, or thoughtless, or unkind ; she will perhaps love him too, for women have a way of worshipping the temple where their idol dwelt, long after the idol has fallen, face downward, on the threshold, — an

w

unfortunate habit, I cannot help thinking, for if a man feels that his wife will love him whether or no, he will naturally be less careful to make himself lovely. If he could be brought to understand that his wife's affection depends upon his behavior, and that, when he falls away from grace, she will fall away from love, he would take more pains to be agreeable. But, as I was saying, such love and service are not the love and service which love and consideration will bring out. Do not men know that to a woman love is a despot? For her love's sake there are no paths so crooked that she will not make them straight, — no places so rough that she will not make them plain, — no heights she will not level, no tides she will not stem, no perils she will not brave. In her love she is strong, wise, brave, patient, untiring, ingenious, — I had almost said, invincible. Nor are women, as a general thing, exacting. They do not demand constant or foolish petting. Only let a woman be sure that she is precious to her husband, — not useful, not valuable, not convenient simply, but lovely and beloved; let her be the recipient of his polite and hearty attentions; let her feel that her care and love are noticed and appreciated and returned; let her opinion be asked, her approval sought, and her judgment respected in matters of which she is cognizant; in short, let her only be loved, honored, and cherished, in fulfilment of the marriage vow, and she

will be to her husband and her children and to
society a well-spring of pleasure. She will bear
pain and toil and anxiety, for her husband's love
is to her a tower and a fortress. Shielded and
sheltered therein, adversity will have lost its sting.
She may suffer, but sympathy will dull the edge
of her sorrow. A house with love in it — and by
love I mean love expressed in words and looks and
deeds, for I have not one spark of faith in the love
that never crops out — is to a house without love
as a person to a machine. The one is life, the
other is mechanism. The unloved woman may
have bread just as light, a house just as tidy, as the
other, but the latter has a spring about her, a joy-
ousness, an aggressive and penetrating and pervad-
ing brightness, to which the former is a stranger.
The deep happiness at her heart shines out in her
face. She is a ray of sunlight in the house. She
gleams all over it. It is airy and gay and graceful
and warm and welcoming with her presence. She
is full of devices and plots and sweet surprises for
her husband and her family. She has never done
with the romance and poetry of life. She is herself a lyric poem, setting herself to all pure and
gracious melodies. Humble household ways and
duties have for her a golden significance. The
prize makes the calling high, and the end dignifies
the means. Her home is a paradise, not sinless,
nor painless, but still a paradise ; for " love is
heaven, and heaven is love."

Why will men not see the priceless jewel that can be their sure possessing? How can a man be willing to bind to himself a body of death, — to walk through the dreary years with a heavy-hearted, duty-bound, care-burdened, disappointed woman, to whom life has become a monotonous round of uninteresting necessities, when, by a time-ly thoughtfulness, a little attention, a little love lovingly expressed, he might secure the constant, healing, beautiful ministrations of

> " a spirit, ... bright
> With something of an angel light " ?

It is madness to let slip away a love so rich in blessing, so easily retained, so capable of bound-less broadening and deepening and strengthen-ing, — yet men continually do it. Reaching out after wealth, they grasp pebbles, and trample under their feet the " mountain of light." Look-ing for ease, they push aside the downy couch, and lay their cheeks upon a pillow set with thorns. Unutterably blind, they will not see the angel that folds its white wings by their fireside, and with in-sane presumption they brush roughly against their heavenly visitant, or with equally insane indiffer-ence turn coldly away from it, till the pure robes are defiled, the white wings droop, and the sad angel fades away forever. O the phantoms of dead joys that flit through unhaunted houses! O the hopes that lie buried under still lighted hearthstones! O the murdered possibilities strewn thick along the ways, over the lowlands and the uplands of life, — stark corses to which no Messiah shall ever say, "Arise!" Through all the land you shall scarcely find a house in which there is not one dead. There is no speech nor language; their voice is not heard; but the shore is sorrowful with the wreck of brave barques; the sea is dark with ships that started proudly, — every banner streaming from the mast-head, every sail spread to catch the smallest gale, — but that lie now dismantled and becalmed in the dead sea of Sargossa, or float listlessly down the unreckoning tide, or rush wildly over the rocks to swift destruction.

XII.

PRAYING.

PRAYING is one of those things about which it seems useless to argue. Nothing is easier than to make out a case against its necessity, or benefit, or reasonableness. Any one can say that, if God indeed arranged matters before the foundation of the world, he will not be turned aside by the wishes of people who very often do not know what it is that they wish, and who consequently make the most unreasonable requests; and any one can answer back, that in this original arrangement allowance might have been made for praying, — that our prayers may be as truly a part of the gearing of the universe as events, and that consequently, so far from being useless, they are essential. But this is not the strong point. It is enough to say, and to know, that God has commanded it. Though we should see no resulting good, we should submit to, and have faith in, a

" Thus saith the Lord." Furthermore, we all, whether we do or do not believe that prayer effects any outward results, do implicitly believe that its reflex influence is beneficial. We know that the state of mind and heart which sincere prayer produces, is favorable to love and hope and faith and humility and benevolence, and all virtue. It cannot be supposed that God would lure us to prayer by false pretences, — hold out answer to prayer as the main inducement to prayer, — while in fact the prayer has no bearing whatever on the object prayed for; that we should have it or not, just the same, whether we did or did not pray for it, and although we do derive benefit from it, it is an entirely different benefit from the one held out to us. The idea is monstrous. It is an insult to the purity and integrity of the Deity. How could He who forbids us to do evil that good may come, do it himself? Would it be consonant to his character to lead us to the performance of a duty by a falsehood, while the truth, if known, would make the duty absurd? If any one thing is plainly taught in the Bible, it is that prayer will be answered. Nor is the argument less strong, even if we reject the inspiration of the Bible. So long as we admit that prayer has a beneficent reflex influence, we are constrained to admit that human nature is so constructed that an act which is a continual and stupendous absurdity is a continual and stupendous

refiner, strengthener, purifier, — which is of itself
as great an absurdity, to say the least, as any faith
in answer to prayer. The Bible and our own
inner life harmonize in inculcating the duty of
prayer.

Secondly, there is a wide diversity of opinion as
to the things we should pray for. Many think
that spiritual good is the only legitimate object of
prayer. Others admit the actual, physical needs
of life, sustenance, and shelter, but are rather
shocked at the idea of asking for pleasures, or
going into particulars of any kind; but neither the
precepts nor example of the Bible, nor the nature
of God nor of prayer, justify this. God is as infinite in small matters as he is in great. It is a false
and assumed dignity which despises the little things.
of life. True dignity can be sportive without being frivolous. *We* think the sparrows in our fields
and the hairs in our heads to be very small matters, quite too insignificant to occupy the time and
attention of Him who made the heavens and the
earth; yet He numbers the one, and notices the
other, nor for that do the worlds wheel any the
less grandly down their appointed paths, nor is the
music of the spheres jarred by one clang of discord.
In a deeper and truer sense than the old Pagan
knew, God in a thousand ways declares, " I think
nothing human to be foreign to me." Therefore
let us come boldly unto the throne of grace, that
we may obtain mercy and find grace to help in

time of need, — whether the need be of the heart,
or head, or arm, or purse.

Yet I have observed that, when we pray for some
special temporal object, God often seems to answer
the prayer in the letter, but not in the spirit. For
instance, you pray that you may succeed in business and amass wealth, and you do; but your heart
becomes hardened thereby, and your business is a
millstone about your neck. You have set your
heart on your boy's getting through college with
the highest honors, and he does, but broken in
health, and fit only for an untimely grave. You
pray for strength and opportunity to accomplish
a certain journey, and they are given you, but
it turns out that the journey would better never
have been made. If God were man, we should
say we were overreached. He keeps his word in
the letter, but breaks it in the spirit. We wish to
make the journey, but it is for a certain purpose.
God gives us the journey which we ask for, but de-
feats the purpose which we assume that he knows.
But God is divinely upright, and there must be
something behind what we see. *I* infer that God,
seeing things as we do not see them, answers our
prayers sometimes by giving us not what we ask
for, but what is best for us, — which we all admit
is a complete fulfilment of the compact, — and
sometimes by giving us the very things we ask for,
to our own immediate disadvantage or discomfiture, in order to show us that we would better leave

16

these things to him. What is best for us in a temporal point of view, we do not know, and therefore I think he would rather have us lean on him, and trust in him, not setting our hearts on this, that, and the other thing; and though, in our weariness and heaviness and heart-soreness, he is not displeased that we cry out sorrowfully to him, " If it be possible, let this cup pass from me," yet he will fold us more tenderly in the arms of his loving-kindness if we meekly add, " Nevertheless, not as I will, but as thou wilt."

Praying is a duty, because God has commanded it. More than this, it is a privilege, because God has permitted it. Sometimes, by too long looking at the duty, we forget the privilege. It is better to do a right thing because we are forced to do it, than not to do it at all; but better still is it to do it because we like it. The law was our school-master, but in the Gospel

"Joy is duty, and love is law."

We have our stated seasons for prayer, and then we stop. Morning and evening we bow the knee before God, and the thing is done. We feel happy because our duty is performed, and it *is*, and the resultant happiness is natural and right. But prayer means a great deal more than this. There are no set hours during which the Lord holds court, and hears cases. His ear is always attentive. His hand is ever ready. His mercies are

not only new every morning and fresh every
evening, but noon and night overflow with them.
Hour calls unto hour to bear witness to the
goodness of the Lord in the land of the living;
and

> " Hourly as new mercies fall,
>   Let hourly thanks arise."

We need to cultivate a praying spirit. We
want the morning orison and the evening thanksgiving, but we want more. The communication
between heaven and earth should be always open.
Prayer should be a state as well as an act. It
should be natural, spontaneous, involuntary. It
should be

> " The Christian's vital breath,
>   The Christian's native air."

It is well to have a time specially appropriated to
prayer; but if that is all, the supply cannot answer
the demand. After your morning prayer, you
feel strengthened, refreshed, at peace with God
and man, — ready for life's work ; but it will not
last. Virtue cannot be bottled up and kept on
hand ready for future emergencies. The fibre lasts,
but the pungency disappears. By the time you
want to use it, it is good for nothing. Prayer in
the morning is good for just what it is worth, —
that is, it begins the day well; but it needs to be
continually renewed. You pray in the morning
for patience to meet all the trials of the day ; and
the little boy suggested to his father that he should

save time by saying grace over the pork-barrel.
One is about as sensible as the other, — both good
as far as they go, but God gives us grace by piece-
meal. He enjoins us to pray without ceasing.
We ought to be in so constant communication with
him, that whenever a slight trial comes, whether
of faith, or patience, or love, and whenever a little
blessing flutters its white wings softly over our
heads, we shall immediately, naturally, without
preamble, or circumlocution, or hesitation, or stoppage, lift up our hearts to God. Thus only can
we obtain all things which God prepares for us.
He has opened for us the fountain of the water
of life. If we draw only at intervals, even
though they be regular, we shall often walk
athirst. We should keep the little rills always
trickling thence into our hearts, that so there
shall be in us a well of water springing up into
everlasting life.

God might have made us differently, but he did
not. He might have made our bodies so that one
whiff of fresh air in the beginning should sustain us
through life, or we might have taken oxygen as
we do food, three times a day; and he might have
formed our hearts and minds so that a daily, or
weekly, or yearly recourse to him should be all-
sufficient for our wants ; but he chose to make us
so that we need to lean on his arm continually,
and it is because, when we go out into the fore-
front of the battle, where we most need it, we

thrust aside that sustaining arm, that we so often faint and fall. " After my prayers, my mind seems touched with humility and love; but the impression decays so soon ! " said one of the Church's holy ones. One should form the habit of prayer, that all good impressions may be permanent.

I see in sundry religious writings a kind of talk which is to me entirely incomprehensible. Good and pious men lament their coldness and want of interest in prayer,— their inability to commune with God. They say that they pray with their lips, and their hearts will not pray. They seek God and do not find him. They have no sense of his presence. They call themselves dead, and hard, and insensible, and their praying gives them no relief. These people, too, are sometimes the great ones of the earth, giants in intellect, saints of whom the world is not worthy ; and it may seem presumptuous in a humbler individual to sit in judgment upon them. Yet a healthy infant is as good a judge of some things as a dyspeptic philosopher, and I venture to say that this state of heart and mind is morbid. I do not believe that a healthy mind — one that has never been overlaid, or undermined, or interjected with cant — one that has been left to its own natural workings and the Spirit of God — one that has drawn its inspiration and instruction from the Bible, and not from the traditions of men — would ever fall into any such miserable condition. Just apply common sense to it, for prayer is a common-sense thing, just as much as eating and drinking. What is prayer? Request, thanksgiving, confession of sins, expression of repentance, and love and adoration of God. Is prayer anything else than this? But I see here no opportunity for coldness, or deadness. It would seem to be the very simplest thing in the world. You have done something wrong, and you wish you had not, and you determine to do so no more. Why not go to God and say so? You have had a pleasant day; everything has gone well. Why not thank God for it, just as naturally as you thank the friend who sends you the first pansy from his garden? You see the young Spring standing by the watercourses, and breathing over the meadows, and your soul is filled with admiration of God's greatness, and love of his goodness, and that is prayer. Where are the deadness, and hardness, and insensibility, and all those villanous frames of mind to come in? If one goes to God in a straightforward way, I cannot conceive what there is to make an ado about. God has emphatically and repeatedly declared that if we seek him he will be found of us, and I believe it. I believe it just as he said it, — without quirk or quibble. But if we go seeking frames of mind instead of him, we shall likely enough find neither what we seek nor what we do not. " I have not enjoyed communion with

God," says a man whose memoir has perhaps
been more extensively circulated than any other,
"or else there would not be such strangeness
in my heart towards the world to come." But
how can our hearts ever be anything but strange
towards the world to come? We have never
been there. We never saw any one that had
been there. We have no reason to suppose that
we have ever been in a world very much like
it. God has told us very little about it, and what
he has told us only makes it the more strange.
He has expressly tried to satisfy us for our slender
knowledge, by promising that what we know not
now, we shall know hereafter. Of all things in
the universe with which we might be expected
to be familiar, the next world is the last; and here
is a good man inferring that he cannot have had
communion with God, because his heart feels
strange towards this unseen and vaguely-described
world.

But why should the fact of our communion
with God depend upon any such inference, or
any inference at all? You know whether you
are talking with your friend or not. You do
not need any results to enlighten you as to the
fact. If he is over sea, you are uncertain, because
he may be beyond your reach. Even while you
are writing, he "may sleep full many a fathom
deep"; but the God we worship in very deed
dwells with men forever. He is not talking, or

pursuing, or in a journey, or peradventure sleep-
eth and must be awaked, before he can hear
us. He sees us while we are yet a great way
off, and has compassion upon us, and comes out
to meet us.

It is true that we do not always feel alike about
praying. Sometimes the heart overflows. We
see in some special way how God has crowned our
year with his goodness, and made our paths drop
fatness; or we catch a sudden glimpse of some
hidden sin, and are appalled; or we covet earnestly some good gift, and the tongue is loosened.
The heart burns with love, and the eyes grow dim
with happy tears. The soul must pour itself out
before God, and would fain dwell in his presence
forever. At other times we are not moved to
special emotion. We know that we love God,
and we are grateful in a general way, but we have
not a vivid sense of anything in particular. This
may be the result of sin, but not necessarily.
The fondest husband in the world is not always
meditating on his wife's perfections, nor admiring
her gentle grace. He is away from her a great
part of the day. He is not thinking of her all the
time when he is with her, and when he is thinking of her, he is not always thinking of her sweet
eyes and her dear face; but he loves her straight
through, and she knows it, and is content.

It is evident that, when this is the case, we cannot pray as we should when the case is different.

The mouth may speak abundantly out of the abundance of the heart ; but when, for any reason, it is weak, languid, or listless, the mouth should not multiply words. The idea that a prayer must be of any set length in order to be acceptable, is preposterous. Be not deceived. God is not mocked. Not the length, but the depth, of a prayer is the measure of its efficacy. Be sincere. Be in earnest. Be natural in your prayers as in your life. If one has nothing in particular to say, it is not necessary to wrap himself in generalities, for the sake of filling up the time. God wants no such lip-service. Not to such prayers are his eyes open and his ears attent. We may indeed continue all night in prayer to God, and his ear does not wax heavy. But if our burdened hearts can only send up the passionate cry, " Lord, have mercy on me a sinner ! " we shall go down to our house just as truly justified, nay, if we do but touch the hem of his garment, we shall be made whole.

I once read of a young negro's being overheard, at his private devotions, to count out his gratitude on this wise : " O Lord, me tank de for food and raiment, for victuals and clothing, but not for de shoe-buckles, for me bought dem wid me own money." Such a prayer would doubtless be heard, and such gratitude accepted by the Lord ; for the one was earnest, and the other sincere. Though the premises and the conclusion may have been wrong, the reasoning was correct. If the Lord really did not help him to the shoe-buckles, there certainly was no occasion for thanks in that direction ; and in this one respect his prayer furnishes an example for all. It was discriminating. It meant something, and he knew what. There was no vague, indefinite thanksgiving for equally vague and indefinite blessings ; no proper, well-ordered words, that meant everything in general and nothing in particular. The negro boy wished to have a distinct understanding on the subject. He was entirely willing to give unto God the things that were God's ; but he wished to have Cæsar's things rendered unto Cæsar quite as scrupulously, nor did his justice to himself in the least imply niggardliness towards God. We can adopt his wisdom without adopting his theology.

We render gratitude to God for his mercies, which are " new every morning, and fresh every evening." When we enter upon the duty of thanksgiving, we thank him in a general way for many things. If pressed to make out a list of what it is for which we are thankful, we might answer glibly, " health and plenty, peace and prosperity." But do we know what these are ? Do we know what national disease and famine and war and adversity are ? If we really are grateful to God for health, shall we turn away from his temples, and immediately proceed to destroy it by over-work, over-play, over-eating, or over-anxiety? If we indeed thank him for plenty, shall we shut our hearts to the cry of the poor and needy, which comes to us from near and far, the cry of those who lack bread for the body or the soul? Shall we show how highly we value peace, by sitting at ease around our comfortable fires, while the right struggles without in the grasp of strong and vigilant foes? Shall we set up prosperity to be our god, sacrificing to it our noblest principles, our sacred honor? Shall we not rather invest our talents? Shall we not prove our worthiness to receive a blessing by the use we make, and the care we take, of those already given. It is the good and faithful servant, who has been faithful over few things, that shall be made ruler over many things.

In our enumeration of our special blessings, the gleam of shoe-buckles is very apt to discover itself. Our plenty and peace and prosperity are the result of our own industry and prudence and wisdom. It is our own hand that has gotten us the victory. We attribute some remote first cause to the Lord, but we take the lion's share of the credit to ourselves. We look abroad upon our vast possessions, the mighty fabric of empire which has sprung up in a night, and exultantly say, — "Is not this great Babylon, that *I* have built, by the might of *my* power, and for the honor of *my* majesty?" But whence came the skill that planned, and the arm that wrought? Who set the rock in its place? Who formed the mountains, and hollowed out the sea? Who sunk the iron in its bed, and planted the forests where they grow? Who pierced the coasts, and poured the rivers from his hand? Nay, who keeps the air in perpetual equipoise, — just so much of this ingredient, just so much of that? A little less density, a little less heat, a little less moisture, and all life would be suddenly extinct.

The shoe-buckles may have been bought with our own money, but the coin has the Divine image and superscription; therefore it should be rendered unto God as one of the things that are his.

In praying for blessings, our innermost sincerity should be tested. We pray for greater light; do we make the most of the light we already have? We pray for opportunities to do good; do we improve the opportunities that constantly present themselves? We pray for our daily bread; are we doing our utmost to earn it? We pray for peace; do we follow the things that make for peace? We pray that Christ's kingdom may come; are we straining every nerve to bring it? What folly — to call it by no harsher name — is it to implore God to add still further to a blessing of which we already possess more than we use! To ask him to help us while we are

not doing all we can to help ourselves! To ask
him to allay discords which we are careless in
fomenting! To ask him to purify our hearts, and
then let evil spirits come in and riot there! In
short, to ask him to do the work which belongs
to ourselves, or to give gifts of which we have
already shown ourselves unappreciative and unworthy!

No! Let us not on the one side weary the Lord
with our words; and let us not on the other side
dishonor him with slavish fear. He is the Lord
God strong and mighty; he is also the Lord
God merciful and gracious. He is a jealous
God; but he is our dearest friend. Eye hath
not seen, nor ear heard, neither hath it entered
into the heart of man, such love as that wherewith
God loves us; and he behaves towards us as if
he loved us. He not only once sent his Son to
die for the world because he loved it, but he continually watches over it for the same reason. He
wants men to pray to him because he loves them.
He does not drag them by violence into his presence, thrust them down upon their knees, command them to pray, to feel, to adore, to have such
and such emotions on peril of his wrath. He opens
his arms to them. "Come, my children, you are
weak and weary. The way before you is long.
Come, rest with me awhile, and get strength.
Come for a little peace and patience and joy.
I have enough of everything you need. I can

give you all you want. 'Come unto me, all ye
that labor and are heavy-laden, and I will give
you rest.'" And suppose we do come after a
hard day's work, exhausted, void of emotion, almost of desire, will God be angry if we only
whisper a good-night prayer? Is a mother angry with her baby who falls asleep in her arms
in the middle of her lullaby? And does not
God who made us know our frame, and remember that we are dust? And if he is not strict
to mark our iniquities, will he be strict to mark
our weaknesses? Oh! let us be simple and sincere. Prayer should not be made a complicated,
uncertain, difficult, and elaborate thing. It is too
precious, too delightful, too heart-healing, to be
turned into a bugbear.

Old or young, happy or wretched, strong or
weak, draw nigh unto God, and he will draw nigh
unto you. Never mind good people's diaries.
Come boldly unto the throne of grace, and find
grace to help. Hear his loving-kindness: "Fear
thou not, for I am with thee; be not dismayed,
for I am thy God: I will strengthen thee; yea, I
will help thee. And the Lord thy God will hold
thy right hand, saying unto thee, Fear not; I will
help thee. When the poor and needy seek water,
and there is none, and their tongue faileth for
thirst, I the Lord will hear them, I the God of
Israel will not forsake them."

XIII.

FORGIVENESS.

CHARLES SUMNER, a man who makes the name of Senator illustrious; who has been truer to the Republic than she has been to herself, inasmuch as, while she has sometimes faltered in the way, suffering herself to be overborne by wicked counsels to her own misdoing, he has known no wavering in his allegiance, but has always been "true to truth and brave for truth"; who, free from the vulgar ambition of place, is fired with the noble ambition of power, but of power based only on what is excellent in himself, and bearing only on what is excellent in others; who has approved the majesty of right as well as the calm steadfastness of genius, by returning, after years of enforced absence, to the battle-ground, and taking up the sword on the same spot where rage and cowardice and wounded iniquity had wrested it from his grasp; who, deserving well of the Republic for services faithfully rendered, and sufferings heroically borne, deserves not less for this, that he has brought down into the arena of politics the culture of the scholar, the courtesy of the gentleman, and the catholicity of the Christian, demonstrating thereby that a nation's work needs not to be done with unwashen hands, but that the most devoted patriotism may consist with the widest learning, the truest refinement, and the purest morality, — Charles Sumner, referring, in a recent speech before a popular assembly, to the aggressions of the slave power upon the rights of man, said : " Forgiving those who trespass against us, I know not if we should forgive those who trespass against others. Forgiving those who trespass against us, I know not if we should forgive those who trespass against the Republic. Forgiving those who trespass against us, I know not if we should forgive those who trespass against God."

The duty of forgiveness is inculcated in the Bible with no more distinctness than is the fact asserted that certain conditions must precede it. This part we are very apt to forget in theory, and though it will hardly be conceded that men in general are too ready to forgive injuries, and therefore need to have the conditions clearly defined, yet all theoretical flaws produce more or less mischief in practice. The particular harm occasioned by this oversight is, that a certain indiscriminate and wholesale forgiveness is enjoined, against which

healthy minds revolt ; the result is that they, with
equal indiscrimination, reject the whole. Consequently, to many, forgiveness is synonymous with
meanness and cowardice. It is attributed either
to a want of spirit enough to feel an insult, or of
courage enough to resent it ; undoubtedly, a good
deal of what passes for forgiveness and amiability
is only this ; but this is not forgiveness any more
than the hide of the rhinoceros, or the horns of the
deer, are forgiveness ; and by as much as forgiveness is a noble, manly, and Christian virtue, by
so much should its character be understood and
rescued from the imputation of being milk and
water.

When the sun goes down behind the hills to-
night, the listening ears of angels, and the always
open ear of Christ, will hear thousands and thousands of sweet child-voices lisping, " Forgive us
our trespasses, as we forgive those who trespass
against us," and as the little night-gowned babies
kneel by mothers' knees, and rest in mothers'
arms, and smile in happy sleep, it will seem as if
no being ever could be so cruel as to trespass
against their innocence, and that even the pure
eye of the Son of God, looking into those little
hearts, will scarcely find any trespass there ; but
when the white-robed cherubs get up in the morning, the angelhood ebbs, and humanity sets in
strong. They are no longer a choir of shining
ones, but a troop of Johnnys and Susys and

Franks, who do not like to be washed, and see no beauty in smooth hair, and have a special aversion to old frocks when new ones are hanging in the closet, and a special knack at setting each other by the ears whenever opportunity does or does not offer.   Consequently, the differences that arise are numberless, and armed interference on the part of parents becomes a continually recurring necessity. Here the matter begins.   In the nursery the battles of life are fought, the perplexities of life are encountered, the drama of life is enacted.   Here the great moral principles that should guide and harmonize life are brought into play and strengthened for future use, or (alas! too often) stretched and strained and ruined.   Here the theory of forgiveness in all its ramifications needs to be thoroughly understood and correctly applied, or incalculable confusion will arise in a thousand forming minds.   Mary will not pull Willie's hair if her mother bids her not, though it seems to her that it would be no more than strict poetic justice in return for his pulling hers; nor will the verse that she is made to repeat about rendering evil for evil, make all the crooked places straight before her.   Harry cannot see why grown-up men put into jail those who rob them of their property, while he is expected to forgive and forget Bob's running away with his ball.   Nor do we, his father and mother, see quite clearly through the whole subject ourselves.   An injury has been done or attempted against us. We feel that we must forgive, because it is right and Scriptural and Christian to do so; yet we cannot feel towards the offender just as we did before, because it is not natural or possible to feel so; and we compromise between *ought* and *is*, and say, " We will forgive, but we never can forget."

But look into this matter a little. We want no compromise with wrong or right. If anything is right, do it wholly, — if wrong, do it not at all. At all events let us know where we are. If it is not possible to forgive and forget, it is not our duty to do it; for God never did and never will require us to do what it is not possible for us to do. Ability is the limit of duty. If it is our duty to do it, we can do it, and we must do it, and — we will do it!

The New Testament draws a parallel between man's forgiveness of his brother, and God's forgiveness of man. If ye forgive not men their trespasses, neither will your Father forgive your trespasses. Even as Christ forgave you, so also do ye. There must, therefore, be a similarity between the two acts. How, then, does God forgive us? The Bible furnishes plenty of answers.

" If my people, which are called by my name, shall humble themselves, and pray, and seek my face, and turn from their wicked ways : then will I hear from heaven, and will forgive their sin, and will heal their land."

" It may be that the house of Judah will hear all the evil which I purpose to do unto them ; that they may return every man from his evil way; that I may forgive their iniquity and their sin."

" Take heed to yourselves. If thy brother trespass against thee, rebuke him ; and if he repent, forgive him. And if he trespass against thee seven times in a day, and seven times a day turn again to thee, saying, I repent ; thou shalt forgive him."

This is the point : repentance must precede forgiveness. God does not forgive wicked men till they humble themselves, and seek his face, and turn from their wicked ways ; and we may be sure he does not require us to do differently, for his ways are equal. He does not even leave us to infer this. He says directly, " If thy brother trespass " — what? "*Rebuke him.*" And then adds: "*If* he repent, forgive him." This is unnecessary, if we are to forgive him whether he repent or not. If a man wilfully or wantonly injure us, by word or deed, in mind, body, or estate, we are in no wise bound to treat him, or to feel towards him, as we should if he had not injured us. We are not only not bound to do so, but we are bound not to do so. It is, generally, not possible, and if it were possible, it is not desirable. We shame the dignity of right, when we allow right to be sinned against with impunity. We encourage evil-doing when we receive the evil-doer with open arms. We set a premium on slander when we welcome the slanderer to our hearths and hearts. Until he repents and brings forth fruits of confession and retraction, meet for repentance, we ought to stand aloof from him, — holding ourselves too high and pure for a friendship with anything unclean. Is not this the doctrine of the Bible?

Here comes in a danger on the other side. We are to stand aloof, but for the right's sake, not for the sake of malice, or revenge, or pride. We may feel and say, " I am better than thou," but not in a Pharisaical spirit. We see that the act is mean, and we despise it, and we cannot help rejoicing, and it is right that we should rejoice, in the consciousness that we are above doing it ; yet he who is versed in the lore of human hearts will hardly indulge greatly in such self-gratulation. He knows how often freedom from special sin may be owing to freedom from special temptation, and his feeling will be less of exultation than of active gratitude to God, who has kept him from the horrible pit and miry clay. Though we cannot look upon the sin but with abhorrence, nor receive the sinner without protest, we should be scrupulously careful not to let the injury rankle and fester in our souls. A wound is terribly hard to heal when the proud flesh gets into it. We cannot look upon our offending brother with the love of complacency, but we can and ought to cherish the love of benevolence. We can pity him, for sin and crime are the worst calamities that can befall a man. We can pray for him, that his eyes may be opened, — not simply to see his sin against us, but to see his sin. We can watch for opportunities to do him good, if so be he may be shamed into repentance; and when the opportunity comes, we can improve it. Here, again, we have God for an example. This is the attitude in which the Bible represents him, — " a God ready to pardon, gracious and merciful," "good and ready to forgive, and plenteous in mercy unto all them that call upon him." Everywhere He stands waiting, longing to forgive, watching the first symptoms of repentance, seeing the returning sinner when he is yet a great way off, going out to meet him, and not only receiving him as a son, but feasting him as an honored guest, and dearly beloved. Is this our attitude? This is what it should be. For the right's sake we should be unswerving, but for the sinner's sake, for our own soul's sake, for Christ's sake, we should not be punctilious. When repentance comes, we should forgive freely, fully, entirely, — like God, who abundantly pardons. Let us have no half-way measures, for so shall we be verily guilty concerning our brother. The word " forget " need give no trouble. We are to forget as God forgets when he says, " I will forgive their iniquity, and I will remember their sin no more." It is not an absolute, intellectual for-

getfulness, for that is not a part of his nature.
Nor can it mean so to us, for we are made in the
image of God. Even if absolute intellectual forgiveness is ever possible to us, it does not come
within the scope of our will. We cannot forget because we are willing to forget, nor because
we wish to forget. The very effort would only
fix the fact more firmly in our minds and memories. Alas! alas! how many know this too sadly
well! How gladly, if we could, would we erase
the little memories from our hearts! How happy,
if, "in the silent hour of inward thought," no
remembered sin, long long ago committed and
repented of, no folly, no weakness, no shame, no
pain, should rise from a long-forgotten grave
to haunt, perhaps to reproach! But memory is
the avenger of conscience, and no repentance can
stay her hand. Not even the abounding love of
Christ can wrest the sting from this worse than
death, — the victory from these relentless graves.
Christ may be glorified thereby, and we rejoice in
that; but we must be forever abased. Man and
God may forgive, but the soul is its own sternest
janitor, and cannot forget.

The forgetfulness wherewith God forgets the
sins of his repentant children is of the heart, not
of the head. It is such forgetfulness as the mother
bestows upon the little one who weeps out his
sorrow on her bosom. Remembering the act, she
remembers it without a vestige of anger or dis

pleasure. She remembers it only to help more generously and to love more deeply. So should we forgive and forget the trespasses of those who trespass against us.

Looking at it in this light, forgiveness is no passive, negative stolidity, the despicable birthright of ignoble souls, but an active, positive, and most Godlike duty, demanding for its accomplishment the exercise of man's noblest qualities, — those that separate him from the beast, and make him but little lower than the angels, — nay, rather, that place him higher than the angels, — allying man to Him who is above all principality, and power, and might, and dominion, and every name that is named, not only in this world, but in that which is to come.

Looking at it thus, the bravest boy may not fear lest his reputation suffer by its exercise. So far from indicating a mean spirit, it presupposes a spirit not only manly, but, since it is in the image of God, divine. A mean spirit may feel an insult, a grovelling spirit may resent it, but only a lofty spirit can forgive.

Looking at it in this light, we shall not find it hard to conduct ourselves justly, as well as Christianly, towards those who have trespassed against others, or against the Republic, or against God. Rightly esteeming the blow struck at the least of Christ's little ones to be a blow struck at ourselves, — rightly feeling those injuries most sensi-

bly which do not affect our own persons, — rightly
shuddering through every nerve when the Republic is endangered by treacherous friends, and the
hurt of the Church is slightly healed, — we will
not be implacable when God forgives. When
those men, North or South, who have sinned
against human rights; who have sought to place
chains upon the necks of freemen, or who have
not sought to remove the chains from the necks
of the enslaved; who, in the pursuit of their un-
righteous ends, have desolated homes, destroyed
life, and publicly perverted justice; who have
trampled upon the Constitution that would not
be wrested to their evil purposes; who have
counted the blood that was shed for freedom of
.little worth; who have sinned most deeply in this,
that they have sought to poison the fountains of
virtue; who have wrought ill to the Republic
most in this, that they have not assaulted her
from without, but have laid hold of her strength
within, — pouring into her veins the turbid flow
of vile self-seeking, instead of the vigorous pulse
of universal right, hastening her on thereby to
premature senility and decay; who have even
gone into the sanctuary, and laid unholy hands
upon the ark of the covenant, making the word
of God of none effect by their traditions; who
have uncovered the nakedness of the land that
gave them birth, causing her name to become a
by-word, a reproach, and a hissing among the

nations ; — when even these shall bethink themselves, and repent, and make supplication unto the Lord, saying, " We have sinned, and have done perversely, we have committed wickedness " ; and so return unto the Lord with all their heart, and with all their soul, then will we too, remembering the plague of our own hearts, join our voices with theirs to the Lord God of Israel, crying, " Hear thou their prayer and their supplication in heaven thy dwelling-place, and maintain their cause, and forgive thy people that have sinned against thee, and all their transgressions wherein they have transgressed against thee ; for they be thy people."

Thus, in all times of our adversity and in all times of our prosperity, in the hour of death and in the day of judgment, shall we be able to say without rebuke, " Forgive us our trespasses, as we forgive those who trespass against us."

XIV.

ERROR.

IT is no matter what a man believes, provided he is sincere in his belief, — is a somewhat common affirmation. It comes chiefly from those who seem to think that liberality consists in having no boundary lines, that there is no such thing as religious truth, and that, though convictions must be tolerated among the masses on account of the shallowness of their minds, and the narrowness of their views, yet the true condition of the highest humanity is a vast and barren negation; or it comes from those who are too indifferent or indolent to search among the foundations of faith, and, either too blind to recognize, or too disingenuous to confess such indifference and indolence, endeavor to satisfy and excuse themselves by believing that the object is insignificant and the pursuit unworthy; or from men of warm hearts, and acute, but not large observation, who see in every sect benevo-

lent, virtuous, and Christian individuals, and who
can in no other way reconcile discrepancies of
faith and uniformity of practice.

" No matter what a man believes, if he is only
sincere ! " rejoin those whose business and pleasure it is to contend earnestly for the faith once
delivered to the saints. " But if a man is awakened at night by the cry that his house is on fire,
and refuses to rise and flee because he believes the
alarm to be false, will his belief save him from the
flames ?   Will he not just as surely perish as if he
did not so believe ?   A man eats poison thinking
it to be food, but shall he not surely die ?   His
belief is sincere, but it does not save him from
death."

And this is called refutation.   The error is supposed to be disproved, — shown to be absurd.

This is not refutation, — not a sound, thorough,
logical, satisfactory refutation.   The cases are not
parallel.   If the cases are parallel, and it is a
refutation, the matter stands thus : As the death
of the body inevitably results from a wrong belief
in the one case, so the death of the soul inevitably
results from a wrong belief in the other case.
It follows that every Universalist and Unitarian
and Roman Catholic will be forever lost ; for they
believe to be false certain statements which we
hold to be fundamental truths.   It follows also,
that every pagan, every idiot, every baby, from
simple lack of belief in the Gospel, whether he

has ever heard of the Gospel or not, whether he has ability to understand its conditions and meet its requirements or not, will be lost, — as the unconscious invalid or the sleeping child would be lost in the burning house. In fact, the illustration is of the most superficial kind. On the face of it, for a moment, it may appear to be accurate, but it does not stand the test of the slightest examination. It leaves the real difficulty untouched, and it assumes what is not true, and so creates a new difficulty, and is an obscuration rather than an illustration. It assumes that moral law is like physical law. Doubtless, in the eyes of God, moral law is just as exactly defined, its causes and effects are just as accurately determined, its logical connections are just as rigorously established, as are those of material law; but not to our eyes. We are not wise overmuch in material law. We know cause and effect to but a limited extent. A thousand modifications come in between our data and our conclusions, and greatly affect the result. But moral law, so far as it falls within our scope, does not pretend to anything like the accuracy of material law. Motives, inducements, temptations, education, — a thousand circumstances of which one mind only is cognizant, — are to be taken into the account. In material law result is everything; motive nothing. A man may burn his house or poison his friend from carelessness or mistaken love, but the house burns and the friend dies as surely as if malice had directed the deed. In the moral world, the result is of less account than the motive, or rather the direct and apparent result is not the real and final result. The actor, not the act, is the important point. God did not forbid Adam to eat the apple because he wished to save the apple, but because he wished to try Adam. Jordan had no medicinal virtue above Abana and Pharpar.

The reason of this is evident. If moral law were rigidly defined, if the details of our faith and practice were verbally laid down, if God had made us so that we could guide our lives with mathematical accuracy, we should have been little better than machines. There would have been no margin for individual endeavor, no elbow-room for love. It seems as if the Bible was made with set purpose to give full sway to our faith and forbearance, our zeal and trust and candor. God could have revealed every article of belief to us with such clearness, that we could no more doubt than we doubt that two and two make four, — that fire and strychnine are fatal to life. It would have been just as easy for him to reveal everything beyond question, as to reveal it as he has. His revelation is such that scores of sects have sprung up, each taking the Bible as its basis, and each understanding it differently. One thinks baptism by immersion is the only real baptism, and one thinks sprinkling is equally Scriptural. One sees universal salvation taught there, and one the final sorrow of the impenitent. One finds God in Christ, and one finds him only in the Father. No one of these sects can be pronounced to be without real and earnest Christians in its bosom. And did not God purposely leave his golden truths somewhat underground, that, by the eagerness and assiduity with which we dig for them, and by the courtesy and kindness which we show to others engaged in the same pursuit, we may at once develop a healthy, vigorous, and refined spiritual life, and prove how highly we prize these manifestations of his will? If we care to take only such truth as lies on the surface, if we do not care to seek the hidden things of God, our love cannot be very warm, our devotion not very hearty. If at every turn in life God stood by us, pointing out, " This is the way, walk ye in it," we could give only a simple obedience ; but if our eagerness to reach him is strong enough to make us pause and ponder, examine the different roads, take observations, bridge ravines, and cut down the underbrush, we have opportunity to show the strength of our attachment and the depth of our desire.

Bearing in mind still that, if the illustration in question be pertinent, it follows that the point believed is all-important, and the sincerity of belief, and its causes, conditions, and other circumstances, of no account whatever, it is worth while to look at our own practice in such cases of moral judgment as fall within our jurisdiction.

John Brown undoubtedly believed that he was doing a just, and right, and humane thing when he disturbed the peace of the country. But he suffered the penalty in spite of his belief. So far the example applies. But though the law does not, the world does, accept his belief in extenuation of his guilt. He died a felon's death, and but for his belief would have been a felon. Civil law doomed him to the gallows; moral law has crowned him forever with the wreath of martyrdom. Now God governs us by moral, not by civil law. Civil law is the endeavor of very deficient, very imperfect, and very sinful beings to do the best they can, — to compass justice as far as possible. It is very bulky and cumbrous. It takes cognizance only of coarse and palpable transgressions. It is hedged about by rules. It is a creature of statutes and precedents. It only approximates justice. By complicated machinery, by close and elaborate reasoning, by circuitous and involved processes, it only succeeds in beating back the great waves of depravity. It just manages to prevent anarchy and maintain society. But moral law is the instrument and the prerogative of Omnipotence. It is delicate, direct, penetrating, instantaneous, infallible. It has no statutes of limitation. It is self-adjusting, self-executing. It does not, like civil law, stop short

at the life. It pierces into the soul. It discerns
the thoughts and intents of the heart. It gives to
every circumstance its just weight. It permeates
everywhere. It embraces everything. It is adequate, exact, perfect.

We may not know the sentence of Divine Justice upon that brave old man whose deeds and
death ring in a thousand songs, but is there in the
whole Christian Church one who believes that his
soul went to God burdened with the guilt of murder and insurrection? Yet if sincerity of belief
and the circumstances which induced it are of no
account, his acts were murder and rebellion.

There are thousands at the South who believe
that they are engaged in a war of right against
wrong, of liberty against slavery, of independence
against servility. They are really engaged in
treason. If the sincerity of a man's belief has no
effect upon a man's character and fate, then every
Secessionist is individually guilty of the most terrible crime which a citizen and the most heinous
sin which a man can commit. There is not in the
rebel ranks one Christian. All their prayer is
mockery. All their virtue is hypocrisy. Every
man is a wretch. Every woman is a monster.
Do we believe this? We believe nothing of the
sort. We believe that there are good and true
men and women among our bitter foes. They
have been misled by wicked men. They have
been deceived by false statements. They have

17 *

been blinded from their youth. They cherish a
false faith. But beneath all the integuments of
falsehood, we discern the royal humanity. Nay,
even the civil law, awkward, unwieldy, and clumsy
as it is, takes cognizance of these facts, and when
the rank and file lay down their arms they will
find mercy, because they did it ignorantly through
unbelief.

So the civil law permits a man to go free who has
killed his neighbor, if it be shown that he supposed
himself to be doing it in self-defence, even though
in reality he were not attacked. Military law
does not condemn a sentinel who shoots one of his
own men under the supposition that he is a rebel
and a spy. If civil and military law, which must,
from the nature of things, be full of imperfection,
and must especially be able to inform themselves
but very inadequately regarding the modifying
circumstances, — if they allow themselves to be
influenced by these, is it reasonable to suppose
that the moral law, administered by a Lawgiver
and Judge who has made the law absolutely perfect, and who knows thoroughly what is in the
heart of man, who judges not by the faltering account which we are able to frame and render, but
by the accurate knowledge which he possesses of
every thought and motive and purpose, more accurate than that of our own hearts, — is it reasonable to suppose that such a one will take into
account only the simple fact of belief, and that the

man will lose or save his soul according as he rejects or receives this or that article of our creed?

Is it then true, that sincerity of belief, and not
correctness of belief, is the point to be attained?
Not at all. Because a thing is not black, it does
not necessarily follow that it is white. The assertion in question is not wholly without foundation.
It is the caricature, the exaggeration, of a truth;
and it is not to be turned aside with a specious remark. It is not surprising that such an opinion
should have gained credence, when we see humble and devout Christians in every sect, and works
of love and mercy wrought under every creed.
But there is a fallacy, though it would appear to
be not easy to point it out.

The assertion is, in the first place, irreverent.
It assumes that truths which God has thought fit
to bring within our reach are not worth grasping,
— that the souls which he made can be nourished
just as well by falsehood as by truth. It puts the
type and the thing typified on the same ground.
The apple which Eve ate was of no consequence,
but the sin which it symbolized is of terrible moment. The brazen serpent was only a molten
image, but he who hung upon the cross was the
Lord of glory. Yet the assertion reduces both to
the same level of intrinsic insignificance.

It is unreasonable. It breaks in upon the anal-
ogy which obtains throughout nature. Falsehood
is always deleterious. Falsehood, rested upon,

and trusted in, as ultimate truth, even in the natural sciences, works derangement, and tends to chaos. Surely, spiritual matters are quite *as* important as scientific. If, in them, a slight error in the premises expands to grievous error in the conclusion, can it be supposed that spiritual error is harmless? It is true that error may not inevitably be fatal in the spiritual, any more than in the scientific world; but as, in the latter, content with and rest in it effectually bar progress in truth, so in the former. In both, wrong is too serious a matter to be tampered with. The possible consequences of wrong opinions are too wide-spread, too destructive, to allow any laxity in pursuit of truth, any indifference to the reception of falsehood. The vertex of an angle rests on a point, but the lines that subtend it may stretch far beyond our vision. Nothing is sure but what is right, and the possibility of wrong demands as great a vigilance as the certainty of wrong. So likewise does the possibility of evil consequences.

So much for the assertion itself. A glance at the appearances which induce it.

Every creed is to be judged by itself, and by its tendencies. The first I leave out of view, as not germane to this subject. Every sect must be supposed to have examined its own creed before it accepted it. Nobody believes that to be true which he judges to be false; but as in point of fact only one of two antagonistic statements can

be true, and as the adherents of each sincerely
believe their doctrine to be true, Scriptural, and
inherently reasonable, we come to the very point
where people say that it is no matter what a man
believes if he is sincere, and where the refuters
aforementioned join issue; and where it is pertinent to bring forward the tendencies of a creed
to disprove the assertion. Looking at individual
members of individual churches, and observing
their patience of hope, and their labor of love, it
may indeed seem that differences of faith are
immaterial; but a creed is to be judged not by
the life of a single individual who professes it, but
by the effect which it has on the masses. One
honest and devout man is a Roman Catholic, and
worships the Virgin Mary; but if you find that
the tendencies of the Catholic creed are to ham-
per the mind and enervate the heart, — if, in
countries where Catholicism has free course to
run and be glorified, you see science stifled by
superstition, literature languishing, the liberal arts
neglected, progress prevented, — if on every hand
you see ignorance, servility, and sloth, — while,
in countries under the influence of a different
creed, you see a different state of things, — you
must judge that creed to be a false one, and
you must see that it is of importance that a man
believe right. So if you see that one faith seems
to chill and benumb the heart; if it freezes the
genial current of the soul; if it closes the avenues

of love and hope and benevolence; if it makes
its votaries proud and disdainful and heedless; if
it works works of selfishness and frivolity and
isolation and self-laudation; or if it makes men
careless of their duties, and thoughtless of God;
or if it culminates in a superstitious rejection of
all creeds, substituting no creed of its own, but
only the ghost of a dead negation; if it exalts
man above all that is called God; if it puts the
works on a level with the worker; if it invests
stocks and stones with Divine attributes; if it invests divinity with infernal attributes; if it deifies
lust and hatred and malice and pride and revenge;—then you must infer not only that the
creed is false, but that belief or disbelief regarding it is a matter of the highest importance.
You see that it does bear fruit, and because its
fruit as well as its nature is evil, it is evil. Two
or three individuals, or two or three thousand,
may stem the current of their creed, and preserve
their integrity.

> "Like the white swan down the troubled stream,
>   Whose ruffling pinions have the power to fling
> Aside the turbid drops that darkly gleam,
>   And mar the freshness of her snowy wing,"

they may be warm in spite of a cold faith, pure
in spite of a vile one, or true in spite of a false
one. But a faith was given for the many, and
the faith that is most firm and sustaining and
ennobling and tender and true is the true faith,

and such a faith is worth fighting for. Nor do I
mean to say that there are *any* who can live just
as well under a false as under a true creed, but
only that some will not be so wholly shipwrecked
as others. No man can bow to an idol, and be as
noble a man as if he worshipped the living God.
Between God and the man who adores him,
there is a perpetual ebb and flow. New every
morning, and fresh every evening, this tidal wave
bears up our mortal adoration to the skies, and
sweeps down the Divine effluence into our hearts.
But the pagan hurtles his soul against a rock, and
all is dumb and hard and cold. Truth will not
be discarded with impunity. If a man's life be
pure with a false faith, it would be dazzling with
a true one. You cannot have falsehood without
friction, and if the chariot-wheels run well in
spite of friction, what speed would they not attain
if the friction were removed !

The very assertion that it is no matter what a
man believes, if he is only sincere, gives us a
glimpse of the frightful gulf fixed in some minds
between belief and practice. It indicates a divorce
between religion and life, between faith and works,
of which one cannot think without dismay. No
matter what a man believes, if he is sincere ? If
a man is indeed sincere, will he not work himself
practically right? If any man will do His will, he
shall know of the doctrine whether it be of God.
Thus alone is sincerity of belief valuable. A sin-

cere belief that does not bear on the life, or that bears it down, is little worth; while if a man is indeed searching for truth, if he goes to the Source of light for light, if he applies to the Fountain of wisdom, he shall receive wisdom and light and truth. No man asks his Heavenly Father for bread, and receives a stone. He may go for a stone. He may be seeking, not for what is true, but for what will build up his opinions, strengthen his party, and give him the victory; and he will probably get what he is after. But the man who seeks to know what is the will of God concerning him, will be sure to succeed. His sincere belief will act on his life, and his life will react on his belief. So far as he is sincere, he will follow on to know the Lord, and as he goes he will see that, though the landmarks are not removed, and though every one saith, I am of Paul, and I of Apollos, and I of Cephas, and I of Christ, yet Christ is not divided. Neither Paul, nor Luther, nor Servetus, nor Wesley, was crucified for us; but the ultimate, the momentous, the essential fact stands, that there is one Lord, one faith, one baptism, one God and Father of all, who is above all, and through all, and in all'those whose life is hid with Christ in God.

XV.

WORDS WITHOUT KNOWLEDGE.

T is not possible to be too familiar with the spirit or the letter of the Bible, nor are people often too much addicted to the use of Scripture language; but it is of great importance that it be used understandingly. A passage of Scripture, aptly quoted, has often more pith, point, power, than anything else could have; but, inapt, it recoils both on him who employs it and on the cause which it was intended to further. Some of the expressions of self-abasement to be met with in prayers, exhortations, and religious books, though transferred bodily from the Bible, are injudicious and disagreeable. It is not uncommon to hear good men call themselves " worms of the dust," but the impression produced is unpleasant. You feel that the statement is not just. Look at man's body only, brimful of hinges, balls, sockets, tubes, cells, bags, and strings, with its more than two hundred beautiful ivory bones, everything ingeniously contrived so as to combine the greatest lightness with the greatest speed, strength, durability, and beauty, — a set of complex and delicate machinery, doing its own oiling and repairing, working without friction, and of which the most admired inventions of man are but a clumsy imitation. Then look at the worm that disfigures your garden-walk after a shower, — a long, raw, writhing, disgusting little fellow, without a bone in his body, — no limbs, no eyes, no lungs to speak of, and not so much of a head but that he can spare it with the smallest possible inconvenience. Cut him in pieces, and he plasters up the ends and makes himself answer. Head or tail, it is all one to him, or all two, or all three, as the case may be; the only difference being that, whereas he was one before, he is now a mob. And a man calls himself such a one as this! When, in addition, you consider that marvellous and awful Thing, which eye hath not seen, nor ear heard, whose substance no man knows, which we cannot define, and can describe only by saying what it does, — it thinks, it loves, it hopes, it suffers, it reasons, it remembers, — that Living Principle which sits inscrutable, in solitary state, behind all nerve and muscle and blood and brain, without which nerve and muscle and blood and brain are but so many particles of dust, — what has a man in common with a worm?

Do you say that his sinfulness is so great that he is an abomination in God's sight? Then you slander the worm; for he is not an abomination to his Maker. I suppose a worm is, in its way, just as pleasing to God as an archangel; that is, the worm is just as exactly what God meant beforehand a worm should be, as an archangel is. It just as truly fulfils the end for which it was created. In its own little sphere — the hole which it has bored in the ground — it is like everything else which God has made, "good." It cannot sin. It never violated law. It never disregarded conscience, nor forgot God; nor has it ever passed, or shall it pass, away from its Maker's notice. There is, in that respect, no comparison to be made between it and a human being.

Do you say, that, although man is so fearfully and wonderfully made, yet, compared with God, he is but as the worm to man? But "God created man in his own image, in the image of God created he him." "Know ye not that ye are the temple of God, and that the spirit of God dwelleth in you? If any man defile the temple of God, him shall God destroy; for the temple of God is holy, which temple ye are." When Deity became incarnate, he took not upon him the nature of worms, but of man; and shall man, the only being created in the image of God, the being honored above all other created beings in lending his likeness to God manifest in the flesh, and furthermore and forever elevated and sanctified thereby, — shall he voluntarily debase himself to the level of a creature with not a thousandth part of his physical, nor a millionth part of his mental faculties, nor any of his divine privileges? This is not honoring God. God is never honored by vilifying his works. An artist is not honored by decrying his pictures. A machinist is not honored by treating lightly the engine which he has built. God is great, yet man is but little lower than the angels. God is great, yet in nothing that we know greater than in this, that the man whom he has made in his own image, chained down to one little world and a few years of time, can, by his own wonderful, God-given powers, sweep the broad heavens, pierce the deep earth, grasp the infinite past, penetrate the infinite future, and be the discoverer and the historian of worlds in numberless ages before he was born, and boundless space where he has never been. Man, man only is made after the likeness of God; man only is bought with a price; therefore glorify God in your body and in your spirit, which are God's.

Probably the phrase in question is generally used without thought, without discrimination, almost without meaning. It is found in the Bible, and, assuming that anything found there must always be available, it is pressed into service. But it should be remembered that the Bible is the revelation of God to man through an Eastern nation; and that Eastern nations, with their warmer imaginations and fiercer passions, have a style far more highly colored than ours. Phrases which are every-day language with them, would be senseless extravagance with us. Phrases which express our ideas, emotions, and sentiments quite adequately, would be bald, dry, and tame to them. Of course, the revelation of God is tinged by the medium through which it passes. That is, the earthly part of the Bible, its physical nature, its body, that part of it which is not divine, is Hebrew, Oriental, — not French, nor Celtic, nor Anglo-Saxon; just as Christ was a Jew, and not a Spaniard or a Russian. Consequently, the Bible has the fervor, the luxuriance, the hyperbole, the warm, poetical, profusely-illustrated style which characterizes the literature and the life of the East. This should be borne in mind in understanding, quoting, and applying it. It is necessary in order to avoid misapplication, and a savor of hypocrisy, or at least insincerity. For example, " The Lord is my rock," would but ill personify God's protective benevolence to a sailor, to whom rocks are the monsters of the deep, — a fear and a dread; but the dweller in a war-like country, where the rock-ribbed hills are fortified posts, surmounted with towers, bristling with soldiers, and a refuge against all enemies, would feel the full force of the Psalmist's exultant song: " The Lord is my rock, and my fortress, and my deliverer; the God of my rock; in him will I trust: he is my shield, and the horn of my salvation, my high tower, and my refuge, my Saviour; thou savest me from violence." So a dweller in sunny lands, who is forced to make toilsome journeys over long, low, level, monotonous tracts, would naturally represent the loving-kindness of God as the shadow of a great rock in a weary land.

It was natural for Job, born and bred in the land of Uz, his children cut off suddenly and simultaneously, in the prime of life, his great wealth gone, his reputation threatened, if not actually destroyed, his person the prey of a foul and loathsome disease, in his bitterness and desolation and fierce self-disgust to say to corruption, "Thou art my father; to the worm, Thou art my mother, and my sister." It was not unnatural that David — an outcast from his country and king; getting his bread by downright lying; feigning madness, scrabbling on the doors, and letting his spittle fall down upon his beard, to save himself from the sword of Achish; hunted by a half-crazy, but strong and savage king, from post to post; hiding in mountain, and wilderness, and dens, and caves, and every available lurking-place; the jest of servile courtiers; the captain of a rabble of malecontents and distressed debtors — should exclaim in despondency, " I am a worm, and no man; a reproach of men, and

despised of the people." But for an intelligent
New-Englander of good habits, good principles,
good conduct, good health; familiar with abstract
ideas, and unaccustomed to metaphor; who understands the difference between moral and natural ability; calls his children George and Jane,
and not " the Son of my Sorrow," or " the Delight of the Lord," — for him calmly to pronounce
himself a worm, is not consistent, to say the least.
His conduct and bearing do not indicate that deep,
prostrating, overwhelming sense of unworthiness
which his words imply. He is coherent, method-
ical, self-possessed, — listens attentively to others,
shakes hands and exchanges salutations with his
friends afterwards, and is extremely cheerful, comfortable, and contented — for a worm. If he felt
as he spoke, would this be so? What did Job do?
He sat down among the ashes, and scraped himself with a bit of broken earthenware, in a grief so
distressing, so profound, and so appalling, that for
seven days and nights his friends dared not speak
a word unto him. It should be a grief akin to
this that should stir our cool blood to such violent
speech. On the contrary, as far as I have observed, it is done with entire complacency, and
the inference can but be that the man speaks not
because he feels, but because he does not feel.
We suspect the sincerity of his humility. A man
must have a pretty good opinion of himself in
private, to risk the defamation of his character in

public. You do not hear a miserly Christian calling himself stingy in the prayer-meeting, nor will
an untrustworthy church-member calmly accuse
himself of lying, or a gossiping sister affirm that
she is a common tattler and mischief-maker. But
a man may confess himself in general terms a
worm, without meaning anything in particular ;
and at the same time soothe his conscience, and
perhaps really believe that he is devoutly and
sincerely humble, or, at any rate, not suspect the
contrary. Let, however, his partner in the shop,
or his political friend or rival, intimate to him in
a secular and special way that he is a little weak
in mind, or morally unsound, and he will soon discover that, unlike worms, he has bright eyes, well-
defined lungs and tongue, not to say fists and feet.

God requires no morbid humiliation, even when
sincere. Job was undoubtedly sincere, yet the
Lord answered him out of the whirlwind, " Who
is this that darkeneth counsel by words without
knowledge ? Gird up now thy loins like a
man ! "

But every *idle* word that men shall speak — idle
words of humility or idle words of pride — they
shall give account thereof in the day of judgment.

True humility does not require a man to rate
himself at other than his real value. It never enjoins upon him to sink below, any more than it
permits him to rise above, his proper level. If
humility consists, as Jeremy Taylor says, in hav-

ing a real mean and low opinion of one's self, then
was he not humble who asserted himself to be the
Light of the world. The sincerest humility does
not prevent a man from recognizing what is honorable in his character, any more than it prevents
him from ignoring what is dishonorable. It will
not make a man accuse himself of sins of which
he is not guilty, any more than it will make him
attribute to himself virtues which he does not possess. This is readily seen in matters which are
cognizable by the senses, and can be testified to in
a court of justice ; but it is not always clearly seen
in points more metaphysical. No honest man,
however sorry for sin, confesses himself a thief ;
but repentant Christians frequently rise in prayer-
meetings, and lament that they are dead in trespasses and sins. Yet it is not possible that they
are so. Dead? The very fact that they say it
— always supposing them to be sincere, and not
hypocrites — shows that they are not. "Dead
men tell no tales." Dead men — I mean, as they
do, men spiritually dead — do not speak at all.
They do not think about their sins. They do not
know that they have committed any ; and if they
did, they would not care. They do evil just as
willingly as good. They are entirely indifferent to
the character and the claims of God. Just so long
as a man feels that he is a sinner, just so long he
may know that he is alive, — perhaps not very
keenly, and watchfully, and jubilantly alive, but

alive enough to have consciousness. He may not
be in a healthy state: his head may be sick, and
his heart faint, but he still lives. Whatever else
is true of him, it is not true that he is dead. To
be dead is to be without life, without warmth,
without feeling, or reason, or desire, or despair, or
hope, or fear, or purpose; and it is wrong for a man,
who has enough of any or all of these to be aware
of his condition, to call himself dead. St. Paul
tells the Ephesians that they *were* dead in trespasses and sins; but they knew nothing about it till
God had quickened them. A knowledge of past
death may come with resurrection; but in death
itself there is no remembrance, no consciousness.

Nor is it at all certain that the Church is as cold
and dead as its members are apt to say in prayer-
meetings. They who assert it are beyond their
depth. Men know very little of the lives, still less
of the hearts, of their brothers and sisters, and they
are generally incompetent to pass judgment. The
brother who seems to you altogether too much given
up to the pursuit of worldly profit, to the accumula-
tion of property, may be cherishing in his inmost
heart, and planning in his eager brain, and shaping
with his skilful hand, some darling scheme, which
shall redound a thousand-fold to the glory of Christ
and the Church. The gay girl who seems to you to
have far too much of the butterfly for life's serious-
ness, may be doing her work just as conscientiously
as the Apostle Paul did his. How do you know

that there is not a method in her gayety? How
do you know that she does not believe it to be her
Christian duty and Divine mission, as well as innocent pleasure, to throw what little sunshine she
may on the severe outlines and sombre coloring of
life? " Be sober, be vigilant," rings in your ears,
but the voice that sings through her soul says, "Rejoice evermore"; and both are divine. May it not
be that the supposed miser, who earns your disap-
probation and contempt, has not one quarter of the
income which you lay to his account, or has four
times the expenditure? What do you know of the
poor relations, the distant dependents, the obscure
charities, the inherited debts, the hampering ties,
that hold him back? You think your brother
who goes to sleep in church must have grown
lukewarm; but suppose you had gone to the
marshes to make hay, for three, or four, or five
days past, getting up at two o'clock in the morning, driving your team half a dozen miles, mowing,
raking, cocking, spreading, loading hay till nightfall, up to your knees in water half the time, — or
suppose you had been carrying that hay to mar-
ket, twenty miles away, driving your team on foot
over the frozen ground, — or suppose you had been
harassed by the complications of your business, by
fears of bankruptcy, and a consequent sacrifice of
your reputation for sagacity, not to say honor, —
or suppose that in any way the perplexities of life
had been unusually aggressive, as they sometimes

are, — would it be the most unnatural thing in the world if, when you had put them away from you on the first day of the week, and were sitting tranquilly in a quiet room, you should fall asleep? It is not necessarily religious indifference. It may be bodily fatigue. The spirit may be willing, and the flesh only weak. I trust I shall not be considered as justifying or excusing avarice, frivolity, or criminal indifference. Undoubtedly people sometimes get more tired than they have any right to do. They fret over their business more than a Christian should. A man with a grand benevolence in view may neglect many small benevolences to which it is equally his duty to attend. But what I wish is simply to suggest that things are not always what they seem, and it is Christian charity, sometimes, to give human nature the benefit of the doubt. The flesh may innocently, nay, perhaps virtuously, be weak. In all matters which lie beneath the surface, God alone is judge. If a church steals, and slanders, and lies, and backbites, not episodically, by an individual here and there, as very likely most churches do, but right on, steadily, without let or hinderance, we cannot help supposing it to be cold; but so long as it behaves properly, so long as its morals are pure, we cannot say that its heart is not warm. Not that morality is all that there is of religion, — not that good morals are the whole duty of man. It is perhaps possible to be quite right in our

relations to man, and quite wrong in our relations to God; but our relations to God lie between ourselves and God, and beyond the range
of others' vision. You may infer that the Church,
is cold, but you do not know it, and it is often inferred from only a partial consideration of facts;
and when you rise in your place and affirm your inference as a fact, you are, with the most innocent,
and probably the most laudable intentions, slandering the Church. Some who hear you know it.
They know that they are neither cold nor stupid.
They *feel* the love of Christ shed abroad in their
hearts. They have constant communion with him.
They draw their life from him, and with them
your sweeping assertion goes for nothing, or for
something very different from what you intend.
There are others who will take your words as true.
They will believe and lament that they are cold
and dead; yet, should you ask them whether
they are interested in the spread of the Gospel,
whether they desire for their children, above all
things, love to God, whether they value for themselves God's approval more than any other good,
whether they endeavor to be honest towards
all, whether they really try to do their best,
whether they are sincerely repentant for sin,
whether they pray every day for pardon and sustenance,—they will answer you unhesitatingly,
heartily, and truly, *yes.* Perhaps they do not
join in public worship so often as you think they

ought. Perhaps they do not pray in the syna-
gogues with much fluency and unction. Perhaps
they do not organize benevolent societies so heartily, or sustain them so wisely, as might be desired;
but what of it? Those things are not religion.
They may be only a screen to conceal its absence. It may be that they have different views
from yours as to the propriety or desirableness
of such measures, or they may not have exec-
utive ability, or there may be no leading mind
among them to direct their piety into these channels. Let a man who knows how to guide men
go among them, and it is quite possible that your
cold, dead church will show at once that the
sap was coursing there ; for leaf, and bud, and
blossom, and ripening fruit, will attest its living
and life-giving presence. I think the apparent
coldness of the churches is often the result of
mismanagement on the part of leaders. They do
not take hold of things by the handle. They
do not get any purchase. They shoot wide of
the mark. They never get at the root of the
matter. Their want of tact and skill may not be
their fault ; and it is unfortunate that the same
incapacity which prevents them from doing the
work prevents them also from seeing that it is
not necessarily the fault of others.

I never can resist the temptation to take up the
cudgel in behalf of those who have not what
George Stephenson called the " gift of the gab."

It seems to me, sometimes, that nobody in the world is so misunderstood and maligned as they. Strange that a man always fluent, and ever ready to take part in exhortation and prayer, will acquire in a month a reputation for active piety which a man just as pure of life, but without his gifts, will acquire only after the lapse of years. It is quite right in judging a man to be a warm-hearted Christian so far as he talks like one, because talking is one kind of action, — one of the fruits by which we know the Christian, and a fruit which comes to maturity sooner than any other, and will of course receive earliest recognition; but it is wrong to go beyond this, and judge a man to be cold-hearted because he lacks this power of expression. It does not materially alter the case if he says so himself. Grind it into a school-boy that he is stupid, and he will think he is stupid. Christians of whom the world was not worthy have been so belabored, so often told that they were lukewarm and backward and worldly by those who ought to have known better, so sincerely and lugubriously bemoaned over by those who did not know better, that they came to believe it themselves, against the facts. They hear a person speak warmly, eloquently, and impressively of religion. They cannot speak so themselves. If they have been brought up to consider that the difference is owing to the other person's superior piety, the probability is that they will accept the statement.

Mrs. Stowe says that her Dr. Hopkins " in general viewed himself on the discouraging side, and had berated and snubbed himself all his life as a most flagitious and evil-disposed individual, — a person to be narrowly watched, and capable of breaking at any moment into the most flagrant iniquity "; and what Mrs. Stowe said playfully of a romance-hero may be said in earnest of many a living Christian. Many honestly seem to believe it to be a Christian duty to have a " real mean and low opinion of themselves." There would be a defect in their orthodoxy if this were not the case. They have read the memoirs of Brainerd, and Martyn, and Page, and Payson, and David, and Paul, and they think, if these eminently holy men felt such an abhorrence of themselves, how much more should common people, who are in no wise eminent for holiness; and having decided, or rather falling into the opinion, that they ought to feel as deeply and deplore as heartily as these men did, it is not hard for them to believe that they do thus feel, and can sincerely thus deplore; and consequently they fall to denouncing themselves in the most emphatic terms. If one should say to them at the close of a summer's day that he did not think he had committed any sin through that day, that he believed God was pleased with him, that he had done nothing that day of which he need repent, they would be almost as much shocked as if he had poured out a volley

of oaths. But is such a thing beyond the limits
of possibility? Is God, indeed, so hard a master
that Christians of five, ten, twenty years' standing
cannot pass a day without falling under his wrath
and curse? Or is Christianity so feeble a power,
that, after eighteen hundred years of effort, it cannot bring the human heart and the human life
into closer harmony with the Divine? It is not
to be supposed. I put the Brainerds and the
Martyns out of view. They were men, and no
inward divine impulse kept them from recording
morbid feelings or false views. Their sorrows
were almost entirely for intangible sins, — sins
which lay within their own hearts, and of which
nobody but themselves and God could judge.
Therefore they ought never to have been spread
before the world. It is the relation between
crime and penalty, between sin and sorrow,
which it behooves men to know. The law is not
magnified by publishing the punishment, and with-
holding the crime for which the punishment was
inflicted. To outward observers, the sorrow of
these men was out of all proportion to their sin ;
because the sin was of such a nature that no outward observer could judge of its magnitude. But
with the Bible people the case is clearer. When
St. Paul declared himself to be the chief of sinners, he gave his reasons for it, — reasons intelligible to every one. It was because he had been
a blasphemer, a persecutor, and injurious. We

are distinctly told how he went through Judæa
and Samaria, making havoc of the Church, entering into every house, haling men and women,
and committing them to prison. It was this
persecution of the Church of God that loomed
up ever behind him, — the great sin of his life, —
that made him in his own eyes unworthy to be
called an Apostle. But I think no one can read
St. Paul's writings with the same candor which
he brings to other books, without seeing that, when
Paul speaks of his sins, he is thinking of what he
was before that great light shone upon him near
Damascus. We are not left in doubt as to his
views of his subsequent character. "By the
grace of God I am what I am." "I labored
more abundantly than they all." Very little self-
denunciation will be found in Paul when he had
ceased to be Saul. David expresses the most vile
opinion of himself: "Behold, I was shapen in
iniquity; and in sin did my mother conceive me."
Well he might, after the commission of a crime
whose greatness was only paralleled by its meanness; but take the Psalms through, and David
seems to have been extremely well satisfied with
himself. He even throws himself back on his integrity. He prays to be judged according to his
righteousness. "My defence," he says, "is of
God, which saveth *the upright in heart*." "The
Lord rewarded me according to my righteousness;
according to the cleanness of my hands hath he

recompensed me." The fact is, Paul and David,
especially Paul, were men of grand good sense.
The sins that they talked about were sins that
you can get hold of. And when they had repented of them, and were forgiven, they let the
matter rest. They did not quarrel with generalities. They were not continually on the lookout
against themselves. They embraced Christ joyfully, fought the Devil within and without man-
fully, till they had finished their course.

Christ's religion is an efficient agent. His
blood *cleanseth* from *all* sin. When he told the
woman to go and sin no more, he did not tell
her to do what she had not moral, natural, and
every kind of ability to do. When he bade his
disciples to be perfect, he meant so. It is, it must
be, just as possible for a Christian to go on day
after day without offending God, as it is for a son
to go on without offending his father. It is not
pride and vainglory to assert this. It is a rob-
bing of God to deny it. If religion cannot do
this, certainly religion is not what it claims to be.
Christ came to save this people from their *sins*.
Is his arm shortened that he cannot save ? O ye
of little faith, wherefore do ye doubt ? God is
not a hard master. He claims to reap only where
he has sowed. He comes to gather in only the
harvest that he has strewed. His yoke is easy,
his burden is light. When he forgives, he forgives wholly, and forever. At any moment we

may begin with a clean record. All the past is
cancelled. He will never again bring it up against
us. We need never again bring it up against ourselves, — never at all, except, as Paul did, to magnify the grace of God. Once pronounced " not
guilty " through faith, we shall never be prose-
cuted on the same indictment. We are pure and
clean in the blood of the everlasting covenant.
The Christ that is within us will so work to will
and to do God's good pleasure, that every day
and hour and moment may be bright with the
Father's smiles, and ring with his " Well done,
good and faithful servant ! "

It may be suggested that it is rather late to
discover that men are apt to think of themselves
less highly than they ought to think. The tendency has been generally supposed to lie in the
opposite direction ; and so it may. That is, the
assertion may be true of human nature generally, and yet untrue applied to certain opinions of
a certain class comprised in a certain other class.
Church-members are but a small part of the world,
and the church-members who have been bred to
this way of thinking may be in small ratio to all
the church-members in the world, though they
are numerous in certain localities. Moreover,
all the people who hold this language towards
themselves do not probably rate themselves so
low as their words indicate. It is a great mistake to.suppose that, because a man is not a liar,

he always speaks the truth. Very few people
get into the inside of words. Expressions of
self-abasement do not necessarily imply self-abasement. A great deal will be gained when men
shall have learned to say exactly what they mean,
when they profess to mean what they say. Men
can confess that they are great sinners, and not
feel very uncomfortable about it, — in fact, take
considerable satisfaction in it. It seems, some-
how, as if one had set one's self right. It
takes off the edge of all censure. I have heard a
good many public confessions of sin that bore no
signs of humiliation. Of course, no one can tell
what is in a man's heart; but the words and the
manner did not correspond. For a sinner is a
thousand removes from a rascal. You can avow
yourself a sinner without forfeiting your position in church or society, and without exciting
suspicion in your own heart. And just here is
one of the evils arising from this wrong way of
thinking and speaking. A legion of little vices
may escape unnoticed under cover of a general
confession, or even sense, of unworthiness. In lamenting over generalities, we pass over specialties.
We confess sins, but forget faults. But there is
no such thing as abstract sins. There is no such
thing as transgressing God's law without doing
something. Sinning is being selfish, stealing,
cheating, telling lies, slandering people, dawdling
away time, eating what is known to be injurious,

making yourself unnecessarily disagreeable, taking advantage of your position to make out your own case, and not giving your opponent any chance for a hearing. Sin is all manner of meanness. Now if, when people make a public confession of sin, they would confess their sins as Paul did, it might be of service. This is sometimes done in what are called " revivals," and it is generally accompanied by unmistakable signs of contrition, and followed by sincere, and often successful, efforts at reformation. I would suggest, therefore, that, when church-members lament that they are dead in trespasses and sins they specify the particular sins in which they died. So their death may serve as a warning to others.

But granting, as of course every one does, that Christians ought not to express emotions which they do not feel, it may be questioned whether good taste would allow them to make their own righteousness prominent. But if good taste allows men publicly to vilify themselves, I do not see why it should not allow them publicly to justify themselves, — especially as their sins are their own fault, and their graces are the gift of God. It is not an individual, not even human nature, but the plan of salvation, that is on trial. Human nature is granted on all sides to be totally or partially depraved. Calvinists and Socinians agree in this, that a child left to himself bringeth his mother to shame. The point to be decided is, whether, when religion is brought to bear upon human nature, it is strong enough to rectify human nature. There are generally many present at prayer-meetings who have not turned their feet unto the testimonies of God. If lamentation and reproaches be uppermost there, will not these people say: " Of what use is this religion that they talk so much about? According to their own showing, it does not seem to make them good, and we are not any worse than bad. We may as well wait a little longer."

St. Paul again stands us in good stead. He does not like to speak of himself. He is profuse of apologies when it becomes necessary. As a gentleman, he shrinks from displaying a personal prominence ; but since the truth requires it, he comes out in full force. His native modesty cannot help holding back a little, but he clenches the fact thoroughly before he leaves it. He who had not thought himself meet to be called an Apostle, because he persecuted the Church of God, now declares himself not a whit behind the very chiefest Apostles. " I speak as a fool," he declares, half indignant at being forced into such a position; " but I will say the truth," interposes his sturdy conscience. " I am become a fool in glorying," he repeats uneasily, " but ye have compelled me : for I ought to have been commended of you; for in nothing am I behind the very chiefest Apostles. As the truth of Christ is in me,

no man shall stop me of this boasting." Why
does he do this? Because they sought a proof
of Christ speaking in him. When they mistrusted
him he asserted himself, and this self-assertion was
honoring God. He assumed to be the accredited
ambassador of Christ, and it behooved him to
show that the grace which was bestowed upon him
was not in vain. "I labored more abundantly
than they all; yet not I, but the grace of God
which was with me." So should we fill ourselves
with Christ, that we be not tormented with a perpetual self-consciousness. When one feels that
any part of his own history or experience is necessary to vindicate truth, and glorify God, he
should declare it boldly, honestly, intelligibly,
definitely, as Paul did; not restrained on the one
side by a false delicacy, nor puffed up on the
other by a presumptuous, ignorant conceit of self-
righteousness. And when the interests of truth
do not require this, he should hold his peace. For
my part, I cannot conceive how a person who has
any consciousness of sin or of sinfulness can ever
talk about it.

But take things at their worst. Suppose a
church is cold, what is the good of saying so?
Few things so lower the mercury at a prayer-
meeting as the doleful periods of a doleful man,
— "church cold and stupid," "ways of Zion
mourn," "few come to her solemn feasts," "left
her first love," "sluggish and worldly." The

very thought of it is chilling. Suppose you *are* cold, is melancholy the only resource? What does a man do when he is cold? He bestirs himself, goes to the fire, rubs his hands, stamps his feet, chops wood, walks briskly, till vigorous blood leaps along his veins, and every finger-end tingles. Go ye and do likewise. The very fact that few are present makes it the more necessary that the meeting should be interesting and inviting, in order that those few may come the next time, and perhaps bring a few more with them. The worldliness of the church is very indifferent fare to those who attend its gatherings. If they are to have nothing better to feed on than their own husks, they might as well stay at home; and they probably will. No. If you are cold, or the church is cold, do not mention it. You will only freeze the harder. Begin and do something to get warm. Read the Bible. Pray more. Pray definitely. Do not pray so much for things in general. Do not repent of your worldliness, but repent that you dropped a three-cent-piece into the contribution-box when your income would have allowed a dime, and be sure to put in seventeen cents the next time. Choose some person to pray for, for a limited time, and then choose another, and be on the lookout for a chance to influence those persons in other ways. Organize a missionary society, or a Sunday-school class. Think of something pleasant, or soothing,

or encouraging, or warning, to say to stray souls.
Find out the old people, and the poor people, and
the blind people, and the drunken people, and the
suspicious people, and the sorrowful people, and
get hold of them. Tell stories to the children,
make the overtasked man laugh, smuggle thoughts
into empty heads, and reflections into careless
hearts, and do not go about shivering. There are
a thousand ways to get warm, and remember that
heat always seeks an equilibrium. If you are
cold you will cool others, and if you are warm you
will set others aglow. If you have been guilty of
public sins, confess them, and see to it that you
forsake them. If you feel called upon to illustrate the loving-kindness, the boundless mercy of
Christ by a relation of any part of your private
history, do it modestly and quietly. Remember that at best you speak as a fool, and that
your only plea can be Paul's, "Yet as a fool receive me."

And whether you confess open or hidden trespasses, and whenever you speak of a state of heart
opposed to God, be sure you do it in the past
tense. Why? Because at the time you speak,
you have, of course, stopped sinning. If you
have not, why are you talking? Do you mean
to confess sins in which you still indulge? By no
means. It is he that confesseth and *forsaketh* his
sins that shall find mercy. You *were* a thief, you
were a drunkard, you *did* shave notes, you *did*

backbite your superiors, but you do it no longer. When you are thoroughly warmed, you can, if you choose, say that you were cold. After God has quickened you, you may thankfully admit that you were dead in trespasses and sins. But when you address your brethren, be guileless. You can be. Forgiveness is entire. However wicked you may have been, begin at once to be good, and if you do not wholly succeed at the first trial, be as good as you can be. Extol the goodness of God. Men are far more easily moved to virtue by a good example, than repelled from vice by a bad. They are far more apt to emulate the good, than to shun the evil. Look on the encouraging side of things. Point out the hopeful signs. Exalt man's capabilities ; in so doing you exalt God, his maker. Magnify his office ; to God is all the glory. Take him at his highest, and he will press on to grander heights. Draw him from the front, as Eastern shepherds draw their flocks, and do not always drive him from behind. "Allure to brighter worlds, and lead the way." If you must record your sorrow, record at the same time your joy. Let God's abundant mercy overshine and dazzle away your guilt. Let every tear be rainbowed in smiles. Let every "Alas! Master," have its "Hallelujah!" Be full of gratitude, and trust, and love, and life. Be helpful, and hopeful, and lusty, and cheery. So shall not only your soul be filled with a joy that no man can take from you, but the cold church around you will insensibly and surely melt away in this new light and warmth which you diffuse, and where it stiffened, a new temple shall arise whose Holy of Holies will enshrine the sacred fire forever.

Besides these words of self-depreciation, there are words of comfort spoken so without knowledge that they irritate rather than console. Their comfort is founded on measurements. Good people see men unhappy, and they undertake to demonstrate that such unhappiness is unreasonable and ungrateful, because there are so many more happy circumstances in life than there are unhappy ones. " Reckon up your blessings," they say, " see how greatly they outnumber your annoyances, and cease to be annoyed. Count the gifts that have been bestowed upon you, and be ashamed that you are so distressed because one or two things go wrong."

This may be unanswerable in point of fact, but men and women, especially women, will never be happy because it is proved in a syllogism that they ought to be happy. The theory may look well on paper, and trip smoothly from the tongue, but the moment it is set to work, it will get out of gear.

For evil and good are not commensurate. Their power bears no proportion to their bulk. A little evil may, from the nature of things, not from the ingratitude of man, neutralize a great good. It may be demonstrably true, that by far the greater number of circumstances that surround a man are pleasant, yet one unpleasant one shall invalidate them all, — not because he perversely refuses to recognize the pleasure, but because the pain is more penetrative and more diffusive. A man has a faithful wife, noble children, honor, and health, and wealth, — but one wayward son, whose life is a constant shame and terror, embitters this paradise. He has more power to make miserable than all the rest have to make happy. He poisons the very fountain of happiness. Even a much smaller evil may work oblivion of good. A severe attack of toothache will make a man for a time indifferent to every advantage. One little tooth is ridiculous, when compared with houses and lands and influences, but one little tooth disturbed will assert its claims with a pertinacity that insures more attention than ambition or love can secure. A single spot on a coat spoils the coat, though not one twentieth as large. An unseen worm bores an insignificant hole in the ship's side, — insignificant compared with the uninjured portion, — but the defect is stronger than the strength, and overpowers it; and the grand and stately ship goes staggering down into the black waters. So in character, a man may be loyal, benevolent, and intelligent, yet so peevish, fretful, or suspicious, that his society is disagreeable, or he may be so self-conceited as to forfeit respect, or so uncleanly

and uncouth as to be justly outlawed.   One evil
expands itself, and usurps the place of much good.
One vice swallows up a thousand virtues.

There is a Divine recognition of this fact in the
Apostle James's assertion, " For whosoever shall
keep the whole law, and yet offend in one point,
he is guilty of all."

Therefore, all comfort based on the ratio of
good and evil is futile.   It is founded on a fallacy, and when the waves of sorrow dash against
it, its fall is certain.   It will do tolerably so
long as we are not in trouble, but when trouble
comes, it is nothing, and worse than nothing,
and vanity — not to say exasperation.   You get
small relief from the man who says, " You have
a felon on your hand, to be sure, but you have
money and fame and troops of friends, and you
ought not to mind it."   Nor is it any comfort
to compare your trouble with somebody else's
greater.   A pin does not prick you any more
gently and agreeably because your neighbor has
had his arm cut off.   The two hundred dollars'
rent which your tenant cheats you out of, is just
as much a loss to you as if your friend had not
been cheated out of his whole fortune.   You may
be glad that you are not in his place, but it does
not make your place any pleasanter.

Sorrow is to be recognized as sorrow.   Nothing
is gained by arguing it out of the way.   It is pre-
supposing and fostering an unmanly weakness, to

assume that a man cannot bear whatever burden God imposes upon him, but must be cajoled into the belief that it is not much of a burden, before he will undertake it. A man loses his property. It is true that he has wife and children, health and honor left, and these are much; but the loss of property is a great loss. Money commands time and space. Money brings beauty and elegance and comfort and culture. Money means eyes to the blind, and feet to the lame, and warmth to the chilled, and clothes to the naked, and hope to the despairing, and strength to the weak; and the man who loses this has met with a severe loss.

But the comfort lies not very much in pointing out what he has left, — for he had all those before he lost anything, — but in remembering that God, in whose hand our breath is, and whose are all our ways, appoints to every man his lot, and all things — pain, sickness, weariness, poverty, length of days, riches, and honor — *all* things work together for good to them that love God. He could, if he had chosen, make every man great and rich and powerful. That he has not done this, proves that he did not will to do it. We feel that, if we were rich, or eloquent, or self-possessed, we could do a great deal more good than we can now, but our very weaknesses may, and should, become "nimble servitors to do His will." The chosen path is barred to our eager feet. One obstacle stands in

the way of success.   A single circumstance, small
but not slight, forces us from the life that we like
to the one we do not like.   One drop of sour spoils
the whole cup of sweet.   But it is of the Lord,
and he means us only good.   Fortitude may be as
heroic 'as courage.   Patience is as sublime as
strength.   " They also serve who only stand and
wait."   " Knowledge by suffering entereth."   In
the immovable shadow of a great sorrow, or in the
flickering shade of many little sorrows, all virtue
may flourish.   The utmost grandeur of character
may be attained by uncomplaining, not stoical,
submission to the Divine will.   Alone with sorrow, alone with trial, man communes with his
Maker, and finds his grace sufficient.   From the
grave of a dead hope we may rise to newness of
life.   From a disappointed ambition we may work
out a far more exceeding and eternal weight of
glory.   There is no strength like the strength
of him who has breasted his disappointments
and overcome them, — whose feet are planted
upon the wrecks of his own plans, and whose
eyes are lifted unto the hills, whence help cometh.

We are told by naturalists that the tones of birds
seem to indicate a certain degree of discontent ;
that " the almost uninterrupted song of caged birds
proves their singing to be no certain evidence of
happiness.   It is well known that, when an old bird
from our own fields is caught and caged, he will

continue his tunefulness long after all others of the
same species, who enjoy their freedom, have become silent."

This is a not inapt illustration of the workings
of the human soul. Some of the finest produc-
tions of genius have been born of a grief that tra-
vailed in anguish, waiting deliverance. It was
" in the narrow chamber of his neglected old age,"
hiding from a hostile king, shut out from the light
of the happy sun, that the eyes of Milton opened
upon the glories of Paradise, and there burst from
his tranced lips " a sevenfold chorus of hallelujahs
and harping symphonies." Still, with a grand
organ-roll, the echoes of that solemn song sweep
down the corridors of time, nor shall any age be
found so base as to close its ear to that Heavenly Muse which erst did soar above the Aonian
Mount.

Cowper's life was one long pang. The cloud
hovered over his infancy, deepened and darkened
above his manhood, and settled around his dying
bed with an impenetrable gloom. Occasional rifts
show how brilliant was the light beyond, but never
its silver lining was turned towards him ; and
Death came, no King of Terrors, but a divine
messenger, at whose word

> " Heaven opened wide
> Her ever-during gates."

Now in a million hearts the songs that warbled

19   BB

up from this breaking heart awake an answering
thrill, and the prayer of all sighing souls is voiced
in that mournful lyre,

> " O for a closer walk with God,
> A calm and heavenly frame,
> A light to shine upon the road
> That leads me to the Lamb ! "

Thus it has been, and thus it shall be under the
sun.   It is the crushed grape that gives out the
blood-red wine.   It is the suffering soul that
breathes the sweetest melodies.   That Holy Life
which eighteen hundred years ago lit up forevermore this valley of shadows, was exceeding sorrowful, even unto death.   The Blessed One trod
the wine-press alone.   From an agony into which
mortal eyes may never look rang out the new
song of peace on earth, good-will to men.   Ever
since, as ever before, the voice of humanity is a
loud and bitter cry.   Genius smites his harp to
relieve the unsatisfied want of his soul.   His verse
is tremulous with gathered tears.

Fear not, little flock.   It is your Father's good
pleasure to give you the kingdom.   Somewhere,
and at some time, the redeemed soul shall realize
its loftiest conception, — nay, rather, the truth
shall transcend his idea ; for eye hath not seen,
nor ear heard, neither hath it entered into the
heart of man, the things which God hath prepared for them that love him.   The white blos-
soms of hope shall then ripen to purple fruit-

age, and the full soul shall bask in the glory
of her God.

> " The poet now hath entered in
> The place of rest which is not sin.

> " And while he rests, his songs, in troops,
> Walk up and down our earthly slopes,
> Companioned by diviner hopes.

> " ' Glory to God — to God !' he saith :
> KNOWLEDGE BY SUFFERING ENTERETH ;
> AND LIFE IS PERFECTED BY DEATH ! "

Cambridge : Printed by Welch, Bigelow, & Co